THE CASTOFF PRINCESSES

TWELVE DANCING PRINCESSES
BOOK TWO

ROWAN MALLORY

ISBN 978-1-956158-04-5

Book cover and map design by Far Shore Design

www.rowanmallory.com

Far Shore Design Publishing

For Ari, Fred, & Charlie, for giving me hope for the future.

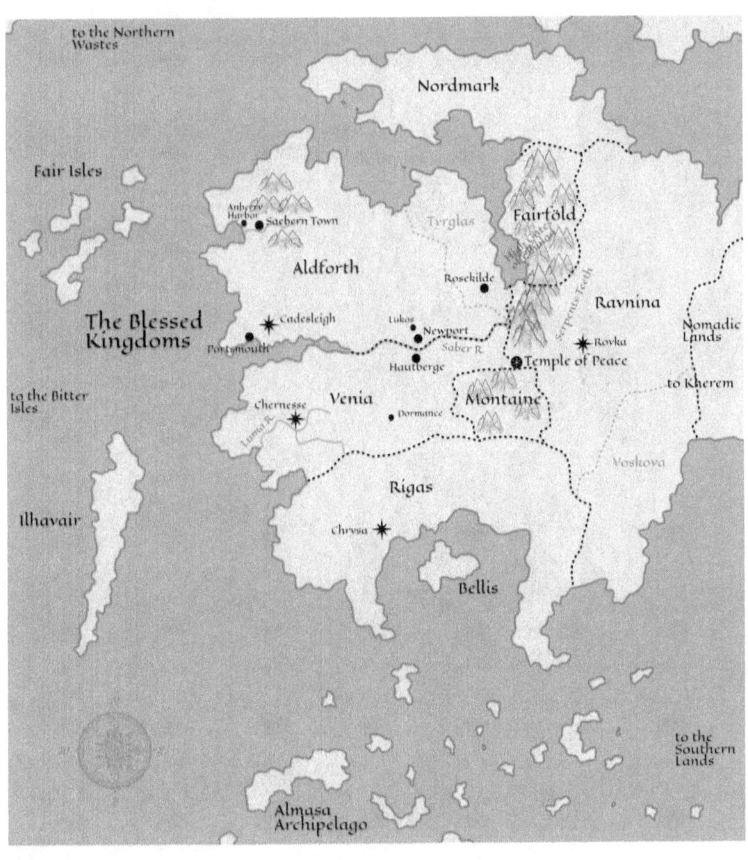

to the Northern Wastes
Nordmark
Fair Isles
Anberry Harbor
Saebern Town
Aldforth
Tyrglas
Fairföld
Rosekilde
Ravnina
The Blessed Kingdoms
Cadesleigh
Lukos
Newport
Serpent's Teeth
Nomadic Lands
Portsmouth
Saber R.
Rovka
to the Bitter Isles
Hautberge
Temple of Peace
to Kherem
Chernesse
Venia
Dormance
Montaine
Lumir R.
Voskova
Rigas
Ilhavair
Chrysa
Bellis
to the Southern Lands
Almasa Archipelago

CHAPTER ONE

6. All she talks about is peace, but she's never *still*.

— Top 10 things I despise about Princess Eira, as listed by Princess Marjani of Almasa

"If you want war, I'll give you war," Eira warned, digging an elbow into Princess Marjani's side.

It was bad enough that Eira had to suffer this endless delay on the dock, mere yards from boarding the vessel that would set her free from confinement in Lukos Castle—or possibly drown her, but she wasn't thinking about that. *Definitely not.* But it was appallingly unfair that she be forced to stand between striking, ebony-skinned Princess Marjani of Almasa and haughty, elegant Princess Raisa of Ravnina.

They didn't have to crowd her, too.

Holy Mother had provided Eira with new clothes for this competition—she had never worn linen so fine, not even back in Nordmark when she'd been a real princess. Yet the snowy white acolyte's robes made her ghostly skin even paler than usual and her ivory-blond hair more ashen. To the crowd on the shore, she must look like a washed-out daisy between two magnificent royal roses.

No matter. She hadn't come to Aldforth expecting to win Prince Theodor's hand with her beauty or her pedigree. King Wulfric claimed he wanted a princess who could protect his son from danger. Eira would be that princess.

She didn't need to be more glamorous than the others. She only needed to be more deadly. This quest to kill the monstrous bear terrorizing one of King Wulfric's northern counties was her chance. And that meant she needed to get on that boat at the end of the dock behind them.

Unfortunately, she would probably die of boredom before she got the chance.

"Stop squirming," Marjani growled, nudging Eira's boot with the butt of her iron-tipped spear. Her blood-red cloak was swept off one shoulder, exposing an arm sculpted by practice with the aforementioned spear. If the Temple of Peace approved of gambling, Eira would give good odds Marjani would be the one to fulfill their quest.

Fortunately, Eira had experience making good against long odds.

She shifted the bow slung over her back so the end jabbed Marjani's calf. "Give me room, and I'll give you peace."

"You are the one who began with strife," Marjani hissed. "You can't complain now."

"I'm not the one holding a stupid grudge." Eira's smile showed only the tips of her teeth. No one in the crowd that packed Newport's narrow streets would guess she wasn't on the best terms with her companions. For surely the onlookers would be eager for gossip to distract them from Castellan Kenrick's endless speech about King Wulfric's foresight, generosity, and benevolence—although Eira had to admire the castellan's flare for invention.

"You told the other princesses I should have been murdered at birth as a sorceress." Marjani turned her head just far enough to glare at Eira with her mismatched eyes, one amber, one green—what Eira's Nordish ancestors would have called wraith eyes.

Unsettling as they were, glaring at her with undisguised contempt, Eira couldn't help noticing how beautiful they looked in Marjani's austere face.

"I said the Nordish *used* to kill babies they thought were sorcerers," she said, as fiercely as she could with her teeth locked together in that false smile. "My mother would never have allowed it. And the Temple of Peace teaches that all human gifts come from the One Goddess. It's up to us to use them for good or ill. You need to let go—"

"You need to stop squawking at each other like angry crows," Princess Raisa advised in an icy whisper. Wulfric had allowed *one* additional princess to accompany them to the boat to see them off, and it just had to be the one who hated Eira most. Or second most. Marjani probably hated her more than Raisa did. "The king is watching. If you anger him and spoil this chance for me to shine, I will toss you both into the river."

The thought of the king's anger made her throat dry, but *the river …*

Eira glanced through the narrow gaps in the dock under her feet. The cold, dark water of the Saber slid by beneath them, coiling and hissing like a malevolent serpent—

She gritted her teeth and forced her gaze upward. The dock was perfectly sturdy and safe, and she was several feet from the edge. She concentrated on the courtiers sitting astride their mounts on the solid, dry land just a few yards away. Castellan Kenrick stood before them, black-clad and shrewd-faced, spouting nonsense about King Wulfric's noble motives for sending her and Marjani on this far-fetched quest to County Saebern.

The longer he talked, the colder the water whispered beneath her and the smaller the vessel waiting behind them seemed. *Focus.*

The king loomed beside the courtiers, dark and brooding atop the breathtaking black stallion Raisa had brought from Ravnina as a gift—or a bribe—for the man who would choose one of the competing princesses as his daughter-in-law. He sat the horse like a warrior, wearing a simple black tunic with a silver wolf's head emblazoned on it, his graying black hair and beard trimmed with military precision. Only the haughty impatience of his pale blue gaze showed the power he wielded over his companions—none of them dared display anything but rapt attention to the praise being showered upon him.

The rigid set of his jaw told Eira that the malicious good humor that had driven him to escort her and Marjani to the dock that morning had drained away, leaving his accustomed seething resentment in its wake.

If she hadn't seen Wulfric's brutality first-hand, Eira might have felt sorry for him. Just a few hundred feet above, on the cliff overlooking the river port, Prince Theodor and his Rose Knights perched on the very spot where Wulfric's eldest son, Crown Prince Guntram, had been attacked and killed by a horrifying manticore not four months earlier.

Today, a very different mythical creature circled far above the prince and his cohort. Tenzin, Princess Anara's dragon companion, glimmered blue-green in the slanting dawn sunlight, her sinuous grace showing no hint of her recent injuries. Her wings spanned nearly six feet across, though her body wasn't any larger than a lean barn cat. Anara had sent her to remind the king that she could warn of any danger to the prince long before it arrived, but Eira guessed the need for a sentinel in the sky reminded him of darker things, as well.

Prince Guntram's murder had led the king to invite Eira and the other eleven princesses to Aldforth to compete for Prince Theo's hand. After Princess Jax had proven herself by rescuing the prince from an angry giant king, King Wulfric had offered this chance to hunt County Saebern's allegedly enchanted bear to any princess brave—or foolish—enough to take it.

"This is *my* quest," Eira reminded Raisa. She had been the only volunteer. A calculated gamble. Even an average bear made dangerous prey, but she was sure and steady with a bow. Fear and superstition probably accounted for the creature's monstrous reputation. On the other hand, who *wouldn't* jump at the opportunity to see if sorcery was real? "It's my chance to shine, not yours. And not Marjani's."

At least, it would be her chance if she ever got to board the wretched boat and get started on the hunt.

"I never wanted to come," Marjani spat. "I am not a fool. King Wulfric chose me to join you."

"You could have said no."

The other two princesses didn't deign to reply. No one who valued their life said no to the brutal Wolf of Aldforth.

"You're fortunate Marjani is accompanying you, darling." Raisa offered a toss of her amber-blond hair to the populace watching from the shore—especially the handsome prince on the clifftop. "She will probably kill the bear before it mauls you. Then again, no one will miss you if she doesn't."

"That's not true!"

But Raisa's cool, superior smile said the truth didn't matter. It didn't matter that Eira's friends, Princess Jax, Princess Beatrix, and Princess Anara, had begged her not to get herself killed and had given her the jade frog charm she was wearing on a silver necklace for good luck.

All that mattered was how foolish Raisa would make her look to the king and his court, to Prince Theo and his Rose Knights, if she died on this twisted joke of a quest—the pallid Nordish exile that no one mourned.

That was fine. Eira had no intention of giving them a reason to mourn.

She touched the smooth ash wood of her bow—a gift from Prince Theodor after her previous bow had been destroyed before the princesses' first archery competition. She stood between her two top suspects for that sabotage, but the loss wouldn't stop her. She was an excellent shot with any bow, and this one was good and deadly. The Saebernians claimed weapons bounced off their bear's thick hide, but not even an allegedly enchanted beast was going to walk away from an arrow through its eye.

When she returned with the creature's head as her trophy, King Wulfric would have to take her seriously as a contender for his son's hand. And when Prince Theodor became king and she ruled at his side, just let anyone try to disregard her value then. She would turn Aldforth from war, bringing an age of peace and prosperity to all seven of the Blessed Kingdoms.

It was just hard to remember peace when her fingers tingled with both anticipation and dread, the river breeze tugging at her plaited hair, the scent of water and tar and fish guts in her nose. To the hells with protocol. Another moment and she was going run up the dock and fling herself onto the boat—before her misgivings about sea travel and the lure of returning to her friends in Lukos could undermine her courage.

"—we wish them fair winds and true aim," Kenrick's words tickled her ear like the breeze, *go, go, go,* "that their hunt may bring relief to County Saebern and glory to His Royal Majesty, King Wulfric of Aldforth, Lord Protector of Nordmark and the Fair Isles, Most Glorious—"

"Finally," King Wulfric barked, the black stallion's ears lying back at his tone. "By all the gods, Kenrick, I thought you'd drone on for the entire morning. Were you trying to put all the game to sleep, to rob me of my hunt?"

Obligatory chuckles rose from his courtiers, but even his appreciative audience brought only an aggravated snarl from the king. With a dig of his heel, he sent his horse surging past the courtiers and onto the dock. Kenrick had to dodge to avoid being knocked into the river.

Eira was suddenly glad she stood beside Raisa as the king urged the snorting stallion toward them, looking as if he'd decided to trade deer for princesses as his morning's prey. Surely the horse wouldn't trample his own mistress.

"*You,*" Wulfric sneered. His cold, pale eyes settled on Marjani as he reined the beast to a halt right before her. "Do you really think to marry that disappointing, worthless whelp of mine?" He jerked his head toward the cliff behind him. "You dare so high, the princess of a jumble of strategically placed rocks?"

To her credit, Marjani held herself like a warrior in her crimson robes, head high, stance wide, as if she'd grown up riding the sea on swift boats. Which she probably had. The Almasa archipelago stretched hundreds of miles across the Central Sea.

"I am my father, King Lisan's representative," she said, holding Wulfric's gaze. "I will prove myself worthy of that duty."

An odd phrasing to Eira's ears, but Wulfric had already turned to his next victim.

"And you," he spat. The stallion danced close enough Eira could have patted its neck. If she hadn't valued her fingers. "Not even your uncle, our vassal, Einar of Nordmark, deems you fit to be a princess."

Good sense warned Eira to keep her mouth shut. But her mouth rarely listened to sense, good or otherwise.

"Holy Mother sent me to represent the Temple of Peace, not Nordmark, your majesty," she said brightly. "At your invitation."

The king's hand whipped toward her, quick as a snake, and he grabbed her chin. His thumb pressed her lip against her teeth hard enough to draw blood. Eira's fingernails dug into her palms as she fought to keep from crying out.

"I don't find you entertaining," Wulfric hissed, his icy tone more frightening than his previous hot irritation. "Nor do I think the Temple of Peace would have sent you if they believed you irreplaceable. I suggest you take this quest seriously. You won't get another chance."

He shoved her chin, sending her stumbling backward. The cold breath of the river tickled the nape of her neck as the sole of her boot landed half off the edge of the dock. Eira's arms spun in a ridiculous windmill. Time felt so slow, yet too fast for anyone to help her, even if they had dared.

Below, the great river flowed swiftly, mercilessly. Eira's bow swung her sideways, and her foot skidded on the wet wood—

Something struck her back, digging into her shoulder. Just enough of a blow to slow her momentum, giving her time to lurch forward and fall to her hands and knees on the dock.

Needles pinched her skin, and her savior smacked the back of her head.

Eira's squawk nearly matched the one ringing in her ear. Shimmering blue-green scales flashed in her peripheral vision, and a puff of smoke blew up her nose, making her cough.

"Tenzin!"

The little dragon settled firmly on Eira's shoulder with a scolding hiss, wrapping her long, sinuous tail around Eira's neck before easing the pressure of her golden talons.

Eira lifted one hand from the rough, stained, solid wood to stroke Tenzin's warm chest as she'd seen Princess Anara do. She hoped the little creature could feel the affection and gratitude in her trembling fingers. She tasted blood in her mouth as she rose on weak legs to face the king.

He glared at her with a mixture of spite and distaste that quite successfully hid any relief he might feel at not managing to murder one of his twelve princess guests. It also hid any alarm at having a dragon swoop down right in front of him. The horse, however, proved less sanguine. Well-trained as it was, it had skittered back several yards at Tenzin's arrival and showed no intention of coming any closer.

Tenzin's silver-tipped crest rose around her head like a fan, and she warbled in outrage. Eira hadn't had time to learn much of the dragon's musical language. Still, she understood enough to be glad no one else on the dock knew it was a language at all. In the dragon's home country of Kherem, a man—any man—touching a royal princess in anger could be punished by death. Unfortunately, they weren't in Kherem, and the curses Tenzin was spewing at the king would have been worth Eira's head if he'd deciphered them.

"It's all right," Eira murmured under her breath. *So fortu-*

nate to be breathing. Though her pulse still beat uncomfortably fast, she offered King Wulfric a respectful acolyte's bow. "I understand, Your Majesty. I give you my oath that I will not squander this opportunity you have given me. I swear to rid Saebern of its bear."

"Is that so?" The scorn that slid across the king's face mingled with anticipation of her failure.

That was fine. This was her one chance to make a difference. She had no intention of failing.

"And you?" he demanded of Marjani. "Have you no oath to make to me?"

Eira had to give the gloomy, grudge-holding princess credit. She held her ground.

"I vow to take full advantage of any opportunity I am given," Marjani said, as much a challenge as an oath.

"You'd better." From anyone else, it would have seemed a petty, resentful response. No, even from King Wulfric, it seemed petty and resentful. It was just that everyone listening knew that petty and resentful was his most dangerous mood.

Eira tensed, aware of the dock's edge still much too close to her back. But he merely gave a dismissive snarl and hauled viciously on the black stallion's reins, turning the horse down the dock and driving it into a fluid canter up Newport's steep, twisting streets toward the clifftops.

The courtiers hastily followed, leaving only Castellan Kenrick behind to finish loading the princesses onto the ship.

Raisa's expression soured as she gazed at the lone groom left on the bank with her borrowed horse.

"I guess you're not invited on the hunt," Eira said.

Raisa tossed her head and offered Eira a smile predatory enough to scare a catamount.

"Goodbye, Princess Eira," she purred. "I would say, 'farewell,' but that would be disingenuous of me. I hope the bear eats you."

Eira smiled back. "I'll bring you one of its teeth."

"I'll settle for one of yours." Raisa turned to blow air

kisses at Marjani's cheeks. "*You* must return safe and sound, darling. None of the rest of these girls have the brains for this war of a courtship. I need my best general at my side."

"I will return victorious," Marjani said with her usual galling poise. But then, a competition wasn't any fun if your opponent wasn't committed.

Raisa turned to glide toward her waiting horse, so only Eira saw the flash of what looked like remorse twisting Marjani's face.

Marjani noticed her looking and scowled. "*That* is a true princess."

Then she spun and strode toward the ship, which meant Eira had to wait *again*, a mere half dozen yards from finally boarding the blasted boat, so it didn't look like she was following in Marjani's wake like a forgotten child.

Which would have annoyed her a great deal more if she hadn't been the one with the dragon perched on her shoulder.

Tenzin warbled a query, shooting a speculative glance at Marjani's back.

"I don't think drowning an Almasan princess would reflect well on an acolyte of the Temple of Peace," Eira said primly. "Jax says I should apologize for the baby-killing story and start fresh. Though I don't know why I should apologize for telling the truth."

Tenzin hummed agreement, but Eira heard Holy Mother's voice in her ear. *Insistence on being right is one of the nine paths to war.*

She sighed and stroked the dragon once more. "You'd better get back to Anara before she starts worrying about you overtaxing your wing. You can report on my good behavior."

Tenzin made a sound that could only be described as a snicker. Her claws tightened briefly on Eira's shoulder as her wings unfurled. A graceful leap and the little creature was sky-born, wings flashing in the sunlight.

Eira watched her circle upward, past the king's retinue, high above the cliffs. Eira envied the dragon's ability to fly free of the politics, intrigue, and backbiting that enveloped the humans below like a massive spiderweb.

"Pardon me, Your Highness. Princess? *Princess Eira!*" Castellan Kenrick appeared at Eira's side, frowning.

Speaking of spiders …

Eira had the uncomfortable feeling the castellan had been trying to get her attention for some time. There were just so *many* princesses in Aldforth at the moment, and she wasn't used to being referred to as "Your Highness." Even when her mother had ruled Nordmark, everyone had mostly called her "girl" or "pest." The Nordish took care not to lavish too much favor on their children—it might draw unwanted attention from a mischievous god.

"It is time for you to board, Princess Eira," Kenrick said. "Steward Tarben is anxious to be underway."

The graying, sour-faced steward of County Saebern stood at the bow of the ship that would carry Eira and Marjani down the Saber on the first leg of their quest. He stared forward, pointedly ignoring his companions, the delightfully handsome Reeve Hartwin and the less delightful Princess Marjani.

"He'd rather be leaving with a cohort of knights," Eira said, not entirely without sympathy. "When he begged the king for help, I don't think he envisioned a pair of girls."

The castellan smiled, a twist of his lip that didn't quite reach his eyes. "Don't presume that I underestimate you princesses like the steward does—or like the king."

It might have been a warning. Probably was. Eira smiled as if it were a compliment and headed for the ship, schooling her stride into the smooth serenity taught all acolytes of the Temple of Peace.

Yet, beneath her white robes, her feet ached to run— forward to the ship and adventure, back to Lukos to compete for Prince Theodor's hand. It didn't matter which direction when her heart was pounding, and her muscles thrummed with excitement.

"Princess Eira!" Reeve Hartwin hurried across the deck to meet her at the top of the gangplank. He reached out a hand, then paused and started to bow, then stuck out his hand again when she didn't slow.

Recklessly ignoring the narrowness of the gangplank and the rocking of the ship, she grabbed his hand and let him help her aboard.

As soon as her feet touched the deck, the young reeve bowed, his fair hair falling over his eyes. "Please forgive me, Your Highness, I—"

"You don't need to be so formal," she assured him. "I'm really not much of a princess."

The deck shifted, and she whirled to clutch the railing. She covered her nerves with an airy wave at the Rose Knights, but Prince Theo and his friends had already disappeared from the clifftop. Probably wise, staying out of King Wulfric's way. She waved instead toward Lukos, the half-ruined tower lurking high on its small plateau behind Newport Castle.

She could just make out the window of the room she shared with her friends. They probably couldn't see her from so far away, but they would be watching. She touched the little frog charm at her throat. *A Kheremese charm for luck,* Anara had told her. *A creature who leaps with as little thought as you,* Beatrix had muttered. Jax had hugged her. *Something to remind you we're waiting for your return.*

The deckhands called around her, and the ship eased from the dock. Never mind Wulfric's scorn or Raisa's taunts. She'd made it. The first step of the path that might lead her to death or glory.

The dark, implacable Saber and the rolling Venian hills on its opposite bank bore little resemblance to the fjords and rough, rocky shores of her childhood, but the feel of the deck rolling beneath her feet filled her with unexpected nostalgia.

To be on the water once more, however little she'd missed that, on a journey north, the direction of a home she would never see again …

She could almost hear Holy Mother's voice. *You cannot dwell in the past, for the past is not a place. Nor can you build your hearth in the future, for there is no solid ground there. Settle in the present, and there you will find your true home.*

Eira closed her eyes and breathed in the murky scent of the great river. She did her best every day to let go of the past. She worked hard in the present to create a foundation for her future.

But *settling* just didn't seem to be one of her talents.

CHAPTER TWO

5. *She* doesn't like *me*.

— Top 10 things ~~I hate~~ I find difficult to appreciate about Princess Marjani, as listed by (former) Princess Eira of Nordmark

Marjani gripped the ship's rail, hands aching with frustration as she watched the dark water slide in the wrong direction past the prow. Sails creaked above her head, catching the upriver breeze, and the rowers' oars splashed rhythmically behind her, all to prevent the boat from careening too fast down the Saber River Narrows with the implacable current. Still, she felt Prince Theodor—the competition, the ball, the crown—receding behind her swiftly as a fading dream.

She had traveled up these same narrows just over a fortnight before, her slender Almasan caravel hauled upstream through the channel by mule teams and pulleys. Yet the towering cliffs still awed her, their scale and their sunless shadows making her shiver.

Princess Eira would mock her for it. *How can you be cold? The Almasan sea must boil if it's hotter there than it's been here in Aldforth this summer.*

Marjani pulled her cloak tighter against the spray misting her skin. She would happily throw the white witch into a boiling sea if only she could find one. Of all the eleven other princesses trapped with her in King Wulfric's depraved competition, it was just her luck to be yoked to the Nordish devil for this quest.

Of course, she understood the king's impulse to send her away. That wily old baboon might treat the princesses as powerless political pawns and breeding stock, but he was too vengeful himself to discount the potency of others' hatred. Instinct alone must prompt him to keep Marjani at arm's length.

A grim smile tugged her lips. Better for him if he kept her farther than a spear's throw.

Of course, Eira's people had also suffered at Aldforthian hands. Not so recently as Prince Guntram's murder of Marjani's brother, Mosi, the heir to the Almasan throne, at a truce meeting a few scant months ago. But Raisa had told Marjani the story of King Wulfric's conquest of Nordmark not so many years past and of how Eira's mother, Queen Sassa, had died during the last, futile battle before the kingdom succumbed to Aldforthian vassalage. Despite that, it was difficult to take the Nordish girl seriously—parading around in those white robes, blathering on about peace and harmony and all the other sop they served the acolytes at that temple she served.

"Princess Marjani. May I join you?" Reeve Hartwin's accent cut his Common Tongue vowels even shorter than the other Aldforthians Marjani had met. Perhaps the farther north one lived, the less heat one wanted to lose through speech.

She had little desire for company. But every league farther from Newport was a league farther from her goal, and Marjani would never get her chance with Prince Theodor if she couldn't best Eira on this hunt for the bear. To do that, she needed a plan. She needed information.

"Of course." She gestured the reeve forward.

As Hartwin stepped up beside her, the deck lurched unexpectedly. He grabbed for the rail, swallowing hard as he glanced down at the surging river. His eyes were a bluer, paler green than the water, a startling contrast to the dried-grass color of his fair hair.

"I envy your footing, Princess Marjani," he said. "You make it look so easy that I forgot boats always want to throw me to the fish. Is it true that all Almasans are born on the sea?"

"That is what we say." Marjani might have stopped there, but the young man's open curiosity was refreshing after the past weeks of royal intrigue. "The water is as much a part of our archipelago as the land. Some Alamasan islands are large enough to have nearly independent rulers, but some are hardly bigger than the decks of our ships."

"So you were 'born on the sea,' but not born on a boat." His disarming grin almost pulled a smile from her in return.

"Well," she admitted. "In my case, both are true. It is considered auspicious for the king's children to be born on the water, so my mother did not go ashore for the last month of her pregnancy."

"It obviously worked," Hartwin said. Then his eyes widened again, and color touched his fair cheeks. "I mean, having a daughter gifted with such grace and courage must have been especially auspicious, Your Highness."

As if she could be charmed by meaningless flattery. Marjani turned to watch a pair of ducks winging upstream, though her eyes barely registered them. If the location of her delivery had been enough to ensure good fortune, she would not be standing on this boat. Her birth had brought only deception and ruin.

It was time the misfortune fell somewhere other than on her own family.

"It will take more than grace to make a success of this

voyage," she said drily. "I do not think Steward Tarben shares your high opinion of King Wulfric's choice of emissaries."

"Truly?" Princess Eira appeared beside Hartwin, her bright voice contrasting with the unpleasant pallor of her face. "However did you deduce that from his continuous complaining about us over the past sennight?"

"The steward believed King Wulfric would send a company of knights to kill our bear," Hartwin said. "He's furious at the waste of time and money our journey has cost, but it's unfair of him to blame you."

A flicker of anger uncurled in Marjani's heart, a relief from the cold weight of memory. "You agree that the king has wasted your time, sending me and the Nordish exile to deal with your bear. What is it about this creature that a trained hunter is no match for it?"

"I mean no offense." Hartwin ran a hand through his unruly hair, apparently torn between diplomacy and his innate frankness. Frankness won. "Saeberners are used to dealing with bears and wolves and whatever the wilds see fit to send us. If all it took to kill this creature was a sharp blade and a strong arm, it would be dead. I'm not convinced even a royal knight would have better luck against him than our lads."

"And a mere girl has no chance at all," Eira finished for him, an edge of icy indignation in her voice.

"Why not?" Marjani demanded, unable to squelch a certain satisfaction at Hartwin's discomfiture. And not because it wrinkled his nose in what some might think was an adorable way. She wasn't *Eira*, for the gods' sake. "Tell us of this bear."

"The beast is massive, larger than any bear I've ever seen," Hartwin said, steadier dealing with facts than with princesses. "And not black, like our forest bears. Its fur is golden brown, almost the color of honey. It has eluded all our hunters, killed our sheep, and torn down fences. The town council doesn't think *any* mere human can kill it."

From another man, it might sound like wild exaggeration. Holding that steady, blue-green gaze, Marjani saw only blunt sincerity and concern for his people.

"Are you saying you believe Steward Tarben's claims the bear is enchanted?" she asked, unable to suppress a shiver. Raisa's tales of northern sorcery all seemed to involve darkness and violence, nothing like the wise council the Almasans prayed to receive from the spirits of those gone before.

Eira snorted. "Sounds like an excuse for poor aim to me."

"The council wanted to hire a sorcerer," Hartwin said, sidestepping the question of belief, "but Tarben said it was the king's responsibility to protect his people, else what do we pay taxes for?"

"Tarben didn't want to pay for a sorcerer? Even though he thinks the threat is unnatural?" Marjani asked. She shouldn't be surprised. She knew the lengths people would go to save a bit of gold.

Hartwin shot her a wry glance. "We rode to Newport because it was cheaper than boat passage. We're only taking you by sea rather than traveling back with the other men and horses because it's a few silver pieces cheaper than acquiring a carriage fit for two princesses."

"Just my luck," Eira groaned. She clutched the rail as the prow shimmied in the current.

"You don't like boats?" Hartwin asked. "But the Nordish are a seafaring people."

Barbarous seafaring marauders, Raisa had told Marjani, but apparently Hartwin was too well-mannered to say so. Then again, he hadn't called Almasans *pirates* as she'd heard some Aldforthians mutter. He seemed genuinely interested in other cultures and other kingdoms. It was … disarming.

"I love boats." Eira leaned against the rail, sucking in deep breaths of air. "Unfortunately, my stomach does not. Going belowdecks only made it worse."

"If you're going to be sick, do it up here," Marjani ordered. It was bad enough that she and Eira had to share that tiny cabin. It would be unbearable if the horrible girl couldn't keep the contents of her stomach to herself.

"Nothing to do but live through it," Eira said cheerfully. "Should get my sea legs in a day or two."

"It will only take four or five to reach Saebern," Hartwin assured her.

"Excellent news!" Eira paled even more and draped wretchedly over the rail.

Marjani could almost pity her. *Almost.*

"It's a good thing Prince Theo isn't here to see this. I've already got to beat long odds to win his hand." The girl was much too cocky for someone whose face was slowly turning green. "But that will change when I kill this bear."

"You will not be Prince Theodor's bride," Marjani warned her. "And I will be the one to kill the bear. Do *you* believe it is enchanted, Reeve Hartwin?"

"The king's competition, he can't really mean for you princesses to—" Hartwin began.

Marjani could see his consternation at the thought of them battling for the chance to wed the prince. But what could he say that would not be impertinent to them or disparaging of the king? He answered her question instead.

"As far as I can tell, so-called magic is just folks wanting to believe they can change reality by wishing things were different." His frown suggested he'd seen too much reality he couldn't change. "It's best to see the world as it is. My older sister had a fancy for the shoemaker's son, so she bought a love spell off the hedge witch to 'win her one true love.' The concoction made the poor boy so sick we had to call for the apothecary. Now Catrin's married to the apothecary, and I've got two little nephews running around the family bakery."

Eira laughed. "Sounds like your sister got her wish, after all."

"Ask her about that when she's changing the baby's diaper."

Proud of their practicality, these Aldforthians. Only believe what they can hold in their hands.

Marjani touched the gold band around her wrist. The sharp edge of the broken circle that had once linked the bracelet to its missing half had long since worn smooth enough not to cut. Not like the edges of her broken soul. "I don't know what power your people think is working in this bear, but in Almasa, we know better than to make light of forces we cannot see."

"It's not the forces I have a problem with," Hartwin said. "It's the people who claim to control them."

The words were clipped, as if he regretted saying even that much, but Eira nudged him with her shoulder. "Tell us then. We can't help your town if we don't know what's going on."

Marjani *felt* the wave of Hartwin's discomfort. She pulled back automatically, but she hadn't touched him. He was still a seemly arm span away, yet she sensed his spirit as though attuned even from a distance, that extra sense she should not have, that she could not control. Felt his discomfiture at Eira's familiarity, reluctance warring with deference for a princess, and something deeper, more painful. If Marjani told him she could perceive such things, he would undoubtedly say she'd noticed his hands clenched on the rail, the tightness of his jaw.

"A Ravninan sorcerer visited Saebern last year," Hartwin said finally. "Name of Rurik. He'd come from King Wulfric's court in Cadesleigh with a token of passage from the archbishop. The folk at the manor seemed impressed by his tricks. He made Steward Tarben's wife, Lady Silke's ruby ring disappear from her hand and reappear in a cup of wine.

"Rurik claimed he could steal the future from the spirits and turn himself into smoke to travel on the wind, but the spirits didn't warn him that Steward Tarben would catch him in Lady Silke's embrace. He had to jump out a window like an ordinary man to avoid the steward's fists."

Eira burst into giggles, but the story made Marjani shiver. The living were meant to listen to the spirits. What might someone who spoke so boldly of controlling them do when challenged?

"Might the sorcerer have enchanted the bear in retaliation for his embarrassment?" she asked.

"No," Hartwin said, but not in dismissal. The twist of his mouth showed a man who had thought long and hard on the question. "Earl Berengar found the whole incident a good joke. He refused Tarben's pleas to send the sorcerer away. Even if Rurik had some kind of power beyond sleight of hand and his bag of potions, he had no reason to wish County Saebern ill.

"Some folk still believe the sorcerer conjured the bear, but if so, he paid a high price. He was with Berengar on the hunt last summer when the earl disappeared. We didn't find either of their bodies, just Rurik's cloak, drenched in blood. The bear must have carried him off. An evil season all around."

The shadow of deep grief lingered like smoke around the young man's spirit.

Kindness said to let him be, but much as she hated to admit it, Eira was right. Whatever strangeness surrounded this bear, she must learn as much about it as possible in order to know how best to kill it. An outcome that would serve him and his people in addition to bringing satisfaction closer to hers.

"The earl disappeared hunting this bear?" she asked. "I thought Steward Tarben said they were on a boar hunt."

"They were hunting boar." Dredging up the memory made Hartwin appear older than his years. "From what we could decipher of the scene, they cornered the boar in a thicket. It got past the first spear and gored Reeve Wendel— my father."

"Oh," Eira gasped. "How awful."

"I'm sorry. I didn't know." Marjani clenched her fists at her sides, though the pain in Hartwin's eyes made her ache to reach for his shoulder. Touching him would only intensify the phantom scents of blood and fear, and she had experienced enough of both to know she could not lift them from him.

"This is not a 'quest' the king has set you," Hartwin said, jaw tight. "It's a bloodbath. You should know. After killing my father, the boar ripped open Marshal Falk's leg, but Falk managed to bury his spear in the beast's neck before he bled to death. It was still there when we found what was left of the boar after the bear got to it. I hope for Rurik's sake he was dead when the bear found him, too."

"May the One Goddess enfold them in her peace," Eira murmured, now as pale with horror as nausea.

Sanctimonious as always. Marjani shuddered and pulled her cloak tighter. "What about the earl?"

"I hope the bear took his time with the earl."

That rendered even Eira speechless.

"Marshal Falk always gave Earl Berengar first chance at the quarry on any hunt," Hartwin said, his voice hard. "If he'd struck true, they'd all have come home that night. But the boar got past him, and he must have run away. There was no sign he tried to help the others. No sign of him at all. Probably got lost and fell down a ravine or died of exposure. But I hope the bear got him."

If his grief was smoke, his anger was crawling, licking flame. Marjani's skin burned with recognition. Even if Crown Prince Guntram had caused her brother's death by cowardice rather than murder, what was left of her soul would still be tethered to the ravaging darkness of her hatred.

"Your father," she said, her voice empty as her heart. "You said he was reeve, and now you are. But Princess Ellycia told me every Aldforthian town's reeve is chosen by its council."

"The council chose me to follow my father." Hartwin's mouth twisted wryly. "Half the council wanted Kaspar the wool merchant, half wanted Jock the blacksmith. They all agreed to me as second choice. I also inherited my father's bakery. I enjoy that a great deal more."

A glint of amusement shone through the dark emotion in his eyes when they met hers, and her breath caught at the smile it pulled from her.

"The council must have had reason to suspect enchantment," she said brusquely. She needed information, not distraction. "You said they would have hired a sorcerer if not for Tarben's ... frugality."

"I don't mean to be unfair to the man," Hartwin said. "He takes his job as steward of the manor's resources seriously. Control of Saebern's revenues still technically belongs to Earl Berengar, at least until Berengar's niece—Tarben's stepdaughter, Artis—comes into her inheritance a little over a sennight from now."

"The anniversary of Berengar's disappearance," Eira said.

"The council," Marjani pressed. Convoluted Saebernian politics wasn't going to help her kill a bear.

"I don't blame them for their desperation," Hartwin admitted, shifting his gaze to the swift, dark water. "Good hunters have tried to kill this bear. They say a well-thrown spear slides right off its haunches. I myself have seen it emerge unharmed from a shower of arrows. I understand why they say it's no ordinary beast."

"Maybe it's a good thing Marjani followed me on this adventure after all," Eira said. "She might be able to tell if the bear is truly ensorcelled."

"*Ensorcelled?*" The sounds squished like raw octopus in Marjani's mouth.

"It's a word," Eira insisted. "Isn't it?"

"You have an acquaintance with sorcery, Princess Marjani?" A sudden wariness flickered in Hartwin's eyes. So much for his unbelief.

"Princess Eira's people believe babies with different colored eyes are touched with demon magic," Marjani explained. "So they *murder* them."

"It's an *old* belief," Eira shot back. "I've agreed it's horrible. The Temple of Peace teaches us how—"

"Can the Temple teach you how *not* to be a Nordish barbarian? Because slaughtering innocents doesn't seem peaceful to me—"

"Your Highnesses!" Hartwin's eyes were wide as a cornered antelope's, trapped between them.

The ship groaned through a bend in the narrows, and Eira grabbed for the railing, breaking their mutual glare.

"I wasn't talking about your eyes this time," the Nordish girl grumbled. "Beatrix said you got all spooky in the tunnels under Lukos, claiming you sensed something evil. I just wondered if you could do the same with this bear."

A girl can't sense spirits. Her father's scorn raked her memories.

Marjani's nails dug into her palms. She should never have spoken up that night in the tunnels. She knew better than to expose herself that way. Even so, she couldn't turn her back on the challenge in Eira's eyes.

"If I got close enough, I might be able to tell if evil had been worked against the bear," she admitted. Dread—or maybe relief—flickered up her spine like a flame. She'd spoken the truth of it for once, and, whatever their skepticism, neither of them had laughed or struck her or turned their back. She *might* be able to tell. *And what then?* Fear prickled her skin. She was no sorcerer. But perhaps if she could sense an enchantment, she could sense a fissure within it. "If I did, would you even believe me?"

"I never said *I* didn't believe in sorcery. I just don't think it matters that much." Eira grinned. "I'll kill the beast long before you get close enough to tell."

The prow lurched and shuddered, and the Nordish princess drooped over the rail to gag wretchedly.

"What are you planning to do?" Marjani demanded. "Drown the bear in your enchanted vomit?"

Hartwin frowned, the resulting dimples reproaching her, but Eira shook with giggles, even as she moaned.

Marjani turned her face back to the breeze and closed her

eyes. Everything Hartwin had told them only reinforced her determination. She had not chosen this quest, yet she would complete it. She would kill this bear and get her chance at Prince Theodor.

But it was going to be a long voyage.

25

CHAPTER THREE

2. She never thinks before she speaks.

— Top 10 things I despise about Princess Eira, as listed by Princess Marjani of Almasa

The knock on the cabin door pounded like a smith's hammer inside Eira's skull. The bones above her right eye felt as though they might crack under the blows.

"Go away!" she rasped. "Or I'll break your fingers off and stuff them down your throat!"

The door creaked open. "I'm beginning to wonder what they teach at your Temple of Peace."

Reeve Hartwin. The young, strong, *handsome* Reeve Hartwin. Of course. Exactly the person she wanted to find her lying in sweaty agony with her hair plastered limply to her face and her skin the color of a rock lizard's hide.

She cracked her eyelids just far enough to kill him with the razor-sharp blades shooting from her pupils. As long as she had daggers stabbing the backs of her eyes, she ought to be able to shoot them at people.

Peace, Eira. Words should not be used as weapons. Eira sighed. If

26

only the memory of Holy Mother's voice could catch her *before* she felt the impulse to kill people.

"They teach forthright communication," she said, closing her lids against the pity in Hartwin's sea-green gaze. "It's one of the Nine Roads to Peace. If you'd listened to me and gone away, we would be on peaceable terms at this very moment."

She peeked at him again. His unruly, windswept hair fell forward, obscuring those fascinating eyes. He should do something about that. Although, over the course of their endless voyage, he'd usually been too distracted by Marjani to turn his eyes Eira's way. Not that she could blame him. Marjani had fascinating eyes, too.

And none of that mattered because she was going to marry Prince Theo. Who also had lovely eyes. And thank the One Goddess they weren't here to see her like this.

She groaned and rolled her own eyes up into her head.

"Princess Marjani says you have a headache from dehydration," Hartwin pressed, "but you refuse to drink anything."

"I *can't* drink anything. There's a difference," she said. "Marjani keeps telling me seasickness can't kill you, but I love a challenge. Besides, at a low point last night, I swore to the One Goddess that if she got me to solid ground, I would make peace with that Almasan doomsayer. I'd rather die."

"You're not going to die."

Eira made a noise that Holy Mother would *not* have approved of. "I've tried every treatment suggested by every sailor on this ship and said more prayers than Abbess Sofia could fit into a hundred Sevenday services. I think it's obvious I won't survive this interminable journey."

"It's only been four days—"

"That's impossible! It's been *eons*."

"—even with changing ships at Portsmouth. A swifter voyage than we could have hoped for."

"Leave me. Death shouldn't be long now."

Hartwin's footsteps came closer to her narrow bunk. "Unless you plan to expire in the next half hour, you're not going to manage it. We've entered Anberry Harbor. We've reached County Saebern."

"Oh, praise the Goddess!" Eira sat up so quickly that Hartwin had to jump back to avoid a collision. The rest of her body might be shaky as custard, but her abdominal muscles had never been stronger. Holy Mother always said there was some good to find in every situation. "You're not teasing me?"

"I'm not teasing. Come up on deck."

He held out a hand, and she grabbed it like a lifeline. Her fingers looked slender and pale against Hartwin's. His didn't have the rough calluses from sword training and archery practice that hers did, but they were sure and strong, and his arms were powerfully muscled. Baker's arms.

"All that kneading."

His brow knit in confusion. "Sorry?"

"I'm lightheaded from starvation," she said. Maybe her hungry smile showed a little too much tooth, because he pulled her upright fast enough to make her head spin. She clutched her stomach as she followed unsteadily after him into the passageway and up the ladder to the deck.

"Oh." As she stepped away from the hatch, a cooling breeze lifted her hair from her face. She filled her lungs with air scented by the forests that swept down the hills surrounding the rocky shores of the harbor—pine and moss and earth and rock. The stone cottages of a small village clustered by the docks, only a few tantalizing furlongs of ruffled bay water away.

Yet it wasn't the nearness of relief from her endless nausea that tightened her throat and stung her eyes.

If she lowered her lashes and listened to the seabirds crying, she could imagine she was almost home, that only a few craggy promontories, a mountain or two, separated her from the fields and forests she'd known so well in Nordmark. That she would never see again.

"Princess Eira? Are you all right?" Hartwin's hand gripped her elbow as if he feared she might collapse.

She opened her eyes and pulled free. The summer sun warmed her shoulders. And yet, her heart felt suddenly cold, a jagged chunk of sea ice lodged in her chest.

"You've gone white. Whiter than usual." Marjani's red robes swirled at the edge of Eira's vision like a promise of blood. "Though I must admit, it is more attractive than the green."

"I wouldn't get too close," Eira warned thinly. "I would hate to accidentally murder you with my lethal vomit. I'm saving it for the bear."

The red robes stalked away in a huff.

"You swore an oath of peace," Hartwin reminded her.

"We haven't reached land. I don't owe the One Goddess yet," Eira snapped back. "And it's no business of yours, anyway."

"Your Highness." He bowed and left her to join Marjani at the opposite rail. The Almasan princess asked a question, and he pointed to something on the shore.

Eira turned her eyes to the wind, drying the traitorous moisture. This wasn't Nordmark, and no amount of wishing would make it so. Uncle Einar had severed her from her homeland forever.

You will never be a queen. Even at twelve years old, she had heard the grievance and bitterness beneath her uncle's gloating words as he exiled her to the Temple of Peace. She realized years later he had only feared her because he had so feared her mother, but his unease had sparked the knowledge that she *could* become someone to be feared. Someone who mattered.

Now she had her chance to prove it. If she rid Saebern of its bear, it would show King Wulfric she could protect Prince Theodor. As the disinherited princess of an Aldforthian protectorate, she might be an unlikely candidate to win Theo's hand. But Wulfric valued brutal efficiency—hence his obvious preference for the dead Prince Guntram over his current heir. The king might enjoy the idea of a Nordish barbarian on the throne at his son's side, a savage ice witch to frighten his neighbors.

To gain the throne and make a difference, make *peace*, for all the Blessed Kingdoms, Eira just had to convince him that she *was* that savage ice witch of Aldforthian nightmares.

Without becoming one.

After her exile, she had dreamed of returning to Nordmark like an avenging demon and challenging her uncle for the throne. There must be enough of her mother's faithful supporters left that she could foment a rebellion. Enough of the rebellious Nordish spirit left to oppose her uncle's capitulation to Aldforth.

Enough for her to cause a civil war. Maybe even win it. And bring the crushing wrath of Aldforth down on her divided and traumatized people.

It had taken a long time for her to realize that such a war would certainly make a difference to Nordmark—by making life even worse for the people who lived there. It was this competition to marry Prince Theo that had offered her another chance to make a difference. Through peace.

Yet it seemed such an improbable chance for such an improbable princess …

She lifted a hand to the frog charm at her throat, but not even the thought of her friends—her competition—could thaw the frost in her chest. If only one of them were here with her instead of Marjani. They'd figure out how to kill this bear together. If only she were her mother, confident and commanding, she wouldn't need any help.

"I see you are able to stand unaided, Princess Eira." Steward Tarben approached her, stroking the trim, graying beard that sharpened his chin to a point. "I wondered how you would accomplish your boast of killing our bear while lying on your death bed, but now I can rest easy knowing you are mobile, after all."

Her laughter startled the steward and cracked the ice constricting her ribs. So much for terrifying people with her

Nordish savagery. "I am even more surprised and delighted by my vertical posture than you are, Steward Tarben. Thank you. Your condescension has reminded me that gratitude is one of the Nine Roads to Peace."

The man's mouth twisted sourly, settling deep into its accustomed aggrieved lines. "This ship cannot draw any closer to shore. We will transfer to a galley for the journey upriver to Saebern Town."

Eira followed his gesture to the small, single-masted boat rowing steadily toward them from the harbor village. Her stomach lurched.

"That's not Saebern Town?" she asked. No wonder even the king forgot about County Saebern's troubles. It was farther from the rest of civilization than the Fair Isles. "I thought this was the end of our voyage! Shouldn't the county seat be here at the harbor?"

"Not at all," he said, dismissing her misery. "The manor overlooks the finest farmland in the Saebern Valley. The town mills our grain and timber right there, saving time and money. The Saebern River is easily navigable for shipping goods the league from Saebern Town to the sea here at Anberry."

"Only a league!" Relief made her whole body feel lighter. "We can walk!"

The steward's spiky brows pinched together, making her think of caterpillars kissing. "You're in no shape for walking, Your Highness."

That was just insulting. "After being trapped on this boat for all eternity, a brisk hour's stroll will do me nothing but good."

"Don't be foolish. The terrain is rough, and the road passes through the woods. We could encounter the *bear*." He whispered the last word as though afraid the beast might hear him.

"Steward Tarben, you forget yourself." The ice in her heart might frighten her, but it sharpened the edge of her smile. "Encountering the bear is the entire reason I made this miserable journey. You need not fear. I won't let it harm you."

"Indeed." Tarben snorted. "The king told us all about your 'training' for his ball."

Eira stiffened. Wulfric knew about their secret training? Even the Lukos guards had agreed to keep secret that the princesses were working together, teaching each other the skills they needed to survive the king's contest—riding, spying, weapons training …

"Wearing out your *dancing slippers*." Tarben's voice wavered between contempt and outrage. "The bear would be happy to dance you a pavane."

"Oh, *dancing*. I don't think the bear will like my tune." She gave him her most challenging grin as she stifled a sigh of relief. The others were still safe from the king's wrath if he discovered the truth. The dancing story had been her idea. And not a lie. Princess Pia was an excellent dance instructor.

"It is obvious the voyage has taken a great toll on you," the steward said stiffly, though whether the wrinkle of his nose was for her mental state or her odor, she couldn't tell. "As soon as we disembark at Saebern Town, you may make preparations to quit this foolish quest and return to Newport."

Eira drew herself up and inhaled another deep breath of the sweet-scented breeze. She wasn't her mother. She wasn't bossy Raisa or intimidating Marjani. But she was still a Nordish princess, and she'd never given up on a competition in her life. She was going to kill that bear, and she couldn't do that vomiting over the rail of yet another boat.

She turned square to the steward. He stood slightly taller than she, but she could meet his gaze and hold it without craning her neck. "I don't think you understood what I said, Master Steward. I will be disembarking here in Anberry Harbor. I *will* walk to Saebern Town."

She watched him slowly recognize her words as a royal command.

"Very well," he said, his words thin and tight. "I will arrange it. Your Highness."

She held her dignified posture until he turned away to find the captain. Then she bit back a grin. After five years of living as a humble religious acolyte, being a barbarian princess again could turn out to be decidedly too much fun.

CHAPTER FOUR

8. She complains about *everything*.

— Top 10 things ~~I hate~~ I find difficult to appreciate about Princess Marjani, as listed by (former) Princess Eira of Nordmark

Tired as she was of the Nordish maggot's complaints about boat travel, Marjani had to admit it felt good to stretch her legs. And to begin to assess the terrain where her hunt would begin. Dejen used to say the hunted chose the battlefield, but a good hunter knew the choice their prey would make before the prey did. Therefore, the hunter had no cause to complain if he or she did not find it to their liking.

"Isn't this bliss? All this fresh air and blessed peace?" Eira demanded, ruining the peace completely. "Maybe we all died on that awful boat, and we've arrived on the shores of the Summer Lands."

Marjani glanced from the rutted, uneven road to the bleak, rocky hillside they climbed. An unfavorable landscape for stalking prey—or doing much else. A bear would see a hunter from half a league away. "The Summer Lands. Is that your Nordish term for the home of the eternally damned?"

"Look at all this *space!*" Eira spun her arms wide, nearly striking poor Steward Tarben. Despite the girl's claims to be on death's door, a bit of bread and cheese, some fresh spring water, and two feet on dry ground had restored her to thoroughly irritating. "Smell the air. Stone and ferns and heather. And the promise of more forest ahead."

"Not to mention murderous bears," Tarben muttered darkly.

Eira made a rude noise. "Not even an ice bear would attack this many humans all at once."

"We're not worried about an ice bear," Hartwin said.

Marjani studied the young man from the corner of her eye. When he had first arrived at King Wulfric's summer court in Newport, he had seemed overawed in the presence of so much wealth and royalty. The close quarters and lack of court formality on their voyage had eroded his wariness of her and Eira, allowing his sly humor to escape. And now she saw yet another side of him as he scanned the countryside with grim intensity, preparing himself for an encounter with a monstrous bear, despite the awkwardness with which he wore the battered old sword at his hip.

Marjani tightened her grip on her spear. She and Eira undoubtedly had more weapons training than either Hartwin or Tarben—or the two stout, axe-wielding yeomen they'd hired in Anberry Harbor as escorts. Yet, none of their companions showed any confidence in the princesses' ability to protect themselves.

Their skepticism obviously annoyed Eira, but Marjani mostly worried that if they actually met a bear, the men might get in her way. Otherwise, she welcomed them as witnesses. Bluff and pragmatic, they would make reputable disseminators of the tale of a foreign princess slaughtering a marauding monster.

She didn't want Wulfric merely to suffer the justice he deserved for what he had done to her family and her kingdom.

She wanted the fear of it whispering in his ear long before it arrived.

Movement caught her eye. Something breaking the pattern of wind across the heather, cloud shadow across the patchy grasses. Wary eagerness pricked her skin before she recognized the curve of a hat.

"Someone is there," she said, nodding toward a dip in the road up ahead where a gully cut through the rocky slope. A few hardy trees clung to the creek bed, obscuring the man from view.

Apparently, there were more secrets to the terrain than met the eye.

"It looks like Old Lothar," Hartwin said. "What's he doing there?"

"His croft is just yonder." One of the yeomen, a burly, red-bearded man, pointed to the crest of the hill where a small stone cottage blended into the rocky surroundings.

Sheep dotted the meadow beyond the dwelling, looking as if some of the fluffy clouds overhead had strayed from the sky and gotten caught in the gorse. Such odd, graceless, shaggy creatures sheep were. Yet somehow appealing. Unlike their meat. In contrast to most Aldforthian food, mutton had plenty of flavor. Sadly, it was a highly unfortunate flavor.

Marjani preferred venison, more like gazelle. Prince Theodor and his friends—the "Rose Knights," as the princesses had called them ever since they'd dressed as rose-wielding bandits on Presentation Day—sometimes delivered deer to Lukos's kitchens from their hunts. Offerings of their prowess to be admired.

It unsettled her how much the young men reminded her of her brother and his companions. Mosi had been no younger than herself—he was her twin, after all, his soul half of hers—yet he and his friends had been so much more care-free than she could ever be. Like a pack of puppies, eager to be praised and supremely confident in their ability to escape any trouble with their youthful strength or their charm, whichever might be required. Unable to believe evil could ever touch them.

Not Dejen, of course. Mosi's chief spear-bearer had been as careful of her brother's safety and protective of his secrets as she, as quick to sense danger and as fierce in destroying it.

Or being destroyed by it.

Agony pierced her heart, so sharp that for an instant she thought she had been struck by one of Eira's arrows, and she missed a step on the uneven ground. A quick flick of her wrist enabled her to steady herself with the butt of her spear.

She steeled her face against her embarrassment, but no one had noticed. They were all focused on the man crouched in the gully up ahead. A skinny youth was scrambling down the hill to join him, gesturing excitedly toward their oncoming group.

The older man rose from whatever he had been examining and doffed his broad-brimmed hat. "Steward Tarben. Reeve Hartwin. *Wal mecht.*" He said something more in rumbling Aldforthian and nudged the gawking boy beside him with his elbow. The youth bobbed his head.

"Good day to you, Old Lothar," Hartwin greeted him in Common Tongue. "And Young Lothar."

Old Lothar was probably no "older" than Steward Tarben, but hard work and harsh weather had cragged his face and stooped his back. What remained of his hair was a tattered gray. His dark eyes looked quick enough, though.

"I mislike correcting you," Old Lothar responded, with a grim relish that belied his words, "but I wouldn't say it was a good day. Nay, sir. Not a good day at all."

"It's the bear, sir!" the youth burst out, his voice cracking so that he blushed bright red.

Eira whipped her bow off her shoulder and nocked an arrow—as though these two sheep farmers would be loitering on the road if a dangerous predator were poised to attack nearby. Marjani brushed past her to see what Old Lothar had found in the gully.

It took her eyes a long moment to make sense of the scene. The vividness of the red splashed across the rocks and dusty road faded the rest of the world to a dull gray. Bones. A cracked rib cage. The body's head had been torn off and lay several yards away in the center of the gully wash across the road. Its dulled eyes stared at her.

"My gods," Steward Tarben choked out. One of the yeomen turned away, gagging.

A noise tore from Marjani's throat, primal and wretched, even as her mind recognized the dead creature as a … *sheep. A sheep. Not a person. Not Mosi …*

"Are you all right?" A hand on her arm. Eira's white hand against Marjani's red cloak, like the sheep's wool in its blood.

Marjani jerked away, knocking the hand aside. "I am perfectly fine." She turned on Old Lothar. "This animal was not killed by a bear. No wild beast engages in such gratuitous slaughter."

If the man were surprised at being challenged by a foreign woman with a spear, his eagerness to prove his point overrode it.

"Beg your pardon, milady, but it's the bear, right enough." He crouched and pointed to the dirt nearby where a massive paw had imprinted its pad, five toes, and five long, sharp claws. "There's teeth marks on the bones."

"And more prints up the gully," Young Lothar added shyly. "I could show you, if you like."

"We trust your eyes," Steward Tarben said. "Princess Marjani can hardly have much experience with animal attacks."

The boy's eyes widened at the word "princess." Old Lothar grabbed his arm and dragged him into a bow.

"Meant no disrespect to you, Your Highness." The sheep farmer looked as though he might topple, he'd bent over so far.

"It's all right," Eira assured him. "Marjani always glares like that, but we're not like those evil queens from the fairy tales who execute people for looking at us wrong."

"I could make an exception for you, Princess Eira," Marjani snapped. Was it any wonder if she glared whenever the Nordish girl was around? "I have seen my share of animal kills, Steward. Leopards, hyenas, jackals—they may not be tidy eaters, but they do not mutilate their prey for no reason. The only animal I have ever seen do such a thing is a man."

Your Crown Prince Guntram. But she did not say it.

"I can't speak to that, Your Highness," Old Lothar said, straightening as much as he was able. "But you're right that this inn't normal. I've had a bear take a lamb once or twice over the years, hungry as they are in the spring, but never a full-grown ewe. The attacks are getting worse. I'm afraid to take my flock up to the higher pastures, but seems they're not safe anywheres. This coulda been one of mine."

"This isn't your sheep?" Hartwin asked.

"Nay, my mark is a notch in the left ear." Old Lothar walked to the sheep's head and turned the right ear so they could all see the bar shape punched into its center. He glanced uneasily at Tarben. "This is the manor's mark. One of the earl's sheep."

The steward's face paled, then flushed crimson. "This is outrageous. The beast is destroying our property, threatening our livelihoods, terrorizing our people, and the king treats it like a joke!"

Steward Tarben's histrionic tales of the bear's predations had sounded far-fetched in the great hall at Newport Castle. Standing on a barren hillside with the remains of this brutalized sheep, Marjani broke out in goose flesh that had nothing to do with the Aldforthian climate.

She scanned the hillside once more. Had the bear chased the ewe down this gully? Or had it lurked in hiding in the brush? And what drove it to such savagery? An unpredictable adversary was the most dangerous of all.

"Wish the earl were here. He'd know what to do," Old Lothar said. "The old earl, I mean. Earl Hallborn."

The other men nodded solemnly.

"It's sad." Eira crouched beside the head and gently closed the sheep's eyelids, cutting off its blank stare. "Terrible, but sad."

Marjani's heart indeed ached, though whether for the sheep, the people, or her own memory, she couldn't say.

"Funny how it's right here in the middle of the road," Eira continued. "Like it's meant to be looking up at us when we reach the gully."

She glanced at Marjani, and for once, Marjani thought they were in complete agreement. *What in all the world's hells have we gotten ourselves into?*

"We can't leave it here," Old Lothar said. "The carcass will attract other predators. Though the wolves're as chary as everyone else with this bedamned bear around. Pardon an old man's language, Your Highnesses."

"I'll send men from the manor to take the meat and bury the rest," Tarben told him.

If Old Lothar had hoped to gain his supper for his trouble with the sheep, he did a fair job of hiding his disappointment. Then again, who could say how much meat, exactly, was left on the savaged carcass and whether it would be the same amount by the time the manor's men arrived?

"We should hurry," Hartwin said. "You won't want men on the road after dark, Steward, and it looks like a storm coming in."

Marjani glanced up, surprised to see the fluffy, sheep-like clouds clumping into ominous herds.

Old Lothar's lined face creased even deeper. "You're not taking these royal ladies on to the manor now? Through the forest? This ewe'd not been dead more'n a quarter-hour when my dog found her and raised the alarm."

"Bears are dead fast," Young Lothar said. "If our Sheena scared it off, it'll be leagues away by now."

None of the adults commented on the likelihood of the boy's sheepdog frightening this particular bear.

"It's as far back to Anberry Harbor as it is to Saebern

Manor," Tarben said grimly. "The princesses are the ones who insisted on walking. We'll do our best to keep them safe."

A glance at Eira told Marjani they were once again feeling exactly the same thing. Irritation at being underestimated.

Of course, the Nordish girl spoiled it by laughing. The ridiculous witch could not take even indignation seriously.

"You'll have to keep up with us, then," Eira said. "Marjani's the only princess in Lukos who can run almost as fast as I can."

Hartwin's eyes widened in dismay.

"I am not running anywhere," Marjani assured him with a cool frown at Eira. "I intend to keep watch for bear sign. I won't miss a chance to dispatch it."

"Don't kill it today," Eira pleaded, hurrying after her, leaving Tarben to spit out hurried, officious orders to the Lothars. "I need at least a fortnight to recover before I get back on that hellish boat."

"This isn't a game to these people," Marjani reminded her. Their distress swirled around her like an ocean current. "They're frightened and in need of help."

"And we're here to help them!" Eira said. "I don't need them to show us respect or gratitude—and they should thank the One Goddess for that, since they seem incapable of either. But why should I have to be all brooding and miserable for them?"

"Decency?" Marjani suggested. "A shred of simple dignity would suffice."

Red bloomed in the Nordish girl's pale cheeks. "Why bother? You're grim and dismal enough for both of us."

"You're a boor."

"You're a bore!"

Reeve Hartwin stepped up between them, his voice pitched low. "Isn't name-calling one of the Nine Roads to War?"

Marjani scowled at him, and Eira must have done the same because, after a quick glance between them, Hartwin raised his hands in surrender and dropped back. After another exchange of angry glares, Marjani stepped to the right side of the road, and Eira moved to the left.

Marjani fingered the broken edge of her bracelet as she scanned the countryside, the weathered hills and tree-covered slopes. The dead sheep had unsettled her, distracted her from the only thing that mattered. However cunning or ferocious it might be, she needed to find this bear. She needed to be the one to kill this bear. And then, she needed to return to Newport Castle and put the remaining scrap of her soul to rest.

4. She assumes she's always right.

— Top 10 things I despise about Princess Eira, as listed by Princess Marjani of Almasa

Eira stomped along the road, glaring into the forest depths around them. She'd been wrong about Marjani. The Almasan princess wasn't hard to like. She was *impossible* to like.

She's far from home, Eira could hear Jax chiding her. *She must be missing her family.*

As if people whose families were still alive got more credit for missing them! Oh, sure, Marjani had recently lost her brother—

Lost?

Fine, so "lost" wasn't the right word. Marjani had seen her brother brutally murdered by Crown Prince Guntram, who had then paraded the young man's head around the Blessed Kingdoms in a box, like some kind of grisly trophy.

An image of the sheep's head, dead and staring in the middle of the road, flashed through Eira's mind, and she shuddered in sudden, brutal empathy.

Yes, Marjani wasn't the only one who had lost loved ones

to Aldforthian brutality, but … Marjani wasn't the only one who'd acted like a complete witch afterward, either. Eira hadn't exactly made many friends when she'd first arrived in exile at the Temple of Peace, nearly smoking with the fire of her righteous hatred and violent grief.

She shot a surreptitious glance at Marjani striding tall and confident on the other side of the road, searching the woods for bear sign while the men trailed nervously behind them. Only the tension in the Almasan princess's shoulders betrayed her lingering horror over the bloody scene a quarter hour behind them.

Holy Mother always said the One Goddess had a sly sense of humor. It would be just like her to shackle Eira with someone unbearable—and then expose how similar that person's need for compassion and peace was to her own.

The Nordish gods were capricious at best, by turns generous and mean, playful and spiteful, involved and indifferent. When Eira was first exiled to the Temple, she had scorned its goddess, who offered nothing more than love and acceptance and then expected her children to be grateful and share it. Eira certainly hadn't felt loved and accepted. The priestesses were mostly kind enough. But no one knew quite what to make of a girl who wasn't there to become a priestess and yet could never return to her home kingdom like the other temporary acolytes, to spread learning and the message of peace.

Still, years of being immersed in the goddess's teachings hadn't left her untouched. Eira sometimes felt that whisper of serenity in her heart, like a golden thread connecting her to the web of the universe.

So much so that when Holy Mother had chosen her as the Temple's candidate to compete for Prince Theodor's hand, she had dared to dream it might be her destiny. That she might be the one to guide Aldforth away from its history of war and conquest and onto the road of peace for the sake of all the Blessed Kingdoms.

Right. As if she were the hearth maiden in a fairy tale, an orphan chosen for her kind heart to marry a prince and live happily ever after. At least half the twelve princesses sent to Aldforth believed it was their destiny to marry the prince—the other half were just hoping to survive the ball.

If destiny *had* set Eira on this particular path, she'd managed to stumble back off into the wilderness. Now that the sheer joy of being on dry land had faded, the cumulative effects of days of seasickness sapped her strength and her conviction that this quest offered her any advantage in the competition. If she actually did see a bear, she wasn't sure she'd be able to lift her bow, much less kill it. She already looked pitiful compared to Marjani's cool competence. Collapsing in the dirt would just make her ridiculous. If they'd stuck to the river, they'd probably be at Saebern Town by now ...

And she'd be missing this glorious walk.

She shook her head, dispersing the unnecessary wretchedness over what might be to focus on the joy of what was.

Bursts of afternoon light broke through the clouds overhead and showered swaths of pine trees broken by stands of oak and birch. The heady scent of evergreens warmed by the brief northern summer wafted on the breeze. Birds sang in the trees, an occasional flash of dun, chartreuse, or crimson. Red squirrels chided them as they passed, the little animals' tufted ears giving them a perpetual look of vexed surprise.

If a bear attacked and killed her at that very moment, she would be sad to leave the beauty of this world. Whereas, if she were still on the boat, she'd be just as glad to end her misery.

"There!" One of the yeomen pointed into the trees. "There's something over there!"

Goddess! She'd lost her concentration. She unslung her bow from her back. She should have been the first to see the telltale shape. A large animal stood so still it almost disappeared into the bars of shadow cast by the trees—

Leaves crunched, and bushes crashed as the roe deer

bounded from its cover and sprang deeper into the forest, spooked by the humans staring from the road.

One of the yeomen muttered a prayer, and the other kissed his knuckles in a sign against evil.

Tarben turned a sour glare on Eira. "See there? Your refusal to take the boat has put us all in danger!"

"From a *deer?*" Never mind that her heart was probably skittering faster than the poor doe's. She settled her bow back over her shoulder. "It's no wonder you haven't rid yourselves of this bear if you don't dare leave the safety of your walls."

"There is no safety behind our walls!" Tarben shouted. "Have you listened to nothing we've said? The bear has wandered into town in broad daylight. It climbed over the manor wall one morning and tried to break down the door!"

"And yet, you are still alive." Marjani's voice was sharp as her spear. "Princess Eira and I are merely doing what we were sent here for. You may hurry ahead if you like. I am sure we can manage to follow the road without getting lost."

Heat rose from Tarben's pointed beard, turning his face into a torch. He ground his jaw so hard that Eira feared for his teeth, but he only barked at the yeomen to keep walking.

It wasn't fair. If Eira had said those exact words, the steward would have bitten her head off. Maybe there were benefits to Marjani's dour dignity, after all. Or maybe it was simply obvious that the Almasan was impervious to criticism, and Eira had never mastered that skill.

She stepped closer to the other princess and lowered her voice. "What happened to 'they're frightened and in need of help'?"

"I am tired of being told that *I* must be frightened. Are you capable of watching your side of the road, or must I do everything myself?"

Angry retorts bubbled in Eira's throat, and yet … *You swore an oath to make peace with her.* She couldn't think of a single one of the Nine Roads to Peace, but Holy Mother taught that shutting your mouth could sometimes prevent you from walking down the Nine Roads to War.

She flashed Marjani a bright smile. With—yes, all right—maybe a few more teeth than necessary. And drifted back to her side of the road, virtuously ignoring Marjani's eye roll.

They were coming to a fork. The main road followed the gentle curve of the land down to the right while the left branch turned sharply up the hill ahead.

"The manor's not far now." Hartwin gestured left.

Uphill. Of course. Eira straightened her spine and forced herself onward. *Food, rest, a soft bed*, she promised her legs. *Not necessarily in that order.*

The trees began to thin, the ferns and mosses beneath them giving way to grasses and heathers. As the road curved around a knob of weathered gray rock, the forest fell away altogether, giving them a clear view down the mountainside into the gently winding river valley below.

Eira stopped in surprise and delight, not just exhaustion. The gleaming ribbon of the Saebern River wended its way around the knees of rolling hills lined with stands of alder and birch. Sheep and cattle dotted the hillsides above the river, and cottages nestled among fields of oats and barley.

Below their outlook, a neatly laid-out town nestled along the riverbank, with bustling docks and a large market square, all surrounded by a wooden palisade. Mills lined the river—a lumber mill, a grist mill for grinding grain, and a fulling mill for treating the wool of the bucolic sheep. Even a mill to supply water to the town.

Saebern Town was much more prosperous than Eira had expected after their trek through the wilderness.

No more than two furlongs up the hill stood what had to be the manor. A rambling collection of pale, weathered rock and dark slate roofs, the buildings looked almost part of the hill itself. A stone wall surrounded the main house and most of its outbuildings, an ancient defense against prowling beasts

—and probably Nordish raiders, back when the Nordish thrived on raiding.

"It's beautiful, isn't it?" For the first time since Eira had met him, Steward Tarben's voice held neither irritation nor resentment. He gazed at the tranquil scene with an expression of satisfaction—and pride.

Watching him, Eira realized *steward* was more than a title to Tarben. More than a job. It described who he was—the person who stewarded County Saebern to keep it thriving and orderly. His obsession with the bear wasn't just his personal fear or frustration at the economic loss of a few sheep. If Tarben felt responsible for the county's prosperity, he must also feel responsible for protecting it.

"It *is* beautiful," Eira agreed, her own responsibility to help this place suddenly more weighty than when she had made her reckless vow far from its troubles.

"It can't be beauty alone that makes it worth living so far from your kingdom's center of power," Marjani said, pulling her cloak tighter against the massing clouds and freshening wind.

"Saebern provides the trees for all the masts in the Alforthian merchant fleet—and the king's navy," Tarben boasted. "We're increasing harvests to expand our timber exports to Venia and Ilhavair and beyond. Not to mention Saebern produces the best wool in the Blessed Kingdoms. You'd think the king would be eager to help us, considering the taxes we send him. And that the town would be satisfied with the manor's management, which increases its prosperity each year."

"The town is well aware of its debt to Earl Hallborn and to you as his steward," Hartwin said. Duty—or grief—weighed his voice. "It was only the old earl's death and Berengar's inheritance that pushed the council to ask for the independence of a royal charter."

"Berengar's management was less satisfactory than his

father's?" Eira asked. Her curiosity had returned, despite her lingering fatigue from the sea travel. That must be a good sign.

"He was a posturing fool," Hartwin said flatly.

"He was … young." Even that feeble defense seemed to stick in Tarben's throat. He cleared it. "He valued book learning over the advice of his elders, but he is not here now. Does the council disapprove of my management since his disappearance?"

"Of course not," Hartwin said. "Yet if, gods forbid, anything happened to you, the town's future would fall under the control of a toddling child."

"That's your daughter?" Eira asked Tarben.

"His stepdaughter," Marjani corrected. "Haven't you paid any attention at all?"

"Know-it-all," Eira snapped. "It's hard to care about politics when you're vomiting." Which probably did not make her compare more favorably to her rival, now that she thought about it.

"Your *step*daughter will inherit Berengar's title?" she asked Tarben with a haughty glance at Marjani. *I remember things, too.*

"Yes, and if I were to die, Lady Silke is perfectly capable of running the county until Artis comes of age." Tarben's beard quivered in indignation. "I intend for the child to receive her full inheritance, including the town."

"The council trusts the king will make a determination fair to all parties," Hartwin replied, equally stiff.

Eira shared a doubtful glance with Marjani. King Wulfric would do whatever enriched his coffers the most—the best outcome anyone dealing with the Aldforthian king could reasonably hope for.

"This view is so lovely." Eira stepped between the two men. "I bet it's even more impressive from the manor."

Holy Mother would have been proud. Finding common ground was the bedrock for building a road to peace.

And maybe reaching the manor before she collapsed.

Tarben's chest swelled a little, and he even offered her his arm. "You will not be disappointed."

Hartwin gave her a wry smile as he dropped back beside Marjani, out of the steward's line of sight.

"Lady Silke will be pleased to have female company," Tarben told Eira as he guided her up the hill. As if he hadn't spent the past sennight moaning about being sent home with princesses instead of knights. "She was used to a busier calendar of social gatherings before she married Lord Orson and moved to Saebern."

"I thought Lady Silke was *your* wife," Eira said. Hadn't he just said as much? How much of her wits had she lost on that blasted boat? "Who is Lord Orson?"

"Lord Orson was Earl Hallborn's oldest son," Tarben explained. "Lady Silke's first husband. He died of a fever a few months before Artis was born. The earl recalled Berengar from his studies in Rigas to take his place as heir. Earl Hallborn himself passed barely six months later." The steward shook his head. "A black year that was. A black, black year."

"Wait." The sequence of events didn't make sense. "Orson was the *older* brother? Shouldn't his daughter have become the earl when Hallborn died?"

"A woman would be a countess, not an earl," Tarben corrected. "And Artis was a baby. A baby girl."

"A girl." As if that explained everything. Eira pulled her arm from his. These people called the *Nordish* barbarians. At least her uncle had been forced to exile her to steal her inheritance. All the feckless Berengar had to do was show up.

"Artis is the heir now, of course," Tarben continued. "Earl Berengar had no other relatives on his father's side."

"So, Artis will be a child countess, after all," Eira said with grim satisfaction. No thanks to the shiftless uncle who had stolen her inheritance or the men who didn't seem to notice the irony.

"A sennight from tomorrow," Tarben agreed. "When the

year the king set aside for us to await Berengar's return is ended."

Seven days. Time enough to kill the bear and gift the child an inheritance free of the creature's reign of terror. Her jaw set. She would ensure this girl received the future she deserved.

"The town council needs have no concerns about the transition," Tarben droned on. "We already have plans underway to increase the arable land in the valley by expanding logging of the forests nearby—"

Eira's attention drifted to the manor they approached. To the food and rest that waited beyond the wall. To the heavy oak gates that would soon open to admit them … Her focus narrowed. The One Goddess had gifted her with an archer's acute vision. Yet, her mind couldn't quite accept what her eyes insisted on seeing. Something hung from the gates, just off-center, about shoulder height …

"*Is that a heart?*" The words burst out before she could stop them, an all too familiar problem. No one would stick a bloody heart on a manor gate. What a ridiculous idea.

And yet, Tarben shouted and began running up the road. Hartwin chased after him, and then the yeomen were running, too.

As Marjani passed her, some impulse made Eira reach for her arm.

The Almasan princess turned, her one amber and one green eye sharp as blades. "Is it the sheep's heart?"

An unnatural chill lifted the hair on the back of Eira's neck. She had feared it was a human heart. Horrific, yes. But if it were the sheep's heart …

Almost automatically, as if she were with Jax or Anara, she and Marjani turned back to back, scanning the countryside.

There. Her breath stopped. She tapped Marjani's elbow and pointed up the hillside. Beyond the manor wall, at the crest of the ridge, loomed the object of their quest. It was easily as large as an ice bear, but its fur gleamed a rich, honey-brown in the late afternoon light. As if it had only been waiting for their attention, the bear rose on its hind legs. And rose. And rose. It dropped its jaw and huffed.

And roared.

Eira heard the men cry out as they finally noticed the beast. She heard Hartwin shout for her and Marjani to run. The animal was at least a half mile past the manor, and still, she wasn't sure she could run fast enough to reach the gate before the bear reached her.

She lifted Prince Theo's bow from her shoulder. She had accused Marjani of sabotaging her own beautiful bow back when the damage had happened. She hoped now she'd been wrong. She needed the Almasan princess to guard her back, not stab her in it.

Theo had also gifted her a dozen hunting arrows for this quest—poplar fletched with white goose feathers, tipped with broadhead hunting points made for killing. She slid one from her quiver.

If the bear charged, her best chance for a lethal strike would come when it got within a hundred yards. She was quick enough to get off several shots before he closed that distance, but she couldn't forget the dismembered sheep's carcass. Even if every arrow struck true, she wasn't sure the bear would realize he was dead before he reached her. She might be glad of Marjani's spear, after all.

The Almasan princess stepped out to the side, flexing her throwing arm and setting her feet.

Eira nocked her arrow and pulled the string back with the smooth confidence of years of practice. *So much for being too tired to draw.* The surge of excitement made her grin with the joy of being alive for one more moment.

The bear bellowed again, the sound echoing off the hills, rolling down into the valley. He dropped to all fours, and Eira drew the bowstring to her ear.

But instead of charging toward them, the great beast

turned his back and broke into a lumbering run, disappearing over the crest of the hill.

"*Goddess.*" Eira slung her bow over her shoulder and prepared to give chase.

Before she could sprint after the bear, Hartwin barreled into view, cutting her off. He skidded to a stop, battered sword in his hand, breathing harder than the distance to the manor gate could account for.

"Are you both mad?" He waved his sword toward where the bear had disappeared. "Did you not see what it did to that sheep?"

"That's why we're here," Eira said. "To track it down and kill it."

"But now you've *seen* it …" Hartwin grabbed the back of his head with his free hand as if he might literally pull his hair out. "You can't believe the king means for you to hunt that animal. He only meant to make fools of us."

"That was his mistake," Eira said. "Not mine."

And this was her chance to show what a mistake it was. If she could kill the bear on the first day of their arrival—

"There's no point in following the beast now." Marjani tapped the road with the butt of her spear. "With the storm coming, evening will fall soon. We cannot track it in the dark. Unless you have more skill than I, Princess Eira?"

Eira's hands fisted at her sides. Of all the smug, annoying … Marjani could out-track Eira blindfolded. Eira knew it. And Marjani knew she knew it. "If we wait until morning, the rain will wash away its prints."

Marjani sniffed dismissively. "That beast must weigh over a thousand pounds. There will be signs of its passing. It has terrorized this county for months. It will still be nearby tomorrow."

"More's the pity," Hartwin muttered.

Eira plucked restlessly at her bowstring. Energy balled beneath her feet, eager to launch her after her quarry. Something felt off, though she wasn't sure what. Marjani was right

… maybe that was it. Maybe she just didn't want to admit Marjani's plan was better than hers.

Just chase it down and kill it. At least her plan had the benefit of simplicity.

As Eira's adrenaline ebbed, she realized it didn't matter. The charge in her feet was merely the last dregs of her energy draining into the ground. She needed food and sleep and more food. She'd be lucky to make it to the manor house before she collapsed.

"Fine. I'll wait to kill the bear until tomorrow." She forced her body into motion, trudging with the others toward the manor.

Tarben and the yeomen waited by the gate, frozen before the sheep heart still hanging from the blood-stained wood.

"What are they just standing there for?" Eira grumbled. A raindrop landed on her nose. The clouds smelled ready to burst. "Why don't they go in?"

"They're probably afraid the heart is cursed," Marjani said.

"Can you blame them?" Hartwin murmured.

No. An uncanny shiver ran up Eira's spine as she imagined the angry bear ripping out the sheep's heart and carrying it all the way here to the manor to fling it at the gate … *Ridiculous.* She no more believed in enchanted bears than Hartwin did. And indeed, as she neared, she saw that the heart had not simply been stuck to the gate with its own gore. It had been fixed there with a horseshoe nail. On purpose. By a human with a hammer.

The thought of some aggrieved farmer or vindictive merchant using a bloody heart to terrorize the manor was disturbing and creepy, but not nearly as disturbing and creepy as—

The bloodstain on the wood beside the heart.

The unmistakable imprint of a giant bear's paw.

CHAPTER SIX

3. He made it obvious he hated being here in Saebern. (Submitted by Reeve Hartwin, head of the Saebern Town council.)

— Top 10 reasons no one misses Earl Berengar that much

Marjani forced herself to breathe as her companions' fear swirled around her. So much pain colored the air that her own heart felt as though it might have been ripped from its cage. *No, no more.* But she had experience moving forward through pain to do what needed to be done. She reached toward the bloody paw print.

"Don't touch it!" Tarben grasped at her sleeve, then jerked back, not quite daring to lay a hand on a princess.

Ignoring him, she hovered her fingers over the mark on the gate. Even now, far from her father's reprisals, her hand shook at her audacity. *A girl can't sense spirits.* Mosi was the prince, the heir, the inheritor of their father's power to hear the pronouncements of their ancestors.

At least, that was the lie they told. Her parents, the head priest, she and Mosi. Perhaps not Mosi. He seemed to half believe it, that during ceremonies in the ancestors' house, he heard the whispers of voices no one else could hear. Maybe she and Dejen did their work too well, protecting him from doubts or suspicions. Maybe they all believed it in the end.

And, anyway, what did she know? If Mosi thought he heard something, glimpsed the flash of another pair of eyes across the fire, it might have been true. Just because she herself saw nothing beyond their own bright, flickering souls, that did not mean nothing else was there. Just because Mosi used her ability to read the spirits of the living to impress others with his wisdom did not mean she could say for certain that other voices never spoke to him.

A girl can't sense spirits. A girl. A twin. An inconvenient intruder into the glorious royal line. A problem, a fault. The crack in her brother's soul that could never be made whole, even by her death.

Otherwise, her father would have happily made that sacrifice.

Grimly, she steadied the tremor of her hand. Here in Aldforth, her existence was not a catastrophe. Here she would be the *instrument* of catastrophe. And she would use any tool necessary to accomplish it. It mattered not what these people thought of her. If they saw her as strange, if they feared her as a wraith-eyed witch, so much the better.

She brushed her fingertips as close to the blood as she could without touching it. It was not the sheep's terror she needed to understand, but the creature who had brought its heart here to … What? Frighten those within?

Darkness, as if she dipped her hand in shadow, into the very depth of echoing nothingness.

"Any spooky curse energy?" Eira asked.

Could she *never* be serious?

"Anger, despair, pain." Marjani lowered her hand, resisting the urge to wipe it on her cloak. She hadn't expected the lingering impression to feel so … familiar. "Overwhelming anguish. A great evil has been done here."

"A bloody heart's been nailed to the gate," one of the yeomen said. "Don't take a scholar to tell there's evil been done. It's sorcery, clear as anything."

"It's a demon," the other one muttered. "No real bear could do this. It's got to be a demon. The gods are punishing us."

"I have never encountered true evil not done by human will." Marjani gave them a cool glance and saw them flinch from the strangeness of her eyes. "I would not look to the gods to explain this bear's actions.

"I am not a sorcerer." She took a breath to clear the bitter echoes from her mind. She'd never claimed to be able to sense magic, whatever that was, but she understood fury and hatred well enough. "I can't explain what caused the fire of rage and violence that drives this creature, but I do not think it will douse itself. Only the beast's destruction will free you."

In the silence after her words, the rain began to fall in earnest, pelting her face with fat drops like tears.

"Good thing we've come, then," Eira said. Before Tarben could stop her, she grabbed the bloodstained handle and swung open the gate. "Let's get inside before the bear returns."

The uncanny threshold broken, the men surged after her. All but Hartwin, who waited for Marjani to enter before following and scrupulously barring the gate.

"Whatever this evil is," he told her, voice low, "it grows worse. If we can return you to Anberry Harbor before the ship sails tomorrow, you can be back in Newport within the sennight. Now that you've seen what we're up against, you can convince the king to send warriors."

If Eira had heard, she would have laughed, but Marjani saw no humor in the Saebernians' futile hope for King Wulfric's aid—quite apart from the fact that as an Almasan warrior, she should skewer Hartwin where he stood for suggesting she was not the equal of an Alforthian knight. If only with the sharp blade of her words.

"Are you so eager to be rid of us?" she asked instead.

The storm light caught his eyes, dangerous as the clouds, and the corner of his mouth pulled up. "Eager to be rid of the most interesting visitors Saebern has ever had? Speaking with you is as good as traveling to Almasa myself. If I didn't fear the two of you were intent on getting yourselves killed by our bear, I'd beg you to stay."

Dismay contorted his face as if he'd just heard his own words, and he glanced down at his boots, the tops of his ears turning a red that was unexpectedly endearing.

"Rather, it's my duty to beg you to plead our case to the king," he said. He met her gaze again. "My people need his help."

"I will do what I can." Even if it couldn't be what he asked.

"I know." The rain weighed his tousled hair, nearly hiding the bright sea green of his eyes. "You have ever made clear your intention to help us, however desperate our circumstances. Please know I am grateful."

Marjani broke his gaze. Her *intention* meant nothing. Only her success.

She had accompanied Mosi on all his hunts. The head priest had told her parents she must go everywhere her brother went for fear the two halves of their soul might wither if they got too far apart.

He was right about that much, at least.

Leopards were their most dangerous, cleverest prey. Even an armed man might fall to one if his guard slipped at all. Mosi—or a favored guest—always had the honor of killing the leopards they hunted. But Dejen had trained her to be Mosi's equal with a spear. She could do what needed to be done, even against a foe that weighed half again as much as she.

But she had never imagined facing a beast ten times her weight, one that could move with the speed this bear had displayed. An animal that strong and that fast with the preternatural intelligence required to nail a sheep's heart to a wooden gate …

She finally understood Hartwin's conviction she could not kill it. She just didn't understand why she cared about his opinion. She couldn't care, however much his kindness and integrity made her wish to prove herself to him. She needed to focus. Figure out how to kill an adversary every bit as dangerous as Hartwin and Tarben had warned it would be.

As they neared the manor house, the door was flung open from the inside. A woman stood in the doorway, her rich, burgundy gown trimmed with gold, her blond hair bound up with a filigreed net. She looked much more a princess than the two young women who stood travel-stained and dripping on her doorstep. On her hip, she held a child, a pudgy-cheeked girl with wispy brown hair and wide brown eyes.

"It's been here again," the woman gripped Steward Tarben's arm, strain in her voice, tamping down some fierce emotion. "Right at the gate. Did you hear it? Artis is terrified."

The child blinked and stuck three fingers in her mouth, her gaze lingering on Marjani with bright interest.

"It's gone, Silke," Tarben told her, easing her back under the shelter of the eaves. "It was frightened off by our arrival."

That was one way of putting it.

"It's gotten worse while you were away!" Lady Silke's voice stretched thin, as though only force of will kept it from breaking. "What was I to do if it had gotten through the gate?"

"I'm home now." Gentleness warmed the steward's voice, though the hand he placed on her shoulder was almost tentative. "It will be all right. But our guests are tired and wet."

Silke's eyes widened as she finally noticed the others. "I've left you standing in the rain! Come in. Quickly, quickly." And when the yeomen held back, "No standing on ceremony in this storm. You two go on back to the kitchen. Cook will see you warmed and dried."

As the yeomen doffed their hats and ducked their heads

past her down the hall, she turned back to her husband. "Master Kaspar came from town with the porters from the boat. They said the king sent no men. That can't be right!"

"Princess Marjani, Princess Eira." Tarben offered them the welcoming bow of a man finally at home. "May I present my wife, Lady Silke, and my stepdaughter, Lady Artis. Silke, these are our guests, Princess Marjani of Almasa and Princess Eira of Nordmark."

The men from the boat must have mentioned princesses, along with the lack of knights. Although Lady Silke had evidently not believed it—and who could blame her—she was quick to offer a graceful curtsy. "Your Highnesses. It is an honor to welcome you to Saebern Manor."

"I'm just a former princess, really," Eira said.

"Thank you, Lady Silke," Marjani said, stifling a grimace at her companion's lack of grace. "We are grateful for your hospitality."

"Come join Master Kaspar in the great hall," Silke invited them. "Sit and rest. You've had a long journey. Ebba!"

A thin, sharp woman appeared along the corridor, her graying red hair pulled up under a cap. "Yes, milady."

"Food and drink for our guests. And take Artis to Nurse. It's past time she was abed." Silke kissed her daughter's hair and passed her to the housekeeper with more reluctance than her brisk tone suggested.

"I'll be getting home, then—" Hartwin began.

"Nonsense." Authority flicked in Lady Silke's voice like a lash. "Not alone, with that beast out there. You'll stay for supper and go with Kaspar and the yeomen."

Perhaps there was truth to the old Almasan proverb, "Fast ships make fast friends." Marjani was grateful to keep Hartwin's company for a little longer in this house of frightened, unhappy strangers.

Unhappiness? Was that the emotion tamped down so sternly beneath Silke's careful courtesy?

Saebern Manor's hall hardly deserved the designation

"great," at least not compared with the opulent vastness of Newport Castle. Yet, unlike King Wulfric's hall, the fire in this hearth warmed the entire room. The wall hangings displayed scenes of farming and sheep pastures rather than battles and hunts. And the well-worn chairs looked invitingly comfortable.

"Tarben!" A large, black-bearded man crossed the room to clap the steward's shoulder. "I told your lady wife you'd arrive safely. Those of us with lovely women waiting at home aren't going to be denied by some gods-scourged bear."

The man looked half bear himself, with his large shoulders and broad chest, well padded with good living.

"Master Kaspar," Tarben greeted him stiffly.

"And young Hartwin!" Kaspar threw his arm around the reeve like a fond uncle. "You were supposed to bring us a company of fighting men, lad. Or at least a brace of dragon-slaying knights."

Marjani saw Hartwin's jaw tighten, but he only offered a tight smile, as if he were as used to being undervalued as Marjani herself.

"The king sent royalty instead," Tarben said tartly. "Princess Marjani and Princess Eira, allow me to introduce Master Kaspar, Saebern Town's leading wool merchant. He's made a name for Saebernian fleece across the Blessed Kingdoms."

"It's our sheep that's done that," Kaspar rumbled, his modesty belied by his velvet surcoat and the diamond glittering from his pinky finger. "I do have an eye for a good trade, though, I don't mind admitting. Take this wine." He lifted a large jug from a sideboard. "A lovely Rigan red. It will set you right after your journey."

And a fine gift with which to buy himself a front-row seat for the best gossip in Saebern. Marjani wagered the ursine merchant was as proficient a trafficker in information as he was in wool and luxuries.

"Pour us all a glass, Kaspar," Tarben said, with more resignation than gratitude. "And let us eat."

Eira moved to a chair near the fire. "Sit here with me, Marjani. You must be freezing."

Surprise and gratitude overrode Marjani's embarrassment at having her discomfort pointed out. She sat beside Eira with a murmured thank you, suppressing a sigh of relief for the warmth at her back.

Lady Silke took the chair at the head of the table, her noble blood outranking her husband's stature as a wealthy commoner. Tarben sat to her right, Master Kaspar beside him. Hartwin sat at the foot of the table. Keeping an eye on them all.

Marjani tilted her goblet toward him in the faintest of salutes. His smile was so quick and so sharp, it was like the flick of a knife against her throat. The wine trailed fire into her belly, and she set it down with a thump.

She listened more than she spoke as the supper progressed. Noting Lady Silke's despair that the king had not sent the help Tarben requested. Master Kaspar's willingness to hire Ilhavairan mercenaries to kill the bear. The increasingly brittle edge to Eira's good cheer as her references to the princesses' hunting skills were ignored.

"If only Earl Berengar were here," the Nordish girl said finally, blue eyes so wide with innocence that Marjani almost choked on her wine. "He was such a devoted hunter. He would have rid you of this bear."

The well-played barb pricked a variety of expressions from those seated around the table. Grief and longing were not among them.

"Berengar was an arrogant wastrel," Lady Silke snapped, twisting the ruby ring on her left hand. "He went hunting to avoid his duties. He wouldn't give two figs for the terror that beast has caused us."

Tarben cleared his throat in the awkward silence. "Marshal Falk said Berengar was competent on the hunt."

"Falk said many things about the young earl," Master

Kaspar muttered over his wine. "Not all of it fit for polite company."

"What did you think of Berengar?" Marjani asked. Had no one liked the young man?

"I didn't know him well," Kaspar said. "He'd only been home from Rigas a short time before the old earl died. He'd been studying at the university in Chrysa. Thought that made him smarter than the rest of us, gave him the right to interfere in our business. He wanted to go back to the old, inefficient way we cut our forests. Slow the expansion of our grazing land. Even though, from the sound of it, he studied mostly drinking and skirt-chasing."

"The boy never expected to be earl," Tarben said primly. "Perhaps he would have grown into the position."

"The *boy* would have grown into an idle libertine and dragged us all into debt." Silke placed a hand on her husband's arm. "The way he *talked* to you."

He laid his hand on hers, a fervently protective gesture. "What bothered me was the way he spoke to *you*. As if he were somehow your better. His own brother's widow!"

"Everyone must be holding their breath, hoping he doesn't reappear before the year is up," Eira observed.

Marjani heard the icy edge to Eira's bland tone. She, too, had noted the irony that the second son everyone welcomed as usurper of Artis's inheritance had proven less fit than his baby niece.

And yet. "It is sad no one grieves him," she murmured.

"My father insisted he wasn't such a bad lad," Hartwin admitted. "Even if he was always going on about how much better everything was in Rigas. But my father is dead because of his incompetence, so he cannot grieve."

"Your father never had a bad word to say about anyone." Master Kaspar raised his flagon, only the sloshing of the wine indicating how much he had consumed. "Here's to those we lost that day. To Wendel and Falk and 'he wasn't such a bad lad' Berengar. Gods rest their souls."

The conversation lagged after that. Even food and wine couldn't lift the exhaustion of the travelers or dispel the shadow of the malevolent beast lurking in the wilderness outside.

Gathering up the threads of her duty as hostess, Lady Silke finally badgered a wine-drowsy Kaspar out of his chair so he and Hartwin could return to town with the yeomen before sunset. As if anyone could tell when the sun set, with the thick veils of rain obscuring even the nearest hilltops.

As Kaspar struggled into his fur-trimmed cloak, Hartwin moved to Marjani's side.

"I am sorry my father is not here to have met you," he said. "He would have loved to hear your stories of your kingdom. And he would have had better things to say of Earl Berengar than the rest of us did."

"He sounds like a kind man." She wished for an instant she had gotten to meet this man who had raised such a capable son. Her own father hadn't had the luxury of kindness. But then, he hadn't been raising a baker. He'd needed his son to become a strong leader.

Like Prince Guntram? Before Mosi's murder, her father had spoken almost admiringly of the brutal Aldforthian wolf cub. A *worthy* prince. Would he have molded Mosi into a beast like Guntram? As King Wulfric meant to do with Prince Theodor?

Never. Her open-hearted brother would never have slaughtered unarmed men during a parley truce as Guntram had. Wulfric's spawn were rabid, vicious brutes who cared only for power. Her father's huntsman would cull such a bloodline from his dogs. Even the puppies would be destroyed for the good of the kennel.

"If I don't see you before you return to Newport—" Hartwin pulled her from her spiraling thoughts with those sea-deep eyes. "I wish you untroubled seas and fortunate winds."

The profound kindness of thinking to offer the traditional Almasan farewell caught her heart off-guard. The wrench of homesickness nearly made her stagger.

"Back to the sea! That's as much as wishing us a visit to the Santian hells," Eira said, butting in to lean her forearm on Marjani's shoulder as if they were spear brothers. "Even if you think bringing us here was a waste of time, you could at least wish us luck in our competition. Which of us would *you* prefer to see win Prince Theo's hand?"

"I *should* say that Prince Theodor was the lucky one, either way," Hartwin said, only a twitch of his wry smile showing he wasn't falling for Eira's trap. A smile that invited Marjani to share his amusement. All too tempting an invitation. All too dangerous. "Besides, I got to meet both of you. That was not wasted time."

That should have been accompanied by a full grin, turning it into a light comment, a pleasantry of his own. But he only held Marjani's gaze a moment longer and then turned away, following the other men into the storm.

"I wish he would look at me like that," Eira sighed, sagging on her shoulder.

Lady Silke rescued her from the need to reply. "Ebba will show you to your room, Your Highnesses. No doubt you'd like to rest after your journey."

No doubt at all. They followed the housekeeper into the haphazard maze of the old house, up sudden stairs and around random turns. It took the last of Marjani's energy to memorize the route.

Ebba finally stopped at the door to a tidy room with a fire burning in the hearth. "We've put your things in here. I hope it's acceptable."

"More than acceptable," Marjani said. "We are grateful for your hospitality."

"This is lovely," Eira exclaimed. She threw herself on the bed nearest her trunk. "After that horrible ship's cabin, I would have been happy with a blanket on the floor."

The housekeeper blinked. "There is a bell if you should need anything." And then she left, with a sniff of disapproval.

"I didn't mean to offend her!" Eira wailed. "I really *do*

think it's lovely. It's no wonder people gaze longingly at you rather than me. Beautiful *and* gracious."

"People here stare at me because I am different," Marjani said.

She had seen other dark-skinned people in Newport. And not all of the other princesses were pale as milk. Anara, Jax, little Ziva of the Fair Isles. Dora had the olive skin of Rigas. But none were dark as she. Ebony, Dejen had told her once. Dark and gleaming as polished ebony. Like her mother's people.

One more reason for her father to hate her.

"People stare at what is exotic." She pulled a sleeping shift from her trunk. "Or they despise it, like you."

"I don't despise you!" Eira sat upright, her face awash in indignation that slowly gave way to chagrin. "Well, if I do, it's only because *you* despise *me*. And I'm sure none of the other girls dislike you, however much you deserve it."

If she expected a response to that, she was disappointed. But it didn't shut her up.

"Raisa truly seems to care for you," Eira continued, changing into her own sleeping gown, "and I didn't think she was capable of human feeling. Even Isolde never says anything bad about you."

"That's only because she doesn't want a fight with Raisa. She has other ways to torment people." Marjani slipped into her bed. The sheets weren't the fine, costly linen of King Wulfric's household, but they were clean and soft with wear. Maybe it was the room's coziness or simply that the Nordish witch was the closest thing she had to a companion here, but something loosened her tongue. "The day after we arrived at Lukos, Isolde told me that if I wanted to win Prince Theodor's hand, I needed to look like a proper princess. She dressed me up in one of her cousin Pia's gowns."

"Not one of the pink ones!"

"The one with the embroidered flowers. And ruffles."

Eira's horror was gratifying, even if it did dissolve into giggles. "It must have been a foot too short."

"I looked ridiculous," Marjani agreed. "Isolde made Pia offer me the gown as a gift. I graciously refused."

"You should feel honored." Eira brushed the loose hair from her eyes. "Isolde has never even spoken to me. She must see you as a real threat."

"She sees everyone as a threat," Marjani warned. "Not all of her stratagems are obvious. She is always scheming."

"Is Isolde the one who broke my bow?" Eira asked, as abrupt as ever.

Was that her way of acknowledging that maybe Marjani hadn't? "I don't know. But she profited the most from it. King Wulfric will not forget how she outshone the rest of us in that first archery competition."

"Just like he won't forget the princess who kills this bear." Eira lay back on her pillows. "It's going to be more dangerous than I thought. After seeing that heart nailed to the gate, even I'm not so sure there's not sorcery involved."

Marjani could not argue with that. It added a whole new layer of complexity to creating a strategy to defeat the beast.

"But it's still a living creature, and a living creature can be killed," Eira continued. "You and I can do it. If we work together."

"Yes," Marjani agreed, unexpectedly touched by her conviction. "I think you're right."

It would be deathly perilous, even together. But she could see how it might work. Tactics she had observed on Mosi's hunts. A combination of Eira's steely nerves and her own fierce daring. Ice and fire.

She thought of how they had stood shoulder to shoulder earlier, facing the bear. They could work well together. How would it feel to have a companion to watch her back?

"We'll make plans in the morning," Eira said, her words muffled by a yawn. "Tarben won't like it."

"He's afraid the king will blame him if anything happens

to us." So little did he understand the king's reasons for sending them in the first place.

"I can't wait to see Wulfric's face when we get back to Newport." The Nordish girl's voice was fading. "We'll make matching necklaces out of the bear's teeth. He'll notice us then. You can count on it."

He would have to. They'd be the girls who'd pulled off what Saebern's best hunters had failed to accomplish. He might even enjoy showing off the pair of them. Sleek and fierce. Like a brace of well-bred hounds.

Marjani ignored the twinge of regret—of weakness—thinking of the vision of camaraderie in Eira's words. Marjani was no hunting dog, safely part of the pack, killing for the king's sport. She killed only for her own reasons. And when the king looked at her next, she wanted to see fear in his eyes.

5. She's too trusting.

— Top 10 things I despise about Princess Eira, as listed by Princess Marjani of Almasa

Even in the depths of a sleep made dark and syrupy by exhaustion, Eira's carefully tuned ears heard the rustling as Marjani slipped from her bed, the brush of bare feet on the floor as the Almasan princess donned her robes. Her slitted eyes noted the shift in the darkness when Marjani opened the door to creep from the room. Dawn must be coming, despite the rain.

Fortunately, Eira did not need a lantern any more than Marjani had. Trust might be one of the Nine Roads to Peace, but nothing in the precepts of the One Goddess required blind credulity. Under the pretense of restless sleep, she had already pulled on an outfit of soft breeches, linen chemise, and knee-length tunic. She had only to tug on her boots, buckle her sword, and throw her fawn-colored cloak around her shoulders before grabbing her bow and following Marjani into the hallway.

After all that talk of killing the bear together. After

agreeing to share the glory. After it seemed as though her efforts to make peace might actually bear fruit …

A shard of ice lodged in her heart, digging into her ribs as she breathed.

So much for Jax's dreams of getting all the princesses to work together. Eira had been right about Marjani all along. Even here in Saebern, out from under Raisa's thumb, the Almasan princess had chosen dishonesty and betrayal over friendship and cooperation.

That was fine. Eira was used to betrayal. Used to being discounted. Used to having to look out for herself.

She touched the frog charm at her throat and stifled the sudden sharp wish that Jax or Anara or even Beatrix were with her.

One hand on the wall, Eira ran down the dark hall as fast as she dared. She almost tumbled down the first short set of stairs, barely managing to catch her balance at the bottom. Still, her recklessness paid off. She reached the main hallway just as the front door thumped softly closed.

Silently, Eira slipped out into the courtyard. In the murky half-light, through the shimmering rain, she could see the gate was still barred. Marjani hadn't gone that way, which left over the wall. It wasn't more than six feet tall, and the rough-hewn stones offered plenty of toeholds.

Eira sprinted to the nearest outbuilding, some kind of workroom or storage shed, and edged around it.

There. A ripple of shadow at the top of the wall. The soft hush of the rain covered the sound of Marjani's landing on the other side. With any luck, it would also muffle Eira's awkward scramble up the wall, her bow clattering against the stone.

Over and down. The image of the bear on the ridge burned in her memory, its teeth gleaming as its great bellow rumbled across the rocky, sheep-cropped hillside. And yet the lack of cover on the broad slope was still an unpleasant surprise. Other than the huge storage barn towering beyond the sheep pens, its wagon porches protruding from either side, there was nothing to break a watcher's line of sight. Even Marjani couldn't disappear, though she flowed like a shadow from rock to hillock to patch of heather.

Eira snugged her hood down over her ghostly pale hair and face—Beatrix had once claimed she glowed in the dark—and followed after. If Marjani glanced back, she could hardly miss her, but the Almasan princess never turned, apparently already absorbed in the hunt, with no thought for the companion she'd left behind.

Left behind so treacherously.

The sting of it prodded Eira through the sopping weeds and grasping heather. She banged her shin on a boulder that lurched up in front of her without warning, but the rock offered rough cover when her quarry stopped at the crest of the ridge. Eira watched, still as a stalking cat, while Marjani stooped to place her hand where the bear had stood the evening before, then lifted her gaze and scanned the hills as if she might conjure the beast with a look.

Only when Marjani strode on, disappearing over the ridge, did Eira dare move, darting up the slope to where she'd seen the double-dealing princess pause.

If she hadn't known to look for it, Eira might not have noticed the print, blurred by the night-long rain. Compelled as inescapably as Marjani had been, she placed her own hand in the center of the great pad, her long fingers nowhere near the marks of the claws.

Nordish stories were filled with tales of young men—and sometimes women—who set themselves the quest of solo hunting one of the great ice bears of the far north, proving themselves to the gods in order to become a leader for their people in a time of great need. The pelt of such a bear had hung behind her mother's chair in her council chamber, a trophy from a beast her great-grandfather had hunted before the battle that made him king of Nordmark.

Her uncle Einar had not gone on such a hunt before

betraying her mother and seizing the throne. He was much too calculating for that. For the stories made clear that many a strong, smart, brave young hunter never returned from the glorious folly of an ice bear quest.

Easier to lurk cravenly in the background and use the Alforthian army to steal the throne.

Too conscious of Holy Mother's teachings, Eira had never outwardly scorned the Saeberners' fears of their little "monster." But in her head, she'd scoffed at a people so softened by civilization that they could mistake a mere forest bear for a real threat.

Hubris was one of the Nine Roads to War—but apparently only if you avoided being eaten before you reached your destination. For this beast's paws were at least as large as her great-grandfather's bear's had been.

With a hiss between terror and exhilaration, she rose and hurried after Marjani. The fool. She was lucky Eira hadn't slept through her disappearing act. With her tracking skill, Marjani might be able to find the bear on her own, but no single spear thrust would kill that monster.

When she found herself looking into those massive jaws, she'd be begging for Eira's help.

～

"Did you think I didn't notice you following me, you simpleminded witch?" The crimson fury staining Marjani's dark cheekbones nearly matched her robes. "You're stealthy as a blundering elephant. You can't think I'd let you use my tracking skill to bring yourself unearned glory."

Maybe gratitude had been too much to hope for.

Eira had followed Marjani through the morning as the rain eased sullenly into a misty drip. The burning flash of the Almasan's robes had led her across steep slopes and through parklike pine forests.

Miles into their trek, Marjani had stopped by a rushing stream to pull food and a water flask from the bag over her shoulder. The traitor must have stolen provisions for a solo hunt before they had even disembarked from that horrible boat.

Eira had tucked a hunk of bread in her pocket after supper the night before, but only as a hedge against the lingering hunger from her days of seasickness. The poor bit of loaf had not traveled well, going soggy and stale. She'd had to creep through bracken and saplings to the stream bank below Marjani's picnic spot to wash it down with the rushing stormwater.

She'd been kneeling in a patch of moss, scooping water with her hands, when Marjani's boot had connected with her shoulder, knocking her on her butt.

"Stop following me!" Marjani's words were sharp and pointed as the spear she thumped on the ground for emphasis. "Or I will stop you myself."

"I followed you to keep you from getting yourself *killed*." Eira scrambled to her feet, out of boot reach. "You can't bring down that bear by yourself. I don't know why you're acting so self-righteous. This is *my* quest. And you're the one who sneaked out after we agreed to hunt together."

"I did not agree to hunt with you," Marjani said, stiffly enough that Eira wondered if she couldn't even convince herself. "I only agreed that it would increase the possibility of our success."

"Isn't that a good thing? Isn't setting aside our differences worth it to give ourselves a better chance of helping the people here in Saebern?"

A flash of what might have been guilt crossed the other girl's face.

"If I fail, then you'll have the chance to help them all by yourself," Marjani said.

"Do you *want* the bear to kill you?" Even as Eira asked the question, the truth struck her. Marjani's constant gloom. Her grief over the death of her brother. Being sent to the court of the man whose son had murdered him.

"Marjani …" What could she say? What would one of Marjani's friends say? Raisa was a snake, but even she might give Marjani a hug. Of course, Marjani probably wouldn't run Raisa through with her spear if she tried it.

"Life is a gift from the One Goddess," Eira said finally. One of Holy Mother's favorite phrases. It sounded so much more compelling in the temple leader's throaty contralto. How could she convince Marjani to give her life a chance to get better? "You don't want to squander it. Things may seem diffi-cult right now—"

Marjani made a sound that reminded Eira of the bear. "You understand nothing. I have no intention of letting the bear kill me. I simply do not wish to share my success with *you*."

That was meant to hurt. Indeed, it was so obvious a blow Eira ignored it, like a feint in a sword fight, meant to distract from the real attack.

"You want all the credit for killing the bear." That, at least, she could understand. The intoxicating fizz of competition stirred in her blood. "You want to marry Prince Theo badly enough to risk your life for it."

"Bah." Marjani bounced on the balls of her feet, nearly levitating with fury. "Prince Guntram came to Almasa demanding free passage through our sovereign waters. When my father agreed to meet with him, he turned a covenant feast, a meeting of sacred truce, into an ambush, a slaughter-house. He murdered my brother before my eyes. Only a heart-less, amoral coward would marry such a man's brother!"

A sliver of something bitter and sharp stuck in Eira's throat. "You're not the only one who's ever lost someone you love. My uncle betrayed my mother to King Wulfric's army. Aldforthian soldiers killed every last man and woman who fought by her side. When I win this competition, I will marry Prince Theodor and bring peace to all of the Blessed Kingdoms." Her hand squeezed her sword's hilt. She *would* change the world, and this stubborn princess wasn't going to stop her. "Do you consider *me* a greedy, amoral coward, you self-righteous hypocrite?"

"Me, self-righteous?" Marjani barked a laugh. "You're the one preaching sugar drops of peace because you're too timid to take vengeance on the men who killed your mother."

Eira peeled her fingers from her sword by force of will. "There is no honor in vengeance. Vengeance is—"

"—one of the Nine Roads to War," Marjani finished with a sneer. "So you say, over and over and *over* again. Why should I care about war? All that matters is evening out the scales."

A burst of noise in the pines overhead made Eira stumble sideways, her heart thudding in her chest. But the whir resolved into a little crossbill winging deeper into the forest, unable to bear their rising voices another moment.

Eira snorted, suddenly overcome by the absurdity of it. Two sodden girls in the middle of a backwater wilderness, arguing over kings and war and vengeance.

"How is getting yourself killed on this hunt going to even the scales?" she demanded. "Guntram killed your brother, not this bear, and he's already dead. Besides, if you wanted to match vengeance for vengeance, if someone killed your brother, you wouldn't kill him, you'd kill *his* broth—"

The word broke apart in her throat as if someone had punched her midsection. She stared at Marjani. Waiting for a scornful laugh. An angry denial. The blood in her ears echoed the storm-swollen stream plunging down the mountainside.

When she finally found her voice, it sounded lost. "Not Prince Theo?"

With his mischievous grin and that Prince Charming hair. The extra prince suddenly thrust into the role of heir to the throne. The boy unable to win his father's approval, who somehow had a knack for making each princess feel like she could be his favorite.

"*Not* Prince Theo," she repeated more forcefully. "None of what happened to your family—or to mine—is his fault."

"Nor is it mine." Marjani's voice was cold as the rushing water. She touched the odd bracelet she wore, the edges of the half-circle that decorated it looking as ragged as if it had been broken in half. "Yet we are the ones who are left to atone for our families' suffering. I will not be sent back to my father in failure. I will not lose my chance to make King Wulfric pay."

She turned to the stream bank where a row of boulders created the little pool Eira had drunk from. The water swirled angrily over and around the rocks before crashing over a brief fall and tumbling down the steep ravine into the forest.

Using her spear as a balance, Marjani ran the few feet to the stream's edge and leaped to the nearest dry knob of rock. As if it were a child's game, she jumped from boulder to boulder. Her foot slid only once, where she had to touch down briefly on a low rock slick with spray, and then she was on the far bank, looking back.

"Return to the manor," she ordered. "I won't allow you to follow me any farther."

"As if you could stop me!" People always said Eira acted without thinking, as if that were a bad thing. It didn't take prolonged contemplation to know that if she looked for a better crossing place, Marjani would lose her for good. Or that if Marjani tried to kill the bear alone, the bear would kill her. Or if it didn't, and Marjani somehow made it back to Aldforth and tried to kill Prince Theo, King Wulfric would kill her …

Really, thinking just wasted time.

Eira's feet left the ground long before thought could bring up pesky concerns like the angry, spear-wielding princess glaring at her from the other side of the stream, or why she should care if Marjani got herself killed, or even the roaring, watery expanse between the stepping stones.

She landed on the first rock, the foaming water suddenly all around her. She flapped her arms wildly in momentary panic, but the boulder was large and steady, and she quickly caught her balance.

The next stepping stone was trickier. She would have to hit the sloping surface with the ball of one foot and then spring to the great boulder slicing through the middle of the stream.

Her foot nearly skidded out from under her on the smaller rock, cutting the power of her desperate leap. She struck the central rock with her shins, tumbling heavily onto her stomach. The current caught her left foot, yanking her toward the falls. Her scrabbling fingers slid on the slick stone.

"Pull yourself up, you fool!"

Such helpful advice. She never would have thought of that herself. Her right boot caught on a crack in the boulder. If she could keep her toe jammed there, she could drag her other leg up out of the water—

The current yanked her sideways. The drag from the bottom of her bow in the water was too much. She didn't want to lose the weapon, but she didn't want to drown, either. The tricky bit would be letting go of the rock with one hand long enough to get the bow off her shoulder.

The butt end of Marjani's spear slammed into the boulder inches from her fingers.

"You're trying to kill me!" Eira gasped at the Almasan princess, who glowered at her from a low rock just feet away. Why that should come as such a horrifying shock, when the girl had just admitted to planning to kill Prince Theo, she didn't know, but—

"Don't move," Marjani ordered. "I am going to jump over to you. If you move, I will land on you, and we will both fall."

"It's too slippery. There's not enough room." Eira dug her fingernails into the rock and managed to drag her shoulders higher. "Just give me a second. I've almost got it."

One more push with her right foot. Her hips inched upward—

Her boot skidded free, her foot plunging backward into

the icy water. Her cheek scraped against the rock as she pressed herself to it, struggling to hold on.

"Grab my spear!" Marjani shouted. "I'll pull you to me!"

But the three feet of churning water between them was an unbridgeable chasm. Marjani had no more chance of taking Eira's entire weight in the power of the flood than Eira did. A roaring bear could not have dug its claws into her with any greater strength than the violent clutch of the water.

"That's the worst idea you've had so far." She slid farther.

The spear butt disappeared, and she could see the swirl of red robes as the Almasan leaped back to the far shore.

"When you drop, swim this way," Marjani called. "I will pull you out."

"I can't swim!" Even in the frigid grip of deathly panic, Eira had to laugh at Marjani's outraged disbelief.

Then her fingers slipped from the rock, the current yanked her over the drop, and the ravenous water swallowed her whole.

CHAPTER EIGHT

8. She never said she couldn't swim!

— Top 10 things I despise about Princess Eira, as listed
by Princess Marjani of Almasa

Drowning took longer than Eira expected. Mostly because the water couldn't decide how it wanted to kill her. Smash her against the rocks. Tumble her along the stream bed. Strangle her with her bowstring.

Pain, cold, numbness. The current flung her against a boulder, crushing the air from her lungs, then churned her back up again, just long enough to catch a watery, gagging breath.

She struggled to escape the current, but the stream's banks rose steeper and sharper the faster she was swept away. She couldn't remember which side she'd been trying to get to when she fell, but it didn't matter. The water had carried her far beyond Marjani's reach.

Cold as she was, it warmed her heart to know Marjani had tried to save her. Or maybe that warmth was hypothermia. Half the elders in Nordmark had a tale of almost freezing to death because of a blizzard or being left behind on a botched raid or some such thing. They all warned that when you stopped feeling cold, you were close to death.

Could she feel the cold? She didn't feel the rocks striking her anymore. Didn't feel the water tumbling her around …

She'd stopped moving. She opened her eyes to see the stream bottom slipping past beneath her. Not stopped. Drifting. She'd been dumped into a pool of quieter water. If she could get to the bank, she might have a chance of pulling herself out.

But she had to breathe. Up. Which way was up? Away from the pebbles. She kicked, her water-logged boots slowing her sluggish legs. She struck upwards with her arms. Did her hands break the surface? But she wasn't moving upward. Something weighed her down.

Her sword.

Her fingers fumbled at her sword belt. She couldn't even feel the buckle. *Stupid. Taking too long. Just pull the sword from the scabbard.* Had she done it? Was the blade still in the scabbard, or had she dropped it already? She didn't feel heavy. Just slow. Floating. Was she even still underwater? Would it matter if she gave in to her aching lungs and just took one deep breath?

Maybe she was already dead, floating to the Summer Lands on the great river Memory. But who would remember her to send her on? And what would the Old Ones think of her worshiping the One Goddess? Would they let her in?

Her shoulder jerked, tugging her back to cold and pain. Her bow. It must have caught on something. Her shoulder tugged harder. She struggled to move, to care. Water splashed her face.

Water and *air*. She gasped, gagged. Her hip hit the bottom, gravel and dirt clutching her, trying to keep her in the stream. Her head bounced off a rock, and she struggled to lift it.

Marjani. She tried to say the name, but her chest was too busy heaving water from her lungs. *Thank you. Stop. Maybe just let me die …*

Marjani grunted and yanked her onto the bank. The bowstring bit into Eira's neck and armpit. Mud and damp leaves squelched into her clothes.

" 'Nough," she moaned. Then heaved some more.

The bowstring broke with a snap. Her forward motion finally stopped. She dropped her forehead to the ground, and her sodden, aching body tried to curl around her. She heard Marjani's harsh breathing nearby. The Almasan princess must have run like the wind. And then the effort to haul Eira out of the water. Her panting was so loud and so close she must be bent over from the effort.

Although that didn't quite explain the … pungent … scent of her breath. Or the sudden lifting of the hair on Eira's neck.

Eira's own breath whistled with cold and pain as she turned her head and cracked open her eyes.

Up close, the bear was even more than she remembered. More massive, more magnificent, more unimaginably terrifying. Its huge muzzle hung inches from her face, the black nostrils quivering as it sucked in her scent.

"Nice bear," she breathed.

She'd always thought bears had small eyes, and perhaps, compared to the size of their heads, it was true. This bear's head was big enough that the golden-brown eye peering at her seemed large and wild enough to get lost in.

Nordmark. The Temple. Her friends back in Lukos. Herself as queen of Aldforth. So much she hadn't accomplished. So much she regretted leaving behind, so close to her goal, so close to the creature she had come to kill. But she couldn't regret failing to dim the life in that gleaming eye.

A low rumble began deep in the bear's throat. It grew louder as it rose toward the surface. The great jaw opened, revealing four huge fangs.

A Nordish warrior did not cower at death. But her breath caught as she closed her eyes. "My, what big teeth you have, my dear."

The jaws snapped closed.

CHAPTER NINE

2. She always expects the worst.

— Top 10 things ~~I hate~~ I find difficult to appreciate about Princess Marjani, as listed by (former) Princess Eira of Nordmark

one. The witless, stubborn, obnoxious witch had tumbled over the falls and been swept away before Marjani could even cry out in horror. She hurtled down the bank, crashing through a tangle of alders. It took only heartbeats to reach the first bend in the stream, a scramble over boulders, ignoring the scrape of rock on her shin, the sting of a branch against her cheek.

Marjani searched the churning water, trying to catch a glimpse of white hair, white skin in the white foam. She pushed through the underbrush with her spear, her robes snagging on brambles, slowing her down.

The stream plunged into a steeper ravine, forcing her up the bank, high above the water. Surely Eira must have gained her equilibrium by now. Found a way to reach dry ground.

What do you mean you can't swim? Curses fumed in her mouth, but she couldn't waste breath on them. Already she could feel her legs getting heavier. She was a strong runner, but she'd put everything she had into her initial sprint, trying to bring Eira into view. If the Nordish princess had been struck unconscious when she fell, if she couldn't get her head above water, if her limbs succumbed to the frigid temperature ...

Marjani's own breathing sounded as though she'd drowned. She had to slow, let her lungs catch up, despite her desperation.

The little fool. If she had only turned back when Marjani told her to. Was she that desperate to be queen of Aldforth? So willing to trade her life for Prince Theodor's?

That was not going to happen. Fury spurred Marjani on. She planned a clean vengeance, a guilty life for an innocent's death, and no sanctimonious goddess-worshipper was going to spoil it by getting herself killed—

There. Something snagged on a dead tree lodged in the current. Marjani scrambled down the bank, sending dirt and loose stones showering into the water. Holding onto the tree's upturned roots, she leaned over the water to grab the snagged leather strap.

It tugged free with sluggish reluctance. Eira's quiver, waterlogged, several arrows somehow still resting inside. But not attached to Eira's body.

Marjani pulled the quiver to the bank, her hands shaking with relief. She forced herself to lean out once more, to peer deeper into the water. To see if anything else was caught below the surface. No telltale flash of pale skin or hair.

She sank back on her heels and closed her eyes. She had to face the truth. She wasn't going to pull Eira alive from the water. Either the Nordish girl had managed to haul herself out on her own, or she'd been dragged to the bottom of some swirling pool. Or her body would be swept all the way to the sea.

Marjani rose and headed downstream once more. She forced herself to keep a more deliberate pace, checking the underbrush for any sign of an unconscious, hypothermic young woman. She took precious minutes to investigate piles of tangled debris and jutting rocks that might hide a body.

As she made her way deeper into the wilderness, the sun finally broke through the clouds, scattering light across the water, making it harder to see beneath. She glanced up, her stomach tightening as she realized how quickly the morning had slid into afternoon.

How long? That was the decision she had to make. How long did she follow this stream? She'd come too far already. She knew that. Too far for any good outcome. Yet there was still a chance Eira had reached the opposite bank. Maybe she had collapsed in the underbrush where Marjani couldn't see her. Maybe she had headed upstream, trying to make her way back to Saebern Manor.

If Eira's sense of direction was anything like her common sense, that could only lead to disaster.

Hope came from that part of Marjani's soul that had died with Mosi, but no matter how slim the chance of finding Eira alive, she had to take it. The search for a body could wait. It would be no more dead tomorrow. She would search for any possibility of a living girl across the stream. But first, she had to cross it.

She continued downstream until she found a place where the current slowed, widening across a marshy meadow. Her breath caught as she stepped into the water, ice immediately creeping toward her heart. *Curse the north!*

At least she need have no fear of crocodiles in water this temperature. She held her robes out of the current with one hand and used her spear as a walking stick, but the flat meadow had sapped the water's murderous energy. Cold numbed her legs, and mud sucked at the boots Raisa had loaned her, but she crossed without danger.

Back up the stream. More slowly yet, hampered as much by furious despair as by exhaustion.

If the stupid girl wanted to drown herself, why couldn't she have done it their first day on the ship? Marjani would have been happy to be rid of her then. Yes, she'd wanted to be rid of her this morning, too, but not *permanently*. Her hatred of the Nordish princess was more complicated now. Complicated by their conversation of the night before, laughing over Isolde's fashion advice, agreeing they could succeed at their quest if they worked together.

Marjani's throat tightened, remembering Eira's accusation of betrayal, the girl's hurt at being left behind. Her concern when she thought Marjani meant to get herself killed. Laughing at herself over the ridiculousness of being unable to swim.

That last image would haunt Marjani forever.

"If you're not dead already, I'm going to kill you," Marjani swore.

Her eyes were so strained from trying to see through the shifting water that she almost missed the odd shape lying near the shore. Sunlight gleamed at the bottom of the stream bed, a long ripple of silver.

Marjani crouched on the bank, struggling to make sense of it. The edges. They were too precise to be natural. It looked almost like … a blade.

Once more, she stepped into the water. Once more, the cold shocked the air from her lungs and the warmth of sun and exertion from her body. If all the water in the north was like this, she would never have learned to swim, either. The current was deceptive here, strong enough to be dangerous even close to the shore. She edged deeper, up to her knees. She didn't dare risk going any further.

She thrust her spear into the water, automatically adjusting to the optical shift of the ripples. It took both hands to hold the shaft steady and guide the spearhead to hook the end of the long strip of metal.

Yes, a sword. The spear caught on the junction of blade and hilt, and she carefully dragged it toward her until it was safe to plunge her hand in to grab it. The weapon was plain and well-made, with nothing to distinguish it from a hundred other swords. Except it gleamed with recent sharpening, not dulled by time or moisture.

Unless some other fool with an undistinguished acolyte's blade had fallen into this remote stream this morning, it had to be Eira's.

Marjani's pulse jumped. Of course, it might have been pulled from its scabbard by the tumbling action of the water. But for it to come to rest just here, in this calmer eddy—that must mean something.

She scrambled back to the bank.

"Eira! Are you here?" The forest swallowed her words, its only answer a bird fluttering away. No matter. If the girl had come ashore nearby, she'd have left a sign.

Like that scuffed area of mud and grass just there … Marjani's excitement shriveled in her throat. She'd been so focused on locating Eira that she'd completely forgotten the bear they'd come out here to find.

Apparently, the bear had found them.

She placed her hand beside the enormous print in the mud beside the scuff marks. Goosebumps traveled up her arm as she raised her eyes to the trees around her. She wished she hadn't shouted.

She also wished she'd spent more time interrogating Hartwin about the habits of bears. Were they stealthy, like leopards? Could they swim? Climb trees?

She swallowed down her sudden terror, reminded herself to breathe. However stealthy this bear might be, it couldn't climb or hide behind any of the slender trees nearby. It was simply too big. It couldn't be close enough to charge her without her hearing it in time to react. She had her spear. She had the swift water behind her. *She* could swim.

She forced herself to look down, to read the story written in the earth around her.

The bear had come to the stream. Dragged something heavy from the water. As much as she'd rather pretend she didn't know what that something was, the broken bow lying nearby told its own tale.

Her heart twisted inside her. She'd spent so long praying that Eira had managed to keep her head above water long enough to reach the shore. Now she only hoped the girl had drowned before the bear found her.

Marjani's soul and heart had both died before her eyes in her father's truce lodge not six months before. Death meant nothing to her anymore—not her own, nor anyone else's. Yet she had to swipe a sleeve across her eyes to clear them.

There was no blood on the ground, no sign of struggle or the beast devouring its prey. It must have carried the body off into the forest. How far would it go? She could follow it now, finish this with her spear.

She glanced up through the tree branches. In this northern region, the sun seemed to linger in the summer sky forever. Yet, if she did not begin her return journey to Saebern Manor soon, she would not make it back before dark. She had no shelter, little food, and all the available firewood was soaked from the overnight rain.

If she found the bear before nightfall, she might kill it, or it might kill her. She would have her chance. But if she did not find it … The idea of being hunted through the darkness by a monster she could not see decided her.

There was nothing she could do for Eira except say a prayer for the dead. She would return tomorrow with help from the manor, to retrieve what they might of Eira's body.

Her jaw tightened.

Killing the bear that killed a princess. *That* would bring her before King Wulfric with a name of honor and esteem. Proof to the world of her worthiness to take his son's life. Even her own father might make note of such a thing.

Yet somehow, the thought brought her no satisfaction.

CHAPTER TEN

2. *Arkou Devor*. A conjuration to cause thine enemy [to be] wholly (altogether?) and unquestionably/irreversibly consume[d] by a bear. (Not cause him to wholly consume a bear, surely? Although that ought to kill him just as well.)

— Top 10 failed spells translated and performed by Rurik, Ravninan sorcerer (in training)

The Summer Lands should be more comfortable. *Death* should be more comfortable.

Every muscle in Eira's body hurt. Her head ached. It hurt to *breathe*. Although, if she were breathing, she must be alive. That was a good thing, wasn't it? She couldn't quite decide.

She was lying down. On the ground, based on the hard surface making her hips ache. But her cheek rested on cloth. Wool. Soft, but slightly itchy. It wrapped around her, holding in her body heat, despite the dampness of her clothes.

Another breath. Woodsmoke. A cook fire nearby. The comforting scent eased something in her chest. Fear. Why was she afraid? She'd probably have a pretty good idea if she could only remember why she hurt all over. It felt like someone had beaten her with a wooden practice sword.

Marjani. She'd been fighting with Marjani, who wanted to kill her. No, kill herself ... No, *kill Prince Theo.* Eira had tried to stop her, chase after her, but—

The memory crashed over her. Falling. Choking. The tumbling current. The water slamming her against every rock in the stream bed. Drowning her.

Except she wasn't drowned.

She was wet and uncomfortable, but she was definitely breathing. As much as her whole body hurt, she should make sure it was still intact. She wiggled her fingers. Stiff, but all there. Her toes all moved, too, tickled by the wool ... *Where were her boots?*

A shift in the air, a grunt. Something breathing. She wasn't alone.

Oh, Goddess, the bear!

She froze, shutting down the sound of her own breathing much too late. How had she forgotten *the bear?* Those teeth! She must have fainted when they closed on her. Why wasn't she dead? Maybe the bear *thought* she was dead. Maybe he'd brought her back to his lair ... and chewed off her boots for a snack?

The breathing moved closer. She should open her eyes, but she couldn't bring herself to look into that horrible maw.

"Please." Her voice sounded as bruised and shaky as the rest of her. "If you're going to eat me, just make it quick."

A snort, more surprised than hostile. "I guess you're awake, then."

A boot-removing, fire-making, *talking* bear?

Eira opened her eyes and blinked up at the figure crouching beside her. No, this was definitely not the bear. The bear had been better groomed.

A man stared down at her from a thicket of dark brown hair that tangled with his scruff of neglected beard. His loose-fitting clothes were streaked with stains and poorly mended, though they appeared to have been of good quality once. His feral appearance inspired little confidence, but at least he was smaller than the bear.

Young, too, once she saw past the disconcerting facial hair. Not much older than herself. Though she suspected that if he were clean-shaven, that field of dense freckles might make him look even younger.

He grunted and sat back on his heels. "I thought you were going to die."

"Sorry to disappoint you." Warily, she sat up. Amazing how much pain fear could neutralize. Not the chill of her damp clothes, though. She pulled the wool fabric closer around her. It was a cloak, she saw now, though not her own, smelling faintly of smoke and pine.

Risking a glance around, she saw that she was huddled near the back of a rough half-dome of a cave. She'd have to stoop if she stood. The ragged man crouched between her and the entrance, where a small fire burned against the night sky. Another person stood beside it—no, that was her cloak, on a stick propped in the ground, drying before the flames. Her boots rested beside it.

The young man followed her gaze. "You should dry the rest of your clothes, too." His voice rasped as if from disuse. "I thought you might be frightened if I removed them."

A giggle rose in her throat. He said that as if any sensible person wouldn't be terrified by the whole situation. Yet, he was so awkward, it was hard to remember to be frightened. After all, she'd been expecting a murderous bear.

"Where am I?" A perfectly reasonable question, she thought, but his gaze shifted sideways.

"A cave."

"Is that right?" She looked around again, wide-eyed. "I never would have guessed."

"Saebern Manor is the closest habitation," he said. "I can lead you there, but it's a long walk. We should get started."

Relief flickered in her chest. If he was so eager to return her to civilization, he probably didn't plan to harm her. Yet, relief was dangerous. It dissolved the threads of will holding her upright. Much as she wanted to get back to her quest—and a comfortable bed!—her body had other ideas.

"I can't walk anywhere tonight," she objected. "I'm not even sure I can stand."

She held out a hand, and they both watched it tremble in disappointed silence.

"I just need rest. And maybe some food?" she said. Enough confidence would make it true. "I'll be ready by morning."

The young man recoiled, face twisting in dismay. "We should go now. I can't wait until morning."

Really? Even dirty hermits couldn't tolerate her presence? "That's ridiculous. What difference will a few hours make?"

"I have things I have to do!" he growled.

"Then go do them! I'll find my own way back."

"Now who's ridiculous? You don't even know where you are. You'll wander in circles and die."

"Well. That's fair." She pulled herself up straighter. "But I'd hate to interfere with your important activities. Give me directions. I'll leave at first light."

"And waste all that effort I put into saving your life?" For the first time, something almost like a smile pulled at his mouth. "Directions won't help you through the forest. There's not a path." Said as if he preferred it that way. "I will return tomorrow evening and take you to the manor then."

"Tomorrow *evening*?" Her hosts at the manor would be worried sick. About the king's wrath over them losing a princess, if nothing else. A whole day for Marjani to hunt the bear without her. "Surely it would be safer to travel by day?"

"I can find my way in the dark. You did say you needed rest." He gestured at the fire. "Come, dry your clothes. You can eat."

"Food?" That got her moving. Wary of hitting her head on the cave ceiling, she scrambled closer to the flames. The firelight obscured the small clearing outside, but she could make out the silhouettes of towering pines. Overhead, summer stars shimmered in the night sky.

A split log lay a foot from the fire. Two trout had been pegged to its flat side with sharpened sticks. The wild man pulled the log back from the flames and plucked the hot fish off with his bare hands. He dropped them on a smooth rock nearby.

"Eat." He peered at her from beneath his shaggy hair. "I can rip the heads off for you. Can you pick your own bones?"

"Ha. I'd have eaten it raw." Settling the cloak on the ground for a seat, she dropped beside the rock. She flipped open one of the cleaned fish and scraped out a steaming bite. She burned her fingers and her mouth, but it was worth it. No salt, no herbs. But the flaky white flesh was the best food she'd tasted in a long time.

She looked up from the remains of her feast. "Aren't you going to join me?"

"I already ate."

"They're both for me?" She could hardly believe her luck. "Thank you."

He gave that fleeting hint of a smile. "I'm glad you like it."

"My mother taught me to cook fish like this."

"Really?" He tilted his head, gaze suddenly sharp. "Your clothes are made of fine cloth. I assumed you were a noblewoman."

Ah. She hoped he wasn't expecting a reward for her return. He'd be sorely disappointed. "I'm Nordish. Everyone in Nordmark knows how to cook fish."

Not even Princess Beatrix could have handled that more diplomatically. Telling the simple truth without confirming or denying his assumption. At least he'd never guess she was a princess, not after the way she'd wolfed down the fish. Even a wild hermit might be tempted to ask a ransom for a princess.

She looked down at the carcasses. "Is it okay to put these on the fire, or will the smell lure the bear?"

"The bear?" He leaned forward to put more wood on the fire, his hair obscuring his face.

"The bear that attacked me." She stared at him. "The one that was about to eat me, last thing I remember. Didn't you scare it off?"

Even as she said it, she realized how ridiculous it sounded. He didn't even frighten her. How had she thought he'd frightened a bear?

"Oh, that bear." He tossed the fish scraps onto the fire. "I guess he decided you were too bony to be worth the effort. When I found you, he was long gone."

"You didn't kill it, then?" She hadn't even thought to worry about *that*—losing her opportunity to win Prince Theo's hand to someone besides Marjani.

"Kill it with what?" the wild man demanded. "My bare hands?"

"So, it's not dead?"

"Not that I know of."

"That's all right, then. I can still kill it myself." She couldn't fault him for his obvious incredulity. Even a Nordish princess had a hard time looking fearsome crouched in the dirt and smelling of fish. "I admit he got the upper hand in our first encounter, but he won't get off so easily next time. Where is my bow?"

"You had no weapons when I found you. You were wearing an empty scabbard." He gestured to the pole her cloak hung from, and she saw the sword belt peeking from beneath the fabric.

Eira sighed. Empty-handed and weaponless. Not the way she had planned to return to Saebern Manor. Marjani would laugh her head off.

Could Marjani laugh?

None of that mattered. Discovering Marjani's real purpose in beating her at this quest only made it more critical for Eira to complete it first. Not just to give herself a better chance to marry Prince Theo and bring peace to the Blessed Kingdoms.

There would be no hope of peace if Marjani killed Theo. And besides, she *liked* Theo. He didn't deserve to be murdered because his brother had been a blood-thirsty menace.

"Why do you want to kill this bear?" the wild man asked.

"It's why the king sent me. Sent *us*." However odd this young man's manner was, he didn't seem threatening. Still, best if he knew there were others searching for her. They *would* be searching for her, wouldn't they? It suddenly occurred to her that everyone at the manor might assume she was dead. Would they care enough to look for her body? "Steward Tarben begged the king for help getting rid of Saebern's monster bear, and Wulfric sent me and Pr—Lady Marjani."

"He sent a pair of girls?" The wild man eyed her warily from under pinched brows as if afraid she would mock him for misunderstanding.

Tired as she was of people being unable to believe two young women could kill a bear, she couldn't bring herself to take offense. Forget the monstrous beast. She'd been taken out by a mountain stream.

She'd thought when the king proposed this quest, he'd meant it as a grand gesture—and quite possibly a mean-spirited joke. Regardless, she'd jumped at the chance to prove herself worthy of being a queen. And then Wulfric had forced Marjani to join her. The one other princess with a personal reason to hate Aldforthian royalty.

"He may have been hoping to get rid of us," she realized. King Wulfric was still hunting for the assassin who had sent the manticore to kill Prince Guntram. He would see anyone with a grudge against Aldforth as a potential threat.

She grinned. "He's afraid of us."

"I've no doubt." This time, the smile split the wild man's whole face, and even that didn't offend her, because it lit his eyes, which she suddenly realized were a much lighter brown than his hair. Almost the color of the caramel candies Prince

Theo had obtained for Tenzin, Princess Anara's sweet-toothed dragon, as a reward for saving his life.

The little creature had chewed and chewed at the sticky candy until, in a burst of frustration, she'd blasted it from her mouth in a gout of fire that had charred the wall of their room. Carefully blank-faced, Anara had scraped the scorched mass from the stone and given it back to the dragon, who had crunched it between her teeth with a look that threatened dire consequences to anyone who laughed.

Eira broke the wild man's gaze, her heart twisting with the sudden ache of missing her friends. With a flush of panic, she lifted her hand to her throat, but by some miracle, the little jade frog on its silver chain still hung from her neck. Anara, Jax, Beatrix—they would all be doing fine without her, of course, just as Nordmark and the Temple of Peace were doing fine without her. Just as she was doing fine without them.

Lost and battered in a dark cave in the middle of nowhere with this wild ma—

"I can't keep thinking of you as 'the wild man,' " she said in sudden irritation. "What is your name? I'm Eira, of Nordmark."

The light in his eyes died. "I'm nobody. Of nowhere."

And here she'd thought *she* was wallowing in self-pity. "That's obviously not true. You speak impeccable Common Tongue. You have a Saebernian accent but with all the rough edges worn off, as if you've spent time in the south. Your clothes are in abysmal shape, but they've obviously been tailored for you—about fifteen pounds ago."

He drew back from her as if to hide in the shadows, but the firelight gleamed in his startled stare.

"Girls of all ranks and nationalities come and go at the Temple of Peace," she said, smug at his dismay. "You have to be able to size them up quickly. I thought at first you were some kind of religious hermit—"

He snorted.

"But a hermit would wear his god's symbol on his clothing, even clothing made out of such fine wool as this." She fingered the soft material of the cloak beneath her, the edge embroidered in an intricate leaf design with what looked like gold thread. "If I didn't know better, I'd say this wasn't even Saebernian sheep's wool. Prin—*Lady* Dora would know for sure, but it feels like that goat's wool she says all the Rigan merchant-nobles wear. I don't suppose you've been to Rigas lately—"

She stopped and stared at the feral young man across the fire, his features taut with sudden wretchedness. A strangled growl rose from his throat, a warning not to say any more.

But she'd never been good at holding her tongue.

"I know who you are," she said in wonder. "The missing Earl. You're Berengar!"

CHAPTER ELEVEN

6. He complained about everything. It's no wonder he didn't have any friends. (Submitted by Master Kaspar, wool merchant.)

— Top 10 reasons no one misses Earl Berengar that much

An outside observer might have thought Saebern Manor was a beehive that Marjani had poked with a stick. There was a great deal of whirring and buzzing, punctuated by stinging comments on her foolishness in sneaking out of the manor without permission—which a royal princess didn't need; getting lost in the wilderness—which she hadn't done; and letting Princess Eira get herself killed—as if anyone could have stopped the girl from taking absurd risks.

Steward Tarben sent swarms of sheepherders and timber fellers into the hills to search for signs of princess or bear, and twilight brought them swarming home again almost immediately.

The Saebern Town Council held an emergency meeting. Since their reeve was busy coordinating the next day's search, Master Kaspar was dispatched to the manor to demand

Tarben explain how he would deflect Wulfric's wrath after losing one of the king's foreign princesses.

"*I* didn't lose her." Tarben slammed his hands on the table in the manor's great hall, his pointed beard quivering. "She lost herself. The king can't hold Saebern responsible for her folly."

"Of course he can," Kaspar growled back, his narrowed eyes making him even more ursine than usual. "If he'd sent you sheep, he'd hold you responsible for letting one get eaten by a bear. How much more so a princess? You should have penned them properly."

"I am not a sheep," Marjani said, outrage pulling her from the guilt-ridden darkness of her thoughts. The men turned to stare at her as if they'd forgotten she was in the room, sitting by the fire with Lady Silke. "Nor was Princess Eira. We understood the dangers of hunting your bear. As does the king."

Which would not prevent him from blaming Saebern for Eira's death if he decided that was convenient, but there was no need to share that insight.

"I will kill the bear," she said instead, "and avenge Princess Eira. That should satisfy the king."

"Enough foolishness." Kaspar rounded on Tarben, his big hands like paws clenched into fists. "You will send this one back to Newport on the next boat. I told you petitioning the king would lead to nothing but trouble."

"The trouble is not Princess Marjani nor the king," Lady Silke said sharply. "The trouble is the monster that plagues our county. Do not presume to criticize these princesses or my husband, Master wool merchant, for making sacrifices that the brave men of Saebern are so unwilling to make."

The fury lacing her words would have raised welts on more sensitive skin than Kaspar's.

"I mean no disrespect, milady," he grumbled. "I am a simple man, and I sometimes speak too plainly. I commend your husband's commitment to Saebern's welfare. But his solution has failed. It's time to try mine."

"We don't need a sorcerer!" Color stained Silke's fine cheekbones. "We need a *killer*. We need one competent hunter to thrust a spear into that monster's throat and choke it on its own blood. If I did not have the future countess of Saebern to raise, I would do it myself."

Lady Silke had probably never wielded anything more dangerous than her dining knife, but in that moment, she looked perfectly capable of killing a bear with it.

"Excuse me." Marjani rose from her seat, too angry and heartsick to continue an irrelevant argument. She knew her duty, and she would complete it. "I have an obligation of prayer for my—" Not friend. "For my companion. Is there a place …?"

"Of course." Sympathy softened Silke's face. "We have a chapel at the north wall. It's dedicated to the Old Man of the Forest, but I often pray to the Mother Goddess there, and he doesn't seem to mind. I will call Ebba to show you the way."

"That's not necessary. I can find it." Marjani suddenly needed desperately to be alone, away from these people and their fears and anxiety. With a barely polite nod of thanks, she hurried from the hall before anyone could object.

Pushing out the front door, she gulped fresh air, still sweet with last night's rains. The evening breeze seemed to sweep away the residue of the troubled spirits inside the manor. Spirits appalled by Eira's death, yet unable to spare any grief for her loss.

Not that they should. They barely knew Eira. Even Marjani barely knew her. And what she did know, she hadn't liked.

Yet she remembered Eira's conspiratorial tone the night before. *We'll make matching necklaces of the bear's teeth. King Wulfric will notice us then.* As if they were arrayed together against the king.

If Marjani didn't need to kill the bear herself. If she hadn't let Eira try to cross the stream. If she hadn't assumed a girl who grew up by the ocean *knew how to swim …*

She pulled her cloak tighter. The north wall, Silke had said. Marjani made her way through the manor yard, careful of her step in the deceptive twilight. The few servants she passed, hurrying to the stables or the kitchens, were too polite to stare, but she felt their curiosity like ghostly fingers plucking at her clothes, her close-cropped hair, her foreign skin.

She found the chapel more by instinct than any religious adornment of the small, unassuming stone building. A sense of … not peace exactly, but calm. Acceptance. Surely an Old Man of the Forest would be a god of patience, tranquil in his knowledge of the transience of human life, human sorrow, human joy.

A candle burned on the narrow stone altar, enough light to illuminate the small space. Sprays of white flowers sat in the niches around the walls, filling the cool air with a sweet scent, and low benches woven of stripped branches offered seats for contemplation.

Simple, yet inviting. It would have suited Eira.

Marjani sat on one of the benches and ran a finger along the broken edge of her bracelet, murmuring the prayer for the Death of the Young Warrior. She did not expect to hear from Eira's spirit. If she had any ability to perceive the dead, surely Mosi or Dejen would have contacted her. Her father had not allowed her to join the vigil in the ancestors' house after their bodies had been burned to release their spirits. Not a worthless girl with only half a soul.

But she had sat with the court's women through their night of singing and prayers, and Mosi and Dejen could have found her there had they wished to.

Of course, not many spirits stayed to advise the living. Most made their way along the spirit roads to the lands beyond. Some few lost their way, wandering aimlessly until they faded into nothing. Terror that Mosi might not be able to find his path with only half a soul sometimes woke Marjani gasping in the night, but Dejen would be with him. Dejen's spirit was a steady star that would light the way for both of them.

And when Marjani finished her task here in Aldforth, once she completed the vengeance they deserved and lost her own life, the tattered fragment of her spirit would find its way to them and finally become whole.

The thought should comfort her. The joy of seeing Mosi and Dejen again, arms around each others' shoulders. Yet guilty confusion curled like smoke in her chest. The head priest had told her father that she, Mosi's twin, held half his soul. When their soul, *Mosi's* soul, reunited, what would happen to her? Would she become a part of him, forever with the two people she loved most in the world, finally one with the love they shared that she could never quite belong to?

Or would she simply cease to be? An unfortunate mistake finally righted?

With a hiss of anguish, she forced the thoughts away. She was here to hold vigil for Eira's spirit, not worry about her own.

She prayed with what serenity she could muster as the candle slowly burned down, the cool dampness of the evening settling into her bones. The crudely woven branches that formed her bench probably had symbolic meaning, but they grew ever more uncomfortable the longer she sat.

A reluctant smile tugged at her lips. Well suited to Eira, indeed. A real pain in the—

"Don't scream."

A hand clamped over her mouth as an arm wrapped around her chest from behind.

Marjani's father had not permitted her to learn wrestling with her brother. But Princess Anara's lessons for all the princesses at Lukos had included close combat.

Marjani grabbed her attacker's tunic where he leaned over her shoulder, already foolishly off balance. She jerked down and forward, and he fell across the bench. A quick duck out of his hold, a thrust with her legs, and he flipped completely over, landing with a heavy thud on the flagstone floor.

Even as she pulled her knife from the sheath at her waist, she realized three things. Her opponent was unarmed. He was too busy gasping for breath to resume his attack. He looked more afraid of her than she was of him.

"Please," the young man gasped, crossing his arms over his face to ward off her blade. "Never meant. Harm you. Didn't want. Call out."

"Then you should have knocked." She risked a glance around and saw the door she had entered through was closed, but a small door behind the altar now stood ajar. She shivered. Dangerous to be so absorbed in her thoughts she hadn't noticed its opening. She couldn't afford such a slip.

"I didn't want. Anyone to see me. Listen?" He rolled to his side but kept his hands up where she could see them. "One minute. Before you call for anyone."

Calling for help was the sensible thing to do. Except she was perfectly capable of handling this situation by herself and was sorely tired of everyone insisting she *needed* help. Besides, he'd piqued her curiosity. The stranger's accent—a tongue-contorting mixture of scouring wind and soft melody that reminded her of Princess Raisa. His hair—long and dark, pulled back in a topknot over slashing black brows, so different from anyone else she'd met in Aldforth. His clothes—snug tunic over loose shirt and breeches, wrists and ankles cuffed in black bands decorated with silver thread.

"You're Ravninan," she said. But not a member of the elegant, brutal aristocracy that had produced Raisa. "From the steppes."

"The taiga," he corrected. "The great forest." He slowly sat up, wincing at the twist of his bruised ribs. Served him right. "Ravnina claims our land. Of course, Ravnina claims any land it can reach. Same with the Kheremese Empire. The earth must be shrinking, the way the distance between the two keeps getting smaller."

"You wish to spend your allotted minute speaking of geography?" Marjani asked. "What are you doing here?"

He met her gaze with a bold tilt of his chin. "I am looking for the Almasan warrior queen who has come to Saebern to hunt the Great Bear."

"I am neither warrior nor queen." She adjusted her hold on her knife, glad the leather grip kept it from slipping in her clammy palm. Did he think she was a child, to be disarmed by pretty words and a handsome face? He could be no more than a year or two older than she. "Your trifling flattery earns you no favors."

"It is only what I heard." He shrugged. "Rumors are the local entertainment. I was told you were seven feet tall, keep a leopard and a crocodile for pets, and you can kill a man with your spear from fifteen yards."

She snorted in indignation. And amusement. "The last is probably true. I could make a trial with you to find out for certain."

He risked a smile and rolled onto his knees. "Your companion is said to be a Nordish snow witch who kills ice bears by tearing out their throats with her pointed teeth."

Eira would love that.

"Princess Eira is dead," Marjani said flatly. "Killed by the bear. Unless you wish to join her in the lands beyond, stop moving and start talking. Why did you accost me?"

"The *bear* killed her?" he demanded, startled out of his smugness. "You saw it?"

"Of course I didn't see it! If I had been there, she wouldn't have died." His minute was surely up, but she hadn't failed Eira *that* badly. "She was swept away by a flooded stream. I found where the bear dragged her from the water."

"She didn't drown? She'd been mauled?" His obvious distress softened her hostility. No one else had seemed to care what Eira might have suffered.

"I haven't yet found her body. There will be a search tomorrow."

"She might still be alive!" He scrambled to his feet, then jerked back, hands up, when she brandished her knife. "The bear wouldn't kill her."

She stared at him. "The beast nailed a mutilated sheep's heart to the manor gate. Of course it killed her."

"A sheep's heart? How did I miss *that* rumor?" The Ravninan shook himself. "It doesn't matter. The bear has never killed anyone."

"Your sources are dangerously uninformed," Marjani said. "It killed one of the men out hunting with Earl Berengar last year when he disappeared—and probably killed the earl, as well."

"They told you that? Who exactly did the bear kill?"

"He was a foreigner, a Ravninan sorcerer—" Marjani froze.

The Ravninan standing before her offered an elaborate bow he probably thought was charming.

"*You.*" She stepped forward. He retreated. "You're the Ravninan sorcerer."

"Rurik, at your service," he said brightly, keeping a nervous eye on her knife.

"You left behind a bloody cloak." She stepped toward him again, and he scurried back. "You let everyone think you were dead."

"To be fair, I *could* have died. I came very close—" His back slammed into the chapel wall.

"Did you even *try* to help the others? Hartwin's father and the marshal? The earl?" It struck her suddenly, the full extent of his depravity. "You saw what happened to Earl Berengar! You could have spared his family—his people—this year of uncertainty. But you … what? You ran away?"

He swallowed hard. "Just lower the knife. Let me explain."

Her knife was at least a foot from his throat. *Coward.* She stepped back, disgusted. "You can explain to Steward Tarben."

"*No!* I beg you." He held out his empty hands in pleading.

"I daren't go to the steward. I can't let anyone in Saebern know I survived. What happened on that hunt was no accident. Berengar was betrayed."

"You're saying … Earl Berengar was murdered?"

"Someone intended for him to die," Rurik said, with a certainty hard as flint in his voice. "But I don't know who. I can't trust anyone who was here that day. That's why I came to you."

She was close enough to sense the turmoil in his spirit, the thread of darkness in it. His fear was honest, but whether it was fear of the plot he described or of her knife, she couldn't say.

"What do you want from me?" she demanded.

"I need you to lead me to the bear." He took a deep breath. "You've heard the rumors it's enchanted? Those rumors, at least, are true. Or close enough. Cursed is more like it."

"*You* sent this bear to attack Saebern?" She'd forgotten the "sorcerer" part of his being "the Ravninan sorcerer." He was so infuriating she couldn't remember to be frightened of him.

"It wasn't my fault!" His objection sounded like a well-worn response. "I didn't weave the curse. I couldn't make it work, even if I tried. And I had tried," he added bitterly. "But a case could be made that since I brought the curse with me to Saebern, I have a responsibility to try to break it."

From his tone, she guessed someone *had* made that case.

"Can you?" she asked. "Break the curse?"

Rurik shook his head, jaw tight. "I've spent the better part of the past year traveling the Blessed Kingdoms, searching for a way to reverse it. I've finally found it."

"So you *can* break it. And if you'd told someone yesterday, Eira might not be dead."

"That's not my fault, either," he snapped. "I got here as fast as I could. I've learned how the curse can be lifted, but it requires the bear, and it must be done soon. Before the anniversary of Berengar's … disappearance."

He paused. "The curse is meant to kill, but I—I somehow deflected it. It's incomplete."

"I've seen the bear," Marjani said skeptically. "The menace it poses does not seem incomplete."

"I suppose not," Rurik agreed, weariness weighing his voice. "But that incompleteness gives us a chance to reverse it and get rid of the bear for good. No protection spell can last more than one turning of the year. If we don't break the enchantment before the year is done, the—" He gestured with his hands. "The gap, for lack of a better word, in the curse will close, and there will be no undoing it at all."

It sounded ridiculous. And complicated. And she wanted nothing to do with it. Much like the rest of her life.

"Why should I believe you?"

"If I lie, what can I possibly hope to gain?" he asked simply. "If I speak the truth, I can live freely again, and you can accomplish your goal. You wish to kill the bear, but it will be invulnerable until the curse is lifted. I only ask that you allow me to come with you on your hunt."

"The last person who followed me is dead."

"I understand the risk."

Marjani appraised him. She had no reason to trust this man. He obviously wasn't telling her everything, and if what Hartwin had said of him were true, his previous conduct had consisted of fraudulent sorcery and the seduction of another man's wife. She couldn't imagine Lady Silke allowing herself to be kissed by this scruffy-looking rascal, but Silke had married Tarben, and Marjani couldn't imagine her kissing the steward, either.

Rurik owed her hosts answers about what had really happened the day their earl disappeared. He owed Hartwin answers about his father's death.

Surely Eira, the sanctimonious religious acolyte, would tell Marjani to help them find peace.

And yet … All Rurik asked was to follow her to the bear.

As if he believed she could find it. As if he believed she was the hunter no one else believed her to be.

If there really were a curse and he really could break it—and yes, that was taking a lot on faith. But. If the curse protected the bear from harm, being there when it was broken would be her best chance to kill it.

Killing the bear would bring her one step closer to paying her debt of vengeance to Mosi and Dejen. To freeing her soul.

Rurik seemed to sense her wavering. "If we find the bear, I may be able to discover what happened to your friend."

"She wasn't my friend." Marjani grimaced in surrender. "I will go with the search party to look for her body tomorrow. The day after, I will continue my hunt."

"There isn't time—"

"The timing is my choice." She owed Eira that much.

After a moment, he nodded, though impatience crackled around him. "Very well."

"I will come to this chapel before dawn the day after tomorrow. If you wish to accompany me, you may find me here."

Without another word, she swept out the chapel door into the star-strewn night. Let Rurik look after himself until then. If he got caught, the manor would get their answers about Berengar and Hartwin about his father. That would satisfy any self-righteous Nordish spirit lingering nearby.

Who was Marjani kidding? If their places were reversed, Eira would be rushing off into the wilderness with any Ravninan sorcerer who happened to drop by, without a second thought.

No wonder she had agreed to Rurik's ridiculous proposal. Eira's spirit must be goading her from beyond the veil.

If a smile touched Marjani's lips, she trusted the darkness to hide it.

CHAPTER TWELVE

5. He spent more time on his hair than he did running the estate. (Submitted by Tarben, steward of Saebern County.)

— Top 10 reasons no one misses Earl Berengar that much

After the wild man bolted into the night like a spooked deer, Eira's smug glee—she'd found the missing earl everyone had been seeking for the past year, *take* that *Marjani*—quickly faded to a more pragmatic uneasiness. She'd lost the earl as soon as she'd found him, and if he didn't return, she might be in serious danger.

As confident as she felt in her ability to survive a few days on her own in the wilderness, she'd arrived at this cave completely unconscious, with no way of knowing in which direction Saebern Manor lay. She and Marjani had been heading north, so probably south. But that left plenty of room for error. There was a real possibility she could stumble around lost in the wilderness until she died from hunger or exposure.

Then again, it was just as likely the bear would find her and finish her off in her sleep. Yet even that fear couldn't keep her from slipping into an anxious doze as the stars brightened overhead. She finally dragged herself to the back of the cave —maybe the fire would keep the bear away—and sank into a fitful sleep.

She awoke in the morning to discover she'd been worried about the wrong things. *As usual.*

Berengar was nowhere to be seen, but a freshly caught fish was cooking by the fire, and a handful of summer berries sat on a rock beside a crude wooden bowl filled with water. Apparently, the hermit earl hadn't completely abandoned her. He might even return that evening as promised to lead her back to the manor.

Even better, the bear was also absent and had not so much as nibbled on her while she was dead to the world.

On the other hand, every bone and muscle in her body hurt so badly she'd almost rather be dead.

She struggled to sit, discovering that her lungs ached, too, and her skin felt like someone had set fire to tiny mites and let them loose all over her body. *Fever.* Not surprising, really, after nearly succumbing to drowning and hypothermia both in one day. But inconvenient. She didn't have time for anything that would diminish her ability to hunt Saebern's bear.

She *had* to kill the bear before Marjani could.

Forget her dreams of marrying Prince Theo and working for peace. If Marjani succeeded in killing the prince—or if Wulfric stuck her head on a spike over the castle gates because he suspected her of wanting to kill Theo—peace would be a distant memory in the Blessed Kingdoms for decades to come.

First, though, Eira would have to live, unpleasant as that might sound at the moment.

Standing seemed out of the question, but she managed to crawl to the water. She brought the bowl to her lips and nearly gagged on the bitter taste. Willow bark tea.

She eyed the battered iron pot hanging over the fire. Plenty of it to see her through the day.

Oh, yummy.

She took another sip. Crushed mint, as well. She could

imagine Berengar's wary, worried look as he added it to the tea. Rather sweet to know he tried to make it palatable. Apparently hoping she wouldn't die.

Of course, if he was so worried, he could have put aside his obligations for the day—what could those be, anyway? Not social calls; everyone thought he was dead. Skulking and hiding? Whatever his plans, he could have chosen to take her back to Saebern Town for proper medical care instead.

She put a few berries in her mouth to mask the flavor of the tea and struggled to swallow them. Who knew chewing could be so exhausting?

"All right, Wild Man. Fair enough. I couldn't walk anywhere today, anyway."

She pulled Berengar's fine goat-wool cloak tighter around her shoulders and took another sip of the tea.

"*Gah!*" Again, almost better to die.

But then Marjani would kill the bear, complete their quest and return to Newport in triumph.

And that would be *worse* than death.

She lifted the bowl and drank the rest of the tea.

THE WILLOW BARK and the warmth of the morning sun revived Eira enough for her to pick at the fish and bank the fire. She needed rest if she had any hope of walking to the manor with Berengar that evening, but her bruises rebelled against returning to the hard dirt floor of the cave.

Once, on one of those rare times when her mother had escaped the responsibilities of royalty for a few hours to spend time alone with her daughter, an afternoon walk had stretched into an impromptu overnight in the woods. Queen Sassa had shown Eira how to make a pine needle mattress for their bed.

"This is a solemn duty," her mother had said, her mock seriousness making Eira giggle. "I am attending to my responsibility as a teacher and guide to the future queen!"

"And now I will put my education to good use," Eira teased her mother's memory as she forced herself to her feet and shuffled to the trees encircling the clearing.

Even just the thought of walking back to the cave sapped her energy.

"You've made me a lovely bed right here, haven't you?" she murmured to the pines as she laid Berengar's cloak on a drift of needles beneath the trees. "I offer you my gratitude."

Her mother had worshipped the capricious Nordish gods with the devotion due from a queen. But in the deep woods, she had always taken time to thank the tree spirits for their fire, the animal spirits for their food, the river spirits for their water.

Eira sank onto the cloak and brushed the dampness from her eyes. Why did she keep thinking of her mother lately? Sassa, the ice maiden of Nordmark. The warrior queen. Who had taught her how to fend for herself in any situation. To be independent. Not to mope around wishing her mama were there to dry her tears. And feed her soup. And sing her a lullaby.

What if she was too exhausted to be self-sufficient? What if she was tired of being an exile? What if she wanted someone to care if she was sick or in pain or lonely?

Eira curled up on the cloak, breathing in the scent of the pines, feeling the sun's warmth dappling her back through the branches. If she were going to die, lost and forgotten, this wasn't such a bad place to do it, really.

She'd close her eyes, drift off, and maybe she wouldn't bother waking up again …

"Gnngh."

Her eyes flew open, and her breath caught in her throat. *No, not quite ready to die, after all.* She scrunched her eyes closed again, blocking out the sight of the massive bear on the opposite side of the clearing.

"Gnngh-ngff."

Pretending it wasn't there didn't seem to be working. She

peeked through slitted eyelids, watching the beast snuffle at the fish-cooking log, the pot hanging over the fire, her boots—which she really wished she'd put on. Much better than bare feet for fleeing a giant bear.

The great head swung away from the cave, and her eyes clenched shut again. Who was she kidding? She wasn't fleeing anywhere. Even if the terror-induced adrenaline pumping sluggishly through her fevered veins could get her to her feet, her trembling legs wouldn't be any match for a bear. *Never run from a predator. It only makes you look like prey.*

Her best—only—option was to lie still and hope it didn't notice her. *Don't move. Don't whimper. Don't breathe …*

She couldn't hear a thing over the pounding of her heart, but surely she'd feel the ground tremble under those huge feet if it got too clo—

A gust of air blew across her forehead. Hot, raspberry-and-fish-scented bear breath. A great, deep inhale ruffled her hair. "Ngff."

She gave up and opened her eyes. The bear tilted its head, the better to peer at her with its own great golden-brown orbs.

"Found me," she chirped around the fear clogging her throat. "You're really good at this game. Shall we play again? Close your eyes—"

"Hnguh." The bear glanced around the clearing, then drew in a great, snuffling breath of the gentle breeze. Apparently satisfied no other feverish princesses lurked nearby, it looked back down at Eira.

"You know," she warned it, "I don't have the energy to stay terrified much longer. If you're planning to eat me, could you just get on with it? I'd hate to fall asleep and miss my own death."

The bear heaved a sigh that could have passed for a small hurricane and slowly lowered its head … and then the rest of its body, down to the ground beside her. *Now* she felt the earth shake as it flopped onto the bed of pine needles, its giant forepaw mere inches from her hand. It gave her one more uncertain glance before settling its head between his paws and closing its eyes.

Eira stared, immobile. A fever vision. It must be. Except the rough blackness of its nose, the white-tipped hair inside its curved ear, the clove and cinnamon dappling of its coat were so vivid, so detailed.

Just for once, be sensible. Close your eyes. Trust it will be gone when you wake up.

But her hand reached out as if it wasn't attached to her caution-screaming mind … Oh, hells. It wasn't like she'd ever listened to caution before.

Her fingertips brushed the fur just below the great bear's shoulder. A little bristly but yielding. It felt just as real as it looked. She pressed a little deeper, to the softer undercoat. A bit like one of her mother's deerhounds. If the hound had smelled like a dangerous wild beast.

One dangerous, wild eye slowly opened and blinked at her, then closed again with another sigh.

"You can't fall asleep," she chided it. "Don't toy with me. I'm not going to just lie here until you decide you're hungry and need a snack."

It turned its muzzle away from her, its ear twitching as if she were a mosquito buzzing too close.

"That's a bit much!" she objected, shifting up on one elbow. "I'll have you know I was hunting you yesterday. If I hadn't fallen into that stream, you'd be a bear rug by now. You turn your back on me, Master Bear, you're taking your life in your hands. Paws. Whatever."

"Hunngh."

She waited, but it didn't move. Didn't so much as twitch one of those great curved claws.

"Fine. Be that way." With a huff of frustration, she dropped back on Berengar's cloak, looking up through the pine boughs to the clear blue summer sky. She should try to sneak away. Sneaking didn't require as much energy as running. She could do this. If she could just work up the motivation.

The fear of being eaten was a pretty good motivation. But it was difficult to be afraid when the eater showed no interest in digging into its meal. It was almost sweet, the way it was watching over her. The way she'd watch over a plate of molasses cookies when Tenzin got too close.

Besides, she wasn't sure she believed it was really there. If a fever could give you visual hallucinations, why not … what would the word be for hallucinations in your fingertips?

Wouldn't it be best to wait a little while? Another quarter-hour. If it were a hallucination, the bear would be gone by then. And if not, there was a chance it would fall soundly asleep, making it that much easier for her to slip away.

Good to have a plan. Especially one that didn't require her to move just yet.

She marked the sun's location against a nearby tree trunk. Give it time to rise to that next branch there, and she'd be on her way …

CHAPTER THIRTEEN

7. Everyone likes her better than me.

— Top 10 things ~~I hate~~ I find difficult to appreciate about Princess Marjani, as listed by (former) Princess Eira of Nordmark

Marjani had little hope that the search for Eira's body would yield useful answers, but even that was quickly dashed. The day after the bear's attack, Steward Tarben called together nearly a score of searchers for fear of the bear. Between their great, clumsy boots and the thoughtless trampling of their horses, they destroyed more sign than they found.

Hartwin did manage to retrieve Eira's broken bow. The look he shot Marjani, so fraught with anguish for what might have happened to *her* if she had encountered the bear, made her blush like a child.

Tarben stubbornly refused to allow Marjani to attempt any tracking of her own. By the time the search party returned to the manor, exhausted and demoralized, he went so far as to forbid her from leaving the manor grounds at all until he could make arrangements for her return to Newport.

He *forbade* her. A princess of Almasa.

If she had harbored reservations about not telling anyone about Rurik the sorcerer or her plan to take him bear hunting with her, that effectively quashed them. She felt no guilt at all looking up from her breakfast the next morning with all the meekness she could swallow to ask Tarben a favor.

"What is it?" he demanded, barely glancing at her and then away. As though if he couldn't see her, she wouldn't be his problem anymore.

Once more, Marjani found herself an inconvenient reminder of violence and tragedy. A leftover problem no one quite knew how to solve. She felt the serving maids' wary glances, imagined their furtive signs to ward off the evil that must linger near her after Princess Eira's tragic demise.

The indignity heated her cheeks, but she could turn even this into a tool to reach her goal. *No one* kept an Almasan hunter from her prey.

"I do not find myself fit company this morning," she told the steward. True enough. "I would like to spend the day alone in the chapel, if I may. I feel the need of solitude and prayer."

Also not a lie, although she did not expect to experience much of either.

Tarben looked at her now, as though he hardly dared believe his good fortune.

"Of course, of course, Your Highness," he said quickly, obviously afraid she might change her mind. "An admirable endeavor. Take all the time you need."

He practically sighed with relief, as if she were a troublesome child to be kept out of sight and out of mind. He even glanced toward Lady Silke as though she might take the hint and remove Artis from disturbing his breakfast, as well.

The little girl sat beside her mother, a pile of velvet cushions lifting her to the level of the food. She had nearly as much butter on her face as her bread, but she presided over the table with unruffled good cheer.

"Artis is the countess of Saebern," Silke explained to

Marjani, ignoring her husband's hint. She adjusted the grip of the carefully dulled knife in the toddler's chubby fist. "She will be granted the title in mere days when the king's year is over, and we can forget this fanciful wait for Berengar's return. She must learn to behave like a noble. She can't do that locked away in the nursery."

"I do it, Mama!"

"Yes, dear. Like this."

"Her mother can hardly bear to have the child out of her sight," Tarben said, though he sounded more resigned than annoyed.

Marjani had noticed the absence of children at King Wulfric's court. Apparently, sequestering little ones from adult business was common practice among the high-born in Aldforth. Not like the Almasan court, where children were only absent from the halls when they were running riot through the gardens, bright and cheerful as the flowers.

"Can you blame me for keeping her near?" Silke asked. "With that bear terrorizing the countryside? If it keeps coming after us, I will find a way to kill it myself. I will *never* allow it to hurt my baby."

"The bear isn't coming after us," Tarben said, an edge to his reassurance. "It's not *after* anyone. It's a dumb beast."

He shot Marjani a warning glance. As if she would bring up curses and mutilated sheep in front of a child!

"How do you know?" Silke snapped. "Why does it keep coming back? Getting closer? It hates us. I can feel it."

"It's just a bear." Tarben's words sounded feeble in the face of Silke's palpable fear. In the face of a bear who could nail a bloody heart to their gate. A bear who could drag a young woman's body from a stream and disappear without a trace.

Silke would understand why she needed to hunt the bear. But she couldn't risk her chance at avenging Mosi and Dejen by telling her.

"Bear like Arris," Artis said with cheerful confidence.

"Bears are horrible, nasty beasts," Silke told her. "Mama will never let one near you."

"*Bear like Arris*," Artis insisted. She let out a low growl, and Marjani couldn't tell whether she meant the bear was fond of her or the bear was fierce like she was.

Either way, the little girl caught her trying not to smile and grinned back, baring her teeth and curling her fingers like claws.

"See how it upsets her?" Silke smoothed Artis's wispy curls and fixed Marjani with a look as intense as any bear's. "We cannot be happy until the beast is gone. You can make the king listen. He *must* send soldiers to destroy it."

Marjani was saved from having to reply by a commotion in the corridor.

"Master Steward!" A big man Marjani recognized from the search the day before burst through the doorway, his weathered face creased with distress. "Master Steward. In the courtyard. It's a monster!"

Silke's heavy chair screeched on the hardwood floor as she jerked to her feet. Her skin paled, so her dark eyes looked black. "The bear!"

Suddenly noticing the ladies, the man yanked the soft cap from his head and managed a jerky bow. "No, milady. It's not the bear. It's a …" His mouth worked as if he struggled for the words. "It seems to be a dragon."

Marjani's breath froze in her lungs.

"A what?" Tarben demanded. "Have you gone mad, Rodolf?"

Silke fell back into her chair and dropped her head in her hands. "A *dragon*. What next?"

"Drangin?" Artis asked brightly. "Drangin like Arris."

Marjani found herself on her feet, her heart pounding with nearly as much fear as her hosts, but probably less surprise. Leave it to Eira to cause even more trouble in death than in life.

"This dragon," she addressed the bondsman. "Is it a very small dragon? Maybe eagle-sized? Blue-green?"

The man stared at her with awe and suspicion, as if she might transform into a dragon herself, right before his eyes. "It is, yes, milady. I mean, Your Highness. Beg pardon, Your Highness. It's just like you describe. Flew down from the sky and landed on top of the hen house. Scared the hens near to death. It looks to have some kind of message strapped to its leg. Like a pigeon!"

Thank gods he hadn't said that in front of the dragon.

"It's Tenzin." Marjani managed to keep her voice calm. Even reassuring. "Princess Anara's dragon, which she brought from Kherem. Tenzin must have brought a message from Newport for us." *For Princess Eira.* "There is no need to be afraid. She intends no harm."

Not yet.

"I will go meet her." Marjani gathered her cloak around her as if it were her courage and moved toward the door.

"Artis?" Silke's voice fluttered like silk on a knife's edge. The chair beside her sat empty, cushions tumbled to the floor. "Artis, darling? Where are you? *Where did she go?*"

For a moment, the adults all stared around the room as if the child might have engaged herself in some sudden interest other than the dragon in the yard.

And then they were all running for the door. Marjani was closest, as well as fastest. She sprinted down the corridor, forcing away memories of the bloodied rabbits Tenzin sometimes brought Anara. The heavy front door hung open, probably left ajar by the bondsman in his rush. She hurtled through, scanning her panic-emptied mind for some thought of where the henhouse might be.

She needn't have bothered. The dragon had taken center stage in the middle of the paved yard as if to bask in the awe-struck terror of the humans around it. The creature sat on her haunches, her crest lifted around her head, a blue fan tipped with silver. Her wings spread at least a yard to either side, the shimmering patterns of blue and green glimmering like icy gems in the morning sunlight.

A very small dragon. Eagle sized? Maybe not even that. Smaller than the great sea eagles that hunted the waterways of Almasa.

And yet her glittering emerald eyes stared down at the solemn little girl before her. The narrow muzzle was closed, but faint tendrils of smoke curled from her nostrils, and the gold-tipped talon of the claw pointing toward the child rivaled a bear's for menace.

Marjani heard the running footsteps behind her falter to a halt. Heard Silke's gasp and the rustle as Tarben held his wife back. She raised a hand. *Stop. Peace.* Though whether the humans or the dragon would notice …

"Tenzin. Greetings." She did not have Eira's ability to hide her fear in breezy banter. She could only hope her words were welcoming. She had heard Princess Anara and the dragon communicate with whistles and warbles, but Eira, and Anara's other friends, often spoke to Tenzin in Common Tongue as though the creature understood. At the docks in Newport, Eira had even allowed the dragon to ride on her shoulder, a set of deadly talons resting on her hair.

She's not dangerous. That was what the other princesses told each other. Even as they kept their distance. Tenzin had never hurt any of them. Never threatened to. But none of them were small and helpless as a baby lamb. A predator was a predator. If the child lunged. Or ran.

Marjani stepped toward them, slow and deliberate. "Tenzin, this child is Lady Artis. She is soon to be countess of Saebern."

"Drangin." Artis put three fingers of one hand into her mouth and reached the other toward the glittering creature's face.

"Tenzin—" Marjani's voice trembled.

The dragon ignored her. Glittering eyes focused only on the child, Tenzin fluttered her wings and bent her head in a regal nod. Then, so fast Marjani had no time even to cry out, her muzzle opened, exposing needle-sharp teeth, and her long, forked tongue flicked out to tickle the end of Artis's nose.

The little girl shrieked with delighted laughter, and Tenzin turned one eye toward Marjani with what could only be described as a smirk.

"Drangin like Arris." Artis threw out her arms and pulled Tenzin into a hug, squeezing a gasping warble from the startled dragon.

"She certainly does like Artis!" Marjani burst out, more a desperate command than an observation. She swept forward to peel the child away from the creature, brushing the smooth, warm dragon scales, the faintest scent of sulfur and frankincense wafting to her nose. Fortunately, Tenzin appeared unharmed.

"Drangin!" Artis shrieked as Marjani lifted the child into her arms.

"Tenzin is a *royal* drangin. Dragon," Marjani said, her words weighted by respect for the creature's restraint in the face of the girl's assault. "You see how regal she is?"

Artis stopped struggling as she watched Tenzin's crest rise in haughty grandeur.

"We must treat her with the esteem due her station. Like a queen."

Artis's eyes widened. "Queen Drangin."

Tenzin sneezed with what looked suspiciously like mirth.

"Right." Marjani gave Tenzin a sharp look. "Queen Dragon. And now I think it's time for Artis to finish her breakfast."

The child sighed, but her chubby, warm body relaxed against Marjani's side, and she nodded. Before Marjani could step back, Tenzin reached out one elegant, knife-sharp talon and caught the edge of Artis's pink silk slipper. She tilted her muzzle up, her crest falling back against her sinuous neck, and blew out a tiny, perfect smoke ring.

Artis's face broke into the most enchanted smile Marjani

had ever seen, melting the fear that had gripped her heart since the bondsman had announced the dragon's arrival. Tenzin gently released Artis's slipper and settled back to the ground, folding up her wings so she suddenly looked small and charming rather than large and fierce.

Then Silke was at Marjani's side, pulling Artis free. The woman's eyes fairly blazed with terror and ferocious love, but her arms were gentle as she hugged her daughter close and kissed her hair, and her voice barely shook.

"Come inside with Mama, my love." She turned with a swish of skirts and rushed Artis back to the house without a backward glance.

"What possessed the king to send a dangerous creature like that to deliver a message?" Tarben demanded—from a good yard behind Marjani. Angry blotches marred his normally colorless features, and his beard quivered. "Retrieve the scroll for me and send the beast on its way."

Tenzin stiffened with outrage, and only the knowledge that the steward had been frightened for Artis kept Marjani from hissing at him like a dragon herself.

"The message is not from King Wulfric," she said coldly. She'd learned that much about dragons, at least. "Tenzin is a Kheremese princess's dragon. She would never carry a message for a man."

Tenzin turned a slow eye on the steward and bared the tips of two gleaming fangs.

"It is a private message from Princess Anara." Marjani couldn't quite bring herself to say, *for me*. She didn't know if Tenzin would play along with the lie. Because the dragon would know it was a lie. She believed that suddenly. That the little creature understood every word the humans were saying.

Princess Isolde insisted the dragon was a "dumb beast"— though never when Tenzin could hear her. Marjani had leaned more toward Raisa's assessment that the dragon was as clever as a good hunting hound.

She'd been wrong. The glittering intelligence in those

sharp eyes was a good deal cleverer than any dog. Possibly clever as a human.

Tenzin met her gaze, and Marjani shivered.

Possibly cleverer.

"Tenzin will accompany me to the chapel," she told Tarben. "If there is anything in the message you should know, I will, of course, share it with you."

"And you can send a message back with the beast!" His face brightened at the thought. "A message to the king that he must send knights. Surely he must, once he hears what happened to Princess Eira."

If Marjani had possessed the power of sorcery, she would have used it then, shoved it down his throat and stoppered his voice until he choked on the words and his eyes bulged with his own stupidity. Hadn't he seen the dragon save Eira's life on the docks back in Newport?

Tenzin's crest snapped erect, and her teeth glittered in an agitated snarl. Her gaze flicked around the courtyard as if looking for a flash of white-blond hair among the wide-eyed manor residents.

"Princess Eira is gone." The words sounded hard, cold, even to her own ears, but there could be no advantage to drawing it out. "Drowned while we hunted for the bear."

Tenzin's wings flared out, tips quivering, and her head ducked like a snake preparing to strike.

"It was her own fault!" Tarben cried. "A pair of girls going out in the wilderness by themselves. The king must understand we did all we could. Saebern Manor cannot be held responsible for their foolishness!"

The gout of flame that burst from Tenzin's mouth sent the steward scrambling backward, though the dragon poured the fire upward toward the sky. A crackling, visible howl of grief and anger.

Marjani could not say where her sudden courage came from. Perhaps it was seeing the creature's pain. She had lived submerged beneath her own fury and despair for so long that seeing it engulf another being, however different from herself, made her want to reach out to the dragon. Not to pull her to safety. There was no dry land in that sea of grief. But so that she need not drown alone.

Marjani lifted her arm as she would to a hunting falcon. "Tenzin, if you come with me to the chapel, I will tell you everything."

With a keening screech that raised goosebumps on Marjani's skin, the dragon leaped into the air. Marjani heard the beating of wings, felt the brush of morning air against her face. And then the shimmering, glorious, terrifying creature landed on her forearm, the great, gold talons wrapping around it with such precision as not to leave a single scratch.

The dragon was light, like a bird, her sinewy body deceptively delicate. Marjani was not fooled. Scarcely a fortnight earlier, Tenzin had helped to bring down a giant during an ambush on Prince Theo's knights and had survived a blow from another giant's fist that would have crushed a human skull.

Dragging her gaze from the talons around her arm, she turned toward Tarben, expecting demands or an argument, but he was gone, escaped into the house. The rest of the onlookers had also fled, leaving the yard empty as if a wind had blown them all away like leaves.

Still, she had no doubt eyes followed them as she carried the dragon through the yard. Tenzin must have felt it, too. They held their heads high in matching royal hauteur.

"It was my fault." She hadn't said it before, not even to herself. Certainly hadn't meant to say it to this deadly, alien creature. "I was trying to frighten her into staying behind. I wanted to kill the bear myself, and I didn't care how dangerous crossing the stream would be—to either of us."

Tenzin hissed, low in her throat. But the sting in Marjani's eyes wasn't from the dragon smoke. Her vengeance demanded blood, but she had never meant to collect the debt from anyone except the ruling wolves of Aldforth.

They reached the chapel, and she pulled Tenzin in closer to slip through the narrow door before closing it securely behind them.

No candle burned on the altar this morning, and Marjani herself had closed the shutters the night before. Blinking against the darkness, she stepped cautiously forward.

A sudden clatter across the room made her jump, nearly shaking Tenzin loose from her arm. The little dragon squawked and flapped her wings. Something metallic banged, much too close.

Flame burst from Tenzin's throat, illuminating the small chapel in a garish wash of red. In the flickering light, a figure rose from behind the stone altar, eyes ringed white, hair rippling like inky smoke, the great spear in its hand pointed straight at Marjani's heart.

CHAPTER FOURTEEN

10. *Amor Aeternal.* (No need to read further. I'll be as dead as love before I try this one.)

— Top 10 failed spells translated and performed by Rurik, Ravninan sorcerer (in training)

"Rurik!" Marjani raised a hand, trying to freeze both the dragon and the wide-eyed sorcerer. "Put down the spear! It's all right, Tenzin. I know him."

Tenzin snorted, but her flames died away. In the dimness, Marjani could just make out Rurik slowly lowering the butt of his spear—no, *her* spear—to the floor.

With the dragon still hissing softly on her arm, she crossed the space between them in three furious strides and yanked the weapon from his hand. "Give me that."

Don't show a potential opponent your fear, Dejen had taught her. *If he sees you are confident that he cannot beat you, he will begin to believe it, too.*

She found the half-burned candle on the altar. "Tenzin?"

The dragon hopped from her forearm to the altar. A lick of fire brought the candle to life.

"What *is* that creature?" Rurik's expression mirrored the flame, flickering between terror and wonder.

Tenzin whistled indignantly.

"If you can't say anything intelligent, don't speak," Marjani warned. "I won't be responsible for what happens if you insult a dragon."

The sorcerer shook his head, still staring. Eyes wide, he looked even younger than he had two days before. And scruffier. His topknot was loose, and bits of straw stuck to his tunic and the rucksack over his shoulder. He must have been sleeping in a barn somewhere.

"A dragon used to visit our village," he said, "to trade for ivory and reindeer meat. My grandmother was only a child the last time it came. She said it was a golden, terrifying, glorious beast. I don't think I truly believed it was real before today."

"What were you doing with my things?" Marjani demanded, thumping her spear for his attention.

"Waiting for you." His eyes never left Tenzin. "You said you'd be here at dawn."

"I was delayed." Truly, she hadn't expected him to appear. When she'd sneaked out to the chapel the night before to hide her spear and other supplies, there had been no sign of him. She'd half assumed he'd lost his nerve and run away again. "Steward Tarben forbade me to leave the manor grounds."

"But you have to find the bear!" Rurik's gaze finally snapped to her face, dismay rising around him in clouds. "We only have five days before the curse becomes permanent."

"As if I would allow a county steward to keep me from my duty!" Marjani couldn't suppress a huff of scorn. "I told him I would spend the day praying in the chapel. He won't know I've left." She shot Tenzin a sideways look. "I don't think we'll have to worry about anyone coming to check on me."

The little dragon showed an amused tooth. Then with a quick, merciless flick of one golden talon, she sliced the ribbon holding the message to her wrist. She plucked the scroll from the altar and held it out to Marjani.

"Are you sure?" Marjani asked. "It's meant for Eira—"

Tenzin narrowed her eyes.

"Thank you." Marjani took the scroll, shocked by the intensity of her desire to hear the news from Lukos. Had Raisa made new alliances while Marjani was gone? Was Jax still the unlikely favorite to win Prince Theo's hand? What wicked tricks was Isolde up to?

"Who is that from?" Rurik asked.

Tenzin hissed, sending him back a step.

"It is from Princess Anara," Marjani said. "Tenzin's companion. She came from Kherem to attend King Wulfric's ball and compete for Prince Theodor's hand."

Although, now that she thought about it—and she hadn't given the Kheremese princess nearly as much thought as the Kheremese dragon—Princess Anara seemed as little interested in marrying a prince as Marjani. She suddenly wished she had asked Anara more questions about Kherem, as Reeve Hartwin had about her own homeland. And not just because it might give her some insight into navigating this interaction with a dragon.

How petty the shifting factions between the princesses seemed now that one of them had died.

"Wulfric is really making a group of royal princesses vie to marry his new heir?" Rurik asked. "Even knowing you're right here in front of me, it still sounds like an absurd rumor. Something somebody pulled from a grandmother's tale."

Ignoring him, Marjani unrolled the narrow parchment and pressed it flat beside the candle. The writing was so tiny she had to squint. But it was neat and precise as needlepoint.

To our companions, Princess Eira, formerly of Nordmark, and Princess Marjani of Almasa, from your fellow royal inmates in Lukos Castle, greetings.

Marjani glanced up to find Tenzin's glittering eyes not far from her own. "It's addressed to me, too."

The little dragon puffed smoke in her face, making her cough.

Yes, Eira, you are required to share this with Marjani. Jax tells me that *"keep your enemies too close to get a good swing at you"* isn't one of the *Nine Roads to Peace,* but it's served the rulers of *Bellis* well.

"Anara didn't write this," Marjani realized. "Princess Beatrix did."

Which made sense. The fiery-haired Bellisian had probably trained since she was a toddler to write tiny, informative messages to her family's far-flung network of spies.

I told the girls it was foolish to send our only reliable connection to the outside world chasing all the way across the kingdom after you, but Tenzin said she was going regardless, so I took control of the letter. Everyone insists on sending you their hopes and prayers for a speedy and successful conclusion to your quest, etc. Pia implores me to ask if either of you has kissed that adorable Reeve Hartwin yet. This is the frivolous idiocy I have to deal with.

Utterly frivolous! As if they were silly girls who had nothing more serious to think about. Marjani didn't have time to dream about kissing boys, not even boys with sea-green eyes and softly quirking lips that she imagined would be sweet and warm against hers ... She hoped the dim light hid the warmth in her cheeks.

*Information you might actually be interested in: Our favorite despot is anxious to return his court to the capital in Cadesleigh as soon as the heat and summer pestilence ease. But rumor says he may decide to hold the Winter Solstice ball at Newport Castle and leave us locked up in Lukos until then. Enjoy your freedom while you can. The Rose Knights sneak in whenever they can get away with it, which interferes with our training. Duke Jordis is still a—*here Beatrix inserted a Bellisian word Marjani didn't know, though it didn't sound polite—*but he gossips like a kitchen maid, so we get all the news from the court. He told Isolde that Duchess Bianka is definitely pregnant.*

Marjani hissed like Tenzin as her insides twisted. *Duchess Bianka. Wulfric's mistress.* Her father's oath rang in her ears, his promise to slaughter every male of King Wulfric's line and destroy even the memory of Wulfric's blood. Her father didn't want only Prince Theodor dead, but also Theo's eight-year-old half-brother, Prince George, Duchess Bianka's son. And this baby, if it were a boy … as her father's designated representative, Marjani would be bound by his oath there, as well.

Maybe her father was right to believe her inadequate, broken, unworthy of his love. Even in the most venomous depths of her vengeance, she could not picture herself murdering an eight-year-old boy, no matter whose son he might be. As for killing a baby …

She blinked hard, forcing herself to focus on Beatrix's letter.

You remember those silly songs everyone was singing? "The Ballad of King Wulfric's Ball" and "The Song of Jax the Giant Killer," by someone calling himself Foolscap the Bard?

She remembered *Eira* singing them—loudly and off-key. Remembered the other girls, pretending to be offended by the satirical lyrics, arguing about which princess's "star-bright eyes" or "fierce intent" the poet was referring to in this line or that.

It turns out Foolscap is none other than Prince Theo's esquire, Ralf. Anyone considering himself that much of a wit should have been clever enough not to get caught. He was the girls' darling for a day until King Wulfric heard and had him publicly caned.

Marjani winced. Ralf was the most amiable of the Rose Knights—and the one Wulfric singled out for punishment whenever Theodor disappointed him.

"Is there anything in there to help us find our bear?" Rurik demanded. "The morning is passing."

Marjani scowled at him but quickly scanned the rest of the letter. More gossip about the court, anything Beatrix thought would help keep her and Eira safe in the shark-infested waters of Aldforth's royal politics.

Now that the two of you have set aside your differences to kill that bear together—in Beatrix's voice, it was a command rather than a hope—*you will be a good example to the rest of us of working in harmony to protect ourselves from the real monster.*

Marjani understood what she meant. A bear, even an *ensorcelled* bear, even a bear that could kill a girl as smart and strong as Eira, could not destroy families and kingdoms and people's souls the way King Wulfric did.

She appreciated Beatrix including her in this mythical harmony, even if indirectly. But she would never risk involving the other girls. Losing Eira had taught her the dangers of allowing anyone to get even a hint of her plans. The other princesses would be safest if she brought King Wulfric to his knees all by herself.

Yes? A cold whisper in her heart. *And what happens to them if —when—you kill Prince Theo?* He would have to send them home. *Would he?* Yes. Yes, of *course*, he would.

She gritted her teeth and read on.

I fear the king's boredom as the summer drags on. It would be helpful if you came back with good news and a good tale. Jax says to tell you it would be good if you just came back, but I see no advantage in equivocation.

We all hope for and expect your triumphant return.

Marjani huffed in disbelief. "Not Isolde."

Except for Isolde, who daily airs her belief that you will come back beaten and humiliated. Don't you dare give her the satisfaction.

In solidarity—Jax insists on adding "and affection"—we wish you well and beg for news.

Princess Beatrix of Bellis, scribe, and the rest of the Dancing Princesses.

"Bad news?" Rurik asked.

"No." Marjani impatiently swiped the moisture from her cheeks. "It is only that I must return their kindness with evil news. Do you have writing supplies in your rucksack?"

Tenzin spat fire, and the scroll burst into flame.

"What did she do that for?" Rurik demanded, scrambling away.

"Written messages can be read by the wrong people," Marjani guessed, trying to gauge the dragon's expression. Amusement? She hoped it was amusement. "Maybe she's telling me she can report what's happened directly to Anara. No need to write it down."

Tenzin offered a gracious head tilt. Definitely amused.

"Very well," Marjani told the dragon. "Sneak out with us, and I will tell you everything as we walk."

"You're planning to sneak in that?" Rurik gestured at her crimson cloak.

"Of course not." Marjani leaned her spear against the altar and shrugged the cloak from her shoulders, revealing the simple clay-colored gown she'd purloined from Eira's trunk. She'd felt a pang of guilt digging through the other girl's belongings, but it wasn't as though Eira would be needing them.

The Nordish princess was an inch or two shorter than she was, but Marjani had found a pair of woolen hose that covered the gap between gown and boots—northern royalty being bizarrely unwilling to show their legs. Even better, the stockings made the morning chill nearly bearable.

"Not to state the obvious,"—Rurik *clearly* planned to state the obvious—"but you're still unmistakable." He waved a hand in what was either a sorcerous invocation or a vague reference to her dark skin and cropped black hair.

She pushed past him around the altar to get the rest of the gear she'd hidden. She strapped on Eira's sword, in the scabbard she'd begged from Tarben with the excuse she needed to return the weapon to the Temple of Peace. Then she settled her knapsack of supplies over her shoulder before sweeping on Eira's dark winter cloak and pulling the hood over her head.

The sorcerer eyed her critically as he settled his own rucksack on his back. "You might pass for a Saebernian laborer. Unless someone gets close enough to look under the hood."

"People see what they expect to see."

His smile showed the tips of white teeth. "You have the makings of a decent sorcerer."

"What about your disguise?" she demanded.

"I've placed an obscuring spell over myself. I won't be seen."

It took her a long moment to realize he might be serious. "*I* see you. Tenzin sees you."

"I'm not trying to hide from you." Nevertheless, Rurik pulled his hood over the long fall of his black hair. "Satisfied?"

"I don't want anything to interfere with my hunt. If you get caught or can't keep up, I will leave you behind." *Before* he was in any danger of getting himself killed. She might not trust him—or even like him—but she wasn't going to be responsible for another death. Not until she found the bear.

"I'll keep up." In the shadow of his black hood, his jaw hardened, accentuating the hollows of his cheeks and the darkness beneath his eyes. For all his preposterousness, Marjani thought she wouldn't want this young man as an enemy.

She'd do well not to underestimate him.

She opened the flap of her knapsack. "I'm sorry it's not dignified, Tenzin, but there's no other way to disguise your splendor."

The dragon snorted her disdain at the flattery, but she gave Marjani a sly smile as she slipped into the bag.

Marjani led the way to the rear of the chapel. The little back door opened on a narrow walkway between the building and the manor wall. The space served as a storage area for old lumber, equipment needing repair, and other odds and ends nobody knew what to do with. Marjani had shifted some empty crates the night before, and it was a simple matter to scramble up them to the top of the wall and drop to the other side unobserved.

"There," Rurik whispered. He pointed toward the huge barn past the sheep pens, to the right of the ridge she'd climbed the first morning. "The animals are already in the pastures, so there shouldn't be anyone around. If we put the barn between us and the manor, we won't be seen."

Marjani adjusted her hood and touched her knapsack to check on Tenzin. Then, holding her spear to look like a walking stick, she followed the sorcerer across the open ground. She forced herself to move confidently, as though she had every right to be there.

She had years of practice pretending to have a rightful place.

They reached the looming grain storage barn without being challenged. Built of heavy gray stone, the barn rose higher than the second story of the manor behind them, but two single-story extensions stretched from the front and rear of the building.

"Wagon porch," Rurik named the blocky extension they passed behind the barn. It had a small, human-sized door along its side but boasted a massive set of doors like a castle gate on the end. "You can drive a full load of grain through these doors, dump the load on the threshing floor in the middle, and drive the wagon right out the other side."

"I've seen a barn before," Marjani said coolly, "even if I am an ignorant foreigner."

"I'm a foreigner, too," Rurik reminded her. "And I'd never seen a barn this big before I came to Aldforth."

Past the barn, they followed the sheep track through the heather toward the rocky outcropping that crowned the ridge. When the path veered toward the grassy pastures above the river valley, they left it to continue up the hill. They crossed the ridge in the shadow of the rocky crag.

Marjani sucked in a breath at the scope of the wilderness before them. Narrow valleys gave way to rocky hills huddled in dark cloaks of pine, which gave way to more valleys and steeper hills …

Her father's court was located on the Almasan archipelago's largest island. She'd tracked game through seemingly endless jungle with Mosi and Dejen. She'd climbed mountains—some still smoking with the breath of the gods that created them. She'd crossed plains of endless grass that rippled like the sea.

Yet here, the land stretched forever, a great, breathless

expanse as rolling and chartless as the ocean that bounded the inhabited world.

She stared in awe—or dread. Unbound or undone. If she walked into that wilderness, she might lose herself completely. *Be* lost completely. To the king, to her father, to the past. If there was no one to know her, would she forget herself? If she forgot she was broken, would it still be true?

"Why does the bear keep coming so close to town?" she wondered. "Hunted, hated. There must be someplace out there, a sanctuary, where it could live free and unmolested if it chose."

"His fate is tied to Saebern," Rurik said. Marjani had almost forgotten the sorcerer stood beside her, gazing grimly into the distance, as lost in the vista as herself. "He can no more escape it than he can escape himself."

"That, at least, I can pity it for." She hefted her spear. "We will release the beast from its curse, at least."

She started down the steep slope, long years of navigating treacherous footing leaving her nimbler than her companion. She tucked away a smile listening to him scrambling and cursing after her.

Her knapsack rustled, and she lifted the flap so Tenzin could peer out. As she walked, she gave the dragon a summary of events since she and Eira had left Newport. She did not spare her own misdeeds—sneaking out of the manor, arguing with Eira, failing to rescue her from the stream.

"It's my fault she's dead," Marjani concluded as they reached the trees. "I cannot express how much the message you brought from the others heartened me. But I will understand if they no longer wish to communicate with me. Or if you choose not to return. I know Eira was a good friend to you. I wish …"

She swallowed hard with the sudden realization. "I wish I had given her a chance to be a friend to me."

Tenzin climbed from the rucksack, her talons digging into the borrowed cloak as she pulled herself onto Marjani's shoulder. The little creature sighed, smoke curling from her nostrils, and rested her chin on Marjani's head.

Marjani pressed her sleeve against her eyes until she could speak again. "I will avenge her. I swear it. I will kill this bear." She pushed aside the uncomfortable thought that the bear's death would not atone for her own regrets. "Go with the gods, Tenzin. May your ancestors watch over you."

With a clear, lyrical whistle, Tenzin sprang from her shoulder into flight.

Rurik tripped to a stop at Marjani's side. "She can't stay hidden for very far. She'll never be able to fly through those trees."

And yet, she did. Trimming her wings like racing sails, caroming off branches, tail whipping. A shimmering bolt of joyous movement. Within a half-dozen heartbeats, the dragon was gone.

"She has bought us the day." Marjani adjusted her bag. "No one will look for me until twilight, if they dare it then. If we find no fresh sign today, I will say Tenzin is staying in the chapel. That should allow us to try again tomorrow. And the day after that. As long as it takes."

Rurik nodded, but his voice was grim. "I pray it's long enough."

CHAPTER FIFTEEN

4. He was an arrogant, skirt-chasing, self-involved dandy. (Submitted by Lady Silke, mother of Countess Artis of Saebern.)

— Top 10 reasons no one misses Earl Berengar that much

She wasn't dead. Which was good, Eira thought. Probably. But she wasn't sure that she wanted to be awake yet. Hazy memories of pain hovered like storm clouds. Echoes of thirst, fear, and heat. A splitting ache in her head. Wracking chills.

Best to test consciousness tentatively. Breathing stretched the lingering soreness in her ribs. Her head … shadows of misery, but nothing immediate. Much of her body ached as if she'd been bruised all over. But then, she had a vague idea that she *had* been bruised all over not so long ago.

Nothing too awful. Yet.

She blinked open bleary eyes. She was lying on a wool cloak in what appeared to be a cave, not far from a small fire pit. Hadn't she done this already? Waking up in a cave, battered and sick, after … oh, right. After being set upon by a bear.

More memories trickled in. Almost drowning. Wild man. Fish. Fever. Bear. Yucky tea. More wild man? More hallucinating? More bear? More tea? More fish?

Her stomach clenched. "No. Please, no more fish."

She snapped her mouth shut. Better not to let any monstrous beasts nearby know she was awake. She waited and listened. Waited. Listened. Got bored and decided to try sitting up. Her arms trembled weakly as she leveraged herself upright on Berengar's cloak. She pulled her own cloak tighter around her shoulders.

The fire had died, but she felt warm—naturally warm, not feverish. The warmth of a fine summer twilight, if the purplish tinge to the trees outside were any indication.

Thirsty. She reached for the wooden bowl nearby. *Plain water. Glorious.* She drained the bowl too enthusiastically and had to wipe the spillover from her chin. But that felt good, too.

"You're alive?"

She squeaked and dropped the bowl. The wild man stood just outside the cave, one hand on the entrance, peering in at her. His freckles crinkled over his nose, uneasy as his cautious question.

"Apparently so." And maybe that wasn't so bad. *All those adorable freckles.* "Disappointed?"

"No! In case you hadn't noticed, I've been trying to keep you—" He stopped and narrowed his eyes at her. "You'd be less trouble dead."

She gave in to a grin. "Don't count on it."

"Are you hungry?" He stepped into the cave and proffered a wicker basket covered with a plain linen cloth.

"*Real food?*" She winced at how ungrateful that sounded. "Not that fish isn't real food. I love fish. I'd eat fish every day —or at least, every other day—but every *meal*—"

She snatched the basket from his hand as he sat beside her. Dark bread. Cheese. A small jug that might hold ale.

"Is that a hand pie?" Chicken, onion, and carrots in pastry

that flaked in her mouth. She moaned. "Thank you. *Thank you.* Where did you get this?"

When he didn't answer, she looked up to see him staring at his hands. "Berengar?"

He flinched at the name. "I'll return the basket."

She choked on the pie. "You *stole* it?"

"You were so sick. I couldn't do anything, and then I had to leave. I thought I could at least find you something besides fish …" He trailed off and glanced at her from under his thicket of hair. "It worked. You're eating."

"There's nothing wrong with fish! Was I complaining?" She didn't know whether to laugh or be horrified. "You can't go around stealing people's food. Whoever was counting on this for their dinner will go hungry."

"I know." He looked more miserable than defensive. "But you threw up the willow bark tea last night. I could barely get you to drink any water …"

"Last night?" Eira blinked against a wave of dizziness. "The fever only came on this morning."

"Three days ago."

Three days? Eira stared down at the hand pie as exhaustion swept over her. She'd been in a delirious stupor for three days?

This awkward young man had made her willow bark tea, apparently tidied her up when she couldn't keep it down, and stolen food in a desperate attempt to keep her from dying. Strong and healthy as she was, he'd probably overestimated the danger she was in, but still—

Warmth flickered in her chest as though the fever might return.

"Are you going to finish that?" he asked.

"Yes." She took a ravenous bite of the pie. It wasn't as though he could return it to its owner. "This doesn't mean I condone your stealing. What if you'd been caught? They might have beaten you senseless."

"Not likely. Here." He passed her the jug of watered ale to

wash down the pastry. "I'll start the fire. It's been cool at night, despite the summer days."

"And you haven't had your cloak." Eira glanced down at the once-fine garment she sat on.

"Keep it." He touched her shoulder to prevent her from getting up. "I'm not cold."

"I'm not, either." But she shivered when he lifted away the warmth of his hand. Stars sprinkled the darkening sky outside. "A fire is probably a good idea, anyway. To keep the bear at bay."

"There aren't any bears near here."

"Shows what you know. There was a bear in the clearing just this morning." She wrinkled her nose. "Or possibly yesterday. Or the day before."

"I doubt it." He turned away to retrieve a small pouch from a niche carved into the cave wall. "You were feverish. Maybe you saw a pine marten or a hare."

"You think I was scared by a *rabbit?*"

"That doesn't sound likely," he admitted, humor warming his eyes as he pulled a flint and striker from the pouch. "Although a hare attacked me once, when I was out exploring as a child. Maybe I got too close to its babies. It bit my boot and chased me halfway home. I had nightmares for months."

Eira snorted, the watered ale burning her nose. "You're not going to distract me. I know the bear was here. It lay down beside me. I touched its fur."

Which, if she were honest, seemed hardly more believable than bloodthirsty hares. Just how delirious had she been?

Berengar worked on the fire, well-practiced with the striker and flint. His absolute concentration precluded interruption. Eira wondered if he used that careful focus for just that purpose, to keep other people at arm's length.

"There." He sat back on his heels. "That should keep out the cold. And the infamous Saebernian hares."

Eira laughed. "You're ridiculous."

He ducked his head, but she caught the grin that crinkled around his eyes.

She brushed crumbs from her hands and held her fingers toward the flames. "You're not at all what I expected from the way people talked about you at the manor."

He tensed, and she feared he might bolt again. But he only shook his head.

"They thought I was useless," he said. "I've never cut down a tree or sheared a sheep, so what can I possibly know about managing timber or grazing? Never mind that I spent nearly ten years in Rigas with my uncle, learning everything he could teach me about trade and finance. Never mind that I attended the best university in the Blessed Kingdoms, studying history and the importance of maintaining resources."

"Which you apparently mentioned a few times."

"Which means I'm arrogant," he said bitterly. "High and mighty with my foreign ways."

She could picture it. With his reticent scowl and the hint of flame in his eyes. His abrupt way of speaking. Put him in a velvet doublet in the latest Rigan fashion, let him unfavorably compare the fanciest Saebernian feast to the everyday delicacies at his uncle's villa and …

And she could see what the people at the manor had seen. A spoiled, arrogant, selfish rake they were all just as glad to see the last of.

She blinked, and the obnoxious libertine was gone, replaced by this awkward young man in stained clothes, his shaggy hair more lamb than lord. "They said you were quite the ladies' man back in Rigas."

"You needn't sound so skeptical." Heat flushed his cheeks, dimming his freckles, but he shot her a wry grin. "Get yourself an uncle who's one of the richest men in Rigas, and see if you don't have to fight the suitors off."

"How hard did you fight?" She shouldn't tease him, but it was irresistible, watching the red spread up his scalp, the laughter hover on his lips.

"I found flight more effective. Rigan noblewomen are terrifying. You may scoff, but have you ever had one try to kiss you?"

Eira thought of Princess Dora of Rigas's sour discontent and sense of entitlement, remembered her proficiency in the Rigan "art" of *pharmacia*—potions and poisons.

"I see your point. I'd hide, too." She didn't want to scare away his smile, yet she had to ask. "But I don't understand why you're hiding now. Why did you run away?"

His eyes drained of light as if a curtain had drawn across them. "I had no choice."

"You had no choice but to disappear into the wilderness without a word, leaving everyone to wonder if you were alive or dead?" Non-judgment was one of the Nine Roads to Peace, but it seemed so obvious. "I can see you weren't happy, but you owed an account of what happened that day to the families who lost their loved ones. You always have a choice."

"No." The word ground from his throat. "I thought I had no choice when my father ordered me to return from Rigas, but I see now I could have chosen to defy him. I thought I had to stay and do my duty after he died, but I could have run then, despite how much it would have cost. But I could not have chosen to return to Saebern Manor that day. Nor can I now."

"Of *course* you can. You're not making any sense." Or maybe he *was* that petulant, thoughtless good-for-nothing, after all.

He looked at her slantwise, and she could not tell if the flicker in his eyes was fear or fury. "If you don't believe I cannot return, believe that I *will* not. You cannot make me. Not by cajoling or threatening or appealing to my obligation to my family and retainers. If you say they mourn for me, I'll know you're a liar."

Eira stared back at him. *At least you* have *a family and a place you belong. At least they searched for you, day after day. At least they think about you still.* But the words were too sharp to speak without slicing her tongue.

"Fine." She tore a piece of bread from the loaf in the basket.

"If you tell them you saw me, and they come looking, they'll never find me. They'll think you were hallucinating."

"Why would I tell them?"

His puzzled look crinkled those adorable freckles. Curse him.

"I—isn't that what you do?" His voice turned gravelly with annoyance. "Say whatever comes into your head? Why *wouldn't* you tell? You've found the man everyone thought was dead. The missing earl, come back to take his rightful place."

"But it's not your rightful place, is it?" The creeping ice in her veins had nothing to do with the deepening darkness outside the cave.

"What?"

"The earldom. It's not your rightful place."

"You don't believe I'm Berengar?" His smile was melancholy. "That would make things simpler. And true in its own way, soon enough."

"Oh, I believe you're Berengar." She didn't smile back. "Isn't that what *you* do? Complain about Saebern? Wish you were back in Rigas? Shirk your responsibilities?"

The words tasted bitter. She couldn't spit them out fast enough. "Except they're not *your* responsibilities at all."

"What are you talking about?"

"Artis, your brother's daughter." She hadn't forgotten the girl, even if he had. *Predictable.* "By your own country's customs, she should have inherited your father's lands and title when he died. Or am I wrong? Maybe I'm missing some arcane twist of Aldforthian law?"

"Silke was pregnant when my brother died. My father couldn't name an unborn child his heir."

"And after she was born?"

"Saebern is far from the king's justice, vulnerable to

outlaws and raiders. It needs a strong leader." Berengar looked nothing like Eira's uncle. King Einar was tall, fair, icily handsome—apart from the humped knife of his nose. But she had heard that identical tone of justification from his mouth. "A baby girl—"

"And if she'd been born a boy?"

"My father was ill. His heart was failing. He wanted to secure his legacy. If he had lived to see my brother's child survive to adolescence, he might have revoked his choice of me as heir and bestowed the title on Artis."

"If she had been a boy."

He opened his mouth. Paused. Grimaced. "You're right. Not for a daughter. Not my father. Not as long as I might have a son of my own."

"So, your father gave you your niece's rightful place, which has now been restored to her," Eira concluded. "If you don't intend to return, why would I call Artis's title into question by telling people you're alive?"

"You have a strange way of looking at things."

"Says the earl living like a wild man in a cave!"

His snort of laughter appeared to surprise him as much as it did her. She would *not* laugh, too. Artis's disinheritance might not be Berengar's fault, but that did not exonerate him from profiting from it.

Yet, against her will, his sheepish grin melted the bitter edge of the ice in her heart.

"I won't tell anyone about you," she promised, more saddened than satisfied. "I'll return to the manor in the morning and leave you to the solitary life you've chosen."

"You need to rest tomorrow," he objected. "If you're strong enough by nightfall, I'll guide you back then. I didn't put all that effort into keeping you alive just to have you killed by a homicidal hare you're too weak to fend off."

"Ha ha." But he was probably right. Maybe not about the rabbit. But about her need for rest.

Of course, she didn't want to prolong the anxiety

everyone at the manor must be feeling—if not for her, at least for what King Wulfric might do if she wasn't found. She cared about other people's distress, unlike a certain feral earl she could name. And the thought of Marjani getting an extra day to beat her to the bear made her want to start back to the manor that instant. *She* had to kill the bear, save Marjani from herself, marry Prince Theo, and spread peace!

Then again, she had a feeling that she'd been a lot closer to the bear over the past few days than Marjani could have gotten. And now that her stomach was pleasantly full, the rest of her body wanted nothing more than to sleep for the next twenty-four hours.

"Fine," she said. "Tomorrow night. But not a minute longer."

"Fine." Berengar gestured at the cave. "Though I can't understand why you're so eager to leave this life of luxury and ease."

For a long moment, sitting on the hard, uneven floor, with pine needles poking through her clothes, she wondered herself. Returning to Saebern Manor, where no one believed in her, to Lukos Castle, where she had to compete against her friends, to Wulfric's ball, vying to marry a charming, handsome prince with no freckles at all.

Back to being nothing but an exile from the only place she had ever felt at home. A feeling that had died with her mother, as ephemeral as the fire, burned to nothing by morning.

"I won't be nothing," she said. "I won't be ignored and forgotten. I have to finish the quest I was sent here for. I have to do it before Marjani does. I have to kill the bear."

She braced for Berengar's disbelief. His scorn. Even his laughter. But he only glanced at her, eyes too shadowed to read.

"The bear you keep telling me watched over you the past three days?"

Watched over her? It could have eaten her! Truly. It could have eaten her any time. And had not.

Yet that same bear had caused Hartwin's father's death. It had terrorized the entire county for nearly a year. It had *nailed a bloody sheep's heart* to the manor gate. She had to kill it for the good of the people of Saebern.

Eira remembered the rough brush of its fur against her fingers. She turned away from Berengar and closed her eyes.

CHAPTER SIXTEEN

9. She's so *sure* of herself.

— Top 10 things ~~I hate~~ I find difficult to appreciate about Princess Marjani, as listed by (former) Princess Eira of Nordmark

Wake at the first hint of dawn, hide her borrowed clothes beneath her red cloak, collect food from the kitchen … Despite the routine's familiarity, like a recurring nightmare, Marjani's dread of being stopped, exposed, confined to her room ached like a bruise between her shoulder blades as she slipped out the manor door.

This was the fourth morning she had crept away to "pray," hoping her hosts' relief at her absence and fear of Tenzin would cover her flight to the ridge to meet Rurik and continue her hunt. It couldn't work much longer.

Not when a fast ship with an open berth could arrive in Anberry Harbor any moment to carry her, disgraced and defeated, back to Newport. Not when Rurik's panic over the upcoming anniversary of the curse had infected her, so she could barely sleep at night.

The rising sun just gilded the tops of the hills as she crept along in the manor's shadow toward the chapel. Despite escaping as early as she dared, the endless northern summer days were not nearly long enough. Not when each one might be her last chance to find the bear.

She and the sorcerer had hiked what felt like a hundred leagues through the wilderness, up rugged hills, into thick forests, across more rushing streams. And she, who boasted—if only to herself—of being one of the best trackers in her father's kingdom, had found no fresh sign of Saebern's monstrous bear.

Not a single paw print.

Where to try next?

She had already returned to where the bear had dragged Eira from the stream. Despite the trampling by the manor searchers, she'd found a place downstream where the bear had entered the water, but it hadn't come out again. Not that she could see. What kind of animal entered a rushing stream and didn't cross immediately to the other side? As if it knew it might be tracked and had purposefully masked its scent in the water?

An *ensorcelled* one. Her skin prickled as if in a chill breeze, though the morning air was still as she skirted around the stable. What would happen if she did find it? What else was it capable of?

Somehow over the past few days, Rurik's unwavering belief that the bear was cursed had seeped into her bones while his confidence that he could do something about it had not.

Hurry, hurry, hurry. The word beat along with her heart as she picked up her pace, driven by the awareness of time trickling from her fingers ever faster the harder she tried to clutch it close.

She nearly ran the last few steps to the chapel door and grabbed the handle. Now she just had to—

"Princess Marjani."

She spun, pulse jumping. Reeve Hartwin stepped from around the side of the chapel, his tousled hair catching the morning sun with a flash of dark gold. He must have been waiting there, watching.

For her.

Her heart skittered again.

"Reeve Hartwin." Anything more would have betrayed the tightness of her throat.

"The steward says you haven't left this chapel in days."

To her guilty ears, it sounded like an accusation. And why should she feel guilty?

"Tarben forbids me to pursue the duty the king placed on me," she said, her voice cold enough to keep it even. "If I cannot hunt the bear, the steward cannot begrudge my praying for Princess Eira's soul to find peace."

"Steward Tarben is trying to save your *life*," Hartwin said. "Why would you want to throw it away on a hopeless quest? To marry a second-rate prince whose own father never wanted him to be king?"

"Of course King Wulfric wants Prince Theodor to succeed him." Marjani stepped closer to him and lowered her voice. "You should not say such things. In my father's kingdom, it is treason to criticize his heir."

"Aren't you his heir, now that your brother is dead?" Hartwin demanded. "Your father wouldn't want you risking your life here in Saebern."

A surprised laugh escaped her. "My father does not consider women capable of ruling. He scorns my mother's people for their matriarchal leaders. He has already named my cousin to succeed him. If I die in Saebern, he will not mourn."

"That's madness. No one could mistake your value so greatly." Hartwin's clear gaze showed no hint of flattery—or doubt. "I've watched you handle Tarben, keep rowdy sailors in line, take on this impossible task. You are a natural leader. Armies would follow you. Your father could not find a better heir."

"I am a useless girl," Marjani told him bitterly, "confined

to a foreign god's chapel by a county steward. He certainly has no intention of following me anywhere."

"Maybe you need to find somewhere better to lead him than on a suicidal hunt for a monstrous bear."

"It is *my* life. It is my right to choose what to do with it."

"Yes. It is." The words snapped like a trap, catching her unwary step. "You don't have to choose the path others have laid for you."

The snare stung. Marjani clutched the bracelet at her wrist. Hartwin would never understand why she couldn't escape. "I do choose it. I have chosen it."

"You deserve better."

"No."

"You *are* better." His composure slipped, and he lifted his hand as if to touch her.

Surprise stiffened her spine. "*No.*"

He jerked back as if burned. She knew how her imperious tone sounded. *How dare you? You presume too much.*

She had to choke down her true meaning. *How dare you make me wish I were better? How dare you show me a different life, a life where I could step off this path of pain and loneliness and take your hand, when I am locked into this destiny like a prison? How dare you make my heart beat when my soul can never be whole enough to share it with another?*

"No," she repeated instead, sharp with despair.

Hartwin's sea-storm eyes fell still, impenetrable. "I will leave you to your prayers, then. I must investigate the bear's latest depredation."

"There's been a sighting of the bear? And they're sending *you*?" She didn't hide her resentment. Better than betraying her eagerness.

"The beast chased a group of woodcutters from their work yesterday. Fortunately, it focused its attack on their equipment, and they escaped unharmed."

"Where?" Somehow she managed to keep her voice cool.

"Not far." He pointed up the river valley. "Just over that

next ridge there. The bear is long gone by now, but the wood-cutters refuse to return to work until I make sure."

"Take care," Marjani said. "I would not like another of my traveling companions to die on this wasted journey."

The words were stiff, carefully formal. But perhaps not so devoid of feeling as she had tried to make them. The reeve's eyes sparked green before he gave a sharp bow and walked away.

Marjani turned back to the chapel, her heart strangely heavy but her step lighter. *Just over that next ridge.*

It had been nearly a whole day since the sighting. No matter. She didn't need the sign to be fresh. All she needed was a place to start.

CHAPTER SEVENTEEN

3. She has no sense of decorum.

— Top 10 things I despise about Princess Eira, as listed
by Princess Marjani of Almasa

It was a very different thing, Eira thought, to be visited by a massive, enchanted bear while one was delirious with fever than it was to face the same prospect once recovered.

She'd woken to find dawn gilding the pines around the clearing and Berengar gone. Again. She'd built up the fire and then hunkered down to hide in the back of the cave. No cuddles with monsters today! But she'd never been much good at staying quiet and out of sight. Boredom and her own body odor drove her out by midday.

Berengar had told her there was a spring nearby. As she set off down the narrow path, she imagined Jax shouting at her to return to the safety of the fire. Imagined Raisa's mocking glee—*please* do *get yourself eaten by that bear, darling.* Marjani would never be so foolish as to wander into bear-infested woods unarmed except for the knife in her boot, the only weapon the raging stream hadn't stripped from her.

None of it deterred her. Embarrassing as it was to admit,

she'd rather be eaten by a bear than have Berengar return to find her still filthy and reeking. He might be a shaggy wild man with travel-worn clothes and no social skills, but he wasn't dirty, and he didn't *smell*.

Well. He had a sort of woodsy scent, piney and a little musky.

"Rrrr!" Eira picked up her pace, stomping down thoughts of Berengar's smell and the freckles on the bridge of his nose. Who cared what that irresponsible, moody, fugitive earl thought of her, anyway?

She was the one who couldn't stand the stink any longer. It wasn't as though she planned to let Berengar close enough to get a good whiff.

If he wanted to. Which he obviously didn't.

Still, she didn't want her odor to repulse everyone when she arrived back at the manor. It would hardly be a triumphal return if they were all wrinkling their noses and refusing to let her inside without a bath.

Within a quarter mile, the narrow deer track—she refused to think *bear path*—spilled into a rocky meadow dotted with violet-blue harebells. Berengar's spring flowed in a pleasing burble from higher up the mountain, slowed by the meadow to a meandering whisper, gleaming silver and gold in the sunshine.

For a moment, Eira could only stand and breathe. *Blessed peace.* Then she folded her cloak on a convenient rock beside her boots. She stripped off her stockings, breeches, and tunic and carried them to the creek's edge.

She did not remove her shift. She had heard all the cautionary tales of fair, innocent maidens bathing naked in hidden pools. They were invariably set upon by lecherous gods and had to turn themselves into trees or birds or whatever to protect their virtue. Besides, it would save a step, washing the lightweight linen along with herself. She set the rest of her clothes on the bank and stepped in.

Cold. The cold shot right to her teeth. *Refreshing,* she told herself as her jaw clenched and goosebumps prickled her arms.

As the gentle current tugged the hem of her shift, fear swirled up from the deepest, darkest corner of her mind. Memories of being ripped from safety by vicious, clutching water, battered against rocks, tumbled along the stream bed. Water in her eyes, her mouth, her nose, her lungs.

She took a ragged breath, a noise almost like a whimper, as the urge to scramble back onto the bank nearly over-whelmed her.

"*Take hold of yourself!*" she hissed, clenching her fists. This creek was maybe a yard across. It barely reached her knees. "Imagine if Berengar saw you quaking over a little water. *Or Marjani.*"

The hiss turned into a snort of laughter. Even drowning—again—had to be better than that.

She forced herself to look at her pale feet, turned slug-like by the water's distortion. She flexed her toes. Felt the sand, the icy cool, the slow current. All lovely. No more threatening than a bathing tub in the girls' dormitory at the Temple of Peace.

And a good deal quieter.

With a shriek of dread and exhilaration, she half sat, half fell into the water. No voracious grasping this time, just an icy embrace. Without giving herself time to think, she sank back, ducking her whole head underwater. For a moment, the only sound was the sloshing of her blood through her ears, the only view the gleam of light on the rippling surface above her.

A thread of peace began to unknot in her heart until she suddenly, desperately, needed to breathe. She sat up, gasping and laughing, and shook her head so her plait scattered glit-tering diamonds of water.

As good as it felt, the water was too cold to linger. Her hands were clumsy with it, unbraiding her hair. She tilted her head back into the current, working out the worst tangles with her fingers. She scooped sand from the creek bed to scour the most stubborn dirt from her shift and her body. And when the agony of the cold finally outweighed the joy of washing, she returned to the bank to give the rest of her clothes a thorough scrubbing.

A sensible person, aware of the danger of monstrous bears, might return to the cave to dry their garments. Princess Beatrix, for example, would have created drying racks from fallen branches before she ever began doing the laundry.

Eira rolled her eyes as she laid her things on nearby rocks, warm from the sun. The bear had already found her at the cave. She was probably safer right where she was, enjoying the sunshine—and making preparations to complete her quest, beat Marjani, and position herself to win Prince Theodor's hand.

Now that she could stand to smell herself again, it occurred to her that she might get a chance to accomplish all of that before she even returned to the manor. She might not have Marjani's tracking skill, but she'd already found the bear.

More than once.

Yes, technically, the bear had found her, but it amounted to the same thing in the end. All she needed was a weapon. And a little Nordish ingenuity.

Finding an appropriate stick took longer than she expected. Green enough not to snap, not too green to work with. The afternoon sun had warmed considerably when she finally returned to the meadow with a branch that would do. She sat in the shade of the nearby alders and used her knife to carve a little shelf near one end of the stick.

She had no twine, so she ripped open the hem of her shift and tore a strip off the bottom. Setting the butt of her knife onto the shelf she'd made, she lashed the handle tightly to the branch with the fabric.

"There!" Eira lifted her creation triumphantly.

She had little experience with spears. Nordish warriors preferred the bow and sword. But despite her lack of training, she was under no illusions about the quality of her new weapon. The balance was terrible. She certainly couldn't throw it. The pole wouldn't survive more than one or two strikes—if the knife didn't fall off as soon as it hit a target.

On the positive side, none of that mattered. If her first thrust didn't enter her target's eye and penetrate its brain, killing it instantly, she wouldn't live long enough to try again, anyway.

Besides, she wasn't actually *hunting* the bear with this thing. Just being prepared if it turned up.

She remembered the feel of the bear's coat beneath her fingers. The curiosity in its golden brown eyes. She imagined it lying down beside her. Imagined lifting the spear to plunge it into one of those eyes.

Her stomach rolled, and she shook the image away. Maybe that was the bear's sorcery. To beguile its hunters by unexpectedly not killing them.

She understood Hartwin's skepticism of the bear being ensorcelled. Even the sheep's heart nailed to the manor gate hadn't changed her conviction that her skill with the bow would allow her to kill it, given an opportunity. Magic wasn't something that had ever touched her life.

However unlikely her discovery of the presumed dead earl with his wry grin and scattered freckles, it hardly counted as enchantment.

So. She wouldn't let fear of a little sorcery—or the odd behavior of what might be a perfectly ordinary bear—interfere with her goal. She doubted she'd have to worry about its friendliness if it came upon her standing on her feet with a spear in her hand.

Satisfied with her plan—makeshift as her spear, but a plan nonetheless—she returned to her clothes. The undersides were still damp. She glanced at the sun, lazily crossing the high northern sky. Plenty of afternoon left. She could catch up on the Sevenday devotions she'd lost to her fever.

As she settled into a prayerful posture, Eira realized she wasn't quite sure *what* day it was. They'd arrived in Saebern on Fourthday. She and Marjani had sneaked out the next morning. How long had Berengar said she'd been feverish?

Counting on her fingers didn't make the recent past any less of a blur. Maybe Thirday?

Faridag, in Nordish.

Common Tongue allowed no preference for any particular country's gods, but a dry, dull number could never bring a flash of pleasure to her heart like remembering it was Fari's day.

"Trouble today," her mother would say each Faridag morning, mock-serious. "Better make some trouble of your own, or Fari will make it for you. Make some for me, too. It would be unlucky for the queen to come to misfortune."

A breath-squeezing hug, and Eira would be set loose to chase the chickens or steal sweet buns from the kitchen—somehow there were always sweet buns sitting unattended on Faridag—or challenge her mother's household guards to a blindfolded archery contest.

"Fari's my favorite," Queen Sassa would whisper, so as not to offend the other gods, when she gave Eira an extra coin for Fari's altar. "In some places, they despise Fari as a mischief-making god, even a wicked one. In Ravnina, they call him a demon. But only we Nordish know the story of how one of Fari's pranks so angered Lin, the lightning god, that Lin determined to destroy him. To escape, Fari transformed herself into a goddess and fled to Nordmark. Here she found a people after her own heart, who loved to laugh and cause trouble. So she stays with us even now and confounds our enemies with tricks and trials."

For a long time, such memories had filled Eira with rage—so much better than the wrenching grief. Where was Fari when her mother had needed her enemies confounded?

But today, she tilted her face to the sky and lifted a rude finger—Fari scorned piety—and repeated the nursery prayer all Nordish children learned for Faridag. Since all gods were merely different aspects of the divine, surely the One Goddess wouldn't mind.

"O, Fari, god of thieves, be not the one to protect my purse.

O, Fari, goddess of lies, inspire not my lover's lips.

O, Fari, god of mischief, make not my hardship worse.

O, Fari, goddess of jests, turn all today's evil into farts."

It felt good to laugh. Good to be out in the sunshine, breathing summer-sweet mountain air.

Eira settled into a more humble pose and bent her head. She could recite the Sevenday prayers for peace now, content in the knowledge that if any god might help an exiled princess kill a monster bear with a knife tied to a stick, it would be Fari.

Snuffling.

Even rising from the depths of light-dappled dreams, Eira knew snuffling wasn't good.

At least the cave offered some protection. She must have fallen asleep waiting for Berengar after she returned from the meadow.

She didn't *remember* returning to the cave. The last thing she remembered was praying for peace. Sleeping was peaceful. But surely even the One Goddess would agree that falling asleep in the middle of a meadow where a monster bear could stumble across her at any moment was *a little too much peace.*

A soft breeze touched her bare arms, raising goosebumps. She no longer lay in the sun. *Cave, cave, cave.* But her skin still felt hot. Slowly, reluctantly, she lifted a finger to her cheek.

And hissed. Very, very softly.

Sunburn.

Another snuffle. A slight tremor in the ground beneath her. Something very heavy treading at a measured pace across an open meadow.

Eira inched her hand across the expanse of her cloak.

There. Her fingers closed around the haft of her makeshift spear. A stick with a knife tied on the end.

Shame washed over her, hotter than the sunburn. She was going to be eaten by a bear while wearing nothing but her underthings, looking like a fire-roasted maggot and clinging to a child's toy of a weapon. Uncle Einar would get a good laugh when he heard. No doubt Wulfric would, as well. The two kings were equally heartless.

She remembered Marjani's scornful assessment. *You're too weak and timid to take vengeance on the men who killed your mother.*

No. Ice hardened her heart, spreading through her veins like a feathery frost. Her mother had not raised a meek, bashful daughter. Eira was no longer a scrawny, frightened child. She had spent years making herself strong.

No, she was neither too weak nor too timid.

Merely too ridiculous. And when had that ever stopped her?

Her eyes snapped open. The sky overhead was turning ashy with evening, though the gleam of the setting sun still caressed the rocky summits of the mountains. Plenty of light for her to face her fate. She would meet it clear-eyed and brave enough to honor her mother's name.

Eira had never lived in a great palace or worn ornate gowns of shimmering brocade. She wasn't beautiful like Princess Isolde or rich like Dora or regal like Raisa. But she was the daughter of Queen Sassa of Nordmark, the boldest leader Eira had ever known.

Sassa had not raised her to be timid. She had raised her to be *fearless.*

Or at least not to show her fear.

With a savage growl, she sprang to her feet. Maybe it was more of an awkward scramble to her feet, but she ended upright with her improvised spear in her hand.

And there it was. The bear. Only a stone's throw away. Huge. Ferocious. Staring back at her.

Eira's skin flashed hot, then cold. She'd been this close to the beast before. Closer. Yet, even lying helplessly in the grip of fever and exhaustion, even with its nose inches from her face, she had never felt quite so *small.*

It had halted on all fours, yet its shoulders stood nearly as tall as she and twice as broad. If it reared up … Her damp palm clenched the stick in her hand. If it rose, she would barely be able to reach its eye with her makeshift spear, much less drive the blade home.

She swallowed hard and adjusted her stance.

The best thing about an inadequate plan was that it was easy to change. If the beast rose before she could reach it, she would duck under its paws and plunge the spear into its belly. The bear would still kill her. But it would die, too.

Just more slowly. Slowly and horribly, from blood loss. Or it could linger until sepsis poisoned it from within. If she hit strong and true, the spear might go all the way through and sever its spinal cord, bringing it down to writhe in agony for hours or even days.

Eira's chest tightened as she tensed for the attack. Staring into the great bear's eyes as it tilted its muzzle, as if trying to puzzle her intentions, she couldn't push the image from her mind. The awful, awesome beast lying broken and helpless, unable to escape its suffering. She wouldn't wish a death like that on her worst enemy. Not Raisa, not Wulfric. Not even her Uncle Einar.

Weak and timid. Her heart clenched again, this time with self-loathing. A true Nordish princess would do anything necessary to take her revenge. What had Marjani said? *All that matters is evening out the scales.*

But what scales are you evening, Eira? What has this creature ever done to you? Saved you from drowning? Watched over you in your illness?

That was her own voice. Preaching the Nine Roads to Peace. No wonder everyone found her so annoying.

She listened to the bear's breathing, watched the flaring of its nostrils as it took in her scent. Yet, it seemed as rooted in place as she. Deciding whether or not to maul her? Or where to nail her heart after it ripped it from her body?

It's a monster. Wrapped in sorcery. Unnatural and evil.

It is not your uncle. Its death will not make you queen of Nordmark.

Oh, but it might. If it wins me Prince Theo's hand.

Is Prince Theo's the hand you really want?

Of course it is! I will marry him and bring peace, and I will finally be able to live my life somewhere I belong.

This creature's death will not bring your mother back to you.

"Be quiet!" Eira's shout flattened the bear's ears and rang in her own. This wasn't about her, about her mother, about King Wulfric's absurd ball. This bear was terrorizing Saebern—town and manor alike. It had to be stopped. *She* had to stop it.

But she had to kill it quickly. Kill it cleanly. She owed it that.

Her mother would agree.

The bear lowered his head, one great golden eye turning toward her. The perfect target. For a moment, she was caught in his gaze, the sorrow almost like a mirror. Both of them trapped in a grinding mill wheel of fear and vengeance, hatred and duty, mischance and fate.

Had they ever had a chance to escape that wheel? Even now—

The beast's face twisted, a rumpled mask of fury, baring pike-like fangs. A terrifying, huffing roar rumbled up from his throat and struck her like a physical blow. There was no escape. One or both of them would die.

Eira's grip shifted instinctually. She might be inexperienced with spears, but she'd been holding weapons since before she could walk. This one would serve.

She could do this. No thought, no second-guessing, no fear. Only absolute certainty. A bounce on the balls of her feet. A jolt of fierce purpose in her heart.

With a scream of pure, Nordish killing fury, she launched herself at the bear.

CHAPTER EIGHTEEN

4. *Findan.* Self-evident spell to find [that which] thou hast lost. (If what you've lost is the nose on your face, otherwise it's as worthless as every other spell in this godsforsaken book.)

— Top 10 failed spells translated and performed by Rurik, Ravninan sorcerer (in training)

"Politics is a soulless business," Rurik observed as Marjani scanned the forest around them. "All those power-hungry families sending their daughters into the jaws of King Wulfric of Aldforth on the off chance you might be chosen to marry his second-best son. What would your father think of this hunt for a cursed bear?"

He would be wondering why Prince Theodore wasn't dead yet.

Marjani brushed the sorcerer's voice from her ear, along with the mosquito that had been dogging her for the past five minutes. When they had set out their first morning together, Rurik had been a brooding, anxious shadow whose only contribution to the hunt had been urging her to hunt *faster.* But over the maddening days of fruitless searching, his frustration had begun to bubble up into bouts of irrepressible conversation.

And now that they had finally—finally!—found the bear's trail, he could not seem to *shut up*.

Throughout the day, as she'd focused on the scuffing of pine needles here, a broken branch there, he'd regaled her with stories. Tales of his childhood in Ravnina, raised by his grandmother, the matriarch of their semi-nomadic village. Being sent to serve as a sorcerer's apprentice in Rovka after the village healer identified him as having mystical potential. He performed wicked impressions of his master and the other sorcerers that made her laugh despite herself.

But as the stories came closer to the present, they tapered off, suffocated by the darkness Marjani sensed inside him. He'd turned to questioning her—about her childhood, her family, her experiences in Aldforth.

She told him nothing substantive, yet his spinning web of foolish chatter did not deceive her. She feared his sharp intelligence gleaned more from her curt answers than she wanted to share.

She narrowed her focus to the ground beneath her feet—a fern crushed beneath a great paw. To the trees—a tuft of fur caught on the rough bark. To the very air around them—what had the bear scented when it passed this way?

"It is as though I feel the spirit of the animal," Dejen had told her and Mosi, describing his tracking skill as they sat by a fire on an overnight hunt. A rare time when the three of them were alone—except for the dozen guards camped nearby to ensure the safety of their prince. Marjani had hung on Dejen's every word, absorbing the calming energy of *his* spirit while Mosi lifted his lover's braids to twine them in the shape of antlers.

"There, you are becoming an antelope," Mosi had teased him.

Marjani would have swatted him, but Dejen only pulled Mosi's hand from his head and kissed it with a smile.

"But I *am* an antelope," Dejen had said, as impossible to distract from his teaching as from his tracking. "And a leopard, a crocodile, a porcupine. Whatever I might hunt or that might hunt me. I need to think like the animal so I know which way it has gone before I ever see the sign."

"Nothing surprises you, then?" Mosi had demanded. "Not even this?"

Dejen had jumped at Mosi's ear pinch, though he must have known it was coming.

"*You* are the surprise, my prince," Dejen had said, his tone serious even as his eyes danced with laughter.

Marjani had shifted her gaze to the flames, blinking away her jealousy—for Dejen's talent, for Mosi's capturing his heart as easily as he captured everyone else's, for their ease and confidence in their places in the world.

Even now, what felt like an impossible distance and a lifetime away, her eyes stung with tears. But for once, not with grief and fury at their loss. At least, not only that. But with a surge of love that connected that moment to this one. Because, finally, she understood what Dejen had meant, as if he and her brother were there by her side.

She *was* the bear.

She had easily found the woodcutters' camp Hartwin had described, a small cluster of hastily abandoned tents and sheds. The recent rain had churned the loose earth of the tree-stripped hillside. The dried mud provided the perfect medium for preserving the massive prints of a marauding bear.

The beast's trail led deep into the wilderness, where the bear had once again obscured its tracks with uncanny skill. But persistence, luck—a moment of carelessness by the bear? —had brought Marjani back to its sign again and again.

She began to understand the patterns of its route, to guess where it would exit a stream or how it would cross a rocky hillside.

And now, for the past mile or more, there had been no more deception, no more diversion from the animal's goal. The bear had come far enough to believe it was safe from pursuit, and she could follow its trail as fast as the bear had ambled it the day before. Maybe faster.

There would be no turning back now. No returning to the manor for the night, no more pretense of spending the day in prayer. Now that she had the trail, she would not stop until she had run the bear to ground. Until either she or the bear was dead.

The bear's death would make a payment on her debt to Eira, however inadequate, and bring her another step closer to making Wulfric pay his debt to Mosi and Dejen. Another step closer to proving her life worth something other than her family's sorrow, whether her father ever acknowledged it or not.

Another step closer to pouring the black pain from her own heart into Wulfric's. Let him carry it. He could kill her. Would kill her. But that would only relieve her completely of her burden, while his would be never-ending.

Only the creeping shadows of evening threatened to slow her progress through the woods. The shadows and Rurik's chatter.

"All those princesses vying for the king's attention," the sorcerer mused. "Which one has the best chance of winning the prince's hand? Other than yourself, of course."

"King Wulfric will never marry me to his son," Marjani snarled.

"Don't be so sure. Wulfric has rapacious ambitions," Rurik said, apparently misunderstanding her reply. "An alliance with Almasa would strengthen Aldforthian trade routes, squeeze Venia, and pressure Rigas—"

"You're saying he would not hesitate to yoke his son to a wraith-eyed twin if it increased his power." As bitter as her words, she couldn't disagree. The Aldforthian king had no scruples when it came to his greed and self-interest … or to anything else, as far as she could tell.

"In Ravnina, we consider twins lucky," Rurik told her.

"Living with only half a soul is *not* lucky."

"I don't believe twins share a soul."

"You have never *been* a twin."

That silenced him. Briefly. "No. But I have felt as if my soul were being torn in two. I should not have discounted your experience."

Something in his tone made her believe he meant it, and she nodded an acceptance of his apology. Another silence. Nearly an entire, blissful minute of it.

"But why should the king be offended by your eyes?"

"The Nordish used to murder children with eyes of two different colors." She narrowed hers at him in warning.

Which he ignored. "Everyone knows the Nordish are barbarians. Not that the Almasans are any better, telling you that you have a malformed soul because you shared a womb with your brother. The Ravninans, of course, would disapprove of you for your gender. They don't allow women to inherit titles or property."

Do not *respond*. "You told me your grandmother is the leader of your village."

"The people of the taiga are Ravninan now," he said with a shrug, "but we were Voskoyan not so long ago. We may be Kheremese tomorrow. It matters little to us. In Kherem, men are the ones who cannot rule or own property.

"Here in Aldforth, families may disinherit children who love others of their own gender. My beloved, Kazmir, was banished from his family's Alforthian holdings. He had to flee to Rovka, to his grandmother's people. Where he died, far from home."

For an instant, she could almost see the grief shimmering on his skin. "I'm so sorry, Rurik."

He forced a careless shrug and pushed on. "Then there is Bellis, where they put secondary children through brutal initiation rights that sometimes maim or kill them to make them more useful retainers to the firstborn. In Rigas, siblings are just as likely to poison each other as—"

"As come to the point? You'd be at home there."

"The point is, why would you let the Nordish decide your worth? Your eyes are extraordinary." He paused. "*You* are extraordinary, Princess Marjani of Almasa."

"*Enough.*" She glared at him. "I am tracking a dangerous, cursed beast, and, as you constantly remind me, we are running out of time. If you cannot stop chattering and flirting, I will use your tongue for bear bait."

"I'm not flirting. I'm *charming*." His smile showed gleaming white teeth.

Marjani didn't smile back. "Is that what you told Steward Tarben when he caught you making advances on his wife?"

"I did not make advances on Lady Silke!"

"You didn't have to jump out a window after Tarben caught you kissing her?"

"No! I mean, yes, I did exit through a window, but I didn't kiss her. I mean, my lips touched hers, but … " He was actually blushing, fiery red blooms flushing his high cheekbones.

"Forgive my Common Tongue," Marjani said, too sweetly. "In Almasa, when lips touch, we call it 'kissing.' Perhaps it's different in Ravnina?"

"*She* kissed *me!*" he huffed. "So, perhaps she also misinterpreted my charm as flirting. I found her waiting in my room one evening, but I do not gossip about my conquests."

"Just everything else," Marjani muttered.

"What about you?" the sorcerer asked with a sly grin. "It's interesting that Reeve Hartwin tracked you down so early this morning just to tell you about a bear sighting."

"He was checking up on me," Marjani said, turning from those too-observant eyes. "Making sure I obeyed Steward Tarben's instructions."

"I don't know the reeve personally," Rurik mused. "I only saw him a couple of times last summer. But he was hard not to notice. That wheaten hair. Those eyes … What color would you say they were? Turquoise? Teal?"

The blue-green of the Almasan sea …

"Sadly, he obviously finds you more fascinating than he

did me. Seeking you out in the early morning hours to make sure you're safe and protected—"

A pale flash caught Marjani's eye. The inner wood of a broken sapling too far to her left. She'd almost lost the trail.

"Silence your chatter," she hissed as she corrected course. "Or I'll silence you."

"Don't tell me you've never been tempted to touch lips with our handsome young reeve."

"*Be quiet!*"

The shout expressed Marjani's frustration so perfectly that it took her a moment to realize the voice wasn't hers. The young woman's cry rang in her ears, its location confused by echoes from the hillsides around them.

"That way." Marjani started through the trees toward where the air seemed to brighten. A clearing of some sort.

"What are you doing?" Rurik grabbed her arm. "We don't want anyone to see us!"

"We came out here looking for trouble. I think we have found it."

The voice had jolted her, a shock of recognition along her nerves—an expression of grief and guilt so sharp they could cut a soul. So familiar they could be her own.

Whatever was happening in that clearing, nothing good could come of it.

"We came looking for a *bear*," Rurik objected, but Marjani shrugged free of his grip.

So familiar. Heart pounding, she ran through the woods, leaping fallen logs, slapping away branches, finally bursting into the stillness of a mountain meadow, where she stumbled to a halt. The last rays of sunlight, as reluctant as any child to leave the sweetness of a summer evening, lingered on the mountaintops. Yet twilight pooled at Marjani's feet, rippling purple across the grass and the pewter ribbon of a creek a half dozen yards ahead.

Defying the fading light, the figure in the meadow's center

fairly shone against the shadows. Pale shift, pale skin. Icy white hair shimmering loosely around her shoulders.

Chills ran down Marjani's arms, and the hair on her neck prickled. Even her father, who claimed to hear the voices of the ancestors as clearly as those of the living, had never *seen* a spirit, though his priest sometimes told stories of the unquiet dead, those unable to accept that their time on earth had ended.

If any spirit were contrary and pigheaded enough to refuse to start its journey to the lands beyond—

A low, growing rumble shifted Marjani's gaze to the edge of the clearing. Another uncanny creature hulked there. Massive. Powerful. Eyes gleaming in the dimming light.

She'd found the bear.

The girl's pale spirit shifted, lifting a … a stick. A stick with a knife tied to the end. And suddenly, Marjani saw the rest. Clothing scattered on the rocks. Fading bruises on bare legs. Sunburned cheeks.

The bear began to rise.

Eira! Marjani's throat closed in horror. Even so, her feet set themselves with practiced precision, and her arm drew back her spear as the Nordish princess lifted her pitiful, ludicrous weapon and prepared to charge the beast.

Marjani had the strength and accuracy to kill a forest antelope from this distance, with a whisper of luck. But she'd heard Hartwin's tales of weapons sliding off this great beast's hide. She would have to make a perfect strike. If she didn't kill the bear outright, it would kill Eira. For certain this time. And then it would kill Marjani, for her spear would be gone, and a sword against that beast would be folly.

Smarter to move closer, but there was no time. Marjani couldn't watch that foolish, ridiculous witch die. *Again.*

She set her back foot. No wind. One last adjustment—

"*No!*" A blow to her shoulder sent her spear clattering to the ground. A flash of dark clothes, dark hair.

Rurik, running past her.

Even as she scrambled for the spear, the sorcerer sprinted across the clearing, leaping the creek almost as though he really could fly. He and Eira, black and white, both rushed toward the bear.

Marjani snatched up her weapon, but she couldn't throw it now. She might hit one of them. She could only chase after.

Knowing she would never reach them in time.

CHAPTER NINETEEN

9. My father said Berengar was too self-conscious to reveal his true nature. It couldn't have been worse than the nature he did show. (Submitted by Reeve Hartwin, head of the Saebern Town council.)

— Top 10 reasons no one misses Earl Berengar that much

There was nothing in the world but that huge golden eye. No sound but the bear's roar rumbling in Eira's chest. No thought as she ran except the knowledge that even as she adjusted her aim, even as the beast bared its massive teeth and lifted its huge paws from the ground, she had made the wrong choice.

Which choice was wrong, she wasn't sure. Time seemed to have slowed so she could see them all laid out before her. Leaving Nordmark instead of forcing her uncle to kill her. Traveling to Newport to compete for Prince Theo's hand. Volunteering to kill an enchanted bear. Failing to toss Marjani off the boat before they ever reached Saebern, so she would not have followed her into the wilderness.

Whatever had brought Eira to this moment, it came with a grief great enough to break her heart. She should not be here.

Should not be killing this beast that had done nothing to harm her, cursed or not.

But it was too late to turn back. She would kill the bear, or the bear would kill her.

His head turned, eye widening as if daring her to strike. Or giving her a target.

Eira shouted again, in fury and anguish, as she brought her arm forward to drive her makeshift spear home—

A blow hurled her off her feet, heaving her up and away, tumbling her across the ground. Her cheek skidded through the grass. Her shoulder struck a rock. Her knife blade caught in the grass, wresting the spear from her hand.

The bear tumbled with her, landing on her, knocking the air from her lungs … No, if the bear had landed on her, she wouldn't be breathing. The hand digging into her shoulder had no claws. The sharp jab in her back was someone's knee.

The someone who'd attacked her, now struggling to get up.

Good luck with that. With a savage snarl, she twisted beneath the knee, throwing her assailant sideways. He yelped in surprise as Eira rolled away from him, pivoting to her feet. Her bare toes weren't much of a weapon, but she aimed for a soft spot on the stranger's anatomy—

"Wait!" He was impressively fast, deflecting the worst of her kick and scrambling backward, trying to get his legs beneath him. His dark eyes stared past her through the cascade of his long, black hair. "Look out!"

The bear! Eira whirled, but the beast wasn't chasing after her. He had risen to his full, overwhelming height to face the warrior charging him with her spear.

Marjani. Even without her red robes, there was no mistaking that lean, powerful form, the intensity in her eyes, focused wholly on the death of the animal before her.

"No! Stop!" The stranger who'd attacked Eira ran toward Marjani.

Quick as he was, Eira was quicker. A swift foot tripped

him flat on the ground. She retrieved her spear before he could recover.

She could still reach the bear before Marjani. She could bring him down first. This was *her* quest, *her* chance to prove herself—

The bear shook his magnificent head and roared, an echoing call of defiance and despair. This bear that had pulled her from the river. That had watched over her while she burned with fever.

Marjani was going to *kill* him.

All those wrong choices that had brought Eira here with death in her heart … now gave her a chance to make a different choice.

Of all the princesses, only Marjani could compete with her in a foot race, but Marjani had to cross the creek, and the water slowed her down.

With a burst of terror and exhilaration, Eira flashed past the towering bear, close enough that her shoulder brushed his bristling fur. She ducked beneath the mighty paws, skidding to a stop just beyond his reach, between him and Marjani.

Startled eyes wide, Marjani slowed more gracefully and set her feet for battle. "Duck!"

"No." Eira raised her spear between them to hold Marjani back. Only tattered strips of cloth remained on the end of the stick. Her knife must have torn off in her fall. "Don't come any closer."

"What are you doing? *You're going to die!*"

Eira couldn't be sure whether Marjani meant it as a warning or a threat until the Almasan adjusted her aim to point over Eira's shoulder at the beast behind her.

"Wait!" Eira lifted her stick above her head. As if there were a chance in all the hells she could deflect Marjani's throw. She heard the huff of the bear's breath behind her. Imagined she felt it lifting the hair on her neck.

What *was* she doing? She had no idea. She only knew she

couldn't let Marjani kill this bear. This bear that had chosen not to kill her. That had never meant to hurt her.

"Stop!" The black-haired stranger appeared off to Eira's right, gaze snapping between the two girls. "Marjani, please lower your spear."

Eira frowned at Marjani. "You know this person?"

"His name is Rurik." Marjani never shifted her eyes from the bear. "He's a sorcerer."

"*The* sorcerer?" Eira risked another glance. Long, glossy hair, blade-sharp black eyebrows, hawk-fierce eyes. She'd always had a weakness for Ravninan northmen. *Focus, Eira.* "Are you sure? Isn't he a little scruffy for a sorcerer?"

"He said he could lift the curse so we can kill the bear." Marjani shifted her spear once more.

"That's not exactly what I—"

"So, do it," Marjani interrupted him. "Lift the curse, sorcerer. Or I'll kill it without you."

"Hey!" Eira waved her stick to reclaim Marjani's attention. "Back off. No one is going to kill my bear."

"*Your* bear?" Marjani's gaze slipped from her target to Eira's face. "That monster is *going to eat you.*"

"Does he look like he's going to eat me?" Eira demanded, hoping she looked bold rather than terrified.

Marjani and what's-his-name-the-sorcerer stared past her, the lengthening shadows obscuring their expressions.

After a long moment, she couldn't help repeating more urgently, "Well? *Does* he?"

A soft thud shook the ground beneath her bare feet. The bear dropping to all fours. Standing down? Or about to charge?

"Of course he's not going to eat you," the sorcerer said, keeping a wary gaze on the animal behind her. "He's not a killer."

Eira couldn't help wishing he sounded more certain.

"It killed Hartwin's father," Marjani said.

"A boar killed Hartwin's father," the sorcerer retorted. "I

was there. I saw it happen. The curse is to blame for Reeve Wendel's death, not the bear."

"The curse," Eira repeated. Apparently, she'd missed a few things being lost in the wilderness.

"So, break the curse," Marjani repeated, in that infuriating, imperious tone Eira had forgotten in her unexpected joy at seeing the other princess again. "And then I will kill the bear. If the Nordish witch chooses not to help, I will be content to receive all the credit."

"You would take the life of this magnificent beast that has never done you any harm?" Eira shivered with relief that the sorcerer—*Rurik*—had saved her from doing just that. "Your grievance is against King Wulfric. Killing this bear won't bring back your brother or heal your soul."

"I am not looking for healing." Marjani's ferocity was hot enough to burn. "I am looking for vengeance. And if I were you, I would not stand in my way."

She shook her spear in warning, and Eira gripped her stick with both hands in defense.

"Listen to me! Just listen." Rurik's voice thrummed with impatience. "You can jab at that bear all you want, but it won't do you any good. The curse won't let you kill him before sunset, but he might accidentally maul you if you do something stupid. Any moment, nightfall will make him vulnerable, and then we can decide what to do next."

Behind Eira, the bear gave a sudden bellow of such agony that she cried out herself. She turned to see the great beast's muzzle lifted toward the sky, where a faint streak of orange cloud was dimming to ash.

"Don't run!" Rurik stepped toward the beast. "Stay and let me help you."

The bear lowered his head and bared his teeth in a vicious snarl that sent the sorcerer scrambling backward. But instead of charging, the animal spun himself sideways with his front paws, turning his bulk toward the woods with surprising grace and speed.

"*Enough!*" Marjani's spear streaked past Eira's head.

With a shout of horror, Eira leaped after it as if she might catch the shaft in the air. She knew Marjani's skill, her strength and focus. Had never seen her fail to hit a target. At this distance, she could not miss.

The spear's head struck just beneath the bear's jaw.

Yet, whether it was a shift in the bear's gait, a gust of the breeze, or the curse's power protecting him as Rurik claimed, the spear slid past the animal's jugular, carving a line through the thick fur but drawing no blood. The bear grunted and lumbered on, gathering speed.

Marjani growled in frustration, and Eira heard the sharp whisper as she drew her sword. Breaking into a desperate sprint, Eira caught up to the bear. He was far too big for her to shield his body from Marjani's blade.

Passing his huge flank and the mountain of his shoulder, she flung herself at the animal's head and wrapped her arms around his neck. The bear's momentum pulled her off her feet, but she dug her fingers into the rough fur and hung on, guarding the beast's throat. The bear's scent filled her nostrils, wild and dangerous.

"For gods' sake, what is wrong with you?" Marjani shouted, her feet pounding the earth behind them. "Don't you dare get yourself killed again, you lunatic witch!"

Eira would have laughed, but she had to concentrate on clinging to the bear as his rolling, loping stride tried to shake her free.

And then, suddenly, she *was* falling. She hadn't let go, hadn't felt a blow, but she hit the ground in a tangle of flailing limbs that weren't her own. Her fists clenched in her assailant's shirt, in his hair. She fought to get to her feet, to get back to the bear. Somehow the sorcerer's arm had entwined with hers, and he grunted when she jabbed an elbow in his ribs.

"Let me go, you Ravninan menace!" But even as she shouted, she realized it wasn't Rurik after all.

Her attacker's hair was shaggy and brown, his frame taller and more tightly muscled than the sorcerer's. Teeth bared, face twisted in an agony that tore at her heart, he was almost unrecognizable, except for the eyes that caught hers with fierce desperation, as if he stood on a precipice and her gaze were the only thing keeping him from falling.

She felt as though she might be falling again herself, a dizzying plunge into those unguarded eyes. His heart pounded against his ribs, against *her* ribs, through his shirt and her shift.

She was lying on a man's chest in her underclothes. An appalling scandal. Raisa would be delightfully horrified. Or horrifyingly delighted. Her reputation was ruined. So, really, shouldn't she just kiss him?

"Oh, Goddess!" She pushed herself up. "What have you done, Wild Man? Marjani is going to kill my bear—or he's going to kill her."

She scanned the twilight woods but saw no sign of the bear. Marjani stood only a few yards away. Despite the horror on the other girl's face, she appeared unhurt, all her limbs still attached to her body. And Rurik lurked a few paces behind her, his face haunted by shadows.

"What ..." Marjani shook her head, her voice breaking. "*Who?*"

"Him?" Eira glanced down at the man lying in the dirt beneath her. "He looks feral, but he means well. Are you hurt?" When he shook his head, she grabbed his hand and pulled him unresisting to his feet.

"He ... he was ..." Marjani's voice sounded wrong, as if she couldn't open her throat all the way.

"Trying to save my life," Eira said, his mute wretchedness making her generous, despite his interference. "He's made that a kind of habit. Princess Marjani, may I present Earl Berengar of Saebern."

Holy Mother would not have approved of her glee, anticipating Marjani and Berengar's mutual shock—You found the missing earl? You know a *princess?*—but their expressions didn't change, Berengar miserable, Marjani horrified.

Disappointing, but Holy Mother liked to say that hoping to be admired was setting yourself up for disappointment. *Peace is its own reward.* Eira smothered a sigh.

"I know this is all very confusing, but I'm really glad to see you, Marjani." Eira was surprised at how much she meant it. "If you give me a minute, I'd like to put on my boots." And the rest of her clothes. "Then we can go back to Berengar's cave and catch up on what's been happening since we were last together."

"But—" Marjani shook her head again. "The bear."

"It's getting dark," Eira said. She'd be lucky to *find* her boots, the shadows were thickening so fast. "Even you can't hunt a giant bear in a strange wilderness at night. Who knows how far he's gone by now?"

They were staring at her now, Marjani and Rurik-the-sorcerer.

"*Eira*," Marjani snapped, her strange stiltedness giving way to familiar fire. She pointed over Eira's shoulder. "It's. Right. There."

Eira whirled, nearly slamming into Berengar. Night was swallowing the forest. She couldn't see anything beneath the trees, not even the glimmer of light reflecting from the bear's eyes.

"Where?" She stepped forward, but Berengar grabbed her arm. "Let go. I just—"

"Eira." He turned her toward him. There was the light she sought, caught in his eyes, a flicker of something beyond hope or despair. His lips remained parted as if to let out words he couldn't seem to speak.

Staring into those tormented brown eyes, so achingly familiar after only a few short days, Eira felt suddenly dizzy again. Two sets of golden brown eyes, superimposed on each other.

She shook her head, trying to keep them apart. But Berengar tightened his grip on her arm, holding her steady.

"Eira—"

"You," she said. For once, laughter refused to come, drowned in the sudden stinging of tears. "You're the bear."

CHAPTER TWENTY

3. She has no sense of humor.

 — Top 10 things ~~I hate~~ I find difficult to appreciate about Princess Marjani, as listed by (former) Princess Eira of Nordmark

"It took you long enough!" Marjani didn't know whether to rescue the Nordish princess from her monster earl-bear or thrash the girl for her sheer cluelessness—or both. At least exasperation freed her from the paralysis that had seized her as the bear began to change …

Change into *what* exactly?

Marjani shuddered. Her sword—Eira's sword—had fallen from her numb fingers as she'd watched the uncanny melting of that horrifying beast into this shaggy creature that looked like a man. A man Eira called Earl Berengar.

She crouched to lift the sword from the forest floor. "Step aside. We can end this now."

"End what?" Eira asked, looking lost.

"Princess," Rurik interrupted, drawing both their gazes. "Princess Marjani, I know this is a shock—"

"I was not talking to you." Marjani's arm might be trembling, but she was pleased to note her voice did not. "I was speaking to *it*."

She pointed at the beast with her sword. "Step away from Princess Eira, and I will end this curse."

"*Princess* Eira?" His voice raised goosebumps on her arms. It sounded so human, so haunted.

Marjani's own voice sounded like steel. "I promise to make it swift, creature."

"He's not a creature!" Tears streaked Eira's face, but she still managed to roll her eyes. "He's a person, just like you and me." Even the pious witch had to pause at that. "Maybe not *exactly* like you and me …"

"Eira." The *creature* lifted his hand to brush Eira's pale hair from her cheek. "Princess Eira. It's all right. I'm ready for it to be over."

He stepped toward Marjani, hands up in surrender—or supplication. "Good men died because of me, the day I was cursed. I have spent this past year regretting I did not die in their place. And now you have come to release me."

"No," Majani snapped. How dare he speak of mercy? A creature whose very existence was a curse, a wrong that needed to be righted. She ignored the sharp stab of empathy between her ribs. *A wraith-eyed, spirit-sensing twin girl who should never have been born.* "I have come to kill you and to fulfill my oath of vengeance for the deaths of my brother, Mosi, and his spear-bearer, Dejen."

She blinked hard, forcing away the images of her dead and the man who'd murdered them—Mosi's blood on his hands, Dejen's blood spattered across his face. Whatever Prince Guntram had suffered at the teeth of the manticore that killed him did not pay his debt. Her grief and fury would never be satisfied until King Wulfric had paid that cost, until his entire kingdom had paid and paid and paid …

She knew nothing of swordsmanship beyond the rudimentary skills Eira had taught the princesses at Lukos, but she knew enough to kill an unarmed, unarmored man.

"You can't do this!" Eira cried. "You're not a murderer."

"This isn't his fault," Rurik chimed in.

But it wasn't their protests that made her hesitate.

It was the bewilderment that wrinkled the freckles across Berengar's nose as he stared at her.

"Your brother?" he asked, eyes dark with desolation. "Can you tell me, please, what … what I've done? I don't always have clear memories from my time as a bear. I don't remember encountering any Almasans. I don't remember killing anyone at all."

As Eira, the self-destructive Nordish witch, threw herself in front of Berengar like a shield, and Rurik commenced shouting melodramatic nonsense that was probably supposed to be some kind of protection spell, Marjani lowered her sword and turned away.

Only a fool would turn their back on a giant, enchanted, murderous bear—even if he did look like a confused, forgotten hermit. But better to turn away than let anyone see her tears. Gods only knew what she was crying for. Certainly not this man she did not know. Not Eira's judgment. Not even Mosi's and Dejen's deaths.

Surely she wasn't crying at how close she had come to killing Berengar. He was a *monster*. And whatever Eira might say, she *was* a murderer. Prince Theodor's murderer. She had long resigned herself to this unholy purpose, separated from the rest of humanity—

"Marjani?"

Not separated far enough.

"It's all right." Eira touched her arm. "We're all shaken up. Are you crying?"

"No." Marjani swiped a sleeve across her eyes. "It is you to blame, as usual. Spreading your sappy weeping like a contagion."

Eira snorted with laughter, easing Marjani's shame. Snot bubbles were definitely more embarrassing than tears.

"Here." Marjani shifted her knapsack and pulled out a handkerchief. "You look appalling."

"You look as gorgeous and intimidating as ever," Eira grumbled as she took the cloth. "Even in those ill-fitting clo— Wait. Are those *my* clothes?"

Marjani trusted the dark would hide her flush. "Tarben forbade me to leave the manor, so I required a disguise. I didn't think you needed them anymore."

"I don't mind," Eira assured her. "Only, I can't help wishing you looked more homely in them." She leaned closer. "Is that my *sword?* You tried to kill my bear with my own sword?"

"Your bear!" How could Marjani have forgotten, even for an instant, how aggravating this girl was? "I *found* your sword where you lost it in the stream. I planned to avenge your spirit by using it to kill the monster that murdered you."

"Really?" For the first time since Marjani had met her, Eira sounded uncertain, almost shy. "You would have done that for me? You weren't just glad to be rid of me?"

Without warning, the Nordish girl threw her arms around Marjani's shoulders and pulled her into a bone-crushing hug. Marjani hugged her back, purely reflexively, the delayed relief at seeing Eira alive washing over her like a flood. But when tears threatened to return, she pushed the girl to arm's length.

"Of course I was glad to be rid of you. Look how much trouble you cause."

Even in the gloom, Eira's pale face beamed. "I prefer to think of it as offering enriching experiences. Admit it, you never expected me to be rescued from drowning by an enchanted earl."

"Truly," Marjani muttered, "I should not have been surprised."

A throat cleared nearby. The earl and the sorcerer stood where the girls had left them, awkwardly looking anywhere but at the emotional reunion.

"Your Highnesses," Rurik said. "We should seek shelter."

"My cave isn't far." Berengar waved an arm vaguely behind him. "If you can tolerate my company, I can lead you there. I'm used to finding it in the dark."

"I, for one, can't tell you how glad I am to see you again, my lord," Rurik said, sounding roughly sincere for once. Indeed, he looked as if he might throw his arms around the ragged young man but settled for clapping him awkwardly on the shoulder instead.

"I could almost say the same," Berengar said with an unexpectedly disarming smile. "I didn't know whether to hope you would return or hope I would never have to see your sorry face again."

Perhaps it was the encroaching night or simply the very human irony in his voice, but no one raised an objection to following a cursed bear-man through an untracked wilderness. Marjani collected her spear, and they somehow managed to locate Eira's clothes without anyone falling into the creek.

Marjani followed the others through the woods more by their stumbles and curses than their fading shapes in the murk. Even Eira's icy-pale hair was barely a shimmer, only a pace away. Marjani was grateful when her feet found the smoother ground of a narrow path.

"I haven't much food," Berengar warned from up ahead. "Just fish."

Eira snickered, and Marjani understood it was a joke between them.

"He's not what we were led to expect," Marjani observed.

"The bear?" Eira asked innocently.

Marjani would have punched her if she could have been sure of her aim. "The earl."

"No," Eira agreed. "He's not. No one on this quest has been exactly what I expected. Not even you."

Marjani trusted the dark to hide her smile. "You've been exactly what I expected. Self-righteous, unreliable, obnoxious. The only unexpected thing is how glad I am you are not dead."

Eira laughed, and her blow to Marjani's shoulder was painfully accurate. "I'm glad to see you, too. Even if you did try to kill my bear."

"Your bear." Marjani shivered. "You really did not know it was the earl?"

She heard the emphatic swish of the other girl's head shake.

"I feel a little thick," Eira said. "I mean, he was only around at night. The bear was only around during the day. He never seemed worried about the bear attacking us. All those *fish*."

"I saw him transform, and I still have trouble believing it," Marjani admitted. "It's like a children's story."

"A fairy tale," Eira agreed. "But with dirt and sunburn. And a curse on someone I *know*. I finally understand why he hasn't returned to Saebern Manor."

"It doesn't explain why *you* haven't come back." Marjani found outrage easier to express than terror or relief. "Leaving us to mourn. Tarben and the town council are terrified King Wulfric will punish Saebern for your death. I hope whatever you've been doing with the earl for the past five days has been worth all our pain."

"We haven't been doing anything!" Eira objected. "I mean, *I* haven't been doing anything. I was out of my head with fever most of the time. Berengar promised to return me to the manor tonight if I was able to walk that far. He's been taking care of me."

"I'm sure he has." Despite the dark and the danger, Marjani smirked.

"Not like that!" Eira hissed. "He wants me healthy so I can leave. He can't wait to get rid of me."

"Is that why he looked like he wanted to eat you back there?"

"The bear never tried to eat me," Eira said. "He rescued me from the river. If he'd wanted to hurt me, he could have done it any time."

"We weren't talking about the bear," Marjani said drily. "We were talking about the earl. He definitely looked ready to do *something* to you with his mouth."

Eira's squeak made the laughter bubble from Marjani's throat. It was worth another smack on the shoulder.

"It's not like that," Eira said. "And, anyway, he hasn't seen another girl for almost a year. Now that you're here, he's bound to stop looking at me at all."

"He's an enchanted monster," Marjani reminded her, sobering. "And all that *hair*. You're welcome to him."

"Wait until you see his eyes," Eira sighed.

"His freckles are horrifying."

Her companion giggled. "You're just too swoony over Reeve Hartwin to see how adorable they are."

"I am *not*—'swoony?' That's not a word."

"Yes, it is. It means you tend to swoon whenever a certain azure-eyed baker glances your way—"

"I do not!"

"Are you ladies—*princesses*—all right?" Berengar called back.

"Princess Marjani had a friend return from the dead," Rurik's amused voice came from not nearly far enough ahead. "They need some time to catch up."

"I wasn't dead."

"We're not friends."

"And anything we 'caught up' on is purely confidential," Eira warned. Even in the dark, Marjani caught the flash of the Nordish girl's teeth. "On pain of death."

"Literally," Marjani added, in case Rurik hadn't understood the threat. She tripped over a root and added a curse.

"Of course." The sorcerer still sounded amused, but he hurried ahead a few paces.

Eira hooked her arm through Marjani's, tugging her back onto the path. "Did you really mourn? When you thought I was dead?"

"I should have known better."

"That's comforting to know." Eira sounded utterly sincere. "I feared no one in Saebern would care. I appreciate your holding vigil for me. If anything were to happen, I would say memorial prayers for you, as well."

"I thank you." It *was* oddly comforting. "Even if they are not my prayers, I think the gods will hear."

"The Temple of Peace teaches that we are all children of the One Goddess," Eira said, "whatever aspect of her we worship."

There was the syrupy piety Marjani remembered. "That doesn't make us friends."

"Of course not," Eira agreed cheerfully. "It makes us *sisters.*"

Marjani's shocked chortle whistled through her nose, and they both dissolved into such helpless giggles that Rurik had to drop back and tug them the last few yards to Berengar's clearing.

CHAPTER TWENTY-ONE

1. We're doing just fine without him. (Submitted by Master Kaspar, wool merchant.)

— Top 10 reasons no one misses Earl Berengar that much

The fish was delicious. Eira didn't know if it was the absence of fever or the healthy hunger of her recovery—or the vial of salt the Ravninan sorcerer pulled from his rucksack. Maybe it was just relief that no one had tried to kill anyone else in the last hour. But she could hardly remember a meal that had tasted so good.

In addition to the salt, Rurik offered up a sprinkling of Ravninan spice that burned Eira's tongue, and Marjani shared a hunk of bread and a handful of sweet-tart plums she had brought from the manor.

Through it all, the fire crackled cheerfully, keeping the night at bay.

It might have been a merry evening if all her companions hadn't been stone silent. Maybe they were each afraid to be the first to speak. They must all be burning to ask the same question.

Why didn't you tell me …?

Eira glanced at Berengar, up on one knee, as if ready to bolt, the flames flickering in his wary eyes. At Marjani playing with the gold circlet around her wrist, staring into the distance as if she were somewhere else altogether. At Rurik, hidden under his hood, despite the night's warmth. He finally looked like a sorcerer, almost uncanny, brooding in the dark. How far could they trust him?

Eira sighed. She could win a war of patience if she wanted to. But why on earth would she want to? Everything she thought she knew, all of her plans, had been transformed as abruptly as the bear. She needed to figure out what to do about it.

"Berengar." She might as well go first. "I didn't tell you I was a princess because I was afraid you might try to hold me for ransom, and I knew no one would pay."

"An earl holding a princess for ransom?" he scoffed.

"Don't pretend it's never happened." Although, from the others' expressions, perhaps such things were more frequent in Nordmark than elsewhere. "Anyway, I didn't know you were an earl at first. Afterward, there didn't seem to be any point in airing my ancestry. You said you'd never return to the manor."

And maybe it had been nice not to be a princess for a while, not even a former one.

No uncomfortable formalities. No weight of unmet expectations. No responsibility to win King Wulfric's twisted competition. To bring peace to the Blessed Kingdoms or restore her family's honor. No duty to marry a prince—not that she'd considered marrying the gorgeous Prince Theo a *hardship*, exactly, but he was a bit … frivolous. And what would it be like if he resented marrying *her*?

"But what is a Nordish princess …" The freckles on Berengar's nose danced, far more enticing than Prince Theo's more obvious charms. "What are *two* foreign princesses doing in Saebern, hunting an enchanted bear?"

"It's a long story." One she suddenly wanted to share with him. Wulfric's ball, the competition for Prince Theo's hand, the almost-war with the giants. She wanted to make him laugh at Jax knocking over seven knights with one blow of her hammer, gasp with shock at Theo's kidnapping of the giant princess, simmer with outrage at Wulfric's threats against the royal girls in his care. But … "The short version: King Wulfric is looking for a bride for Crown Prince Theodor. He was hoping your bear would make sure it's not me or Marjani."

"I don't …" Those *freckles*. "Does the long version make more sense?"

"Not really. Your turn."

"I didn't tell you I was a bear—" He poked at the fire with a stick.

Unspoken reasons spilled around them in the silence like sparks from the fire. How could Eira be angry at his deception when every excuse would burn? Why should he trust a complete stranger with such a deadly secret? She would not have done so in his place.

Yet it hurt, all the same.

His hand fisted against his knee, and he grimaced as if he had snatched one of those sparks from the air and clutched it in his palm. "I didn't tell you I was a bear because I didn't want to see your horror when you looked at me. I can't remember the last time anyone saw me as just Berengar, not the disposable son, the second-choice heir, the disappointing earl. I … wanted you to keep liking me."

Warmth curled deep inside Eira's chest. She sent a brief prayer of gratitude to Fari for her sunburn, hiding the heat staining her cheeks.

"What is *your* excuse?" Marjani challenged Rurik, shattering the moment. "Why did you let me believe the bear killed Earl Berengar instead of revealing the true nature of the curse?"

"Would you have believed me?" Rurik brushed back his hood, his teeth showing in a grimace. "Or would you have thought me out of my wits and refused to let me accompany you on your hunt?"

Marjani's eyes flashed in the firelight. "I believed that if I found the bear, you could lift the curse. Was that a lie, too?"

"I didn't lie." Rurik waved a long-fingered hand dismissively. "I never said I could lift the curse—"

In a blur Eira could hardly follow, Marjani's spear point was at Rurik's throat, the shaft steady in her hands.

"No tricks, sorcerer," Marjani growled. "Your promise to lift the curse is the reason I allowed you to accompany me. Why are you here? What is your real purpose?"

Rurik swallowed hard, offering no reply. To be fair, it would be hard to speak with that sharp, glinting spear tip against one's jugular.

Still, Eira wished she hadn't lost her knife in the meadow. It had been easy to forget about evil curses with Berengar's freckles dancing in her eyes. But this dark stranger in his dark cloak with his dark eyes ... she hadn't noticed the diamond sharpness of those eyes when she'd been admiring his handsome features. Hadn't been thinking of gored reeves or eviscerated sheep while they all ate together.

How simple it would be to claim someone else had laid a curse. Claim that you had found a cure. And come back to finish off your hapless victim with only a couple of foreign girls for witnesses. It would be easy enough to curse them, too.

Or would it? Eira had been clinging to Berengar when he had shifted from bear to man, and she still barely believed in sorcery. She couldn't claim to know what was possible for a Ravninan sorcerer bent on malice.

It didn't matter. If this sinister rogue had been lying to Marjani—

"Don't move your hands," she advised him, hefting a rock from the fire circle. "I don't know how sorcery works, and I might get nervous."

"No quote about the roads to war?" Marjani asked. "No warning about the dangers to my soul if I commit murder?"

Eira shook her head, as surprised as Marjani at her trust

in the other girl's instincts. "You know him better than I do. If you think he means harm, I'll be happy to clobber him."

"Don't hurt him!" Berengar rose, hands up in supplication. "I've wanted to clobber Rurik myself more than once, but the gods know he's tried to lift the curse. That day, after I … after it all happened, he followed me into the wilderness, even though he was injured himself. He stayed with me for weeks, trying every spell, every potion, every incantation in his wretched book. Even a spell that was supposed to set my ears on fire."

"I thought magical flame might break the link between the curse and its source," Rurik explained, voice tight against the spear.

"I was relieved that one didn't work," Berengar admitted, rubbing an ear. "The thing is, he may not be a very good sorcerer, but he's done his best to help me. When he left last fall, he said he was going to look for help, but I thought he'd given up. I never expected to see him again. Yet here he is."

"There's a darkness in him." Uncharacteristic uncertainty haunted Marjani's eyes. "Whether it is something he has done or something done to him, I cannot say."

"Should we let him tell his story?" Eira asked. She might not trust Rurik, but she trusted Berengar. Goddess help her. "He's done nothing to harm us."

"Besides lie to us." But Marjani pulled back her spear.

"I didn't lie," Rurik said, rubbing his throat. "I said I'd found a way to lift the curse, not that I could lift it myself."

"We need a different sorcerer?" Marjani demanded. "You said we only have two more days. Or was that a lie, too?"

"Two days? Is that all?" Berengar asked, as though he understood what Marjani was talking about. Something in his eyes sent a shiver down Eira's back. He tossed his stick into the fire. "You've come to tell me there's no hope."

"That's not what he said." Eira stood, too, her heart beating faster. "A better sorcerer—"

"There's no time!" Berengar's growl suddenly reminded her very much of the bear.

"Eira." Marjani's pity scared her more than Berengar's hopelessness. "If the curse isn't lifted by the anniversary of its casting, it becomes permanent. Two days from today."

"He'll be trapped like this?" Eira struggled to breathe. "Bear by day, man by night?"

"Just bear," Berengar corrected, voice cold and bleak. "Rurik says I'll stop transforming back and forth. Lose what little humanity I have left."

His despair rolled down his bowed head, his hunched back, the fists pressed against his thighs. It crashed over Eira in waves.

"But—" She spun to Rurik, her fist hardening around her rock. "Why didn't you bring a sorcerer who could lift the curse? Why return at all if you could do no good?"

"*I* can't lift the curse," Rurik repeated. "But someone here in Saebern County can."

Even Berengar looked up.

"*Who?*"

"*Who?*"

"*Who?*"

They sounded like a bunch of owls.

"*That's* the tricky part," Rurik said, wincing. "I don't exactly know."

And if Eira gave into the surge of Nordish bloodlust icing her veins, none of them ever would. She took a slow, careful breath. "*You don't know?*"

Rurik flinched. "Just hear me out before you bash me."

Eira forced her fingers to let go of her rock. *Look at me, Holy Mother. Not killing him at all.* She held up her empty hand. "I'm listening."

"True listening," Marjani commented, settling her spear across her lap, "is one of the Nine Roads to Peace."

"You've been paying attention!" The day continued with its shocking surprises.

"I found the list in your trunk when I borrowed your clothes," Marjani said. "Along with a note from your high priestess admonishing you to follow them."

"Which I *am*," Eira insisted. "I didn't know the bear was an earl when I tried to kill him." She folded her hands piously as she sat beside Marjani. " 'May our thoughts and words and actions here foster peace.' Did you cast this curse, Sorcerer Rurik?"

"No! Of course not. I never cast—"

"The truth." Marjani touched her spear in warning. "Why does that question trouble your spirit so?"

Rurik glanced at Berengar. "I did not cast the *Arkou Devor* curse on the earl here."

"But you *have* cast it on someone else," Eira realized.

"Yes." The word hissed between his teeth. Firelight reflected in his dark eyes, giving the eerie illusion that flames flickered behind them.

Eira's fingers curled on her knees as she resisted the impulse to make a sign against evil. *Peace. Peace.*

"I *attempted* to cast that curse on the man who killed my beloved." Rurik lifted his chin in defiance. "I spent two years traveling the Blessed Kingdoms, hunting the man who ran him down in the street with his horse like a dog because Kazmir got in the way of a race he wanted to win. I stole my master's darkest tome, left my apprenticeship at the sorcerer's guild, and I set out to commit murder."

For a moment, Eira could almost see the darkness Marjani said she sensed in him. She thought maybe she recognized it in herself. "You killed a man? With sorcery?"

"No," Rurik said bitterly. "I cast every deadly curse I could find, from melting the skin off his bones to stopping his heart with a lightning strike. Even one that was supposed to cause a festering rash in his nether regions. None of them affected him at all. The bastard feasted and caroused and thrived, and I realized that even the darkest, deadliest book of sorcery in all Ravnina held no power against wealth and privilege."

Ice coiled in Eira's heart. She knew how it felt to be helpless in the face of evil.

Rurik struggled a moment to gather his thoughts—or suppress his tears. "I forswore my oath of vengeance and reconciled myself to a life of sucking the blood of that wealth and privilege like a charming leech."

"You abandoned your revenge?" Marjani demanded. "How can you rest with Kazmir's killer still alive?"

Rurik laughed, then, a laugh as broken as his smile. "But he's not still alive. When I heard that Prince Guntram had been torn apart by wolves—"

"Prince Guntram!" Eira gaped at him. "Crown Prince Guntram killed your friend?"

"How many people wished to murder that monster?" Marjani's eyes flared with anguish. "His death robbed us all of our vengeance."

"Prince Guntram is *dead?*" Berengar's freckles wrinkled.

"You've missed a lot this year," Eira told him. "But Guntram wasn't killed by wolves—"

"I knew that wasn't true," Rurik scoffed. "As soon as I heard it, I knew the wolves were just a story to cover the fact that he was murdered by his own guards, probably paid off by a member of King Wulfric's court."

The princesses had heard all kinds of wild rumors about Guntram's death before arriving at Newport for King Wulfric's ball. Like Rurik, Holy Mother had told Eira she suspected Guntram had fallen to court intrigue. But Eira had heard the true story directly from Princess Ellycia, who'd been at Guntram's side when the manticore attacked, a story even more incredible than the speculation.

"I know it's hard to believe," Eira said, "but Guntram was actually killed by—"

"And where was *I* when this happened?" Rurik interrupted, jumping to his feet. "I was halfway across the Serpents Teeth looking for a counter-curse, because just when I found a credulous, wealthy host"—he grimaced an apology at

Berengar—"someone stole a page of my master's bedamned book and tossed off one of its most difficult curses like it was a child's nursery rhyme."

"Is it such a surprise that there are better sorcerers than you?" Marjani asked. "You've admitted you're merely an apprentice who stole his master's spells. You're nothing but a charlatan."

"*Yes*. A charlatan." Rurik thumped a fist against his chest. "A good one. Good enough to intrigue dukes and entertain earls. I studied with the best sorcerers in Ravnina. I learned their tricks, watched their showmanship. And I stopped believing in sorcery long ago."

"But—" Eira met Berengar's bleak gaze. "How do you explain him?"

"*I don't know!*" Rurik threw up his hands. "I attempted that curse half a dozen times. Never felt a flicker of power, never so much as killed a spider on the wall. Someone else tears it from the spell book and sets it off—to gods-damned spectacular results—and *that's* when I light up like some kind of sorcerous lightning rod, somehow deflecting its full effect …"

He shook his fingers at them in outraged frustration, and Eira half expected to see sparks.

"When I saw Berengar's transformation, I knew it was the *Arkou Devor* curse." Rurik sat down with a defeated sigh and slapped his rucksack. "I thought maybe I could use the same words to reverse it, but the page had been torn out."

"Stolen from the book *you* stole from your master," Marjani muttered darkly. "Convenient. Why didn't you return to the manor? Tell them what you knew?"

"They would have blamed him for the curse," Berengar said.

"That's not—" Rurik took a breath. "Yes, I feared suspicion would fall on me. But I was also afraid that whoever cast the curse might think I could unmask them. I worried I would be the next to die, before I had a chance to help Berengar."

It had been a very long day, but that wasn't why Eira

hadn't seen the implications before. No, it was simpler than that. She hadn't *wanted* to see them. "You're saying someone at Saebern Manor stole that curse and used it to try to kill Berengar."

"The notes I'd written in the book said the *Arkou Devor* caused its target to get eaten by a bear." Rurik looked sheepish. "Quite a surprise when it turned the earl *into* a bear."

Eira suddenly wished she could return to that morning, to the simple pleasures of bathing in a mountain stream. Or to the evening before. Just her and Berengar by the fire, wondering if he was wondering what it would be like to kiss her. Back to before she'd found out about the curse. Before she knew Berengar was doomed. Before she discovered that the people she'd come here to help might not be innocent victims after all.

But such cowardice was unworthy of Queen Sassa's daughter.

"Someone tried to kill Berengar with that curse," she repeated, her voice hot with an outrage that ignited her sunburn. "They killed two innocent men and turned another into a bear. And then they brought me and Marjani here to finish the job."

CHAPTER TWENTY-TWO

1. *Restvrivo.* Performed [with/by?] the proper/appropriate heart [action], restores that which hath been changed [by?] hate. (And if you've managed to change the actions of your heart, you're a powerful enough sorcerer not to need this stupid spell.)

— Top 10 failed spells translated and performed by Rurik, Ravninan sorcerer (in training)

Marjani tensed as Eira leaped to her feet, rock once more in hand. Even in the dark, the Nordish princess had deadly aim. The missile struck a tree across the small clearing with a thud.

So much for peace.

"You have made a serious charge against our hosts, sorcerer," Marjani said, keeping her voice cool despite her own indignation at Rurik's deception. "But we have no proof beyond your word."

"A curse, a sorcerer." Rurik's smile was grim. "One and one make two."

"You didn't see Rurik that day." Berengar held Marjani's gaze from under his ridiculous hair. "He followed me all afternoon as I raged through the forest, terrified. When I changed back that first night, when we—" His face twisted in misery. "When we thought I'd escaped the curse, he wept with relief."

"Perhaps it was regret," Eira suggested, hard as ice. "He had a change of heart, and he's trying to make it right."

"Why would I curse the man paying my fee as his household entertainer?" Rurik demanded.

"It makes no sense," Marjani agreed. It would be easier if the sorcerer were the villain, but when had her life ever been easy? She was supposed to be killing a bear. Simple. Supposed to be killing a prince. Perhaps not simple, but at least straightforward.

What was she supposed to do with this earl-bear and his sorcerer and these accusations of murder? She still had to return to Newport and face King Wulfric. Avenge her beloved dead. None of the rest of it was her concern.

Except, somehow, these ridiculous people were drawing her into their ridiculous drama and making her want to help solve their ridiculous problems.

"Who *did* have something to gain?" Eira crossed her arms. "Who could possibly have wanted Berengar dead?"

Marjani stared at her.

"Besides Steward Tarben," Eira conceded. "It's obvious he resented Berengar ordering him around. And Lady Silke was furious the old earl named Berengar his heir instead of Artis. And Master Kaspar was angry about his governing style. But besides them—"

"Everyone?" Berengar gave a soft, humorless laugh. "Reeve Wendel campaigned hard for Saebern Town's royal charter. He knew I would fight it."

Rurik shook his head. "If Wendel cast the curse, it should have lifted when he died."

"Killing the caster lifts the curse?" Eira asked, going eerily still. Vengefulness might be one of the Nine Roads to War, but the acolyte of peace looked as though her feet itched to walk it.

"That's often how it works," Rurik said. "But it's also possible it could make the curse permanent instead. Either way, I don't think Wendel could have cast it. He was right beside me when it struck."

"Reeve Wendel shouldn't even have been there," Berengar said, his voice low with grief. "It was supposed to be Master Kaspar and a couple of the wealthy local landowners, but I couldn't bear another day of them badgering me about increasing their profits, so I took Wendel instead. Perhaps his son, Hartwin, cast the curse, not realizing his father was on the hunt."

"Hartwin would not curse you!" Marjani objected, the heat of her response startling even her.

"Why not? He's too handsome?" Rurik asked archly.

"He's too honorable!" Marjani snapped. "He wouldn't curse anyone." But could she be certain of that? She'd known him less than a month. Why couldn't he be a murderer? Because he looked at her as if he saw her? As if she mattered?

When he'd first told her and Eira about Berengar's disappearance, he'd said he hoped the bear had killed the earl. He'd hoped the bear *took his time* killing him.

She had understood that anger at the man responsible for his father's death. But cold-blooded murder to get rid of an inconvenient overlord? She didn't want to believe it.

"He's not a fool." *That* much she knew. "He would have known his father was with you. You said Master Kaspar was supposed to be on the hunt. Perhaps he felt slighted enough to plot murder."

"Master Kaspar, Master Philip, Master Horst, Mistress Susanna—the entire town council wanted me out of the way," Berengar said bitterly. "Whenever I refused to expand the tree harvest or allocate more land for sheep, I saw the loathing in their eyes. I studied history in Rigas, you know. I told them how our ancestors stripped the land and depleted the soil until their economy collapsed. Some left. Some starved. Nordish raiders and the Devastation killed most of the rest. It's taken five hundred years for Saebern to return to prosperity. I wanted to protect that prosperity, but all they saw was arrogance."

They were the most words Marjani had heard him say at one time, and he clenched his jaw as though he regretted them escaping. She could understand the town leaders' response. Hard enough to hear unpopular ideas from one of your own. Easy to dismiss them from a prideful young man who was practically a foreigner.

Easy to believe that if that young man were gone, their problems would be solved.

"The curse isn't *all* bad," Berengar admitted quietly. This must be the Berengar Eira saw. Shy rather than haughty. "Bears don't mind if no one wants them around."

"Your bear ripped out a sheep's heart and nailed it to the manor gate," Marjani pointed out, as much to remind herself as him. She already felt halfway responsible for Eira's safety. She didn't want to be drawn into caring what happened to this unsafe, inconvenient earl.

"I'd forgotten that." Berengar ran a hand through his shaggy hair and ducked an embarrassed glance at her. "I think I had some vague idea of nailing my own heart to the gate to convince everyone I belonged to Saebern, after all, but that didn't seem feasible."

The others shared an uneasy glance.

Eira sat beside him and laid a hand on his. "The good news is that someone here in Saebern can lift the curse."

"No." Marjani had already glimpsed the dark end to Rurik's tale. "I think that is the bad news."

"All that time I wasted trying to undo the curse," Rurik mourned. "I roamed for months, searching the Blessed Kingdoms for a cure. I didn't dare return to Rovka, of course. I knew an apprentice who had his thumb cut off for spilling tea on his master's robes. I didn't want to find out what they would do to someone with the skill and audacity to steal a book of dark magic from under a sorcerer's very nose—"

"Give us the short version," Marjani commanded.

"Fine," he huffed. "It was a blessing I couldn't return to those old frauds in Ravnina because that's not where the answer lay. After months of failure, I was ready to succumb to despair when I remembered a story my grandmother used to tell. A legend, of sorts—"

"Shorter," Eira interrupted. "You said we only have two days."

"The trackless forests of the Serpents Teeth. Giants. Monsters. Cheating death. And so forth." Rurik waved a hand. Ever the showman. "I sought out an old witch who lives deep in the mountains. There was a question of whether or not she might cook me for supper, but I charmed her into hearing my plea."

"She must have been desperately lonely," Marjani muttered, making Berengar snort.

Rurik heaved a long-suffering sigh. "She knew of the curse, *Arkou Devor*. It comes from the ancient Santi Empire, before the Devastation, back when the Santi split their worship between gods and demons."

"Hedging their bets," Eira said. "Holy Mother says the Santians made the mistake of denying the dark aspects of their own humanity and attributed them to—"

"Now who's digressing?" Rurik asked. "She said the ancient Santi death curses all had one thing in common. They require a dark focus, generally hatred or fear, although greed or jealousy may work, and can only be cast by an almost superhuman malicious will."

"Is that why you couldn't cast it?" Eira asked.

The darkness in Rurik's spirit shifted. Marjani could almost see it writhing around his heart like a snake. She half expected him to feed it with a lie, but instead, he shook his head.

"That's what I thought. That my will wasn't strong enough. That I had failed to avenge Kazmir through weakness. I begged the witch to help me, to teach me how to strengthen my hatred so I could complete the spell, but—"

"But she refused to endanger your soul by helping you become a murderer," Eira finished, shooting Marjani a smug glance.

"No. She said I had a deep well of hatred. That wasn't the problem. I hadn't been able to cast the curse …" His words faltered, and color rose in his cheeks. "The witch said Kazmir's love was protecting me from the evil I wanted to do."

He shrugged, suddenly looking more boy than sorcerer. "I asked if it was the memory of his love that protected me or if his spirit was still watching over me, but she said I was a hopeless idiot, and if I didn't stop bothering her, she would chop me up and feed me to her chickens."

"And you expect us to take advice from this violent recluse?" Marjani asked.

"*I've* threatened to chop Rurik up more than once," Berengar said. Red suffused his freckles at Marjani's raised eyebrows. "Oh. I see your point."

"Princess Raisa told me her father's sorcerers claim they are the only practitioners of true magical knowledge in the world," Marjani told Rurik. "It is hard to believe a sorcerer would go to a hedge witch for wisdom."

"Are you saying sorcerers are arrogant?" Rurik demanded, his back stiffening, dark eyes flashing. Then his teeth flashed, too, in a sharp smile. "Haughty, self-important, vain. It's all true. But I learned more wisdom at my grandmother's hearth than I ever did in Rovka. Grandmother said the witch in the mountains was already ancient when she was a child and that she knew more about the old sorcery than anyone else alive."

He held Marjani's gaze. "I felt the curse when it struck Berengar. Whoever cast it hated him with a will deadly enough to kill."

A chill crept up Marjani's arms. She understood such hatred. If she had possessed such a spell while Prince Guntram was alive, nothing would have stopped her from casting it. For although she had surely loved Mosi and Dejen as much as Rurik loved Kazmir, no one had ever loved her as much as Kazmir had loved Rurik.

"I believe you," Eira said quietly, fingering the little charm she wore around her neck. "Someone here in Saebern tried to murder Berengar. So tell us who can lift the curse."

Marjani had teased her about the way Berengar watched her. How had she missed the way Eira looked at him? Of course, Eira got "swoony" half a dozen times a day. But this was not her sighing appreciation for Hartwin's eyes. Or the strategic flirting she used on Prince Theodor. Something fierce burned in her gaze. An understanding, perhaps. The connection that came from understanding. Along with a fierce determination to save Berengar from his curse.

And Rurik had misled the impractical, idealistic fool into thinking they had a chance in all the hells of doing it.

"Why did you even bother to return?" Marjani asked. "Tell them. It's impossible."

"It's *not* impossible," Rurik said. "Santian death magic derives its power from the will of the caster. Therefore, if the caster has a change of heart, he can undo the curse at any time with a simple spell. And I still have *that* spell in my book."

"The caster." Marjani might have chopped him up herself if she hadn't already returned Eira's sword. "The person who hated Berengar enough to steal a sorcerer's spell. The person still hoping someone will kill the bear and finish the deed. That's the one person in the entire world who can lift the curse."

She knew Berengar had already reached the same conclusion. He sat with head bowed in silent resignation. He'd never expected a reprieve from his fate.

Eira, on the other hand … Her skin had a sickly pallor beneath her sunburn, but her eyes were stubborn as ever. "Then we just need to figure out who it is and make them cast the counter-curse."

"Whoever it is will never agree," Berengar told her.

"Of course they will." Steel laced Eira's bright tone. "I'll convince them."

Marjani gritted her teeth against the surge of grief cracking her heart. How cruel could the gods be, to make her watch Eira break under the same inability to save those she cared about that had severed her own soul?

Berengar clenched his hands and stared up at the stars. "Hasn't it occurred to any of you that it might be better if I don't return? When the curse is complete, my bear will be just a bear. It can be killed. The county will be safe. No one will miss me if I just stay gone."

"Leaving a murderer at large?" Eira shot back. "You can't just give up!"

"Tell her it's impossible—"

"Tell him we can do it—"

For some reason, they were both looking at Marjani—Eira in hope, Berengar in despair, and she couldn't decide which infuriated her more. She had one purpose here in Saebern, one chance to earn her way close enough to Prince Theodor to kill him, and these two had ruined it.

"If I could say something here—" Rurik began.

"No." Marjani rose, her emotions thundering about her. "There's nothing more to say. In the morning, we will return to Saebern Manor, find the person who cast the curse, and compel them to lift it."

Eira jumped up, her smile blinding. "I admit it. I was wrong. You're not so bad, after all, Princess Marjani."

Even Marjani's sharpest glare couldn't douse the girl's grin.

"Don't read too much into it, Princess Eira," she warned. "I swore I would rid Saebern County of its enchanted bear. I always keep my vows."

CHAPTER TWENTY-THREE

5. *Dyrna Hythan.* An evident and simple (ha!) incantation to render thyself [immune?] from the sight of thine enemies. (Yes? Or maybe it just makes thyself *more* visible, you stupid, worthless tome of gibberish.)

— Top 10 failed spells translated and performed by Rurik, Ravninan sorcerer (in training)

Berengar was gone by morning, but the bear brought them fish for breakfast. Eira glimpsed him in the early dawn light, though she pretended to be asleep like the others. How had she not seen Berengar in the bear sooner? The wariness of his approach, nose up in arrogant-seeming defense, the sly humor as he dropped the fish near Eira and nudged them closer. The duck of his head as he paused at the edge of the clearing, glancing back with a heartbreaking longing that reminded her of his words the night before.

Hasn't it occurred to any of you that it might be better if I don't return? No one will miss me if I just stay gone.

Not true. Eira's heart constricted as she watched the bear pad into the woods, the gold of his coat melting into the dappled light beneath the trees. He'd promised not to disappear. He might be ambivalent about returning to Saebern but not about protecting his people. That would be enough to keep him close.

It had to be.

But there was so little time to help him. And so much to lose if they failed.

How much better it would be for Berengar if Eira were one of the other princesses vying for Prince Theo's hand: Princess Jax, with her almost uncanny ability to get people to work together. Princess Beatrix, trained to dig out anyone's deepest, darkest secrets. Even Princess Isolde, who could probably convince the curse caster to reveal himself by simply batting her eyes.

Instead, Berengar had to rely on an exiled former princess who had failed to keep her mother safe, failed to prevent her uncle from stealing her crown, failed to complete the quest that might convince King Wulfric she was worthy of marrying his son and bringing peace to the Blessed Kingdoms.

Of course, if she hadn't failed at Wulfric's quest, Berengar would be dead.

He's alive. There's a chance.

She tried to focus on that desperate hope as she trudged after Marjani and Rurik through Saebern's rugged wilderness, retracing their route following the bear's tracks the day before. Yes, she might have chosen other champions for Berengar's rescue than a fraudulent sorcerer and her own worst rival. But Rurik had deflected a curse once. He might be able to do it again.

And Marjani …

Now that she'd committed to helping Berengar, Marjani was too unspeakably stubborn to give up. Eira smiled. It still warmed her heart that the Almasan princess had been so happy to discover she was alive.

"If only you'd actually drowned," Marjani grumbled as they crested yet another hill and stared down the steep slope ahead. "I would have dispatched Saebern's bear and be on my way back to Newport by now. We won't even reach the manor until afternoon."

"We'd be farther along if Rurik hadn't spent all that time fussing over my hair," Eira said. "Cutting it off would have been faster."

"I've never seen such straight hair that tangled," Rurik marveled.

Eira lifted a self-conscious hand to the elaborate plait circling her head.

"Don't muss it," he ordered, swatting her hand away. "Appearances matter. Appearances and attitude. Half of Ravninan sorcery is skill with fire powders and sleight of hand, and half is how sinister you look performing it. If we're going to trick the curse caster into revealing themselves, we need to be intimidating."

"How is Eira's hair intimidating? She might unwind it and strangle someone?" Marjani scoffed.

"It looks like a crown," Rurik said. "It reminds everyone you're princesses. To people under the thumb of a despot, there is nothing more intimidating than royalty—unless it's a sorcerer."

He straightened his back, lifted his chin, and raised a single, slashing eyebrow. And suddenly, despite his travel-worn clothes, Eira's attention was caught by the embroidery at his cuffs, the haughty gloss of his black hair, the dangerous flash of his dark eyes.

An uncanny shiver ran up her spine, fearful and thrilling. In that moment, he *was* a Ravninan sorcerer.

"Impressive." She glanced down at her stained tunic and battered boots. "You make a better sorcerer than I do a princess."

"What do you think a princess should look like?" Marjani asked. "Isolde of Montaine? All golden hair and silk gowns?"

"Yes. Just like Isolde. She is *definitely* intimidating."

Marjani thumped the butt of her spear into the dirt of the deer track they followed. She beat a complicated rhythm as she walked that made Eira's heart pound with the cadence of the hunt. "You think she is more intimidating than I?"

A sennight ago, Eira would have thought Marjani was offended. Of course, maybe a sennight ago, Eira would have tried to offend her.

Holy Mother's favorite form of discipline was to assign aphorisms for wayward acolytes to memorize. On more than one occasion—possibly several more—she had given Eira the text, "How difficult it is, once one's feet are set, to step off the path of war."

Each time, Eira would tell her, "I know that one already."

And each time, Holy Mother would reply, "But you obviously don't understand it yet. You'll know when you do."

Goddess. Holy Mother was right again.

"No one is more intimidating than you, Princess Marjani." Eira offered her a sweeping bow.

"Not even a merciless Nordish barbarian with all the self-discipline of an adolescent monkey?"

When she put it that way … Eira's hand moved to the sword on her hip. She lifted her head as though her hair were a circlet of gleaming gold and narrowed her eyes to icy slits.

Marjani sniffed. "If you get rid of that ridiculous grin, people might take you seriously."

Eira widened her smile so her teeth showed. "Appearances and attitude."

"Enough!" Rurik shuddered. "I'd confess anything just to get the two of you to stop."

"I'd feel fiercer if I had my bow," Eira admitted as the path narrowed down the steepest part of the slope. She fell in after Marjani, Rurik behind them.

"You stood up to a bear last night in your underclothes," Marjani said, "with nothing but a knife tied to a stick. You don't need a bow to feel powerful."

Eira was glad Marjani couldn't see her blush. Did she really see a strength in Eira that everyone else seemed to overlook? That almost sounded like admiration in the Almasan princess's voice.

"But that was stupid," Rurik said.

Eira swallowed her protest. He had a point.

"If we succeed in our plan, we will be confronting someone willing to murder to get what they want," Marjani said. "We must convince a cold-hearted killer to perform a spell to save an enchanted bear that person wants dead."

To save a young man who never deserved to be cursed. Eira's heart tightened. An awkward young man with a good heart, a thoughtful mind, and impossibly adorable freckles. And if they didn't succeed, he would be doomed to live as a bear for the rest of his lonely, brutal life.

Doomed, abandoned, betrayed, just like Eira's mother. Another person she cared about lost because she wasn't strong enough, brave enough, smart enough to save him.

"And we only have until tomorrow to do it," Marjani concluded. "This is a quest that *requires* stupid, foolish courage. We could not ask for a better exemplar than Princess Eira."

Which was obviously meant to offend her, right out of her gloomy self-pity. Gallingly, it worked, sending a bracing spark through her veins. Foolish courage might as well be the *motto* of Nordish royalty. Surrender—to an enemy, to fate, to some ridiculous curse—that was the only failure. Queen Sassa had died, but she had never *given up*.

Eira smacked Marjani's shoulder. "Foolish courage and mule-headed resolve, an invincible combination. It's good we're finally on the same team. See how wrong you were to try to leave me behind?"

Marjani snorted. "Only because it didn't work."

"I *did* find the bear first."

"If you think the bear dragging you from the stream where you were *drowning* counts as 'finding' it—"

"A whole *four days* before you found him."

"Oh, look." Rurik pushed past them as they reached the bottom of the hill. "There's the woodcutters' camp. Only

another league or two of your bickering to suffer through
…"

His voice trailed off as he stepped into the clearing.

"What's wrong?" Marjani demanded. "Is something different?"

Rurik shook his head. "I think … I think it's my eyes that are different."

Eira followed Marjani out of the trees. In her head, "woodcutters' camp" had somehow translated itself into "woodsman's cottage." She had pictured something from a fairy tale, a small cabin in a meadow, smoke from a cook fire, a little garden. Perhaps a pair of children playing among the herbs—a happy time before their parents abandoned them in the forest to be eaten by a wicked witch because the parents couldn't afford to feed them anymore.

This camp was a work site. A couple of rough canvas tents. An open-sided cooking shed. Another shed for tools—she could tell because its door had been ripped off by an angry creature with very large claws. Saws and axes lay scattered in the dirt.

But that destruction was paltry compared to the devastation around them. Nearly every tree in the shallow valley had been cut down. Smaller trees lay flattened by the larger trees' falling. Stripped limbs scattered the scarred earth, removed for easier transporting of the trunks.

I told them how our ancestors stripped the land and depleted the soil until their economy collapsed. It's taken five hundred years for Saebern to return to prosperity.

Eira's lungs squeezed in her chest. How long would it take *this* forest to return? Or would it be turned into more sheep pasture and never recover? At the moment, she couldn't imagine even sheep finding anything to eat amid the desolation.

"Saebern is renowned for its tall, straight pines," Rurik said, staring at the destruction. "They provide masts for many kingdoms' fleets. A highly profitable export. You can understand why the lumber merchants didn't want Berengar to curb their trade."

"Do your people cut the trees of the taiga like this?" Eira asked.

He could only shake his head.

"Profit is a powerful motive," Marjani said darkly. She strode into the maze of detritus. "Our quarry could be a wealthy man hoping to increase his wealth even more."

"Or wealthy woman," Rurik said. "It isn't only men who are greedy or vengeful."

Eira knew that well enough.

"But who had the opportunity to steal the spell from your book?" she asked, tugging her cloak free from a pile of discarded branches. The smell of pine sap stung her nose.

"Berengar considered it his duty to host dinners for the county's merchants and minor nobles," Rurik said. "They might not have loved him, but they loved eating his food and drinking his wine." He shook out his sleeves, making the silver threads glimmer. "And he offered them excellent entertainment. Which means I spent those gatherings focused on illusions and timing—"

"And flirting," Marjani suggested dryly.

"An essential part of the craft," Rurik acknowledged. "Anyone might have slipped into my room on their way to the privy, and I would have been none the wiser. I kept the wretched book in my rucksack under the bed. I hadn't opened it in months, so I have no idea when the spell went missing."

"Perhaps next time you steal a collection of deadly curses, you could safeguard them more carefully," Marjani suggested, stepping gracefully over a broken sapling. "It would be helpful if we could narrow down our culprit."

"I *know*," Rurik snapped. "I thought the spells were worthless. I actually sold one in Cadesleigh for traveling money. A ridiculous bit of nastiness that no one could ever use. It turns an assassin into—"

"It doesn't matter," Eira interrupted. The weight of the

curse and its deadline lay heavy on her shoulders, but Holy Mother always said you couldn't walk the roads to peace if you were mired in despair. "We can't fix the past. We can only act on the assumption the curse caster is someone who knew Berengar was on that hunt a year ago. Someone we can flush from hiding if we do this right."

"We will not relent until we have lifted the curse or the deadline has passed," Marjani said, holding Eira's gaze. "We will have nothing to regret."

A half-smile tilted Rurik's mouth. "You two are the least likely sorcerer hunters I can imagine, but you don't know how to give up. It doesn't matter who cast that curse. They're no match for you."

"Appearances and attitude," Eira said, mostly to make Marjani roll her eyes. "Nothing can stop us now."

"Halt!" A commanding voice echoed from the hillsides around them, startling Eira into obeying. "Don't move! Stay right where you are."

A dozen armed men burst from the trees ahead of them. From gangly boys who looked more like shepherds than soldiers to a white-bearded grandfather wearing what could pass for thousand-year-old pre-Devastation armor, they appeared to be a fairly hapless outlaw band. But why would outlaws be attacking a woodcutters camp …

Bear hunters. Not outlaws at all. They probably thought she, Marjani, and Rurik were outlaws.

"It's all right!" Eira called. "We're guests of Steward Tarben. We're just returning to Saebern manor."

The men didn't lower their weapons as they began to spread out.

"You tell them." Eira nudged Marjani. "You're better with people."

But Marjani didn't move, limbs frozen as still as if she were a figure carved from one of the fallen trees, her eyes wide with what looked like anguish.

"Marjani?" Eira prodded, eyeing the men beginning to encircle them.

Marjani shuddered and blinked hard as if awakening from a nightmare. But confusion lingered in the furrow that deepened between her brows.

"Hartwin?" Even Marjani's voice sounded strange. "What's going on?"

One of the men stepped toward them. He wore a leather cuirass and a battered helmet that hid his face—except for the blue-green eyes that showed on either side of the nose-piece. Eyes as hard as sea stone.

It might be Hartwin, if more had changed during her absence than Eira had imagined.

And the older man beside him, with the great black beard and a breastplate that barely covered his broad chest, was the wool merchant, Master Kaspar. These men who looked like shepherds and tradesmen … bear hunters, just as she'd thought.

So why did she suddenly feel so uneasy?

"Princess Marjani. Princess Eira—I see you are not dead. Set down your weapons," Hartwin ordered, voice as cold as his eyes. "I am taking you into custody."

CHAPTER TWENTY-FOUR

4. She never expresses her feelings.

— Top 10 things ~~I hate~~ I find difficult to appreciate about Princess Marjani, as listed by (former) Princess Eira of Nordmark

Ambush, betrayal, death. No! Not again. Marjani shook her head, pushing away the images that tried to fill her mind. Bloodied swords, her brother's body, Dejen's blank eyes, wide with surprise.

She was not unarmed this time. Her hand clenched around her spear's haft until her palm ached with the pressure. But she could not seem to move her arm. Could not even seem to breathe. She watched as if from far away and underwater, unable to cry out in warning, as Eira gaped beside her.

"You're not arresting us!" Eira said. "This is all just a misunderstanding."

Staring into Hartwin's stormy eyes, Marjani doubted that.

"We understand quite well," Master Kaspar said, one beringed hand on the hilt of his sword. "You have deceived your hosts, betrayed your oath to King Wulfric, and are even now aiding and abetting a known sorcerer and suspected murderer."

"Rurik of Ravnina," Hartwin said. "You're supposed to be dead."

So much for that obscuring spell.

Rurik moved up to Marjani's side and curled his lip. "I'm hard to kill."

"Is that a challenge?" Hartwin snarled.

He stormed forward, but Marjani stepped between the two men, her limbs suddenly obeying her. *No more slaughter!* She lifted a hand to Hartwin's chest, his momentum making her stumble. He cursed and caught himself—then caught her arm before she could fall.

Even through his leather cuirass, she felt the heat of his anger. Confusion and betrayal roiled the depths of his sea-green eyes. His fingers tightened on her elbow, but he didn't shove her aside.

Of course, he wouldn't dare. She was a princess. Her father would lop the hand off anyone who touched her in anger—anyone but himself. It was only her imagination that Hartwin held her a moment longer than necessary.

His gaze shifted to Rurik as he stepped back. "You have colluded with this sorcerer, Princess Marjani, knowing he is a swindler and a murderer."

"Don't be silly!" Eira said. "He didn't kill anybody."

"Rurik has spent the past year learning how to lift Saebern's curse," Marjani said, her voice thick but steady. "He's returned to make things right."

"Make things right!" Hartwin's scorn cut more sharply than his rage. "You can't be so naive as to believe that. If there's a curse on our county, he's the one who laid it. He killed my father."

"Your father saved my life." The anger drained from Rurik's voice, weighed heavy with regret. "He pushed me aside when the boar charged, when everything went to hells."

"After you cast your curse?" Master Kaspar accused.

"You abandoned him," Hartwin said. "You left him there to bleed to death."

Even his concealing helmet could not hide the agony of a boy who'd lost his father. If Marjani had a heart left, it would have cracked for him.

"By the time I reached Reeve Wendel, he was dead," Rurik said. "As was Marshal Falk. There was nothing I could have done."

"You could have brought us word." Hartwin's voice was cold. "Instead of leaving us to find their bodies."

"An innocent man," Master Kaspar put in, "wouldn't have left us to wonder whether or not our earl would return."

"*Please*," Rurik scoffed. "None of you wasted any tears on poor, missing Earl Berengar. I saw how you all treated him. Resentment. Scorn. The only one to offer him any kindness was Reeve Wendel."

Master Kaspar bristled. "Marshal Falk tried to teach him—"

"Falk treated Berengar like a spoiled puppy who might yet be re-trained into a decent dog."

The wool merchant tugged on his sword. Fortunately, the hilt caught on the bottom of his breastplate.

"Stop this!" Marjani commanded. Despite the memory of screams that still rang harshly in her ears, her voice cracked like a whip. Not even her father could have managed a more imperious tone. A sudden wariness flickered in the eyes of the men around her. Appearances and attitude, indeed. "I have brought this sorcerer back to lift your curse and rid you of your bear. You will escort us to Saebern Manor so I may complete my duty to King Wulfric."

"You have brought two people back from the dead," Hartwin noted bitterly. "Just not the two I would have chosen."

"Ouch." Eira's bright smile didn't quite mask the hurt. "I know I wasn't the knight you were hoping for, but I thought we'd become friends on that awful boat."

"I thought so, too." Hartwin's gaze slid back to Marjani.

"Until you betrayed that friendship. All that talk of your duty to rid us of our bear, and you return with a snake instead."

Anger flared through the clouds of horrific memory. But guilt came with it. She *had* lied to him.

"*Goddess.*" Eira sheathed her sword with a loud sigh. "Just let us explain. We need that snake to get rid of the bear."

"Hey!" Rurik objected.

"Sorry. Rurik isn't a snake, and the bear isn't the curse. The bear *is* cursed." Eira paused. "Well, it's not so much the bear that's cursed. The thing is, you don't have a bear problem because the bear isn't actually a *bear*—"

"*Eira,*" Marjani cut her off. How had everything gone so wrong so fast? This wasn't their plan. She herself had suggested explaining everything to Hartwin. But Rurik had pointed out that undoubtedly the only reason the curse caster hadn't tried to curse Berengar again was that the caster didn't know he was still alive.

Rurik and Eira hoped they could trick the caster into lifting the curse by asking everyone in the manor to try the counter-curse. Surely the caster would be eager to get rid of the bear if they didn't realize the spell would restore Berengar.

Hartwin's strange coldness now made Marjani fear they had chosen rightly not to confide in him.

"Ignore my babbling," Eira said. "All these weapons pointing at us are making me tense. I'd hate to have to slice anyone to pieces today."

The men stiffened, raising those weapons.

"Step back," Hartwin ordered them. He held out his hand to Marjani. "Give me your spear. It's for your own safety. They're nervous."

"*They're* nervous?" Eira said in disbelief.

But, of course, they were. Marjani could see it in the men's rigid grips on their weapons, the fearful suspicion in their eyes as she reflexively pulled her spear out of Hartwin's reach.

They were facing two slender women and an unarmed

man no taller than Marjani. Yet what they saw were three strangers. Three foreigners. One with mismatched eyes—*wraith eyes*. One the descendent of barbaric Nordish raiders. One who claimed to be a sorcerer.

"Demonization of the outsider," she murmured.

"One of the Nine Roads to War," Eira agreed.

"A dozen against three isn't a war," Rurik said apprehensively. "It's barely a skirmish."

Marjani had sworn never to be defenseless again. Never to be rendered helpless and forced to watch while those she loved were slaughtered. *Pain, terror, death* … She forced down the scream in her throat.

She wasn't defenseless now. She had her spear. She could fight. None of these men knew the fury that burned inside her. If Hartwin ordered them to attack, she would spill gallons, lakes, oceans of blood before they could take her down.

Hartwin's blood? Master Kaspar's? That youth, so jerky with nerves she feared that he would hack his own thigh with the hatchet he carried before he ever got a chance to swing it at anyone else?

And then she would be dead. Her vengeance would be left undone. Eira left dead again. Berengar lost and Saebern still cursed by its monstrous bear.

Beside her, Eira sighed. "They're taking us where we want to go, anyway. We don't want to hurt anyone."

There it was. They'd come to Saebern to help these people. They couldn't do that by killing them.

As Eira unbuckled her sword belt and Rurik passed his knife to Kaspar, Marjani handed her spear to Hartwin. When his fingers wrapped around the wooden shaft, the storm of emotions he was keeping so carefully in check crashed over her, mixing with her own. A rush of grief and rage and betrayal and … guilt.

"You *knew*," she realized, suddenly sick with the knowledge. "When you spoke to me yesterday morning, you knew I was sneaking out of the manor to hunt for the bear."

She remembered his seemingly offhand words. *The beast chased a group of woodcutters from their work yesterday. Just over that next ridge there.* Hartwin hadn't accosted her at the chapel to woo her. He'd laid a trap. And she'd walked right in.

"I gave you a chance to tell me what you were doing." His eyes were hard, but they didn't quite meet hers. "To trust me. You lied to me instead."

The tightness in her throat nearly swallowed her words. "Why didn't you just ask?"

"I'm reeve of Saebern Town." The tendons in his hand on the spear looked so tight they might snap. "I have a duty to protect it from those who wish us harm."

"You believe I wish you harm?" Her words tasted like tears. Where was that fierce warrior princess Eira seemed to see in her?

Hartwin jerked his chin toward Rurik. Master Kaspar was tying the sorcerer's hands behind his back, presumably considering them potential weapons. Several of the men carried coils of rope. Had Hartwin planned to truss them all up like game if they didn't surrender quietly?

"I meant only to follow you, to see what you would do." Hartwin's voice ground from pain into accusation. "Until I saw your companion. Saw you conspiring with the man who murdered my father."

"Rurik didn't kill your father."

"Then let him prove it." He pulled the spear from her nerveless hand. "If the sorcerer is innocent, he can convince Steward Tarben and the town council. It doesn't matter what I believe."

He gestured for her to follow the others as they started up the track toward Saebern Manor.

Show nothing, girl. Pretend to have courage. Her father would scorn her injured feelings. Scorn her having any feelings at all, especially toward a common-born northerner. A baker! *If I must tolerate your existence, you must at least* appear *to be a princess worthy of my tolerance.*

In truth, her father scorned her regardless of her adherence to his commands. He hadn't sent her to Aldforth as his representative. He'd sent her as his assassin, fully aware that if she fulfilled his vengeance, she would die far from home, undoubtedly in the most brutal way King Wulfric could invent.

What did he know of her courage? Agreeing to be sent, knowing that completing her mission would not only satisfy her father's revenge but also rid him of the inconvenient daughter he'd never wanted.

The courage it took to look Hartwin in the eye. "What you believe matters to me."

She brushed past him to stride after her fellow captives.

CHAPTER TWENTY-FIVE

7. She's too obnoxious for anyone to like.

— Top 10 things I despise about Princess Eira, as listed
by Princess Marjani of Almasa

"You don't realize how much trouble you are in," Master Kaspar said. He walked the broad track at Eira's side, watching her narrow-eyed as if he suspected she might bolt back into the wilderness. "I've always said that bear was enchanted. Anyone involved in such dark magic must face justice."

"I agree." Eira offered him her most amiable smile. At least, the most amiable she could manage around her fury at being treated like a criminal. He actually flinched away from her slightly, but she pressed on. "That's why we're here. To help you find the person responsible."

"We have the man responsible." The wool merchant nodded toward Rurik, who walked just ahead of them, flanked by two burly young farmers.

Despite his bound hands, the sorcerer held his head high, chin jutted with hauteur. Appearance and attitude. It seemed to be working on Kaspar.

"Rurik did not enchant the bear," Eira said, already tired

of repeating it. "If you'd just listen to us, you'd save yourself a lot of embarrassment later."

"He's a sorcerer," Kaspar said, face stony above his generous beard. "He has cursed our county, and we will hold him to account. There has been no death magic in Aldforth for centuries, but the laws still stand. The punishment is death at the stake."

Rurik's back stiffened, and a chill ran down Eira's spine.

As foreign royalty, she and Marjani were exempt from Aldforthian capital punishment. Theoretically. Of course, King Wulfric would face no serious consequences if he executed *her*—Uncle Einar would be overjoyed at the news. Even Marjani might not be safe, not with the king eager to blame someone for Prince Guntram's murder by manticore. But neither of them was as vulnerable as a common-born Ravninan sorcerer's apprentice.

She had judged him a coward for not bringing the news of Berengar's curse to the manor the previous summer. Now that his fear had proven all too real, she respected his courage in returning now.

Eira lifted her chin as if her carefully braided hair were indeed a crown. "You have no evidence Rurik has used death magic, and we mean to flush out the true villain. Once the curse is lifted, your justice may be served. I do hope, for your sake, that it doesn't turn out to be you."

Something flickered in the merchant's eyes. Surprise? Fear?

"Don't concern yourself with me," he flung back, pulling a handkerchief from his pocket to swipe the sweat from his ruddy face. "Look to your own soul's deliverance."

He didn't speak to her again after that. The entire company lapsed into an edgy, distrustful silence as the forested hills opened to rocky fields and crofter cottages. As the day wore into afternoon, they trudged to the top of a narrow ridge. Below stretched the Saebern River valley, town and farms, tamed and prosperous. Ahead, the ridge stretched between the forested wilderness on one side and Saebern Manor on the other.

The sight softened Eira's resentment. These people worked hard to carve a good living from this place they loved. A place not so different from the wild valleys and sea villages of her homeland. People not so different from the herders and fishers her mother had ruled. The people Queen Sassa had given her life to protect from King Wulfric and his army.

Berengar had spent his childhood among these hills and pastures. This might be the very track along which he'd made his desperate flight from that homicidal Saebernian hare. A smile tugged her mouth, even as her heart broke for that little boy, sent away from his home and family to a place so distant and different that when he returned, he might as well have been a stranger.

Uprooted. Unmissed. Socially … inexpert. No wonder she and Berengar understood each other. They were like two arrows fletched from feathers of the same goose.

Except for the whole turning-into-a-bear thing.

What if she were cursed, too? She could imagine disappearing into the hills, padding alongside Berengar's great beast, shoulders brushing, breathing huge bear breaths of pine-scented air. And if she got hungry, she could just meander over to a mountain stream and …

Fish.

She grimaced. Anyway, it wasn't as if she could let a killer go free. And if she didn't break Berengar's curse, his freckles would be gone forever. An incalculable loss.

Master Kaspar dropped back and ostentatiously waved Marjani ahead to walk with her. The merchant slowed and drew Hartwin back farther. Still, he was breathing hard enough that his words reached their ears.

"We need to take them to the town hall," Kaspar huffed to the reeve. "The cells there are better equipped to hold dangerous criminals than the manor."

Eira caught Marjani's eye, the Almasan's green and amber

gaze as appalled as her own. They had to expose the curse caster before morning. They couldn't do that from a cell.

"Steward Tarben wants them brought to the manor for questioning," Hartwin said curtly, as if he'd made this same argument before.

"Tarben isn't our earl—"

"He speaks for our countess."

"A child whom his orders endanger!" Kaspar growled back.

"You overstate the threat," Hartwin said. "I will not put princesses in a thief's cell. They did not come to Saebern meaning us harm—"

"You saw your father's body," Kaspar reminded him. "The ground soaked with Falk's blood. Gods only know what fate that halfwit Berengar suffered. These *princesses* conspired with the sorcerer who killed them. You can't believe a word they say."

"You seem awfully determined not to let us speak, Master Kaspar," Eira called over her shoulder, ice sharpening her voice. "What are you trying to hide?"

"*Hide?*" The merchant's beard quivered with indignation. "I am trying to protect my friends and neighbors."

"Protect them from the truth?"

Kaspar sputtered, but it was Hartwin who spoke. "You made a pretense of your own death. You have no right to lecture anyone on the truth."

"I wasn't pretending!"

Kaspar had the gall to snort, and the nearest of the armed men laughed.

Eira opened her mouth, but Marjani gave her a tiny head shake. Eira guessed she was right. Arguing with that pig-headed Kaspar would get them nowhere. They should focus on Tarben, though Eira couldn't help a burgeoning dread that the steward might prove no more reasonable than the merchant.

The track split just ahead, one branch leading down

through the sheep pastures to the town, another continuing along the ridge. The men paused, glancing back to Hartwin for direction.

"To the manor," he ordered.

"The council will not approve," Kaspar warned. "As reeve, you serve at our discretion."

"And you can replace me," Hartwin said. "When the council meets." He strode past Eira and Marjani at a brisk pace, leaving the wool merchant huffing behind.

"Toadying to a *steward*." Kaspar's voice bit with scorn. "That's what we get for putting our trust in a callow young man."

Ironic, Eira thought, because for the first time, she truly saw Hartwin as a reeve, not just as her formerly genial traveling companion. He'd made a decision that might cost him his position, and he meant to see it through because he thought it was right.

Glancing at Marjani, she caught the flicker of longing and loss that darkened the eyes of her competitor … her accomplice … her frie—

No need for labels.

"He's doing his duty, not what his heart says," Eira murmured. "He'll listen when we explain what's happened. He'll forgive you."

"For what?" Marjani snapped, voice low, eyes flashing. "For doing *my* duty? For trying to protect his precious county and find justice for his father's death?"

Eira did not point out that self-righteousness was one of the Nine Roads to War.

"For not trusting him enough to tell him the truth," she said instead. *For breaking his heart.*

"He didn't trust me enough to tell *me* the truth!"

"You've known each other barely a fortnight," Eira reminded her. "You both need to realize that trust takes time."

"The only people I ever trusted are dead."

"I trust you," Eira said, surprising herself almost as much

as she'd obviously surprised Marjani. "More than I ever thought I would—despite you sneaking out on me the day after we got here. People always say trust is earned, but no one can earn your trust if you don't let them. I'm glad I gave you another chance."

Marjani's brittle anger cracked, showing the uncertainty beneath. "Hartwin tricked me. He brought an armed force to capture us. What if Hartwin is the one …"

Who cast the curse. Eira swallowed hard. She understood why Marjani couldn't say it, as if the words themselves might make it true.

"He wouldn't," she said. "His father—"

"What if his father was the one who told him it needed to be done?" Marjani's face was a mask of misery. "He's so angry. So bitter about his father's death. What if he blames himself?"

"I can't tell you it's impossible, but …" Eira leaned closer and lowered her voice. "I still think Master Kaspar makes a better villain. Imagine him with wolf's teeth and a grandmother's cap …"

That pulled the hint of a smile from Marjani. "Yes, we have a children's story like that, too. His beard does remind me of a lion's mane—"

"Stop that!" Kaspar barked, laboring behind them. "Stop whispering, or I'll tie you up like the sorcerer."

"What did I tell you?" Eira asked. "I'll huff, and I'll puff —"

"Quiet!" Kaspar grabbed Eira's arm, slowing her to his pace. He might be struggling with the climb, but his grip was an iron shackle. "This is not a joke. This is our lives. Our livelihoods."

"What about us?" Eira demanded. Fury was supposed to be hot. Her blood felt icy enough to freeze. "We came here to help you, but you've never taken us seriously. If you don't start listening, your county will never be free of its curse, and it will be all your fault."

Kaspar's free hand clenched into a fist. Eira tensed. She hadn't been struck since her uncle had dragged her aboard the ship that took her from Nordmark. For an instant, she was that twelve-year-old girl again, her grief and fear and rage so thick in her throat she thought she would suffocate. Breathless.

Helpless.

Not anymore. She didn't have her bow or her sword, but Princess Anara had taught her a few tricks from her training as a royal bodyguard. Eira hoped Master Kaspar didn't plan on siring any more children.

When the furious roar began, she thought for an instant it came from her own throat.

"*Bear!*"

Shouts rose around them. Kaspar's hand squeezed convulsively on Eira's arm as he swiveled wildly in alarm, but Eira saw the source of the men's panic first. *There*. The rocky outcrop at the crest of the ridge. The bear stood with paws squared, head lowered, jaws wide. The afternoon sun gilded his massive shoulders, and his teeth gleamed like daggers.

"What is he doing here?" Marjani asked.

Eira's heart leaped and then fell like an arrow-shot deer, understanding even before her mind could catch up. He'd followed them. To protect them from the dangers of the wilderness—drowning, wolves, vicious rabbits.

"It's the curse." For the first time, Rurik jerked against the rope at his wrists. "It's so close to completion that it's driving him to attack the manor."

"No." Eira met the bear's golden-eyed gaze, and her pulse fluttered with unexpected joy and helpless exasperation. He'd not shown himself or made a move until Kaspar grabbed her.

He was protecting *her*. The endearing, maddening fool.

"Arm yourselves!" Hartwin shouted, trying to direct the men into some kind of formation. "Swordsmen, protect the prisoners. Bowmen, nock your arrows. Fire on my mark."

"Stop this!" Eira twisted free of Kaspar's grip and

stomped up the path toward the bear. "The only thing we need protecting from is you."

"Princess Eira!" Hartwin shouted in alarm.

She ignored him, waving her hands at the bear as if shooing chickens. It wasn't like there was an *approved* way to shoo a bear. "Go away. This is all a misunderstanding. We've got it under control."

"Archers!" Hartwin bellowed. "Stop the bear! Don't hit the princess!"

Eira whirled to see the four archers readying to fire. "Don't shoot!"

Another roar drowned her words, and the arrows whistled past. She turned to see the bear lumbering toward her, his shoulders rolling as if shaking off a shower of fall leaves.

"Stop!" Her voice tore with her heart. She lifted one hand toward the bear, one toward the men. "Don't hurt him!"

"She's mad!"

"He's possessed her!"

"They can't harm him, Eira," Rurik yelled. "Not during the day."

She knew that. In her head. Her heart could only feel the terror of all those frightened, angry men with their arrows and blades and hatred, all bent on killing an innocent man …

"Murderers!" she spat. "All you've ever wanted is to get rid of him."

The bear stood frozen, halted by her raised hand a dozen yards up the path, yet she could feel the rumble of his fury through the balls of her feet.

"Archers—"

"Stop!" Marjani grabbed Hartwin's arm. "He thinks you're going to hurt her. Have the men lower their weapons. She can get him to leave."

"She can control the beast?" Kaspar's face twisted in a mix of horror and disbelief.

"He's protecting her," Marjani said. "She just needs to convince him we're not in danger."

"Show me." Kaspar strode forward, teeth clenched against the fear Eira saw in his eyes. "If what you say is true, tell him not to attack me."

"He's not a dog," Eira snapped. She glanced at the great beast. Berengar had said he wasn't always aware of what he did while a bear. If he charged ... Hartwin's men would fight. Arrows would fly. Swords would swing. The bear might be impervious, but none of the rest of them were.

Peace, Eira. If the bear scented her fear, if Kaspar panicked ... She had to *be* the peace. *Please, Goddess.* She took a long, shaky breath and let it out slowly as Holy Mother had taught her.

"It's all right," she told the bear, her voice calm and confident as she could make it. "They don't mean us any harm."

The beast snuffled, nostrils flaring. Those eyes. Not quite Berengar's, but not quite not-Berengar's. He heard her. Maybe he didn't follow her words exactly. Still, he understood.

"They're just scared," she told him. "Show them there's nothing to fear."

She heard Kaspar behind her but kept her gaze locked with the bear's. Slowly, the bunched muscles in his shoulders eased, and his ears relaxed.

"That's right," Eira said. "Back off and let us fix things at the manor."

"That's right," Kaspar repeated, his breath surprisingly close to her ear. "Let's fix this once and for all."

A burly arm wrapped around Eira's torso, jerking her against the wool merchant's leather breastplate, squeezing a shocked gasp from her lungs.

The bear's eyes widened in alarm. Marjani cried out.

"What are you doing?" Eira wheezed. "He's backing off."

"It's not going anywhere. It's coming with us." Kaspar's arm was an iron band. "The sorcerer says we can't kill it. But we can lock it up until it starves. Boys, bind it with your ropes!"

The bear's ears flattened, and a savage growl rumbled

from his massive chest. Eira doubted any of the "boys" were eager to follow Kaspar's orders.

"Just go," she yelled at the bear. "Get out of here. I can handle this."

The beast shook his head, snarling his distress.

"Quiet!" Kaspar squeezed her so hard she gagged. "Let us tether you, bear, or she'll pay the price."

Arms pinned, Eira tried to stomp his foot, but he jerked her sideways, half off her feet. The bear rose, taller than the giants that had visited Newport earlier that summer. Tall enough that ten yards seemed incredibly close.

"Let her go!" Rurik yelled. "He's about to charge—"

Eira heard a thud as his voice cut off.

"Keep the sorcerer down and out of the way!" Hartwin ordered. "Kaspar, stop. It's going to kill someone."

"It won't," Kaspar said. "This girl's going to make it surrender."

Something glinted in his free hand, and suddenly a knife blade pressed against Eira's cheek. Her heart lurched in her chest.

The bear dropped, his forepaws striking the ground with enough force to rattle her teeth. He lunged forward a step, shaking the ground again, his mouth opening wider than seemed possible.

"Not one more inch!" Kaspar shouted. He slid the blade under Eira's chin, and she couldn't bite back a hiss of fear.

"Are you mad?" Marjani shouted. "Let her go!"

Eira wished Marjani didn't sound quite so panicked. She was having a hard enough time holding still against the press of the knife.

"Let *me* go!" Marjani demanded, sounding more like herself. Hartwin must have had the sense to grab her before she could rush Kaspar. If Kaspar were startled and drew blood—

"Release Princess Eira," Hartwin ordered. "She is under the king's protection. And mine."

"She's in league with that monster," Kaspar snarled, his breath hot in Eira's ear. "You saw. She must be a sorceress herself. Not even the king can protect her. I will not release her until the bear is bound. You hear me, bear? Go on, men."

Six men approached the bear. Two carried slip-knotted loops, and the others gripped the rope behind them.

A low growl rolled from the bear's throat, and he whipped his head toward one of the men, shockingly fast for such a huge creature.

Kaspar's knife tip touched Eira's cheek. "Put your head down, monster!"

The growl shifted into an aching, desperate sound that broke Eira's heart.

"Go!" she screamed. "Just get out of here! He doesn't dare hurt me!"

But the great beast stilled, dropping his head, his shoulders. He seemed to shrink before her eyes.

"No!" Eira struggled against Kaspar's grip, but the knife point pricking the skin beside her eye melted her strength.

The men moved warily, yet the bear remained motionless, drained of savagery, of violence, of spirit. Emboldened, they tossed their ropes over his head. Only an ear twitched as the rough hemp slid across it. The men pulled the nooses taut around his neck and backed as far from his teeth and claws as the ropes would allow.

"*No!*" But Eira's voice was as hollow as her chest, emptied of air, of life, by the sight of the great bear bound and defeated.

"You can't choke him to death," Rurik warned, his voice sharp and bitter. "Yet you could still make him angry enough to forget everything except breaking free."

The men sized up the situation. Six of them. One bear. Not even a contest. The ropes slackened just a little.

"Now, the girl," Kaspar ordered. "Bind her tight. She's slippery as a Nordish eel."

Other hands grabbed Eira, and Kaspar's knife lifted away.

She barely felt the men bind her wrists. Caught just a glimpse of Rurik's look of hopelessness as a guard heaved him to his feet. Of Marjani being bound, as well, Hartwin's objections unable to curb the men's instinctual fear of the unknown and uncanny.

She could focus only on the bear, the great golden eyes seeking hers in confusion and misery as his captors tugged at his neck, leading him toward the manor.

"Go," she whispered, her words lost in the tears of a girl as helpless and useless as a twelve-year-old.

"Don't fret, Your Highness." Kaspar's dark eyes glinted. "The king sent you to Saebern to rid us of our bear, and you've succeeded beyond all expectations."

CHAPTER TWENTY-SIX

9. *Apen Veret.* A charm to run one's eye [over? around?] the truth. (Right. With my luck, my eye would literally run out of my head, and then how would it know when it found the truth?)

— Top 10 failed spells translated and performed by Rurik, Ravninan sorcerer (in training)

Bound like a criminal. Or an animal. Armed guards at her side, eyeing her with dread and suspicion. Shame chafed more painfully than the ropes at Marjani's wrists.

This quest should have been an opportunity for glory, gaining her access to Prince Theodore so she could enact dramatic, bloody vengeance against King Wulfric. Instead, she was a prisoner, accused of sorcery, feared and despised by the very people she had come to help. Bested by farmers with axes.

Her father had been right to value her as less than nothing. She had failed to help Saebern, failed to avenge her brother, and failed to uphold her kingdom's honor. Even if Wulfric declined to prosecute her for sorcery, her father would disown her. She would have no name, nowhere to go.

Her own fault, trusting Hartwin. Whatever distaste the reeve felt for Kaspar's tactics, he'd been quick to take advantage, leading them to the grain storage barn outside the manor walls. With the heavy oak doors on the ends of its protruding wings—what Rurik had called the wagon porches—and its thick stone walls, it certainly looked capable of containing a massive, ensorcelled bear.

The huge beast balked at the threshold, but a rough growl from Kaspar, still holding Eira at knifepoint, sent him through. A lost, lonely bellow echoed from the cavernous structure.

"Let me stay with him," Eira begged. "He'll be terrified."

The men stared at her in disbelief or spat a defense against sorcery. Kaspar ordered her gagged. He looked as though he expected tears, but Eira drew herself up like a true Nordish princess, her eyes cold as ice. The look she gave the man who gagged her brought sweat to his brow.

"Poor bastard," Rurik muttered in mock sympathy, making the young man shudder with dread.

The Saeberners might be nervous about the Ravninan sorcerer, but they obviously feared the girl who could talk to ensorcelled bears even more.

Whereas they have hardly any fear left for an Almasan princess, however foreign.

The great doors at the end of the wagon porch closed, and Marjani heard the men inside slide the bar across to keep them that way. The men came out through the small door on the side of the wagon porch, which they locked with visible relief. The youngest boy had run to the manor house to get the key, but no one from the manor had returned with him— even bound, the bear kept the residents imprisoned in fear.

Kaspar prodded Eira forward, and the men surrounding Rurik dragged him after her, heading around the manor toward the front gate.

"Did you know?" Hartwin demanded, falling in beside Marjani. "That she could control beasts with sorcery?"

Marjani's heart twisted at the accusation in his voice. Yet, there was one unlooked-for benefit of disgrace. It released her from the fear of losing his good opinion. And if she had lost her claim to worth as royalty, she could speak simply as herself.

"No," she said simply. "I did not know Princess Eira could control animals, because she cannot."

"I saw what I saw." Indignation hardened his jaw. "She told the bear to back off, and it did."

"It's a question of knowledge, not eyesight," Marjani said. "You ascribe to Eira magical powers because you believe she controlled a beast. But I know the bear is not a beast."

"A bear that is not a beast? You speak in riddles."

Words fluttered in her throat. So tempting to let them escape, to tell him about the curse, about Berengar and the murderer lurking in their midst. They had fallen behind the others. No one else would hear, and time was running out. Convincing Hartwin to help might be their best chance to uncover the person who cast the curse.

Unless Hartwin laid the curse.

Her skin prickled. She had fallen into the trap he had set for her the day before. She couldn't trust herself to judge his innocence.

"A cursed bear is unnatural, with unnatural powers," she said instead. "This bear nailed a sheep's heart to a gate. He understood Kaspar's threats. Does that seem any less strange than his response to Eira?"

"How should I know? I have no knowledge of sorcery," Hartwin said brusquely.

"I hope not." The truth, so sharp it ached.

Ahead, the manor gate swung open. In a moment, Steward Tarben would take charge of her fate.

Marjani lifted her bound wrists to place a hand on Hartwin's forearm. A hand? Her fingertips. The mixture of hurt, doubt, guilt, and self-righteousness that radiated from him might as well have been her own. Impossible to follow a single thread with confidence. But she wasn't trying to read him. Only to turn him toward her, to meet his sea-storm gaze one last time.

"You told me once that you prefer to see the world as it is rather than how you wished it were," she said. "I failed to trust you with the truth yesterday. Now I am forced to trust you with my life. I must hope that the man I thought I knew, the man I … admired … will not allow bitterness and prejudice to keep him from seeking the truth."

"Are you sure you want to do that? Dare me to search out the *truth*." A challenge. An accusation.

A promise?

"Yes." A truth of her own. Because if he sought it, if he found the truth, he would not flinch from it, even if it wasn't what he wanted to find. Whatever her doubts, whatever she questioned about his motives, she suddenly realized she did not question that.

"What is the meaning of this?" Steward Tarben sounded even more disgruntled than usual as he met the procession at the gate. "What have you gotten us into, Kaspar?"

"What about the bear?" Lady Silke demanded. "You didn't really bring it here? Endangering my family, my daughter. I had to shut her in her room with her nurse to prevent her from rushing out to see it. What were you—Princess *Eira!* You're alive? Why is she *tied up?*"

Time had run out. Marjani's fingers slid from Hartwin's arm. No, *down* his arm, to catch involuntarily on his hand. His fingers curled—a reflex?—a brush against her own. If only she could control the curse of her birth, the sensing of spirits that should have been her brother's gift. If only she could use it to share with Hartwin her own regret, the honesty of her plea, this confusion of emotion in her heart …

A spark of energy burned her fingers where they touched his, near hot enough to set her skin aflame.

Hartwin startled, his hand closing on hers for the briefest of moments.

"Someone here cast that curse, Hartwin," she whispered

urgently. "They didn't care how many people it killed. They might be capable of something even worse. I know you want to believe it was Rurik, but if there is any doubt in your mind—"

"The sorcerer!" Steward Tarben's voice spiraled to unexpected heights, and the moment was gone. "What new devilry is come upon us? Reeve Hartwin, have you lost your senses?"

A brief glance only. Did she imagine Hartwin's misgiving, the crack in his armor of judgment? And then he was striding to the gate, his shoulders squared under the weight of his duty.

Marjani could only follow.

"We've bound the sorcerer's hands," Hartwin told the steward. "He is powerless to cause more harm."

"I've never harmed anyone," Rurik objected with a dramatic sigh. "More's the pity."

"You've left him his voice," Tarben accused.

"What about his book?" Silke asked. She hissed at the men's blank stares. "His book of spells? He boasted often of its power."

One of the farmers flanking Rurik spoke. "The only thing he's carrying is that rucksack."

"You didn't take his bag?" The tip of Tarben's beard quivered with disbelief. "Stop! Don't untie him, for gods' sake! Cut the strap."

Rurik jerked away from the man reaching for his rucksack, but another farmer grabbed him by his hair, wrapping it in his fist.

"That book is dangerous," the sorcerer warned as the first man lifted a wicked-looking hunting knife to the strap across his chest. "It could curse anyone who dares open it without proper precautions."

A gambit to keep anyone from reading it? Or perhaps to frighten the curse caster into revealing themselves? Marjani searched the faces of the gathered group and saw Eira doing the same. Flashes of fear, disgust, skepticism. If there was any sign of guilt, it passed too quickly for her to mark it. She caught Eira's eye, and the Nordish girl shook her head.

The knife-wielding farmer tugged the rucksack off Rurik's shoulder and held it at arm's length as though he gripped a venomous sea snake about to strike.

"Only a fool trifles with sorcery," Lady Silke said, voice sharp with scorn. She held out her hand, and the farmer passed her the bag with obvious relief. "I will lock it in the strongroom. No one will touch it there."

"Careful," Rurik advised. His smile showed the tips of his teeth. "I would hate for someone so lovely to lose a hand. Or an arm."

The strap slipped in Silke's fingers, but Marjani had to give her credit. The lady tightened her grip and held on.

"You think my head easily turned," Silke said, only the color in her cheeks hinting at her shame at having kissed him. "But I assure you, I will keep your evil spells secure until we can find a priest to safely destroy them."

Eira moaned around her gag and looked wild-eyed at Marjani.

"You can't destroy that book," Marjani said. "That's why we're here. There's a spell in it—"

"To curse us again?" Kaspar growled.

"To reverse the present curse!" Rurik snapped. "That spell can save you if you let it. Lady Silke, for your daughter's sake, listen to me."

Silke's eyes blazed. "How dare you bring Artis into this?"

"How dare I?" Rurik nearly struck himself in the face trying to wave his bound hands. "It's her people who are paying the price for this curse. If you'll just let us try—"

"Enough," Tarben barked. "Kaspar should have gagged you. One more word, and I'll remedy that. Hartwin, put them in the cellar, then join us in the great hall."

"The cellar?" Silke had turned toward the house but now looked back at her husband. "You are not going to put royal princesses in the cellar."

"Just until we get this sorted out, my dear—"

A flick of her fingers cut him off. "Not until *any* time. Not in my house. Reeve Hartwin, Ebba can show you to their room, where they will be unbound and ungagged."

"You can't keep them in a bedchamber," Kaspar objected, his chest swelling with indignation. "These girls are traitors, sorcerers, *dangerous*."

One of Silke's slim eyebrows rose. "Are you dangerous, Princess Marjani?"

"I mean no harm to you or your family, Lady Silke." Sometimes a partial truth was better than the whole.

"There, you see. No danger." The smile Silke offered Kaspar was dangerous enough for both of them. Her expression softened as she glanced at the princesses, to something like sympathy. "I must allow Reeve Hartwin to lock your door, as you have a habit of straying. But you are guests in my house, and I promise you will be treated as such."

"But they … The sorcerer—" Kaspar sputtered.

"The sorcerer can go in the cellar." Lady Silke's long skirts swirled, and she strode away.

Marjani sought her companions' eyes. Fight? Run? Tell their mad story of missing earls and enchanted bears?

Rurik shook his head, but whether in warning or simply because he had no idea himself, she didn't know. Eira's glare seemed to be offering to rip Master Kaspar's throat out with her fingernails, but that would only get them thrown into the cellar with Rurik.

"Follow me, Your Highnesses," Hartwin said formally, and any other option slid away.

Ebba, the housekeeper, met them at the door and led them through the labyrinthine hallways to the princesses' room. All of the things Marjani wanted to say, needed to say, *couldn't* say crowded her throat.

Hartwin inspected the room, the lock, and the window—a fifteen-foot drop into the kitchen garden, Marjani knew— before he untied her. His eyes darkened at the chafing on her wrists, but he offered no comfort. She almost wished he had. She could have hated him then, if he'd treated her as less than a warrior.

He glanced at Eira's dagger-sharp eyes, then back to Marjani. "I'll let you release her when we close the door. There's no need for more violence today."

"Tell that to Master Kaspar."

The blow struck true. Hartwin faltered. "If I had known what he intended, I would have stopped him."

"Is that the truth?" Marjani had sworn to avenge Mosi and Dejen, no matter the cost. Would she be willing to hold a knife to Eira's throat if that's what vengeance required? "It got you what you wanted. Kaspar said it himself, he would do whatever it takes to keep Saebern safe."

Hartwin's hands clenched, but she felt more disquiet in his spirit than anger. "Maybe Kaspar would be a better reeve than I. Myself, I cannot be sure that he has made Saebern safer. I can only assure you that I will not allow him to hurt either of you again."

He gave her a stiff bow and retreated to the hall. The key Ebba had given him scraped in the lock, and Marjani and Eira were left alone.

CHAPTER TWENTY-SEVEN

7. He acted like Saebern was a prison he couldn't wait to escape from. (Submitted by Tarben, steward of Saebern County.)

— Top 10 reasons no one misses Earl Berengar that much

Eira sat hunched on her bed, pressing her face against her knees to keep from screaming. Her wrists burned from the ropes that had bound her. She still tasted the old rag that had gagged her.

None of it distracted her from her terror for Berengar.

Boot soles scraped the chamber floor, rubbing her raw nerves. She pushed the heels of her hands to her ears. "Stop pacing, or I'll be forced to strangle you."

"I'm not pacing." Tension crackled in Marjani's voice. "I'm monitoring the guards."

Only two guards—one outside the door, one below their window in the kitchen garden. Proof of how maddeningly little their captors feared them. Or feared their chances of escaping without being seen.

The window had a pretty view of carrots and parsnips,

"""

cabbages and beets, fennel and leeks, as well as large pots of herbs, both flavorful and medicinal, and bright beds of summer flowers and sweet roses. A lovely, quiet haven from the outside world—which seemed to attract far more gardeners and cooks and clandestine kisses than could possibly be normal for a small country manor.

A bronze-faced sundial on a stone pedestal ruled over the garden's center, its gnomon in the silhouette of a prancing unicorn all too quickly counting down the minutes of Berengar's last day. The princesses had been trapped in this room for hours already, and Eira couldn't bear it much longer.

"I just need the courtyard to be deserted for a moment, so I can jump down," she said. Yet again. So far, her fellow prisoner had refused to listen. "Landing on the guard will take him out of the equation."

"Breaking your neck won't help Berengar," Marjani snapped. "Tarben will send for us eventually. We must use that opportunity to discover who cast the curse."

"Hartwin and Kaspar wouldn't listen to us." Eira swiped at her mouth, trying to rub away the horrible memory of being gagged. *Silenced.* "Do you really think Tarben will be any different?"

"Lady Silke—"

"Didn't let them toss us in the cellar. For which I'm grateful," Eira admitted. "But she despises Rurik, and she's terrified of the bear. She won't listen to anything except how to destroy him."

"Hartwin might listen." Marjani paused her pacing, her mismatched eyes dark with turmoil. "Would such an honorable man kill someone through sorcery? I cannot believe he would be so cowardly."

"You don't *want* to believe it. Not that I blame you." Eira didn't want to believe it, either. But she couldn't risk Berengar's life on a wish. "I'm going out the window as soon as it's dark. You can't stop me."

There were any number of ways Marjani could stop her, of course. Warning the guards being the simplest. Smothering her with her own pillow being an unexpected option—

But Marjani simply shifted the pillow out of the way to sit beside her on the edge of the bed. "If you try to escape, they will see it as evidence of guilt."

Eira looked out to where a few stray clouds were beginning to gild themselves with the colors of the setting sun. Each passing moment tightened the iron bands of grief around her chest.

"This is the last night he'll return to human form." The words peeled strips from her heart as she spoke. "We're his only chance. I need to get him out of that barn and bring him to the manor. They'd *have* to listen to him then."

Listen to a raving wild man who claims to turn into a bear each day? Listen to the missing earl they'd all be just as happy to have never return?

Her fists clenched so hard they ached. "I'll *make* them listen."

Marjani didn't look up, just turned the broken bracelet at her wrist. "I doubt Tarben or Silke have any interest in bringing a sorcery charge against us, regardless of Kaspar's accusations. But if you are caught trying to release the bear, they will have no choice."

"They won't catch me releasing the bear," Eira objected. "He won't *be* a bear."

"Eira—"

"*Don't say it!*"

"We can't be sure he'll ever be human again."

The words hung in the air, even sharper and more dangerous than they had been when unsaid in Eira's heart. She brushed them away. "The anniversary of the casting isn't until mid-morning tomorrow."

"If Rurik is right that the time matters, not just the date," Marjani said.

"King Wulfric won't execute us for sorcery whether I get caught or not," Eira said, ignoring the likelihood of Rurik being wrong. That didn't matter. They had to act as though he were right until they found out otherwise. "I'm sure he suspects both Nordmark and Almasa of plotting Prince Guntram's assassination—"

"I only wish we had."

"But his solution was to send us to Saebern, not kill us. No one would allow their princesses to stay for the ball if he did."

"Nordish fool," Marjani hissed, leaping to her feet. "King Wulfric wouldn't have to execute you. He could just send you back to Nordmark."

Ice washed across Eira's skin. None of the other girls' families could object to the king sending her home, after all. Not his fault her uncle had vowed to kill her if she ever set foot in Nordmark again.

Yet even the thought of Uncle Einar's satisfaction at being able to finally put her to death couldn't quash the sudden warming of her heart.

"You're worried about me."

"Don't make too much of it." Marjani's growl rivaled the bear's. "I promised King Wulfric I'd bring you back safely to Newport. I can't do that if your foolhardy rescue plan fails."

Eira gifted her a Nordish warrior's grin. "Then I guess you'd better make sure it doesn't fail."

Planning might not *always* be a terrible idea. Not that Eira would admit it to Marjani—the Almasan princess spent too much time plotting already. But she had to concede that this alternative to just jumping out the window had a certain flair. And was somewhat less likely to result in broken bones.

Eira squeezed the little jade frog in her palm one last time. It had kept her friends close when she'd been most alone. But they had given it to her for luck, and now she needed every last bit she could get.

"Are you sure?" Marjani asked. "Maybe the pewter cup —"

"Too big." Not only was the frog charm small enough that the guard would never find it in the dark, but she knew its weight and proportions better than anything else in their room. Her fingers gripped it with instinctual confidence.

She tossed the pendant in the air a couple of times to settle her nerves and stepped to the window. They had waited through the endless summer twilight, the light supper Ebba had brought them, and another hour after they had extinguished their candle and pretended to go to bed. Now the only light in the garden below came from the river of stars above and the guard's single lantern.

Eira could barely see her chosen target, but she didn't waste time on doubt. She drew back her arm with all the strength of hundreds of hours of archery practice and hurled the little frog into the night.

It struck the unicorn on the sundial with a sharp ping and ricocheted back, drawing a grunt of surprise from the somnolent guard.

"Hey! Who's there?"

"Struck him right above his ear," Marjani breathed with approval.

Now to see how the guard would react. If he tried to raise an alarm, she would have to drop down on top of him, after all.

"Is that you, Neddie? I told you to stay home with your ma. If I catch you out here while that bear's nearby, you scamp, I'll tan your hide …"

Eira peered over the sill, Marjani at her shoulder. The guard stomped over to the hedge beyond the sundial and poked the handle of his axe into the bushes, muttering imprecations at the unjustly accused Neddie.

"Quick," Marjani whispered.

Eira climbed onto the stone sill, careful not to rattle the

open shutters. She wore Marjani's red cape, as good as black in the shadows, with the hood pulled over her pale hair and face.

The nearest strut for the roof eaves was to the left of the window rather than directly overhead. She'd have to lean farther out to scramble onto the rough-hewn beam. She just needed to get a hand on it to steady herself …

Her fingers slipped on the cool stone of the window, and she had to crouch back down to catch her balance.

"Here." Strong fingers gripped her wrist. "I'll anchor you."

Eira glanced over her shoulder, barely able to see Marjani's face in the darkness. She suddenly remembered their first morning in Saebern, the punch of betrayal when the Almasan princess sneaked out to hunt the bear alone, driven by her unquenchable need for vengeance.

If Eira were caught trying to free the bear, if the two of them were tried for sorcery, Marjani would never get the chance to avenge her brother's murder. But if Eira died trying to escape … Marjani might even get credit for the bear's capture. Releasing Berengar from his curse would technically fulfill their quest to rid Saebern of its bear, but there was no guarantee it would please King Wulfric as much as the bear's hide.

The scene played in Eira's mind. Marjani seated beside Prince Theodor at the king's feast, a bear claw necklace around her neck, rising to her feet with a knife in her hand … and if this idea had just occurred to her, Marjani would have thought of it ages ago. What had really changed in the past few days? They were still at odds. Still opposites. Still rivals.

Still the only two people in all of Saebern who could save Berengar and make things right.

Eira released a breath and nodded. *I trust you.* Marjani's fingers tightened, tethering her as she rose from her crouch, that iron grip the only thing keeping her from falling.

She wrapped her right arm over the beam, and Marjani squeezed her wrist, a silent *good luck*. Then she let go, and Eira launched herself forward, scrambling up onto the beam to hunch like a Venian gargoyle in the dark beneath the eaves.

The brush of her clothing, the scrape of her boot against the side of the building sounded deafening to her ears, and she held her breath, waiting for a reaction from the guard. But he continued to poke through the bushes, less as if he might find someone, more as if trying to stave off boredom.

The next eave strut was barely a yard away. An easy stretch …

From beam to beam, she made her way along the underside of the eaves to the end of the long wing. There, it was an easy drop to a shed roof, then to the ground. Silently, swiftly, she followed the directions Marjani had given her to the chapel and over the wall behind it.

She slipped across the open ground outside the wall, hunched low, trying not to trip on Marjani's cloak. A lantern flickered outside the great barn's front wagon porch. She could see two figures hunched on the ground nearby. She'd expected guards, considering the monster imprisoned within. But the fickle starlight hid more than it exposed, allowing her to reach the end of the barn without being seen.

She pressed against the rough stone wall, willing her heart to slow. She'd managed the easy part. The real difficulty would be getting inside. The barn windows were mere slits set high in the stone walls. The doors offered the only entry.

Eira touched the braided crown on her head and found the hairpin she'd stashed there. Beatrix had given her a lesson in lock-picking back at Lukos. She would sneak around the back of the building and hope there was another small side door on that wagon porch. With a simple lock. And no guard. And—

The panic that had been building in her ever since the bear's capture filled her chest so she could hardly breathe. She had to get Berengar out of this barn. Had to expose the curse caster. Had to make them reverse the curse.

Had to save Berengar's life.

No lanterns illuminated the rear of the barn. There was nothing but darkness. Eira crept forward fast as she dared.

There. The deeper darkness ahead must be the rear wagon porch jutting from the center of the barn's length. She patted her way along the expanse of stone, feeling for a wooden door.

Nothing.

Eira's fear whistled in her ears like a Nordish winter storm as she made her way around the end of the porch. There were the huge loading bay doors she expected. She shoved against them with her shoulder, but they were barred from the inside.

Hurry, hurry, hurry.

She swung around the corner to the other side of the wagon porch.

"Oof!" The obstacle was solid enough to be part of the barn, but its baritone grunt was distinctly human.

Eira jerked back, but the man's hand caught the edge of her borrowed cloak and yanked, spinning her sideways.

"Let *go!*" She kicked out blindly, striking something that made him squawk. "Let me go, or I'll step off the Road of Peace."

"Princess Eira?" A feminine whisper on her other side startled her into holding back the punch meant for her opponent's gut. "How did you get out of your room? What are you ...? Rodolf! The lantern."

The hand holding Eira's cloak let go, but before she could bolt, a light flared in her eyes. Blinking against the glare, she took in the man before her. The low angle of his lantern made him look taller and broader than he was. Surely. Because, really, no one but a bear was that tall and broad.

The light also revealed the three other men moving to surround her. And the cloaked figure at their center.

"I told Tarben he should have set more guards on you." The slender woman drew back her hood.

"Lady Silke." As Eira's gaze darted around the scene, calculating the possibility of escape, she took in two more details. The narrow wooden door just a few feet away. And the ring of keys Silke held in one slender hand.

The woman's dark eyes gleamed in the flickering light. "Shall we go see this bear of yours, Your Highness?"

CHAPTER TWENTY-EIGHT

7. *Onthynan.* A spell to open any lock. (Lock of *hair?* Because
it hasn't worked on any other kind.)

— Top 10 failed spells translated and performed by
Rurik, Ravninan sorcerer (in training)

Marjani wasn't pacing because she was anxious for
Eira's safety. If the Nordish witch didn't break
her neck, it was merely a delay in the inevitable
consequences of her reckless approach to life.

But if Eira's desperate gambit were to succeed, she would
need every minute of freedom she could get. Marjani had lit
the lamp by her bed and taken up this anxious pacing to reassure the guards that their prisoners were present and
accounted for.

It had nothing to do with the dread crawling across her
skin like spiders, making it impossible to lie still in the darkness. Nothing to do with the bloody images swirling through
her mind. Eira swinging from a gallows. Rurik burning on a
pyre. A huge bear rug covering the flagstones in the manor's
great hall.

Nothing to do with the coldness she imagined in her
father's eyes as he cast her out for her failure to kill the prince.

Would he have her whipped bloody and dumped in a leopard's hunting grounds as he did for captured enemies? Or pushed out to sea in a rudderless boat as he did for traitors?

She'd paced a good mile or more before she realized she didn't care which. He had judged her worthless the moment she'd been born—a girl, a firstborn girl, beating his longed-for son into the world by mere moments. Nothing she had ever done had changed that judgment. Nothing ever would.

He could condemn her as an enemy or a traitor—either would be more recognition than he had ever given her before —and it wouldn't cause her a sliver of the grief of knowing Hartwin thought she'd betrayed him.

She froze mid-step, one foot hovering over the timber floor. She had carried the burden of her father's disapproval and disappointment for so long, only to recognize now … it wasn't hers to carry. His judgment showed a great deal about his character and nothing about hers.

She could set it down, finally. Nearly crying out with the pain of relief.

But if her father's opinion wasn't worth all the effort she put into earning it … what was?

Answers pricked her like wasp stings. The vengeance she'd sworn for Mosi and Dejen's murders—*that* she pursued for her own sake, not her father's demands, however much they aligned. Punishing King Wulfric. Avoiding execution. Safeguarding her dignity. Placating the spirits of those no longer encumbered by earthly forms.

All the myriad things she had cared about for months. The things she *should* care about.

But here, this night, what actually mattered to her … were the living. The people in danger right this moment. Eira, Berengar, Rurik. Hartwin, who deserved to know the truth about his father's death. The people of Saebern, suffering under the curse that had been laid on their earl. Steward Tarben, Lady Silke, and especially little Artis, in danger from the cold-blooded killer who had cast it.

What mattered were the people who needed her. People she could help because she chose to, not from duty or someone else's command, but because she cared about them.

People she couldn't help from inside a locked bedchamber.

Her lifted foot finally struck the floor. Why had she let Eira escape alone? The Nordish princess might be surprisingly tough for someone so stringy and pale, but her chances of breaking into a guarded stone barn by herself were nearly nonexistent. She needed assistance.

Waiting to be called before Tarben that afternoon, Marjani had donned her most striking gown, a shimmering, fluid garment of rich scarlet silk. The sleeveless bodice showed the strength of her shoulders and arms. As intimidating as even Rurik could have asked for but hardly practical for an escape attempt. Still, she didn't have time to change.

Boots.

Marjani snatched her footwear from beside her bed. After a wasted minute of awkward hopping, she sat on the nearby chair with a hiss of frustration. How did northern women have time for anything if they had to spend half a day on their bootlaces?

She blew out the lamp and padded to the window. She was just enough taller than Eira that she should be able to reach the beam under the eaves without help. The shy light of the crescent moon did nothing to illuminate the garden, but she could make out the guard in the soft glow of his lantern. He sat against the house wall, his shoulders slumped, head canted to one side.

He couldn't actually be asleep. That would be too much to ask for. Yet, as she held her breath, she heard the faint whuffling of a snore. Maybe her luck was turning, after all—

A murmur of voices at the chamber door spun her around, heart slamming in her chest. No, her luck was just as bad as ever.

Hartwin was in the corridor outside her room. She couldn't hear the words, but her heart warmed to the timbre of his voice, even as her hopes of escape burned to ash. Tarben had finally sent for them—probably to accuse them of sorcery. Even so, it was a chance for her to ask him to attempt to lift the curse. A desperate chance—praying Tarben would listen, *anyone* would listen. But a chance, nonetheless.

A chance they wouldn't get if Hartwin discovered Eira missing.

Marjani rushed to the door and put her hand against it. She needed to prevent Hartwin from seeing Eira's empty bed. *Eira is sick.* But not sick enough to need a doctor. *Eira is sick with grief.* But then Marjani would have to explain about Berengar, and there was no time for that. *She has cried herself asleep with fear, and I refuse to wake her for your ridiculous questions.*

Appearances and attitude. She was still a princess, after all.

The voices stopped. All was quiet in the corridor. Hartwin hadn't come for them, after all. He'd only been checking on the guard.

But before she could release her held breath, a key scraped in the door's lock. A pause. And then the door pressed against her hand as it inched open, spilling lantern light through the crack.

"*Who's there?*" The strangeness of the silence made her words sharp.

"It's Reeve Hartwin." Hartwin's voice was a rushed whisper. "Princess Marjani—"

"You can't come in." She pushed against the door. "Eira is sick. I mean, she's sick with grief. I mean she—"

"I need to talk to you."

"No! You'll wake her. I'll come out."

"*Shhh.* Let me in before someone sees me."

The urgency in his voice pushed her back, despite herself. He squeezed through the narrow opening and swiftly closed the door. Their two hands pressed against the warm yellow wood, his broad and pale, hers long-fingered and dark. He was so close she could see the day's shadows beneath his eyes, the sandpaper of stubble on his chin.

Close enough to feel the crackle of lightning in his spirit.

"Tarben didn't send you," she realized, her pulse jolting.

"He thinks you are less of a problem than the giant bear in his barn," Hartwin said. "He and Kaspar have spent the evening inventing ever more outlandish ways to dispatch the beast, if they gather the courage to open the door. When I left them, Kaspar was arguing for burning the building to the ground."

Marjani pressed her fist to her mouth. *Berengar. Eira.*

"Tarben will never agree to it," Hartwin assured her. The barest hint of his wry grin tugged his mouth. "A new barn would cost a fortune."

She stifled her matching smile. Hartwin was not her friend, nor was she his. His duty had called him to betray her once, and if it asked again, he would answer the same way.

"If Tarben has dismissed us for the night, why are you here?" she asked, almost coldly enough to be convincing.

His eyes met hers, clear and sharp. "This afternoon, in the courtyard, you said there was a spell in the sorcerer's book that could undo Saebern's curse."

"Yes. Maybe," she agreed warily. "Rurik thinks it will work."

"I don't trust Rurik."

She couldn't blame him for that. "He's a terrible sorcerer."

"You believe that he didn't cast the curse."

"If you'd seen how much it hurt him to admit he *couldn't* cast it, you might believe it, too."

Hartwin shook his head, eyes hard. "When I saw him with you, alive, I knew he must be responsible for my father's death. I wanted to watch him burn." He took a deep breath, and she could almost feel the fires of rage he struggled to control. "That sounds horrible. It *is* horrible. But I can't let it go. I feel like I could breathe the flame that would set him alight. I can't explain it—"

"You don't have to." Marjani's fingers twitched, but she refrained from reaching for him. "My brother—"

To her horror, her voice cracked on the word, but Hartwin nodded, his eyes showing grim acknowledgment, not pity.

"But that fury, it's not real." He grimaced. "I mean, the feeling is real, but it's not reality. The reality is, I don't know who cast the curse. You said if I had a shadow of a doubt, it was my duty to find the truth."

The conflicts she had felt roiling his spirit earlier seemed to have woven themselves together into a unified purpose, taut as a bowstring or the snap of a hunter's snare.

Marjani stilled, unsure if she was the arrow or the rabbit. "Does that mean you are seeking it?"

"I was furious at you, too." His jaw tightened, but he held her gaze. "You lied to me. You trusted that foul sorcerer more than you trusted me."

"Rurik didn't tell me I was incapable of fulfilling my duty or try to dissuade me from my vengeance." Her voice was a scathing sword, but she couldn't help rolling her eyes. "You honestly think I would rather hunt a cursed bear with *Rurik* than with you?"

"No." Hartwin's eyes flared in the lantern light.

Her recriminations died in her throat. "What?"

"All afternoon, I kept telling myself you betrayed your oath to kill the bear, betrayed Saebern, betrayed *me* to align with a murdering sorcerer and bring destruction to my home. But I couldn't make myself believe it."

He ran a hand through his hair. "You grew up with the cunning and pretense of royal politics. I know you would risk your life to gain an advantage in whatever game of revenge you're playing with King Wulfric. You *lied* to me. And yet, I can't stop believing in you."

If Marjani could have looked away, she could have hidden the heat that rose from her core all the way to her cheeks. *The depths of those eyes.* Still, she could do haughty and dangerous, even with her face aflame. "What do you mean?"

"I told you armies would follow you." He lifted his hands, palms up. "Here I am."

Marjani clenched her fists against the coil of emotions swirling inside her. The light in his eyes wasn't just lightning. It was laughter, too. Though whether he laughed at himself or at her, she couldn't say. Probably both.

Her chest ached. She'd broken a rib once, training with Mosi, and for a moment, it felt like the same pain, something breaking inside her. Except she wanted to laugh, too. And weep.

There wasn't *time*.

"The door guard," she said.

A fierce grin. "I volunteered to take his place."

A flash of something almost like hope seared through her, making her heart leap. *No. The truth.* It wasn't *just* hope making her pulse flutter. But the hope first. Berengar.

"We have to get Rurik's spell book," she said.

"No need. Princess Eira has it." Hartwin flicked a wry glance toward Eira's empty bed. "I checked the strongroom and found the book gone. I knew one of you must have escaped and taken it. I assume she's headed for the barn to cast the counter-curse?"

That was the danger with hope. When reality came along and swatted the pesky vermin, it released a poison that took your breath away.

"Are you all right?" Hartwin grabbed her elbow, steadying her. "Marjani?"

She shook her head. "Eira did go to the barn. *Straight* to the barn. She didn't take Rurik's book."

Which meant someone else had. Someone who dared to touch a book of dark, cursed sorcery. Someone who had touched it once before?

"Are you sure?" Hartwin raised an eyebrow. "Eira is almost as reckless as you are."

"I am not reckless! We're nothing alike!" But that wasn't the point. "She knows she can't cast the counter-curse. She was planning to bring Ber—" No, too much time to explain. "She's hoping to find the person who can."

Confusion wrinkled his brow. "Rurik?"

"No." Desperation swirled around her. Hartwin was here, listening, but it would take the rest of the night to tell him the whole story, to convince him this wasn't all some "fairy's tale" or whatever Eira had called it. There was no time. And she was only a foreign princess, a lying stranger, a girl with only half a soul …

And Hartwin was here.

"You trust me?" She could hardly believe it, even now.

"Yes." A simple statement. "Do you trust me?"

Caution said no. But her heart said otherwise. "Only one person in Saebern has successfully cast a spell from that cursed book."

"But you said Rurik can't—"

"It's not Rurik."

His eyes widened as his hand tightened on her elbow. "Whoever took that book from the storeroom might just be someone who doesn't know they can't work the spells."

"Or—" A chill ran down Marjani's back. "Or it might be the one person who knows all too well that they can."

9. She's always getting under people's skin.

— Top 10 things I despise about Princess Eira, as listed by Princess Marjani of Almasa

"You can't get inside on your own." Silke gestured at the solidly built side door. "You may as well join us."

"But—" Eira's mind raced as she glanced around at the men. Were they here to try to kill the bear? A few yeomen with old swords? Where was Tarben? Why was *Silke* here? And, "Why are you sneaking into your own barn?"

Silke offered a conspiratorial smile. "As my daughter's trustee, I have authority over what happens at the manor, but sometimes I tire of waiting for the men to listen to me. Perhaps you understand."

"None of them listened to *anything* Marjani and I said," Eira had to agree, the frustration grinding in her chest.

"I did." Silke chose a sturdy iron key from her ring. "And when Kaspar and my husband began talking about trying to hack the bear apart with axes—"

"*What?*"

"Yes, it was obvious they wouldn't come up with anything

useful. Yet, you said something that made Kaspar believe the curse lifted at night, that the bear might be vulnerable?"

Eira pressed a hand to her mouth. She might have said something, all right. When she thought she could reason with them. Before Kaspar held a knife to her throat.

"You claimed tonight was the last opportunity to lift the curse," Silke continued. She turned her key in the lock and paused with her hand on the door. "I thought it best to see for myself before any axes got involved. Will you help? I understand you have some power to control the beast."

Eira sucked in a deep breath. *Finally.* Finally, someone was willing to listen and try to understand. Only because Silke thought this might be the best chance they had to kill the bear. But now Eira could show her the truth.

It was her turn for a conspiratorial smile. "You don't have to worry about the bear." Then it struck her. "How can you be so calm about this? You've always been terrified of the bear."

"I was terrified because I never knew what the monster would do next," Silke said. "I was terrified it might catch my husband on the road or break into the manor and attack my daughter. Now, I know exactly where it is, and I can do something about it."

Her keys jingled with the trembling of her fingers. "I'm still frightened. Of course I am. But you've brought me hope I can end this curse and protect my daughter. I would risk *anything* to protect Artis."

"Let me go first," Eira said. "I'll make sure it's safe."

Rodolf spoke behind them. "Master Kaspar says she's a witch, milady."

Lady Silke rolled her eyes. "Master Kaspar thinks anyone with a womb is a witch. I am more concerned about King Wulfric's reaction if Princess Eira gets eaten by a bear. We've already drowned her. Another death seems excessive."

"The bear won't harm me," Eira promised. "Let me ensure no one else gets hurt."

Silke gave her an appraising glance, then nodded. "Philip, give Princess Eira the other lantern."

An older man carrying a leather rucksack and a dark lantern stepped forward. He opened the lantern's shutter to release a beam of light and handed it to Eira.

"You have five minutes to calm the beast," Silke said. "After that, I will take matters into my own hands."

"Five minutes." That's all she would need. If Berengar was all right. If he was still human. *He had to be still human.*

Really, five minutes was all she would need, either way.

Silke's men shifted nervously, and one breathed a prayer, but they didn't break and run as she opened the door. Brave, Eira thought, considering the monster they believed waited within. But all that poured from the doorway was darkness and silence.

"They tied it up good," Rodolf rumbled, only the sheen of sweat on his forehead betraying his fear.

"Maybe it choked itself to death," another man suggested hopefully.

"Hush," Silke commanded in a fierce whisper. "Princess Eira—"

"Five minutes." Eira slipped through the narrow gap and closed the door.

The emptiness struck her first, the sense of echoing space that spread far beyond the feeble rays of her lantern. The hush, the coolness, the arching beams overhead. They reminded her of the One Goddess's sanctuary at the Temple of Peace.

She stood in the wagon porch, the huge entrance doors closed and barred behind her. Ahead, the broad hallway of the porch led into the main barn, where the ceiling rose into shadows, and she could barely make out the entrance to the other wagon porch on the opposite side.

Tamping down her nerves, she strode to the building's central aisle. Large bays lined the barn in each direction. This late in the summer, before the autumn harvest, they appeared mostly empty, though bits of straw and hay flecked the flag-stone threshing floor.

She wanted to shout for Berengar, but a shiver of dread closed her throat. Didn't he see her light? Why didn't he call out? Maybe he'd fallen asleep.

Or maybe he hadn't returned to human form, and a massive, murderous bear hid in the dark, waiting to attack anyone who dared enter.

Stifling her panic, Eira crept down the righthand aisle. She peered into the open bays, great wooden-walled rooms, like stalls for giants' horses. A few bales of straw in one. Scythes and flails and other farming equipment in another.

She neared the barn's northern end seeing no sign of man or bear. No sound except a rustle from the rafters high above. Maybe bats. She swept the weak beam of her lantern across the openings of the last two bays. Nothing but shadows.

Except, as she turned away, her gaze caught marks in the floor.

Away from the flagstone threshing surface between the wagon porches, the barn floor was bare earth, packed hard as the stone. At the entrance of the final bay, dark streaks marred the surface, gouges dug into the ground by something sharp and powerful.

Something like bear claws.

"Berengar!" Of course she regained her voice now, when caution said all she'd found was evidence of a monster.

Curse caution. Eira ran to the bay, her lantern splashing light wildly across the wooden partitions. A figure stood in the center of the bay, disheveled, head drooping with exhaustion. Taut ropes led from the tight loops around his neck to iron hooks in the walls.

She nearly spilled the lantern, clanging it to the ground so she could run to him. She would have flung her arms around his chest if she hadn't been afraid of knocking him off his feet and hanging him. Instead, she touched his shoulder. He flinched.

"Berengar?"

She brushed his wild hair from his face. His teeth showed in a flash of feral despair, and the eyes that met hers were flat and opaque. They showed no recognition, as if his human form were a mere shell already inhabited by the soul of a beast.

At Eira's moan of dismay, he moved with a predator's speed, grabbing her arms with iron strength. Panic fluttered her throat, but before she could react, his eyes widened, then warmed, like dying coals fanned to life by a gentle breath.

"Eira?"

She nodded, swallowing back tears. "You're alive."

"Apparently so." His freckles crinkled. "Disappointed?"

"You'd be less trouble dead." Choking on a laugh—or a sob—she reached for the ropes at his neck and hissed when she saw the abrasions beneath.

"I couldn't get the loops wide enough to get my head through," he rasped.

"Who tied you like this?" she demanded, struggling with the knots. "I will kill them."

"I don't think murder is one of the Nine Roads to Peace."

"That's not funny." Her fingernail snagged in the rough hemp and ripped. "*Goddess.*"

"When they noosed me like this, I was a bear," he said. "They were terrified. I was terrified. I didn't know what Kaspar had done to you. I must have nearly strangled myself to get the knots that tight."

"But the bear's neck is huge! The ropes should have loosened when you changed." She gave up on the noose's knot and moved to the hook screwed into the barn wall.

"The ropes must be like my clothes," Berengar said. "Part of the sorcery. I've always thought it was a mercy that the change doesn't rip them to shreds, and I don't come back naked. But it wasn't to my advantage in this case."

Eira primly turned her mind from imagining Berengar without his clothes. Well, maybe just a *quick* peek.

"Gah!" The knot at the hook was just as bad as the ones around Berengar's neck.

Silke and her men couldn't see Berengar like this. He was their earl. He should be standing free. If only they stored weapons in the barn—

"Wait! I'll be right back."

"I'll be here," he said with a wry smile.

She grabbed the lantern. Two bays down. Right side … no, left. The scythes glinted sharp and wicked in the flickering light. She grabbed one and sprinted back, the lantern swinging wildly.

Berengar's eyes widened. "You look like one of Lady Moon's holy hunters come to reap my soul for the afterlife."

"Grab this rope with both hands and hold it tight," she ordered. "I don't want to kill you now."

She'd never wielded a scythe, and the rope was thick and tough, but the well-honed farm implement slashed through the rough strands in seconds. The severed ends slapped heavily to the ground, and Eira let the scythe drop. She ripped a nail free, struggling to loosen the nooses around Berengar's neck. She pulled off the first, and Berengar worked off the second, tossing the rope aside with a gasp.

He stumbled, and she grabbed his arm.

"My legs." He put a hand on her shoulder to steady himself. "They were getting a little shaky."

"If you'd fallen …" Eira pressed her fist to her mouth.

"Strangling might have been less painful." He glanced at her sideways, those dangerous eyes fully warmed now. "But I knew you'd come for me. I couldn't let you think me a coward."

That called for a response. Something grand that a warrior princess of Nordmark would say in a legend song.

"Don't be a goose." They didn't have time for a song. Besides, Nordish legends tended to end with everyone dying, and she wasn't going to let that happen. "I'm taking you to the manor to lift the curse—"

"Of course you are." He laughed. "I've never met anyone as stubborn as you. Unless it's Princess Marjani."

"I'm not stubborn!" Eira objected. "Marjani and I are nothing alike."

"But just in case." His voice lowered. "Just in case I don't get another chance."

She didn't understand what he meant until his mouth had almost reached hers. Or maybe she had understood, somewhere deep inside, because she was already leaning toward him.

Their noses bumped, and she laughed. Until she met his gaze, and the look in his eyes silenced her, even as her blood fizzed like that sparkling Rigan wine Princess Dora was always going on about. Then their lips met, and for the first time in forever, there were no princesses, no princes, no queens and kings and deadly royal games.

Heat pooled in her very center, spreading to her fingers, her toes. He tasted of wild berries and hope and sorrow. She found her hands on his chest, felt his heart beating beneath his tunic. His palms cupped her cheeks, his mouth drinking hers as if she *were* that Rigan wine, bright, deep, intoxicating.

Good sense wanted to pull her back. *Take caution.* Why would Berengar kiss a sunburned, exiled Nordish girl, except that she might be his last chance for a kiss in this life?

But her heart didn't believe a word. *Caution?* It laughed, full of joy and wildness. *Don't you dare start now.*

Eira's hands slid up his shoulders, pulling him closer, breathing in the scent of pine and musky wilderness. He caught his fingers in the hair escaping from her plaited crown, his light touch against her neck sending a delicious shiver down her spine.

A sudden noise broke the moment. A door banging.

"Princess Eira?"

Lady Silke. She'd entirely forgotten about Silke. About her five minutes. It was possible she'd forgotten her own name.

Berengar's mouth lifted from hers. He didn't duck away, in

shyness or regret, even if the skin beneath his freckles had warmed to a lovely russet.

"Princess Eira!" Silke called again, voice strained.

"I think she's afraid you've been eaten by a bear," he murmured.

Only nibbled …

Eira found her voice, a little ragged at the edges. "Lady Silke! It's all right. There's nothing to fear."

She stepped back and scooped up her lantern. "Let me reassure them."

Berengar nodded, though his shoulders hunched a little. "They might not have liked me much, but at least I've never frightened anyone in this form."

"We'll lift the curse."

He nodded again.

She forced herself to break eye contact and step into the aisle. Silke quivered, taut and anxious in the center of the threshing floor. Her men huddled around her, swords drawn.

"Princess Eira!" Relief warmed the tight pallor of Silke's face. "Where is the bear?"

"He's not here."

Old Philip cursed and spun around. "Behind us!"

"No! I mean, he's right here," Eira said hastily. *That* didn't help. "I mean, he's not a bear. He's a man. That's the curse. He's a bear by day but a man at night. Put down your swords."

"She's mad," Rodolf barked, raising his sword. "You must flee, Lady Silke. The bear could be anywhere."

"Wait." Silke lifted a hand. "She does not strike me as mad. But I don't understand what you mean, Princess Eira."

The shadows shifted as Berengar stepped from the bay.

Rodolf swore. One of the men dropped his sword as he made a sign against evil.

"That's no bear," Philip said. "That's a beggar or a madman."

"I am the bear," Berengar assured him. "*Was* the bear this afternoon and will be again in the morning."

"Damn my soul." Rodolf took a step forward, his lantern raised high. "It can't be … Earl Berengar?"

"Our missing earl and the bear," Silke mused amidst the men's cries of surprise. "One and the same. It is because it must be. Why did I not see it before?"

"Because it's not blooming possible," Philip said, adding a belated, "Milady."

"I hardly believe it myself," Berengar agreed.

"Why has he returned now?" Silke asked, turning her stunned gaze to Eira.

"The curse becomes irreversible tomorrow," Berengar said.

"There's a counter-curse in Rurik's sorcery book." Eira couldn't be sure if the buzzing in her fingers was from Berengar's kiss or the sudden upspringing of hope. Somehow, her desperate plan had worked. Against all odds, Berengar was still human, and Silke and her men had seen and believed it. "If we can collect the book from the storeroom—"

"No need." A faint smile touched Silke's lips. "Princess Marjani mentioned the counter-curse this afternoon …"

She gestured to Philip, who passed her his rucksack. Silke reached in and pulled out a fawn-colored, leather-bound book that looked like it had traveled rough for many more years than Rurik had been alive.

"That's it?" Eira asked, absurdly disappointed. A book of sorcery should be huge, heavy, and black. Very, very black, possibly with smoke curling from the pages.

"I had the same reaction," Silke admitted, though she held the book with wary respect. "Rurik made such a fuss about how deadly his spell-book was. When I saw it, I thought it must be a fraud, just like him. But—"

She gestured at Berengar.

Berengar stepped closer to Eira, and she reached out to take his hand. A spark of elation flashed through her. Yes, they still needed to get the original caster to speak the counter-curse, but for the first time, that actually seemed possible.

"I took the liberty of looking for the spell earlier." As Silke flipped through the book, Eira saw notes and diagrams scribbled in the margins around the carefully calligraphed letters. Silke stopped at a page marked by a bit of ribbon. "*Restvrivo*. Rurik has written beside it, 'tried this a hundred different ways, curse whoever wrote it and gave poor B hope of a cure.'"

She looked up. "He really is a hopeless charlatan."

Strangely enough, true as that might be, Eira's first thought was, *not fair*. Rurik had spent an entire year trying to save a man he barely knew from a curse he hadn't cast. That said more about his character than any failure as a sorcerer.

"Do you think you can cast this spell?" Silke asked her.

Eira stifled a startled laugh, but the yeomen shifted nervously. After all, Kaspar had spent the day calling her a witch. But, it was too late to trick the caster into trying the counter-curse by telling them it would get rid of the bear. That plan was only feasible if no one knew Berengar was still alive. They needed Silke's help now. She had the power to order everyone to try it.

"Princess Eira cannot lift this curse," Berengar said, obviously reaching the same conclusion. "Only the person who cast it has that power."

"Is that what Rurik told you?" Lady Silke fingered the spell's page, a slight frown between her graceful brows. With a sudden, decisive jerk, she ripped the page from the sorcery book's ancient binding.

"What—" Eira began, startled.

"Perhaps he's right." Silke clutched the scrap of parchment so tightly her knuckles turned white. "Perhaps only the caster can perform this spell. But I wouldn't want to wager my future on *Rurik's* judgment. I'm sure you feel the same way."

She dropped the book into the rucksack and lifted the page toward Berengar like an offering.

"I hardly know how I feel." He glanced at Eira. "I haven't had a future in so long."

Eira squeezed his hand. Surely, as long as she held it, so warm and human, they could make this right. They could do anything.

"We ought to try casting the counter-curse before we do anything else," she agreed. "Just in case Rurik is wrong. Is it complicated?"

"No," Silke said. "On the contrary. It looks quite simple."

The parchment trembled in her hand. She had seemed so indomitable earlier, facing her fear of the bear, but suddenly she looked like she might collapse.

"I'm sure it's not dangerous," Eira assured her, "but I can try it first. Make sure it's safe."

Silke stared at her for a moment. Then she laughed, some of the horrible tension draining from her face.

"Oh, my gods, no." Silke rolled up the loose leaf of parchment. "No, that wouldn't do at all."

She reached out to take Rodolf's lantern. "You completely misunderstand me. I'm not hoping to see if someone else can cast it. I want to ensure they can't."

With another incredulous laugh, she thrust the end of the parchment into the lantern's flame.

CHAPTER THIRTY

6. She doesn't trust anybody.

— Top 10 things ~~I hate~~ I find difficult to appreciate about Princess Marjani, as listed by (former) Princess Eira of Nordmark

Marjani followed Hartwin through the empty manor corridors. Despite the day's excitement, the late hour had sent most of the inhabitants to bed, though she could hear Master Kaspar's voice booming from the front of the house.

"Kaspar could have taken Rurik's book," she whispered. "If Tarben won't let him burn the barn, he might try a curse."

"I doubt it," Hartwin murmured back. "Steward Tarben has been plying him with drink to blunt his rash ideas."

A rumble of drunken laughter punctuated his point.

"Or it might make him even more rash." Marjani couldn't forget Kaspar's knife at Eira's throat. She blinked away images of Eira's blood spraying like Mosi's had. "That book is dangerous, whether the person who took it knows how to use it or not. To fight sorcery, we need a sorcerer."

"You mean Rurik." Hartwin's voice was flat.

"I know you don't trust him—" And when had *she* begun to trust the troublesome Ravninan? "But he deflected a portion of the bear curse last year. If someone casts another one, it might be good to have him nearby."

"If you say so," Hartwin growled, a little bear-like himself. "Follow me."

"How do you know your way?" she asked, more lost in the maze of the old house than she liked to admit.

"My father brought me to the manor sometimes when I was little." A flash of a mischievous grin. "I was proud of him, you understand, the town's reeve, advising the old earl. But it was awfully boring. I might have done a bit of wandering."

Light bloomed ahead, spilling softly from a narrow corridor.

Hartwin held up a hand and mouthed, "Wait here."

Blunt and straightforward as he was, he moved with the grace of a stalking leopard, padding to the very edge of the light. He cautiously glanced around the corner, then gestured for Marjani to join him.

She slipped into the short hallway to find Hartwin going through the pockets of a lanky young man who lay sprawled on the floor beside a lantern. Her heart went cold until she saw the steady rise and fall of the man's chest.

She was hunting someone who had stolen a book of dangerous black sorcery, who might even now be plotting another dark curse. Yet, she quailed at the thought of harming one young man in order to stop a greater disaster. A stranger who, now that she looked closer, had aimed a bow at her and her companions just that afternoon.

Weak. Her father's voice. *Cowardly. Useless.*

Compassion is one of the Nine Roads to Peace.

Gods. The lily-faced witch had invaded her mind like some kind of brain-eating maggot.

But she was still glad the boy was breathing.

"What did you do to him?" she hissed.

"Do you remember the story I told you about my sister marrying the apothecary?" he asked.

"You *drugged* him?"

"I brought him some hot cider earlier. He looked cold." That mischievous light in those sea-green eyes could lure the unwary to drowning. With a huff of triumph, he pulled a key from the young man's coat.

"You're the town *reeve*," she scolded through stifled laughter.

"I swore an oath to protect the people of Saebern Town," he said soberly, though his eyes still danced. "That's what I mean to do."

Another realization struck her. "You already planned to release Rurik."

"I feared it might be necessary." His expression turned grim. "Whatever else he may have done, Rurik cannot have stolen that book from the strongroom. He might be the only one who can figure out how to stop the person who did."

He turned the lock. Beyond the doorway, stone stairs dropped away into darkness. Marjani grabbed the guard's lantern and picked her way over his sprawled legs, not daring to breathe until she'd joined Hartwin on the steps and closed the door behind them.

Hartwin's gaze met hers. "I made a terrible mistake this afternoon, arresting you and Princess Eira. You must think me a fool."

"You are one of the most conscientious, honorable men I know, and you did what you thought was right. You are doing that now, despite the danger." Marjani lifted her chin. "I would accept nothing less from my one-man army."

He choked down surprised laughter, his eyes darkening with something deeper. "You deserve a real knight as your champion, not a baker. But I swear I will do my best."

"If all bakers are like you, I don't need knights and princes." She'd meant it to be light. Continue the jest. But it came out sounding like what it was.

The truth.

His position a step below put him nearly even with her height and so close she scarcely needed to lean forward to touch her lips to his forehead.

Hartwin jolted. One foot slid off the stair, landing hard on the next step down. He slammed his hands against the walls to brace himself. Marjani grabbed his tunic with her free hand to hold him steady. A baker's muscles were easily as hard as a knight's—*not* that she was noticing.

"I am sorry." Her ears burned. "That is how my father would accept a pledge of duty from one of his champions. But I am no princess of yours. I take it back—"

"Don't you dare." His arms were still tensed, yet his smile held no strain at all. "It only surprised me, as it is not our custom. Here in Aldforth, our lord—or lady—would hold out their hand."

He released the walls and gently lifted her hand from his shoulder, positioning it in front of her, fingers down, in demonstration. "Then the knight would kiss his liege's ring."

Marjani glanced at her bare fingers, her nails ragged from sword training and archery practice with the other princesses, despite the strict hand care regimen Princess Isolde had required them all to follow. "I do not have a ring."

"I am not a knight." He touched her fingers to his lips.

Heat traveled up her arm, sharp and burning as if a knife had been drawn along her skin and then plunged into her chest. Yet even as she braced against the pain of the blow, the feeling changed. Something light and soft released inside her, unfurling like the wings of a crowned crane, beating in rhythm with her heart.

A fledgling's wings. Erratic, unsure. Only knowing they must reach for the sky.

She glanced at her arms, half expecting to have sprouted feathers, before she realized it was her spirit revealing itself to her. So unexpected and alarming, she feared it might fly away from her body altogether.

"Hartwin …" His name on her lips sounded as soft and wondrous as her soul.

"Marjani." He turned hers into music.

"I love a romantic moment as much as the next man." Rurik's voice rose from the shadows beneath Hartwin's feet. "So, I wouldn't interrupt, but one of the spells I was never able to cast was the one that makes time stop. How does that work do you think? Sorcerous metaphysics was an advanced-level seminar, so I will probably never know. But I do have an acute sense of natural time, and we're past midnight."

Midnight. Marjani's heart still beat too fast, each beat another moment they couldn't afford to waste.

Hartwin dropped his hand to his sword hilt. "Lady Silke ordered you confined, bound, and gagged, sorcerer."

Rurik appeared at the edge of the lantern light at the bottom of the stairs, free hands lifted palms up. With his clothes rumpled and topknot askew, he looked even scruffier than usual.

"I may have no talent for curses," he said. "But I do excel at sleight-of-hand."

Marjani would have sworn his fingers barely moved, but suddenly one fist held a dangling rope and the other a short, sharp blade.

He tossed the rope aside. "At least you've saved me the trouble of picking the lock."

"This isn't a game," Hartwin growled. "People have died."

"And the rest are still in danger," Rurik snapped. "Someone has taken my book from the strongroom. Not to state the obvious"—although, of course, he did—"but we've got to get it back before that someone uses it."

"Not to state the obvious," Marjani said. "But that's why we are here." She'd been so much happier to see him before he opened his mouth.

"Wait!" Hartwin tugged his sword, freeing a foot of gleaming blade from its sheath. "Who told you the book was stolen, villain?"

"I *felt* it," Rurik hissed. "That gods damned book. Never offered me so much as a glimmer of power, yet it delights in warning me when someone else wields it."

"You *felt* it," Hartwin scoffed.

"Like a twist in my gut." Rurik shuddered. "I hoped maybe Tarben had poisoned me, but then I remembered he hadn't fed me. So, I'm left with sorcery."

"Hartwin." Marjani touched the reeve's arm. He'd promised to trust her, but Rurik never made anything easy. "We must hurry."

Hartwin glanced from her to the sorcerer, then slammed his sword back into its sheath. "Has someone cast another curse?"

"I don't know," Rurik admitted. "Last year, I sensed the curse building for a while, like welling nausea, but I didn't recognize it as sorcery until I felt it crackling in the air. Like during a storm, before lightning strikes. When I tried to shield Berengar, it blasted through me. Or around me. It should have killed me."

He glanced down at his hands. "I would have sworn I have no magical abilities, no matter what my grandmother believed. But *something* rose within me then. Enough to deflect a portion of the evil ..."

"And now?" Marjani pressed. "Can we stop it *now?*"

"It could be the book sending a warning, like a signal flare. I don't *think* a curse has been cast yet. But I fear one is coming."

"We must get to the barn as fast as we can." Marjani reached for the door. "Whoever it is will go after the bear."

"The *bear?*" Hartwin asked.

"But the *Arkou Devor* is about to be completed," Rurik said. "Casting another curse on the bear is unnecessary. The caster wouldn't be so foolish—"

"If it were Prince Guntram in that barn," Marjani said, "and you knew he would be executed in the morning, would you pass up the opportunity to stab him in the heart tonight?"

The sorcerer's gaze locked with hers, and he surged up the stairs. "We have to get to the barn."

Hartwin slammed a hand against the door. "Wait. We're going to risk our lives to prevent someone from cursing a *bear?*"

"From cursing a bear a *second time*," Rurik corrected. "Do try to keep up."

"You're not funny, sorcerer," Hartwin told him. "And I don't trust you."

"Fine," Rurik said. "I don't trust you, either. The difference is, you need me, and I don't need you."

"Really? Who rescued you from this cellar?"

"We don't have *time*—" Marjani reached for the door.

"*I* rescued me," Rurik interrupted. "There isn't a cell in this gods-forsaken backwater that could hold me."

Hartwin clenched his fists. "Would you care to wager on that?"

"*Enough!*" Marjani commanded. Not even her father could have managed a more imperious tone. "If we hope to save our friends and stop this sorcerer from turning us all into monstrous beasts—"

"Which is *not* the nastiest spell in that book," Rurik put in. "Did I mention the one that sets your blood on fire?"

"If we mean to do any of that," Marjani said. "*We all need each other*. Which is the only reason I haven't locked you both in here and left you behind."

Now that she had them, now that she had this inconvenient flutter of hope, she could hardly bear that they weren't already *sprinting*. She yanked open the door and stepped over the sleeping guard into the hall outside.

"Turn left," Rurik whispered. "To the garden."

"Right," Hartwin objected. "There's a guard in the garden. Unless you've got an invisibility spell—"

"It's going to work one of these days," Rurik grumbled. "Just you wait—"

Hissing with frustration, Marjani spun around the corner into the hallway, slamming into Steward Tarben so hard her forehead bounced off his nose.

CHAPTER THIRTY-ONE

1. She's reckless.

— Top 10 things I despise about Princess Eira, as listed by Princess Marjani of Almasa

"No!" Eira lunged toward Silke as the spell's parchment began to smoke and curl. She might have thrown herself onto old Philip's blade—to be fair, it didn't look as though it had been sharpened in decades—but Rodolf grabbed her first.

"Eira!"

She heard a scuffle as Berengar tried to reach her, but Rodolf was almost as quick as he was wide, and his massive arms crushed her to his chest. For a moment, helplessness jerked her like an undertow, pulling her back to Master Kaspar holding her captive mere hours earlier.

Unlike Kaspar, Rodolf didn't think it necessary to hold a knife to her throat. His mistake.

Her boot heel struck the top of Rodolf's foot with a satisfying crunch. His grasp barely loosened. That was all Eira needed.

She dropped beneath his arms, swung around, and struck him in the back of the knee with a swift kick. She'd seen

Princess Jax fell a six-foot Rose Knight with a similar move. Rodolf merely grunted in surprise.

Still, she whirled out of his reach, coming around to find yet another guard between her and Lady Silke. And when she dodged him, there was another. And another.

Silke held the flaming parchment like a candle, still smiling as it burned down to her fingers. With a sigh of evident relief, she flicked the smoldering scrap to the threshing floor and ground it beneath her shoe.

Eira cried out in horror as Berengar gripped her elbow and drew her away from the bristling guards.

"Why?" She asked Silke. She could choke out nothing more coherent, her hopes scattered like the ash on the ground. "You can't … I don't … *Why?*"

Silke's fervent gaze met hers. "I told you why. I had to be certain no one could perform the spell and set him free."

"It was you." The ground seemed to tilt beneath Eira's feet. "You cast the curse."

So obvious, really. Tarben, Kaspar, Reeve Wendel, and any number of wealthy landowners might have resented their new earl, the awkward, untried, virtual stranger upending the settled order of their lives. Might even have gone so far as to have wished him dead.

But who had lost the most when the old earl named Berengar his heir?

"You blamed Berengar for his father denying Artis her birthright." Eira shook with fury, grief—and even pity. "She should have been a duchess. You were furious she lost her title."

"Lost her *title?*" Silke's eyes flashed. "When Earl Hallborn broke law and custom to name that witless, worthless boy his heir, he didn't just steal my daughter's title. He stripped her of every scrap of autonomy and power she had in this world."

"Silke, no." Berengar's voice broke. "Artis is my brother's child. She was my heir. She will always be a noble lady."

"A lady." Silke's voice dripped with venom. "A pawn, I

think you mean. Isn't that what a lady is? A game piece to further the ambitions of her father, her brother, her *uncle*."

Eira swallowed hard, thinking of *her* uncle, so quick to cheat the board in his favor.

"Played strategically to create an alliance or secure a border," Silke continued, her dark eyes blazing with a hatred that could sear the skin. "As quiet and compliant as a bit of ivory moved about the table, her worth measured in the children she produces. Expected to go meekly to whatever cold, remote wasteland she is sold to. Cut off from her friends, her family—maybe forever if her husband doesn't 'see the appeal' of travel."

Why had Eira assumed Silke had loved Berengar's brother? Just because she loved the child she'd had with him? For the first time, Eira realized her uncle could have done worse to her than banishment.

Silke laughed, sounding more exhausted than amused. "Do you think I wanted to give birth to a daughter? That I would choose to condemn her to such a life? And then to have her born with a chance to have more. To be free. Only to have that ripped away by a man who made it clear *he didn't even want to be here*."

Beside Eira, Berengar flinched.

"I didn't," he admitted. "If I'd had a choice, I would have stayed in Rigas to finish my schooling and work for my uncle. But when my father called me, I had to answer. You could have come to me. Told me your fears. We could have made provisions for Artis. Together."

"Why didn't I think of that?" Silke's eyes widened in mockery. "After all, you made it abundantly clear how much you valued my experience running the household. How much you wished to listen to my advice."

Berengar reddened, and his chin jutted defensively. For a moment, Eira could see clearly the callow, arrogant youth Silke had seen, as well as the scornful, bitter adversary Berengar had seen in her. What might have been if the two of them had only been able to look beyond each other's worst selves?

Berengar took a breath and shook his shoulders like a bear shaking off falling leaves.

"I should have given more thought to your feelings, losing my brother and then having my father disinherit your daughter," he said. "I never saw the unfairness of it until Princess Eira made me understand. I was wrapped in my own grief and misery, but that is no excuse."

Eira's heart cracked open, knowing Berengar had so valued her words. It cracked for Silke and Artis and all the other girls like them—and herself—used and discarded at the whim of others. It cracked from the knowledge that whatever change she had provoked in Berengar's thoughts, it made no difference in the long run because Silke had burned all their hopes away.

Her heart shattered because it was frozen, deathly cold, black as the soot on the stone beneath Silke's feet.

"Berengar never hurt anyone deliberately," she said, hard as her heart. "He never chose murder. Not like you, Lady Silke."

"Murder?" Silke asked. "Burning a piece of parchment?"

"You cursed Berengar and killed two other men in the process. You're a sorceress."

"You're the one who's been arrested for sorcery." Silke tossed her head. "You're the girl who speaks to bears."

"What bear?" Eira asked, the mockery bitter on her tongue. "I don't see any bear. Just Berengar, the rightful lord of Saebern. Rodolf, Philip, and these other men are his, not yours."

"These men are *Artis's*," Silke snapped. She glared at her little band of guards, eyes blazing as if to burn away their confusion and doubt as they glanced nervously between the menacing woman in their midst and the rumpled wild man at Eira's side.

"Berengar is their earl," Eira repeated, willing the men to listen.

"*Not anymore*." Silke's voice bled from outrage to grim satisfaction. "It's true that King Wulfric, at that scheming Kaspar's request, delayed Artis's instatement as duchess for one year from the day of Berengar's disappearance."

Silke's smile showed teeth this time. "But it's well after midnight."

"The *time* doesn't matter. He's here. *You're here*," Eira cried to Berengar, desperate to staunch the gray resignation flooding his face. She turned to the yeomen. "Your earl didn't abandon you. He's been in Saebern this whole time."

"He's been a *bear* this whole time." Silke spat. "And he'll be a bear again at dawn. Forever. At least, that's what I understood from Kaspar's report of your ravings this afternoon."

When Eira and Marjani had returned from the wilderness with Rurik in tow, Silke must have felt the truth closing in on her, threatening her with exposure. And she had turned it all to her advantage with bold action and a gracious smile.

Eira gritted her teeth against her tears. "You're a monster."

"There is a monster here," Silke said, her outward calm returned. "And no one will be taking orders from him ever again."

She turned to Rodolf. "Seize them!"

CHAPTER THIRTY-TWO

1. She holds a grudge *forever*.

 — Top 10 things ~~I hate~~ I find difficult to appreciate about Princess Marjani, as listed by (former) Princess Eira of Nordmark

"Aagh!" Tarben staggered back from the collision with Marjani, his hand pressed to his face.

Marjani managed to catch her balance, but Tarben stumbled into Master Kaspar, his elbow jabbing the merchant's broad middle. Eyes wide in drunken surprise, Kaspar dropped the jug he carried. It shattered, spattering wine dregs across the floor.

"Left," Hartwin ordered, pulling Marjani away.

"Told you so," Rurik called as they sprinted after him.

"Stop!" Kaspar roared. "I'm go … go … catch an' *beat* you."

Considering Kaspar's inebriation and Tarben's bloody nose, Marjani thought that seemed unlikely. As long as they didn't run into anyone else in the hall—

Rurik turned the corner ahead and gave an incoherent shout. There was a thud as something hit the wall and then the floor. *"All the gods' eyeballs!"*

Marjani skidded around the bend after him, Hartwin on her heels. The light from Hartwin's lantern showed Rurik's sprawled form, a tangle of cloak and hair and limbs struggling to rise from the floor. The obstacle that had tripped him sat in the center of the hall, chubby fists clenched, eyes large and brimming, loosing the first startled notes of a rising, high-pitched cry.

"Artis!" Marjani dropped to her knees at the child's side. "Are you hurt?"

The incipient wail wavered as Artis stared up at her, mouth open in astonishment.

"She's fine," Rurik grumbled as he lurched upright. "Thanks to my quick footwork. Didn't so much as touch her. Let's go."

"But what is she doing here?" The child had obviously woken and wandered from her room, but why hadn't anyone come looking for her? "Where is Silke?"

"Her stepfather is right behind us," Hartwin reminded her. "He'll find her quick enough."

As Marjani pushed to her feet, Artis threw her arms around Marjani's leg. "Drangin! Queen Drangin!"

Tenzin. "The dragon isn't here, child."

"Small mercies," Hartwin muttered as Marjani fumbled to peel away Artis's surprisingly firm grip. "The bear's enough to worry about."

"Bear like Arris," Artis said, sniffling. "Mama go."

Where *was* Silke? Didn't Artis have a servant to watch her? A *nursemaid,* Princess Raisa called them. Raisa had been horrified to learn that Almasan royalty nursed their own babies. Almost as horrified as Marjani had been to learn Ravninan royalty didn't.

"Let's go," Rurik urged, grabbing Artis's shoulders to pull her away.

"Mama go! Bear!" Artis shrieked.

Rurik jerked back as if she'd bitten him, and Marjani

scooped her up, an involuntary reaction to the wailing toddler. The little girl's arms wrapped python-like around her neck.

"Arris go bear," Artis sobbed into her shoulder.

"*Marjani*," Hartwin warned as footsteps thudded in the hall behind them.

"Just bring her with you," Rurik urged. Even in desperate circumstances, he could make Marjani roll her eyes.

"We are not endangering this child. You go," she said. *No time. No time.* "I'll slow them down."

But Hartwin thrust the lantern at Rurik and put a hand on his hilt as Tarben and Kaspar lurched around the corner. Blood trickled from the steward's nose, though he looked more alarmed than injured.

Kaspar staggered, grabbing the steward's shoulder to keep himself upright. The merchant's mouth contorted as he jabbed a finger at Hartwin's chest, but the only vocalization he produced was an incoherent growl.

"Artis!" Tarben paled at the sight of the girl in Marjani's arms. "You monsters! If you hurt a single hair on her head—"

"*Us?*" Rurik's voice cracked in outrage. "You're the one letting a baby wander loose in the middle of the night. *We're* trying to prevent a magical catastrophe."

Firmly, Marjani detached Artis from her neck and held her out toward Tarben. "We found her sitting alone in this hallway."

"Scoundrels!" Kaspar roared. He slapped at his waist as though reaching for his sword, but fortunately for everyone— *especially himself*, Marjani thought—he was unarmed.

Tarben snatched Artis from her arms.

"Tarbie! Tarbie, Arris go bear."

"Reeve Hartwin." Tarben tugged Artis's fingers from his beard. "I demand to know what you are doing with these prisoners. You are sworn to protect Saebern!"

"I am," Hartwin agreed, wary eyes on Kaspar's flailing. "And that's what I intend to do."

"We're not staying to argue," Marjani told Tarben. "You can hunt us down after you put Artis to bed."

She turned to Hartwin. "Let's go."

"Shtay away from that barn!" Kaspar roared, then tipped over against the wall. "Gods take that bear!"

"Arris go barn! Tarbie! Arris go barn!"

Artis's cries and Kaspar's bellows followed them as they raced down the hall. When they reached the kitchen garden, they caught a breath of luck. The hapless guard still snored peacefully beneath Marjani's window. A small archway in the opposite wall, nearly hidden by the hedge, held an iron gate.

Rurik made quick work opening it, nearly as adept at picking locks as Princess Beatrix.

"I'll lock it behind us," he said. "Slow them down."

Hartwin shook his head. "Tarben and Kaspar didn't steal your book. They think we're up to no good, but we might need their aid before the night is out."

"Gods help us," Rurik muttered as he led them into the earthy, heather-scented darkness.

The barn lay only a hundred yards from the manor, but she couldn't make out the building through the thick, inky shadows ahead. A summer night, the warmest moon-span of the cold-cursed north, and yet the unnatural chill racing down her spine seeped into her very marrow.

They could see nothing, but their lantern made them visible to anyone who looked their way.

She turned toward Rurik to warn him to shutter it, but the brightness of the light made her blink and stumble backward.

"Watch your step. Twisted ankle won't do us any good," Rurik said, before his eyes widened at her expression. "What? What's wrong?"

"What are you doing?" she asked, breath suddenly tight. "You're ... glowing."

"*Where?*" he demanded in alarm, hopping sideways as though he'd stumbled into a campfire. The lantern jounced with him, its light flickering wildly, but that didn't change the aura that seemed to radiate from his skin. "What do you mean, glowing? Get it off me!"

"Stop that!" Hartwin ordered. "You're going to spill the oil. There's nothing wrong with you. Nothing more than usual." He looked at Marjani. "What do you mean he's glowing?"

"You can't see it?" But even as she spoke, she realized the problem. "It's not Rurik that's glowing—not his body. It's his spirit ... It's *brightened*."

That wasn't the right word, but as close as she could come. It wasn't that his darkness had left him. More as though the rest of his spirit had expanded and ... clarified. She had never seen a spirit so distinct, so vibrant that it obscured his physical form.

"Like someone lengthened the wick in a lamp." She gestured at the lantern Rurik carried, though that, too, was a poor metaphor. She sensed no evil in the sorcerer's new intensity, yet it raised the hair on her arms. "Can't you *feel* it?"

"You mean that tingling?" Rurik hunched his shoulders. "It's just a storm brewing."

They all glanced up at the stars glimmering overhead.

"It's a storm," Rurik insisted. "It feels like lightning is about to strike."

"Which is exactly how you felt when the bear was cursed last year," Marjani said.

For a wild moment, she hoped he would contradict her. Instead, his face paled, startling against his black hair.

Hartwin yanked his sword from its sheath. "Is it coming from ahead of us?"

Rurik closed his eyes, his body tensing in concentration. The brightness in his spirit seemed to stretch, pulling his body forward.

"Yes." His eyes popped open. "*Run!*"

Marjani was already sprinting for the barn.

CHAPTER THIRTY-THREE

2. He never thought of anyone but himself.

— Top 10 reasons no one misses Earl Berengar that much (Submitted by Lady Silke, mother of Countess Artis of Saebern.)

"Don't touch her!" Berengar's order cracked like a whip in Eira's ears.

His ragged, unshaven appearance might have allowed Silke's men to forget he was a lord. But that voice, cold and sure, held the confidence of a man used to being obeyed. The yeomen hesitated long enough for Berengar and Eira to retreat out of their reach.

Yet, Eira could see the standoff wouldn't hold. Silke was the men's mistress, from her dignified bearing to her elegant clothes, whereas Berengar might transform into a terrifying beast at any moment.

"Princess Eira is no part of this," Berengar told Silke. "Allow her to leave, and I will not fight you."

As if she would desert him! Eira gritted her teeth, but his ridiculous chivalry might gain her a few moments to come up with a plan …

"Fight me?" Silke scoffed, gesturing around at her men. "I

don't think that would go well for you. Still, I have no quarrel with Princess Eira. I will ensure she is treated kindly in her madness rather than executed for sorcery. You, however, are a clear danger to Saebern that must be destroyed to ensure the peace and safety of our people."

Eira edged closer to the bay where she had found Berengar, quelling her snort of disgust. The destruction of another human life was never a road to peace. Lady Silke could have benefitted from a year under Holy Mother at the Temple.

"You expect these men to murder me for you?" Berengar asked.

"I don't expect them to wait for a cursed bear to slaughter us all," Silke snapped.

"There will be no slaughter tonight!" Eira grabbed the scythe she'd used to cut Berengar's ropes. It wasn't a sword, and she was half Rodolf's size, but she was a Nordish princess. Give her a blade, and she could make these men think twice about murdering anyone.

"Honestly," Silke sighed. "Do be sensible. Very shortly, this man will become a bloodthirsty beast. The counter-curse is destroyed. The only way to protect ourselves now is to kill him."

"You're the one who burned the counter-curse!" The scythe shook with Eira's outrage. "Give me that book, and I will find another way to help him."

"I *can* help him." Silke pulled the sorcerous tome from her bag and opened it. "I can release him from his cursed existence. Something quick. I think he would prefer that to living his life as a monster."

"She's right," Berengar said, his eyes bleak and pleading as he met Eira's gaze. "Rurik claims the bear will be vulnerable when the curse completes, but I might still kill or maim these men before they can kill me. I might hurt you."

She saw the pulse of fear in his throat, the bravery it took to choose others' lives over his own. This good man who wanted so badly to do the right thing. And Silke meant to take that from the world.

Eira's veins burned as if her blood had turned to venom. This was the hatred Rurik had spoken of. A hatred pure enough to take any curse in Rurik's book and slam it into Silke's heart with no shred of pity or regret.

"Let's see …" Pages rustled as Silke flipped through the book. "A plague? Not fast enough, and it might be contagious. A pack of wolves? I think we've had enough of wild beasts. Invisible knives might be difficult to aim … Ah!"

She glanced up, eyes bright with triumph. "A lightning bolt to the heart. Quick and unambiguously deadly. A merciful solution to our little problem."

Eira tightened her grip on the scythe, but Berengar gripped her arm.

"No one can save me now," he said, his voice rough. "You've done all you can. More than I deserved."

"No, this is my fault," Eira realized. No wonder her hatred of Silke burned so bright. She needed it to blind herself to her own guilt. "This afternoon, when Kaspar's men captured you, I was so frightened for you that I blurted out too much of the truth. That's why Silke came to the barn tonight, to see it for herself."

"*Deca onni zeii thi demonii* …" No longer harshened by fear or anger, Silke's face held an austere beauty as she read the spell in her clear, dignified voice.

The words reminded Eira of ancient Santian, but though the language was flowing, almost lyrical, the sound curdled her stomach, making her want to retch.

Fear hollowed the faces of Silke's yeomen, whitening their knuckles on their weapons. But Eira could see they had made their choice. Their lady might be performing sorcery, but she was doing it to protect them from the cursed bear that had terrorized them for months.

Even though it was Silke who cursed him in the first place.

Eira couldn't defeat all four guards with a scythe, but one

good swing would stop that spell. She lunged, only to be brought up short by Berengar's iron grip.

"Killing Silke won't save me." His voice was sharp as any sword. "But I can save you. Take cover."

"I'm not going to hide! I'm going to kill them all!" She'd shouted those exact words at Uncle Einar when he'd told her of her mother's death at the hands of King Wulfric's army. *I'm going to kill them all.*

Uncle Einar had laughed at her. Banished her. Rendered her helpless and alone.

"You won't kill them," Berengar said. "Those men don't deserve to die."

"She's going to *kill you.*" The words tore from her throat. *"Because of me."*

"No." Another voice broke in, burning with an anger as hot as Eira's was cold. "She means to kill him because she's a vicious, amoral murderer."

"Marjani!"

The Almasan princess stepped from the wagon porch onto the threshing floor, Hartwin and Rurik on either side.

"Milady! It's the sorcerer!"

"Silke's casting a curse!" Eira warned.

"Is that *Earl Berengar?*"

"Run! Save yourselves!"

"Igniste!" Silke intoned the final word in a cry of triumph, and Eira felt the curse awake.

Rurik, racing toward Berengar, jerked abruptly, as if struck by an invisible blow. He stumbled, and Eira had to drop her scythe to catch him.

"The curse," she cried. "She's hit you."

"No, she hasn't released it yet," Rurik gasped, gripping her shoulder. His eyes didn't quite focus on hers, his pupils dilated to black pools. "Get behind me. Both of you."

He sagged suddenly. Berengar grabbed his other arm, holding the sorcerer steady as his head lolled sideways.

"Too close," Rurik croaked. "She's grown more powerful. Don't know. If I can. Deflect it."

Eira could have wept for his bravery.

"Put down that book." Marjani's order held the force of a royal decree.

Silke's yeomen turned sluggishly, slowed by their fear or their proximity to Silke's power. Eira couldn't tell which. They hardly seemed aware of their own actions as their swords came up to block Marjani.

"Stay back." Energy flickered along Silke's arm like sheet lightning as she pointed a finger at the Almasan princess. "I am protecting Saebern from that cursed monster. I won't hesitate to cut down anyone who tries to stop me."

"Can she do that?" Hartwin demanded. "Can she strike more than once with the same curse?"

"I don't know." Rurik winced as he regained his feet. "But you can't risk attacking her. If she loses control, she could incinerate us all."

"I could." Silke's voice rang with triumph as though she relished the power building within her. "I could burn this whole building to the ground in an instant and be the only one left standing. Your sword would melt in your hand before you could draw it, Reeve Hartwin."

"Back away." Rodolf's voice sounded hollow, though he held his own sword steady. "Before she kills us all."

Marjani touched Hartwin's sleeve, and he lifted his hand from his weapon. Whatever his skill with a sword, Eira knew he wasn't faster than a lightning strike.

"I only want Berengar." Obsession burned in Silke's eyes. "If the rest of you step aside, you need not be hurt."

Eira saw the entreaty in the glance Marjani sent her. *Don't be a fool. You can't save Berengar now.* And something more. *Don't you dare get yourself killed. I can't watch another friend die.*

Eira blinked back tears. So many years of exile, of belonging nowhere, to no one. Now, unexpectedly, she had people who cared about her. Jax, Anara and Beatrix back at

Lukos castle. Berengar—who'd *kissed* her! Even this Almasan princess she'd once considered her enemy.

It didn't seem fair to die *now*.

"Go," Rurik croaked. "I can't shield you both."

"Can you shield Berengar?" Eira asked.

"That's why I'm here."

But she could see the real answer in his eyes.

"I won't let you die with me," Berengar said. He tried to step away, but Rurik's grip on his shoulder brought him up short.

"I brought this curse to Saebern," the sorcerer said grimly. "I never questioned Lady Silke's motives when I found her in my room. To be fair, I found it plausible she might want a kiss from a handsome young heartbreaker."

Eira choked on a laugh. Trust Rurik. Even on the brink of death …

"She stole my spell, blamed her curse on me," he continued. "I can't let her win."

The men shared a determined look, which Eira had to acknowledge was moving and all, but she knew what they'd say next.

"No, I will not run," she said. *Appearances and attitude.* She lifted her head high, her veins cold and hard as ice. Implacable as the northern winter. Yes, she was afraid, but she was *not* helpless. For once, she would make a difference.

"Lady Silke," she shouted, drowning out Berengar's objection and Marjani's hiss of frustration. "You think no one will care if you kill a foreign sorcerer and a cursed bear. But I don't believe you'd risk King Wulfric's wrath by murdering a Nordish princess invited to Aldforth as a potential wife for his son and heir."

Not that she thought Wulfric had lost any sleep when he'd heard she had drowned. She had never been one of his favorites. But Silke didn't know that.

"Reeve Hartwin, remove her!" Silke commanded, curt

with annoyance. "Quickly, unless you want her to die. I can't hold this power back forever."

"Please, Lady Silke. You don't have to do this." Hartwin edged slowly between Silke's threat and Eira's glare. Earnest, sensible. *And those sea-blue eyes.*

But no. Eira had to fall for the awkward, quarrelsome one with unfortunate claws and big teeth.

"Lay the curse aside," Hartwin urged. "No one needs to get hurt tonight."

"Fool!" Silke snapped, and Eira heard strain in the curtness now. "A curse isn't a sword. I can't just 'lay it aside,' even if I wanted to. I have to cast it."

"No, you don't," Marjani said, voice hard with a warrior's authority. "You started this. You can stop it. Rurik, tell her how to let it go."

Rurik shook his head. "As I believe *I may have mentioned*, I've never successfully cast a curse. I don't know if she *can* stop it."

Sweat sheened Silke's forehead, and Eira saw tension tightening her jaw, accentuating the tendons in her neck.

"Eira, you must go. For me. *Please.*" Berengar's voice cracked, but those golden brown eyes were always more eloquent than his hard-won words. Begging her to go because he couldn't bear to lose her. Just as she couldn't bear to lose him.

In the space between heartbeats, it felt as if nothing else mattered. The curse, the fear, the grief. All of no consequence compared to that thread of connection between his heart and hers.

"Bear!" The high-pitched shriek broke the fragile moment like glass shattering. A tiny figure burst from the front wagon porch and plowed across the threshing floor, her wispy hair stuck up at odd angles, her brown eyes wide with manic sleeplessness.

"Artis!"

"No, child, watch out—"

"Stop her!"

Undaunted by the horrified shouts, the little girl flew by Marjani's outstretched hand, darted around Hartwin, and pushed past Eira to fling her arms around Berengar's legs.

"Bear!" She grinned up at him. "Bear like Arris!"

After a hushed, breathless second, Berengar bent to lift the child. His face crumpled only a little. "Yes," he said. "Uncle Ber likes Artis very much."

"*Artis!*" Silke's voice skittered across bright octaves of panic. "Let go of her, you monster!"

"Mama!" Artis cried. "See! 'S Ber!"

Berengar hugged her close, blinking hard. "How do you even remember me?"

"Berengar." The name sobbed from Silke's depths, her face contorted with the effort of holding back the power straining within her. "I can't stop this curse. I can't control it much longer. Please, *I beg you* ..."

Berengar's eyes found Eira's as he kissed the top of Artis's head. "You have to take her out of here. Get her far away."

No. Hartwin could, or Marjani. Or that nuisance Rodolf.

But Berengar was pressing the girl into her arms, murmuring in Artis's ear. "Go with Princess Eira, dear one. Don't fuss. You're a countess. You must be dignified. You'll do that for Uncle Ber, won't you?"

Still looking into Eira's eyes.

No, no, no.

"Come, Countess Artis," Eira croaked as she settled the girl on her hip, still holding Berengar's gaze. *Don't make me leave you.* "It's past bedtime for both of us. You know what happens to princesses after midnight, don't you?"

Artis shook her head and stuck three fingers in her mouth, the universal sign for *you had better tell me all about this.*

"*Hurry!*" Silke's voice cracked as though she were splitting in two.

"Hurry," Berengar echoed. "Save her. For me."

Still shaking her head, Eira backed away. Tears blinded her. Hartwin touched her shoulder, turning her toward the barn's front door. She'd find a guard. She could leave Artis with him …

"Keep her away," Marjani murmured as Eira passed her. "I will bear witness."

With a sob, Eira fled down the suddenly endless length of the front wagon porch. Steward Tarben burst through the side door, two guards close on his heels. He grabbed her arm, eyes wild. "Artis! Thank the gods. I only turned my back for a minute. Where is the bear? Give me the child!"

Silke's anguished howl filled the barn. "*Let her go!* Get out of here!"

"*Silke?*"

Pulling free of the slack-jawed steward, Eira stumbled out the door into the dark, dark night. It was desperately dark, even with the stars so thick above. Dark enough to hide her streaming tears from the child in her arms.

"Ber like Arris?" the little girl mumbled through the fingers in her mouth.

"Ber loves Artis. Very, very much." Eira forced the words through the agony in her heart. "Remember that, always."

She staggered away from the door. How far was safe enough? A dozen yards? Fifty? She couldn't go farther, unable to breathe for the pain in her chest. She wrapped Marjani's cloak around the both of them, her back to the barn, hunching over Artis like a shield.

They might have crouched there for an instant or an hour. Time had no meaning. But just as she began to believe time might have stopped altogether, a sudden charge sizzled the air around her, bringing the sharp, sweet scent of a summer storm.

10. She's *dangerous*.

— Top 10 things ~~I hate~~ I find difficult to appreciate about Princess Marjani, as listed by (former) Princess Eira of Nordmark

Marjani's thoughts raced desperately as Eira rushed Artis from the barn. Once the child was safe, Silke would have no reason to hold back. Her guards looked dazed, as if the curse held them captive. They wouldn't stop her. And no one else could get close enough.

"Is that … *Earl Berengar?*" Steward Tarben stumbled to a halt, blinking in confusion. "Silke? What is going on?"

"I'm doing what you couldn't." Silke's dark hair crackled around her head. The black pools of her eyes reflected flames Marjani couldn't see. "I'm protecting my daughter. Ridding Saebern of its monster, once and for all!"

"Monster? Wait." Tarben's gaze whipped around the barn. "Where is the bear?"

"Berengar *is* the bear!" Silke cried. "Only I can stop him from slaughtering us all."

"*Lies.*" Marjani threw off Eira's fawn cloak, revealing the brilliant scarlet of her gown. *Appearances and attitude.* She threw back her shoulders to highlight the power in her arms.

Silke wasn't the only one who could look like Vengeance.

She strode to Hartwin's side, planting herself between the sorceress and Berengar and Rurik. A faint glow still surrounded the Ravninan sorcerer, though the strength of the curse seemed to have dimmed it, and he looked haggard with the effort of standing on his own.

Whatever power Rurik might have to deflect sorcery, Marjani didn't think it would stop Silke this time.

Very well. She would have to make Silke stop herself.

"Lady Silke, even as a beast, Berengar has never harmed Saebern's citizens." Marjani's voice rang in the echoing, empty bays. "*You* brought this curse upon them. You are responsible for the deaths of Reeve Wendel and Marshal Falk. You are the monster. A danger to your brother-in-law. A danger to your people. A *danger to your daughter.*"

"I would never hurt Artis," Silke objected. "*Never.* I'm doing this for her. I was *protecting* her—and Saebern—from that selfish, irresponsible *boy.*"

"I don't think it's the spell you burned that matters," Marjani told her, ignoring the sparks dancing on the woman's fingers, focused solely on the tangled emotions buried in the ragged turmoil of Silke's spirit. "It is your will that brought the curse to life. Your will can stop it."

The only thing that could. How to make Silke see it?

"You can't understand such righteous anger," Silke said, the shadows surging wildly around her. "This is bigger than my will."

Marjani's own anger danced fiery on her tongue. Had this woman watched a brother cut down in front of her? Watched the man she adored bleeding out at her feet? What gave her the right to claim righteousness for her evil?

"I'm making things right for my daughter." Silke lifted her chin imperiously.

There. The barest crack in the bitter spite. Marjani nearly missed it, blinded by her own dark emotion. A flash of … not light. Doubt, fear, yearning.

"For your daughter?" Marjani's fury burned out, pooling cold around her feet. "It is for Artis that you mean to murder a man willing to sacrifice himself to protect her?"

"He's a *monster*—"

"Princess Eira rescued your daughter from this curse you plan to cast," Marjani pressed, seeing again the pale girl in a blood-red cloak, face streaked with tears, clutching an innocent child to her chest as she ran. Her throat tightened, threatening to close.

Hartwin's fingers touched hers, and she clutched his hand tightly.

"You are responsible for Hartwin's father's death," she told Silke. "Yet even now, he is trying to save lives, not seek vengeance. You refuse to let go of your hatred even to save your own child."

Silke stared at her, dark eyes unfathomable. The power surging around her felt so loud Marjani wasn't sure she'd even heard her.

"Tarben?" Silke's voice crackled like the sparks on her skin. "I did it for Artis."

"What?" Tarben's face was ashen. "What did you do?"

"And for you. You've run Saebern for so many years," Silke said. "It wasn't right you had to bow and scrape to a callow youth. As my husband, you're the earl now, in all but name."

"But … my love," he shook his head as if that might wake him from the nightmare he found himself in. "That wasn't what I wanted."

"Then you're as much a fool as Berengar," Silke snapped. "What did you want, if not the power?"

"I just … wanted you."

Silke blinked. For a moment, her eyes were entirely her own, a clear, dark brown. "You … I—"

Doubt swirled around her like a whirlpool.

"You can change your will," Marjani said. "You can choose love over hate."

"You can choose love," Rurik repeated behind her in a voice of wonder. An incredulous laugh escaped him. "*That's why I couldn't curse Guntram. It wasn't because Kasimir loved me. It was because I loved Kasimir.*"

"You've seen them all choose love," Marjani told Silke. *Listen. Please listen.* "Eira, Berengar, Rurik, Hartwin. They chose light, not darkness."

Eira could have said it better. Surely there was a Road to Peace that was perfect for this situation.

"I do love Artis," Silke said. Her voice trembled with uncertainty. "This *is* love."

"It's *not* love," Hartwin began, but Marjani squeezed his hand.

"Of course you love Artis." She had to clear her throat of suppressed tears. Her own sundered spirit ached with longing, whether for the love she had never received from her own father or for the loves she had lost, she couldn't say. "But that is not what feeds this curse."

"This is love," Silke whispered, staring at her sparking hands with growing horror. "This is a love that will kill everyone who stands in its way."

"No one stands in your way." Berengar had somehow slipped from Rurik's grasp. He stood alone at the opening to the rear wagon porch.

"You don't need to hurt anyone else," he said, spreading his empty hands.

"She doesn't need to hurt *anyone*," Marjani growled. *Curse the man. Literally.* She'd been so close to getting through to Silke.

"I'm tired," Berengar said. "I'm tired of being afraid of what I am and what I might do. I'm tired of my failure to be the earl you all wanted me to be. I'm tired of bearing your hatred, Silke. Kill me, and carry it yourself."

"You're pathetic," Silke snarled, teeth bared in hatred.

"You're not worth the effort these people put into protecting you."

And yet, she still didn't strike, despite the struggle to hold the curse back, despite the shadows writhing around her. Maybe she was listening—

"He's definitely not worth cursing," Rurik said, moving to Marjani's side. He cringed at Silke's hiss—or maybe Marjani's glare.

"The sorcerer is right," Tarben said. Pleading. "Just come home. We'll go back to our lives. Forget any of this ever happened."

"I cursed a man. Do you think Marshall Falk's and Reeve Wendel's families will forget that?" Silke's gaze skittered wildly from one face to another. "Do you think any of the people here will forget? How can we go back to our lives when witnesses remain?"

Her yeomen shrank from her, eyes widening with fresh terror.

"Will *you* forget?" she asked Tarben.

Fear inked the gloomy lines of his face. "I—I …"

Marjani dropped Hartwin's hand.

"Princess—" he whispered.

"Trust me." She barely mouthed the words, but his eyes responded with a wordless declaration—not just that he feared for her, but that he saw her. That she *mattered*.

Light shone in her heart, even as she turned toward darkness. The unnerving shadows swirled around Silke's spirit, a whirlpool tugging at the guards, lashing at Marjani's feet, trying to pull her in.

To *entice* her in. She could choose to enter the shadows, she realized. Wade into them. Join them. All that power Silke held by only her fingernails. What might a girl who could grip it with both hands accomplish?

Her father's voice. *A girl can't sense spirits.*

Oh, Father. Yes, I can.

How easy it would be to simply … tug the curse from

Silke's grasp. All that seething hatred. It would mesh with the ragged edges of her own spirit. Perhaps even fill in the missing pieces.

Her finger brushed the broken edge of her bracelet. *Mosi. Dejen.* Alive one moment, gone the next. She could seize the power to avenge them.

Yet, alongside her grief, she felt the tiny shimmering thread of light connecting her to Hartwin. The darkness laughed at such a fragile thing. But she held it tight, afraid to tug too hard for fear it might snap.

The slender strand connected to another thread. *Eira.* Pale and unruly and strong as steel. And another—Rurik's tarnished gold. The under-appreciated strength of Berengar's bronze. Was that silver skein Artis? It pulled with it a thread of smoke and gleaming emerald leading to Tenzin, which led to the other princesses back in Lukos castle. Raisa, Ellycia, Jax and Beatrix, and the rest.

One thread might be weak, but all of them twined together … She grabbed the rope they made, wrapped it around one wrist, and stepped into the whirlpool.

"The question is," she said, stretching her other hand toward Silke, "will *you* forget? Think of how you have lived this past year. In such fear."

"Fear of the bear!" Silke cried. She flung her hand toward Berengar. "Of *him.*"

"Of yourself. Of what you'd done. Of being discovered."

Silke shook her head. "It was that sorcerer's fault he survived. Now I can fix it."

"You think this curse will leave you unmarked, even if you are able to cast it without striking yourself?" The darkness had claws, digging into Marjani's ankles. She clung tightly to her tether. "You think the fear and the guilt won't haunt you? That you will ever be able to break through this evil to reach the love for your daughter that drove you to it in the first place?"

Marjani's eyes blurred. *That is not love.* Love was the frayed, uncomfortable cord around her wrist. Not the power to destroy enemies. Not lack of fear. There was nothing so fearful as those threads of love, the knowledge of how easily they could be snapped and lost forever.

Or perhaps not lost completely. That faint trace of green, the whisper of fiery red. Perhaps her love for Dejen and Mosi still bound her, too.

"I can see the damage this curse has caused you," she told Silke. "Do you think Artis won't see it, too?"

The darkness wrenched at her, trying to engulf her. Yet, in the center of it, she saw another thread brighten. Silke's connection to her child.

"I would never hurt Artis. Tell her, Tarben," Silke demanded.

But Tarben was pressed against the barn wall, braced as if he couldn't stand without its support.

"You must know this curse will hurt her," Marjani said. "If you kill all of us. Her beloved stepfather. Her uncle."

"She will forget them," Silke whispered, tears streaming down her cheeks.

"Do you truly want her to forget?" Tendrils of malice whipped Marjani's face. She could almost hear them hissing. *Love makes you weak. This is power. Kill her! If you cannot take it, you will be destroyed.* She might have believed the whispers if she could not see how the shadows tore at Silke's soul. "Do you want her to forget who you were before you murdered them? Do you want her to feel this taint on you as long as you live?"

"*I never wanted any of this*," Silke cried. "I never wanted to be dragged to a miserable, isolated backwater by a husband I barely knew. I never wanted to be a pregnant widow and have to marry another man to protect my unborn child. I never wanted to be so desperate to protect my daughter that I would steal a sorcerer's curse."

She laughed wildly, a harsh, gurgling sound, as if the darkness were drowning her. "But I've done what I needed to do. Berengar will be gone by morning, and Artis will never have to fear for her title or her inheritance." She sucked in a breath, wretchedness twisting her features. "All it took was murder and dark magic. And the betrayal of the people who cared for me."

She looked to Tarben, still pressed against the wall. "I thought everyone would be better off with Berengar gone. I never meant to hurt you. I know you can never forgive me."

Tarben's face skewed into something almost like a smile. "I could forgive you anything, my love."

Marjani saw then that it wasn't his terror that prevented him from escaping. Another thread shimmered in Silke's spirit.

Silke turned to Berengar, the fragile light of those threads making the shadows hiss and recoil. "I meant the bear to devour you. That's what the curse was *supposed* to do."

"It's in an arcane Old Santian dialect," Rurik said defensively. "I translated it as best I could."

"Magic comes with a cost," Silke continued, ignoring him. "Money for the piper. Clothes for the elves. Your firstborn child for turning straw into gold. I thought the bear was coming for its payment. I thought it meant to take Artis from me. I thought—"

She choked on a sob, and the darkness roiled.

"I knew the bear terrified all of you," Berengar said, his voice husky. "I tried to leave Saebern more than once. But the bear always found its way back. As a bear … all I wanted was to come home. I can't say the bear isn't dangerous. But it would never have hurt Artis. I would protect her with my life. I swear it."

"I believe you." Silke's voice rang with despair, but another tenuous thread flickered to life between them. "I saw you do it. Just now. And Princess Eira. And Reeve Hartwin. And Princess Marjani. And my husband."

"I didn't *have* to come back to Saebern to help you all, you know," Rurik said when the list ended. "I could have just saved myself—"

"Even strangers have shown courage and love, to protect

my child." Silke straightened, the light coalescing into a core of strength, even as the darkness clawed wildly at Marjani's hem. "That is all I wanted for her, and I couldn't see it. She is well protected. From everything but me."

Marjani cried out as the curse raked across her skin and was gone. The sudden absence of darkness was so shocking she almost reached out for it. *Love is weakness.* Only the tug of the imagined cord around her wrist held her back.

Rurik gasped with relief. "She's done it! She's lifting the curse! I feel like I can breathe."

Yes. Marjani realized she could breathe freely, too, no longer crushed by the shadow of the curse. Silke *had* chosen love. *No one has to die tonight.*

She watched the shadows sweep past the four yeomen, freeing them from the grip of Silke's power. They stumbled away, breathing heavily, rubbing at their eyes as if to rub away a film across them.

The darkness moved faster as it shrank, spinning wildly around Silke's form.

"Don't let her forget." Silke's gaze met Majani's, the sorceress's eyes clear and resolute. "Don't let her forget how much I loved her."

And suddenly, Marjani remembered the truth of whirlpools. The faster they spin, the stronger they are. A swimmer or a ship can escape the edges, but at the center, they swallow their victims whole.

"Silke! No!"

The light burned in Silke's core, and flames danced in her eyes. "Don't let her forget."

Marjani reached toward her, only to be yanked backward. Rurik knocked her to the floor as the darkness shattered, shrieking, in an explosion of light.

CHAPTER THIRTY-FIVE

One more thing? Once she decides you're her friend, you
cannot get rid of her. I suppose I am stuck with her now.

— Top 10 things I despise about Princess Eira, as listed
by Princess Marjani of Almasa

A thin wail pierced the awful silence after the
explosion. The child in Eira's arms shifted, her face
scrunched in fretful exhaustion as she cried.

"Shh. It's all right." Eira struggled to her feet, heedless of
what she was saying. It hardly mattered. She couldn't imagine
anything mattering.

Artis blinked weepily and whimpered again. But then she
slipped those three fingers in her mouth and leaned her head
on Eira's shoulder. Her eyes fluttered closed. There was
enough light to see her eyelashes brushing her cheeks.

Eira looked up to see a band of dusky topaz stretching
above the eastern hills. It was almost dawn. *The bear!*

She fought down tears as realization struck anew. There
would be no more worrying about the bear.

The barn stood dark and quiet, with no visible signs of
damage. Silke had said the curse would call a lightning strike,
but whatever force had thrown Eira to her knees hadn't set the

building on fire. Perhaps Rurik had translated that spell wrong, too.

Or perhaps a sorcerous lightning strike damaged only its intended target.

Eira wrapped Marjani's cloak more tightly around Artis. The child's body melted against hers with a heavy sigh. She should take the girl to the manor. She should check on her friends. She should find her sword and make Lady Silke pay the price for murder.

None of that would ease the pain.

It wouldn't change the fact she had failed Berengar.

Frightened, grieving, filled with rage, her twelve-year-old self had stood on the deck of the ship that would take her from Nordmark forever, the impact of Uncle Einar's blow throbbing on her cheek. She had swiped away the tears and looked him straight in the eye, as her mother had taught her.

I am a Nordish princess, she had shouted. *You can send me away, but I will always be a Nordish princess, and you can't break me.*

Uncle Einar had laughed. His retainers had laughed. The sailors had laughed. For five years, the memory of that moment had shamed her. What a helpless little fool she had been.

Now she looked back at that girl, aching and alone, and she saw how much courage it had taken. Not standing up to Einar. That had been the flash bravery of a moment. But to go on. To study hard at the Temple of Peace and never give up. To refuse to let grief and hatred define her.

I am a Nordish princess. She took a deep breath of the pre-dawn air, of heather, pines, the lingering sweetness that sometimes follows a storm.

"I am a Nordish princess," she whispered. "And you can't break me."

The two yeomen who had been guarding the barn's front door stumbled out of the wagon porch, shouting queries at each other as if the curse's blast had deafened them.

"You!" Eira called.

They stopped, staring at her, eyes wide. One reached for his sword.

"Don't be a fool," she snapped. "Go to the manor and get help. You." She pointed at the older man. "Come with me. There may be injured people in the barn who need our help."

A few minutes earlier, they would have ignored an order from a foreigner accused of sorcery, but after being pummeled by supernatural forces, they seemed eager to let someone else take charge. She was a *princess*, after all.

Appearances and attitude.

She strode toward the barn, the anxious guard scurrying to her side.

"The young countess, miss—pardon, I mean Your Highness. Is she all right?"

She'd forgotten the child in her arms. She should have given Artis to the man she'd sent for help, but he was already halfway to the manor.

"She's not injured." Eira shifted her cloak so the guard could see the girl's sleeping face. "Just exhausted."

"She's a right precious one," he said with obvious relief. "You can't mean to take her into the barn, milady. Your Highness. The bear—"

"The bear is gone."

He blinked, but the bitter finality of her voice seemed to steady him. "Be that as it may, Your Highness, let me go in first."

If her heart hadn't already broken, it would have shattered then. She had seen so much evil in the past few hours that his simple act of kind bravery seemed almost unimaginable.

Before she could answer, the door swung open, and Steward Tarben staggered out.

"Steward!" The guard grabbed the man's elbow to keep him from falling, but Tarben shook him off and waved him toward the door.

"Help them," the steward barked. He stared at Eira, but it

seemed to take him a moment to recognize her. "Artis?" He blinked and took a step toward her. "Is she—"

"She's safe." Eira crossed to him. "Here, take her."

He shook his head, blinking faster. "I don't—I can't ... Silke—"

"I can't take her with me," Eira said sharply. "So unless you're going back in there—"

"No ... no, I can't ..."

"Then hold out your arms."

Tarben's care for the child—or perhaps his habitual annoyance with Eira—brought a spot of color to his deathly gray cheeks. He tugged off his cloak and wrapped it around the sleeping girl, taking the awkward bundle from Eira's arms.

"I didn't ... I didn't know—" he stammered.

She turned away, carrying too much of her own grief and regret to bear his. The guard had left the door open behind him. It took all the icy courage she could muster to cross the threshold.

A single lantern flickered inside. In the gloom, she saw figures approaching. The guard she had sent in came toward her, one of Rodolf's massive arms draped over his shoulder, the big man's head hanging toward his chest. The man on Rodolf's other side—

"Hartwin!"

"Princess Eira." The Reeve staggered a little under Rodolf's weight, his hair ragged and singed. "Silke's yeomen. They were closest to the blast. Help them. I can still feel ..."

His voice trailed off, but she felt it, too. A lingering buzz of fear and malice.

Berengar? Marjani? Her throat froze.

"Princess Eira!" Rurik's voice.

She rushed to the next trio of limping survivors. The Ravninan sorcerer and Silke's elderly yeoman, Philip, carried another guard between them. Blood dripped from the young man's nose.

"Is he—"

"Breathing," Rurik grunted.

"Fool," Philip spat. "Not enough sense to run. What'd he think the red princess was distracting her for? That one had nerve, I'll give her that, stepping right into that evil curse."

Eira's stomach dropped. "*She didn't.*" But of course she had.

"She was barely a yard from Silke when the lightning struck," Rurik said. "If I—"

"She said she'd bear *witness*," Eira cried. "*Marjani!* I swear, if you've gotten yourself killed, I will rip out your—"

But there. Another figure, tall and dark, her gown flickering like burning embers in the lantern light.

"Marjani!" Eira rushed to her, nearly knocking the Almasan princess into the last yeoman following her from the threshing floor. She grabbed Marjani's shoulders. "Are you all right? Can you hear me? You are such an idiot."

Marjani gripped Eira's wrists and firmly removed them from her shoulders. "I'm perfectly fine. Must you always overreact?"

"You're limping!"

"A skinned knee—thanks to Rurik."

"*Yes*," Rurik called over his shoulder. "*Thanks* to Rurik. I saved her life, shielding her. And spared Hartwin the worst of it, too. The fool ran toward us instead of away when it all went to hells."

"He did save my life," Marjani muttered darkly. "And I'm properly grateful, but I fear I will hear about it for the rest of my days."

"*You* saved all our lives, Your Highness." The yeoman behind her paused to catch his breath, hands on his knees, but then he straightened to place a hand on his heart and offered Marjani a bow. "The Lady would have killed us all if you hadn't turned the curse back on her."

"You what?" Eira asked.

A mixture of grief and anger washed across Marjani's

face. "I did not turn the curse on Silke. I believe she finally understood how much destruction her hatred had caused. But she could not manage to let it go. In the end, she turned it on herself."

All that violent power. Eira's skin prickled with horror.

"Silke is dead?"

"She's …" Marjani paused, eyes bleak. "She's gone."

The yeoman kissed his knuckles against evil. "The blast knocked me off my feet. I looked back, and there was naught left of her at all. Just the stone charred, where she stood."

"Not just charred." Marjani grimaced. "Melted."

Eira knew she should feel something. Shock. Gratitude for Silke's sacrifice. Grief and anger that a desperate mother had chosen death over facing the evil she had done. But all she felt was a hollow where her heart should have been. After what Silke had done to Berengar—

"But … if she turned it on herself … Where's Berengar?"

Marjani's hands tightened on Eira's wrists. "Silke struck only herself with the lightning curse, but …"

That was not the only curse she had cast.

"*Where is he?*"

"He asked me to tell you goodbye," Marjani said. "It might be easier." But she must have known Eira too well by then to expect her to agree. She let go of Eira's wrists and gestured back into the barn.

Eira ran past her, past the guttering lantern, past the ghastly dark circle on the threshing floor. Down the rear wagon porch, to the little door flung open to let in the cerulean pre-dawn light.

Eira hurtled through the doorway, out into the dew-damp grass. *There.* A figure trudged up the sheep track toward the rocky ridge above the manor. He strode with dogged purpose, but Eira hadn't lost a footrace at the Temple since she'd turned thirteen.

"Berengar!"

He turned, his face twisting in anguish as she neared. "Eira. You can't follow me. I need to be far away by sunrise."

"Don't be a fool." Knowing that her heart was about to break made no difference at all to how it leaped at the sight of him. "I'm coming with you."

"No." Berengar lifted a hand. "When the curse is complete, I will be lost in the bear. I might kill you."

Eira snorted. Loudly. No need to pretend dignity with this young lord. He'd seen her at her worst. Would she ever feel so free to be herself with anyone again?

"I've spent more time face to face with your bear than you ever will," she said. "He would never hurt me."

"Eira." A choking laugh of exasperation and misery—and something so warm, it filled her chest to bursting. "I can't be sure of that. You need to let me go."

"I know." The words broke apart inside her, lodging in her throat. She wasn't sure she could continue to breathe, much less speak. *I am a Nordish princess.*

"I know," she repeated, a rough whisper. "But I'm going to walk with you as far as I can. I won't leave you to do this alone. And when … when it's over, I will watch you go, and I will sing the prayers of departure for you."

"Eira." A prayer of its own. Emotion lit his eyes, and if she could have, she would have stopped the sunrise forever and simply bathed in that light.

She grabbed his jaw with both hands and pressed her lips to his. Her mind knew that any moment the arms that wrapped around her could crush her, the mouth that met hers might lengthen, bristling with deadly teeth. But her heart felt only the joy of being close to him, spreading through her like the sun brushing across her shoulders—

Eira stilled, her heart freezing. An agonizing moment of suspension. A moment that stretched. And stretched …

She pulled back, her hands tangled in shaggy hair—long, unkempt human hair. The sunlight heating her back reflected in the warm depths of Berengar's eyes, highlighting the freckles across his nose.

His breath caught, and his eyes widened as he stared over her shoulder. He clutched her arms as though she were the only anchor holding him to the earth.

His gaze met hers. Terror. Hope. The wild terror of desperate hope. Eira could only stare back. One heartbeat. Another.

Footfalls beat on the sheep path, hurrying toward them.

"You said he'd turn into a bear." Hartwin's voice, caught somewhere between alarm and confusion.

"It's always happened exactly at sunrise," Rurik said. "*Always.*"

Berengar lifted a hand to his sun-kissed cheek, still staring at Eira in wonder.

"Rurik told us the curse might lift if the caster died," Marjani said with a mixture of awe and sorrow.

Clouds dimmed Berengar's eyes. "I would not have chosen Silke's death."

"There's no way to be certain whether or not it was Silke's death that broke the curse," Rurik said. "She turned the force of her hatred away from you. She changed her heart. That might have been enough to dispel the *Arkou Devor.*" The corner of his mouth tilted. "Of course, if you believe the fairy tales—and just now, I can't see any reason not to—the best way to break a curse has always been true love's kiss."

Heat suffused Eira's cheeks, and she couldn't muster a response to the sorcerer's teasing. If that's what it was. A flash of longing crossed Rurik's face, and she wondered if he might actually be serious.

Either way, Berengar's cheeks were red as hers, and he'd taken hold of her hand as if he never planned to let it go.

"We should return to the manor," Rurik said. "Before Master Kaspar wakes. The newly restored earl of Saebern could benefit from a bath and a shave before he faces the town council."

"Appearances and attitude?" Marjani asked wryly as they started down the path.

"No," Berengar stated firmly, then winced at their distressed stares. "Not 'no' to the bath. No to my being the earl of Saebern. Silke had that right. I did not return within the year the king allotted. Artis is the countess."

Eira nearly tripped in her surprise, but Berengar's hand held her steady.

"I'm sure the king will restore you to your rightful place," Hartwin said. He scowled. "Or are you still trying to avoid your responsibilities?"

Berengar's cheeks colored again. "I am not. I will petition to be named my niece's guardian, to guide her and govern Saebern in her name until she reaches her majority."

He ducked a self-conscious glance at Eira. "I never should have been earl to begin with. My father was wrong to disinherit Artis. I will make it right."

Eira squeezed his hand, her heart full enough to burst. On her first day at Lukos, she had told Jax that she wanted to marry Prince Theo in order to make a difference, to help bring peace to Aldforth and all the Blessed Kingdoms.

And here she'd made a difference, just being herself.

"You must ensure Artis receives the love a child requires to thrive," Marjani said. "The consequences of Silke's hatred include depriving Artis of her mother."

Eira suppressed a shiver as they passed beneath the shadow of the barn, thinking of the child she had held, warm and trusting in her arms. Artis slept now believing the world was a place of wonders and safety. She would awake to a life forever changed, to the knowledge the people she loved could be torn from her without warning.

"She's lost even the memory of her mother," Hartwin said heavily. "At least now I know my father died as honorably as he lived, saving another's life. Silke left only a legacy of hatred and death."

"Not only that." Berengar stopped them as they stepped from the shadow. He held his hand up and turned it in the sunlight. "In the end, she could not free herself from her evil, but she freed the rest of us. That is her legacy to her daughter. She gave her life delivering Saebern from its curse."

Watching the fierce light in his eyes, the drive for justice and kindness, Eira could have cursed him herself, the earnest, awkward man. Weren't the freckles bad enough? Anyone might swoon for a wry smile or a pair of golden eyes. She'd swooned often enough for less.

But swooning could be cured.

Eira suspected she might never recover from what she felt for Berengar. The warmth of his hand in hers melted not just the ice in her veins but the cold, hard dreams of her future. Defeating the other princesses to win Prince Theodor's hand. Ruling Aldforth at Theo's side. Seeing the look on Uncle Einar's face when she visited Nordmark as his queen.

Those visions shimmered in the morning sunlight and dissolved, chimerical as fairy tales.

"You should tell her the truth," she advised. "That her mother made mistakes and did her best to make them right. But also that Silke loved her, and that love will always be with her."

Even if Artis couldn't go back and save her.

"Yes," Berengar agreed. "She can leave the evil behind her without letting go of the love."

" 'You cannot dwell in the past, for the past is not a place.' " Eira firmly suppressed the tears threatening to clog her throat. " 'Nor can you build your hearth in the future, for there is no solid ground there. Settle in the present, and there you will find your true home.' "

She sent a sharp glance at Marjani, who obviously needed Holy Mother's advice as much as she did, but Marjani ignored her, squinting at the sky, a hand up to shield against the intensifying sunlight.

"Did you hear what I—" Following her gaze, Eira broke off with a cry of delight. "Tenzin!"

The little dragon screeched and dove, streaking toward her. Hartwin ducked, and Rurik threw up his hood with an involuntary shriek.

Berengar stood his ground, staring in awe but no fear. "Is that a ..."

Eira scrambled to put some distance between them. She was going to have to keep an eye on Berengar. He'd obviously spent too many months as an indestructible bear.

Tenzin hurtled past her so fast and close that Eira's cloak rustled. The dragon skimmed across the grass, then banked up to swoop around again. The whistles and warbles came too fast for Eira to make any sense of them, but she understood she was being scolded severely.

"I told her you died," Marjani said. "She was very upset."

Another pass, another screech.

"I'm sorry!" Eira called, trying not to laugh. She raised her arm in a peace offering perch. "I didn't mean to frighten anyone. I'm awfully glad to see you, too."

Tenzin landed with a great flapping of wings that (probably not) accidentally cuffed the back of Eira's head. But then the little dragon lowered her crest and pressed her forehead against Eira's cheek.

Eira stroked her chest, pretending the tears in her eyes came from the smoke curling from Tenzin's nostrils. She pointed at the little scroll tied to the dragon's foreleg. "Is that from Anara?"

Tenzin swatted her hand away and leaped from her arm, swooping around to land on Marjani's shoulder. The Almasan princess only jumped a little, though her eyes widened in surprise. With a haughty sniff, Tenzin held out her foreleg.

"It's obviously not for you," Marjani said. "Everyone thinks you're dead. It's probably a death threat from Princess Beatrix for losing you."

"Don't worry. Beatrix isn't that fond of me." Eira couldn't

help grinning. It *was* nice to know people missed her. "Besides, she's too diplomatic to murder anyone."

Marjani's brows lifted as she unrolled the scroll. "Perhaps you haven't heard the stories I have about Bellisian 'diplomats.' But even if Beatrix doesn't want me dead, I'm sure the king is ... *displeased*, to say the least."

"King Wulfric isn't mourning me," Eira assured her. "He probably doesn't even remember which princess I am."

"It's not his affection for you that concerns me," Marjani said, peering at her over the scroll, "but his loathing of me. Prince Guntram's death has made him irrational and suspicious and liable to lash out at anyone who vexes him."

"Having your heir murdered by your own nobles will do that to you," Rurik said scornfully.

"It *wasn't* his nobles," Eira said. "I tried to explain the other night. Prince Guntram was killed by a manticore."

"A *what?*" Rurik stared at her, his face turning slowly white.

"I know, it sounds impossible," she admitted. "But Princess Ellycia saw it herself. Wings like a dragon—not as beautiful, of course, Tenzin—the body of a lion, an almost human face, except with lots and lots more teeth ..."

"Someone sent a manticore to kill Prince Guntram," Rurik repeated, though Eira could see he still didn't want to believe it. She was a little surprised that he seemed so shocked. They'd just spent the past few days with *an enchanted bear*.

"When you put it that way," Marjani murmured as she scanned Beatrix's message, "the king's paranoia doesn't seem *quite* so irrational—"

She stopped. Her body stilled as her eyes scanned the message once more.

"What is it?" A sudden chill raised the hair on Eira's neck. "What's happened? Is someone hurt?"

"No. Nothing like that." Marjani's voice sounded strange and distant as she rolled up the parchment. "Apparently, your death has convinced King Wulfric that Saebern's enchanted bear is a greater threat than he'd thought. He has sent Prince

Theodor and the Rose Knights to dispatch it once and for all. They are riding hard and should arrive here tomorrow morning."

Her ironic smile didn't quite reach her eyes. "It appears the king holds you in greater esteem than you supposed."

CHAPTER THIRTY-SIX

One more thing? She never gives up. If she cares about you, whether she admits it or not, she'll keep fighting for you even after you're dead—actually dead or just presumed. I might as well accept the fact I'll never be free of her.

— Top 10 things ~~I hate~~ I find difficult to appreciate about Princess Marjani, as listed by (former) Princess Eira of Nordmark

Marjani crept through the dark, warren-like maze of the manor. She had done this so many times now she no longer worried about getting lost or stumbling down a flight of stairs. The quiet courtyard, the chapel, the boxes against the outer wall. It was all so easy, so familiar.

The piercing regret as she paused at the top of the wall, her spear heavy in her hand—that was new.

She should be done with sneaking out alone, done with deception. But fate had proved fickle as always, and she was an Almasan princess, not some … what did Eira call children's stories? A fairy's tale. Not some naive fairy-tale girl dreaming of handsome princes, magical aunties, and auspicious destinies.

Despite her birth on the sea, her destiny had never been auspicious, and now it had hunted her down here in Saebern, a dark, toothed beast more monstrous than any enchanted bear.

She could not stop it. She could only go out to meet it with whatever courage she could muster. Alone. For she could never explain to her ... her what? There was no other word for them, in Common Tongue or Almasan. She could never explain to her *friends* why she must walk this road.

As it happened, the main road through Saebern followed the river up the valley, a level, well-maintained grade that was easy to travel even in the murky gloom before dawn. By the time the sky began to pale, she had left Saebern Town far behind and was hiking into the county's southern mountains.

As the sun rose overhead, the terrain became steeper, the road winding up a valley that constricted into a cramped ravine. At its narrowest point, Marjani left the road and scrambled up the sharp slope, using her spear and the tenacious trees clinging between the rocks to pull herself on. The ground leveled off at the top of the ravine, a half dozen yards above the road. A screen of scraggly pines shielded her from view but left her a clear line of sight to the ground below.

She inspected her spear as Dejen had taught her, running a hand down the shaft, checking the binding, testing the sharpness of the blade. She hefted it, her right hand automatically finding the balancing point, her wrist bending back so the wood lay along her palm, her fingers gripping either side of the shaft.

The short stretch of visible road, the trees, the downward angle—it would take a quick, decisive throw to strike a target moving past on horseback. There would be no shame in a warrior admitting it was beyond their skill.

Marjani pulled her hand back and bounced the spear lightly behind her, imagining the flow from her calves and hips to her arm and fingers. She could feel the power needed, see her quarry in her mind's eye, hear the point of her weapon striking true.

She had learned this art from the best spearman in her father's court. She had practiced for hours, with her brother and alone, hoping only for a nod of acknowledgment from Dejen when she threw well. Hiding her glee when she outmatched Mosi. Suppressing her disappointment that no amount of success could ever impress her father.

This shot was not beyond *her* skill.

She folded her cloak on the ground and settled herself to wait. Calmed her heart, her mind, her breathing. Let the trees forget her, the birds wonder if they might settle on her shoulder, the breeze play idly with the ends of her cropped hair.

While her eyes watched the road, her heart sorted memories. Some were bright and sweet as the tangerines Mosi always brought her for their birthday. Some were faded and worn as the comfortable leather sandals Dejen had given her to wear on hunting trips rather than her elaborately beaded royal footwear. A treasure box of laughter and arguments, pranks and encouragement, annoyance and love.

All the things the world had lost because a brutal, arrogant prince decided he didn't want to pay the lawful tariff for his ships to pass through Almasan waters.

But Prince Guntram was dead, leaving his account to be paid by those left behind.

Her own debt of love and vengeance hung heavy on her shoulders. Drew tightly around her throat. Living, when the best and brightest were dead. The wrong twin, the torn soul.

She heard the travelers before she saw them. First, the low drumming of hoofbeats, then the call of a voice, the jangle of bridles, and the rumble of baggage carts far behind. Even their scent preceded them, the taste of dust and horse sweat on the soft summer breeze.

Marjani rose. Through the pines, she caught a glimpse of the riders up the ravine. Proud, swift palfreys with pricked ears and gleaming coats. Fit youths with hair as glossy as their mounts, jockeying for position near the tall, dark-haired young man on the bay gelding at the front of the pack.

The handsome prince. Her destiny, as inevitable as the sun rising.

Despair took Marjani by surprise.

Grief, guilt, fury, shame. So hot her skin burned with it.

She reached for her spear, wincing as she released her reflexive grip on her bracelet. She turned her palm to see she'd clutched it so tightly that even as dull as it was, the ragged edge had broken the skin. Yet more blood spilled because of Prince Theodor's brother.

The riders were so close she could hear the creak of their saddles. Recognize Prince Theodor's voice, his esquire Ralf's laugh. A horse moved into her target window, a brash auburn chestnut, ridden by a brash auburn-haired boy. Duke Jordis had pushed his way into the lead.

The prince's bay would be just behind.

Marjani hefted her spear along her palm, felt the wood heat with her hatred of King Wulfric, her desire to hurt him the way his son had hurt her. The darkness that coiled inside her writhed and hissed with anticipation. She adjusted her stance and pulled back her spear.

One more second. Another.

Prince Theodor rode into view, turned in his saddle so Marjani could see his face, the sharp curve of his cheek, the flash of his blue eyes beneath dark lashes. Turned so his chest was a broad, perfect target even from above.

The shadows inside her exulted.

Marjani thrust that darkness into the shaft of her spear. With every ounce of power drawn from her training, her fury, her will, she hurled the spear at her target.

For a moment, the hatred screaming in her ears drowned all other sound. And then it shattered, leaving sudden silence.

Not silence. Again, she heard the creak of leather, the snorting of a horse, the whir of a dragonfly zipping past. Heard the thrum of her spear quivering where it had struck, the point driven deep into the thick summer loam between the roots of the pine trees.

She would need to clean the dirt from the bindings.

The riders continued down the road below. A shout, laughter. Not one looked up. Prince Theodor and his five Rose Knights. And then another group of four or five riders, more dignified, perhaps, constrained by their precarious position as guests, candidates, *prisoners*, but no less colorful.

Marjani did not turn when she heard the soft tread of deerskin boots crossing the ledge to stand beside her.

"King Wulfric has let the girls out on parole," Eira commented on the riders below.

In scattered glimpses through the trees, Marjani recognized Raisa's amber-blond hair, the glossy flare of her prized Ravninan stallion's black mane. The blaze of Princess Beatrix's red hair marked her from the others, her terrible scar hidden on the other side of her face. Princess Anara rode at the rear, her compact form contained and alert on her stocky white mount, her black tunic showing off the glittering dragon sitting on her shoulder.

One emerald eye flicked toward Marjani's hiding place. A puff of smoke drifted up behind the little creature, visible laughter.

"Poor Tarben. All these guests will drive him to distraction." Eira paused, turning contrite. "Not that anything could truly distract him right now."

"I should have known you'd follow me," Marjani said. "You are incapable of keeping your nose out of other people's concerns."

"And I did it without you noticing!" Eira crowed. "To be fair, it helped I knew exactly where you would go."

"Don't be smug." Marjani yanked her spear from the ground. Her hand shook a little, but no lingering darkness stung her fingers. "You didn't get here in time to stop me."

"I knew you couldn't kill Prince Theo." Eira grinned—

quite smugly. "I just wanted to be here for you when you realized it yourself."

"You don't know anything, white witch," Marjani snapped, though she suspected Eira really did know, maybe better than Marjani had known it herself. "I *could* have killed him. I *chose* not to."

"You chose the road of peace over the road of war."

"I'm still holding a spear," Marjani warned.

Eira laughed, but her eyes were sharp. "I'm not saying it was easy."

"Silke risked everything to kill the man she hated, and all it brought was destruction—to herself, to her family, to her people." Marjani brushed a finger across the edge of her bracelet. In the dark hours of the night before, she'd seen that was what she herself might become. A bringer of death and devastation. "My father is willing to pay for his vengeance with a war against Aldforth, but it turns out I am not. My love for Mosi and Dejen … I don't want it poisoned by murder."

She closed her eyes and turned her face toward the sun. Did she only imagine she could still feel those threads of love, connecting them to her?

"I fear they would be disappointed in me."

"If you were the one Guntram had killed," Eira asked, "what would your spirit wish to tell your brother?"

Marjani let the tears run down her cheeks. "I would tell him to make the world a kinder place."

"And maybe live his own life even more fully?"

"I no longer have a life now that I am not my father's assassin. I will never be able to go home." Marjani's voice broke on the word. She'd known when she left Almasa that she would never return, but … "I thought it would be death that kept me away. Not failure."

"*Not* failure," Eira said sharply. "Not yours, at any rate. King Lisan's failure to be the father you deserve is not your fault. It's true that being exiled is a terrible thing. It's hard, and it hurts, and that doesn't go away."

"Are you trying to make death sound more appealing?" Marjani swiped her eyes impatiently.

"Still, there are some benefits to being stripped of all that royal baggage. For instance, there's no longer all that alliance-making nonsense to stop you from marrying anyone you like." The Nordish witch had the gall to grin. "Even someone like, oh, I don't know, a baker?"

Marjani's stomach curled. And maybe so did her toes. "My marriage prospects are none of your concern."

"Really?" Eira asked. "I deserve fair warning if I'm going to be forced to be your neighbor."

"*You and Berengar?*" For just a moment, Marjani forgot the wrack of the life she had expected to live, the dangerous clouds that overshadowed her.

Eira's face burned so red it made her pale hair glow. "He's asked me to return after Wulfric's ball. He wants my advice on raising a girl to become a strong leader."

"*That's* how he chose to court you? He really does need help."

"Actually, he wanted to elope immediately."

Marjani hissed in alarm. "He's spent too much time as a bear. King Wulfric would kill you both."

"That's what *I* said." Eira rolled her eyes, but they glowed with a happiness Marjani hadn't seen in her before. "And when I'm the voice of reason, you know he can't be trusted to his own devices. Now, Hartwin—"

"Hartwin would never dare to propose to a princess," Marjani said. She'd almost knocked him down the stairs with a kiss.

"Of course not! That's why you'll have to do it."

Marjani thanked her ancestors for the dark skin that muted the fiery rose blooming in her cheeks. She'd listened to the other princesses giggle over Prince Theodor and their crushes on the Rose Knights, and she knew what Raisa or Isolde would advise. That she veil her interest with shy glances and flirtatious banter so she could deny it if he did not reciprocate. That she doubt her own feelings, keep her options open in case someone better came along.

But she was an Almasan princess. Or, if not a princess much longer, an Almasan warrior. She did not hide from questions she did not know the answers to. She asked them.

She couldn't help asking … What would that life look like, the one with Hartwin at her side? Not as a guide or a knight, but as a true companion?

Did she dare risk her heart? Risk losing him, as she had Mosi and Dejen? She could hardly measure the fear she'd bowed beneath throughout her life. Fear she wasn't good enough. Worth enough. Whole enough. And where had all that fear gotten her? Exiled in a strange land, reeking of failure. Fear had brought her nothing.

"I can understand if the life of a town reeve isn't exactly the life you imagined for yourself," Eira said, unexpectedly gently.

"I was raised to be my brother's shadow," Marjani replied. "A life of my own … "

Was unexpectedly appealing. She turned to hide her thoughts and began picking her way down the cliff to the road.

"If I married Berengar, you would be one of my subjects." Eira scrambled behind her. "I'm liking this future more by the moment."

"I thought you *wanted* me to talk to Hartwin."

"We're sisters, remember?" Eira caught up and hooked an arm through hers. "I've gotten used to having you around. Besides, the whole 'burning us as sorceresses' thing seems to have settled down quite a bit."

Indeed, whatever stories Silke's yeomen had spread about the events in the barn had apparently featured the two princesses as heroes. The manor staff could hardly find enough ways to make them comfortable or enough delicious food to feed them, and none passed by without a word of gratitude for saving them from the county's curse. Master

Kaspar had made himself scarce—whether from shame or his massive hangover—but had withdrawn any challenge to Hartwin's position as Town Reeve.

Even Steward Tarben, wan with grief but also somehow softened by it, had thanked them for saving his stepdaughter, his own life, and the county he loved so much, even if they could not save his wife. And his staunch, selfless support for Berengar to serve as Artis's guardian had bought the former earl a more enthusiastic homecoming than he had dared hope for.

All in all, the thought of living in Saebern County was not wholly unpleasant. If one could ignore the climate.

Marjani pulled her arm free of Eira's and drew her cloak more closely about her shoulders as the morning breeze brought gooseflesh to her arms. And this was *summer*.

"Part of my soul is anchored in Almasa," she said. "My father can disown me, but I mean to see it again, even if Saebern should become my home harbor."

The thought of standing on the bow of an Almasan caravel, the warm sea breeze carrying the scent of orchids and orange trees … it made her heart sing. She even dared to imagine Hartwin beside her, his face alight with curiosity and amazement at the beauty of her homeland.

"That will please Jax," Eira said. "She has this plan that no matter who ends up reigning alongside Prince Theo, the rest of us will support her as a network of allies to bring peace and justice to the Blessed Kingdoms—and beyond, obviously, with you and Anara. Maybe I'll ask to serve a turn as Aldforth's governor to Nordmark." Her grin turned danger-ous. "To promote peace, of course. Not just to see my uncle's face when I show up on his doorstep."

"You can't believe *that* will happen?" Marjani demanded. She had never even imagined the possibility. "All of us working together? We are speaking of the same twelve princesses?"

"Well." Eira's smile faltered. "If Raisa marries Theo, I'm

hoping you'll convince her not to make Princess Dora poison me."

"Raisa is too practical to discard a useful game piece over a grudge. I can't say the same about Isolde."

"*Goddess.*" Eira blew out a breath. "Our first Princess Pact needs to be to ensure Isolde doesn't become queen of Aldforth."

"*Princess Pact?* I categorically refuse to participate in anything you refer to with those words."

Though she couldn't help laughing at Eira's sly grin.

It felt so good to laugh. Her lungs expanded as if she hadn't taken a free breath since Mosi and Dejen's murders. Her chest filled with the scent of pine and sheep and heather. With the morning sunshine limning the rocky green hills. With the hope of a friend beside her and a freely chosen road under her feet.

Maybe she had never taken such a free breath in her entire life.

"Don't worry about Isolde," Eira said, giving her a sharp nudge with her elbow. "If I can befriend a gloomy, sullen doomsayer like you—"

"You mean, if *I* can befriend an insufferable, sanctimonious witch like *you*—"

"Then Isolde doesn't stand a chance."

"Just because we defeated an evil sorceress and lifted a curse on an enchanted bear, that does not make this one of your fairy's tales," Marjani warned. "This is not happily ever after."

"That's just as well," Eira said solemnly. "Happily ever after means your story is over. I'm not ready for that. I've got lots of story left to live."

Marjani tried to push down the hope bubbling inside her. No happily ever after meant parts of their stories would *not* be happy. There would be pain and loss and boredom and frustration. There was no guarantee Hartwin's story would join hers. That she would see Almasa again. That she would even survive King Wulfric's ball.

But no happily ever after also meant that parts of the story would be better than happy. There would be love and joy and hope and wonder.

And friendship.

This time Marjani was the one to hook her arm through Eira's. "I like that. We can write our own story."

EPILOGUE

3. *Morai ipakro liomandras*. A transformation [curse]. Remake thine assassin into the meat [flesh?] of a manticore; refine [his] blood to venom; distill [his] purpose to death. (A manticore. Oh, right. You can't believe I'm desperate enough to believe this one.)

(Add. note: As it happens, I *was* desperate enough, and no, it doesn't work, either.)

— Top 10 failed spells translated and performed by Rurik, Ravninan sorcerer (in training)

Despite our princesses' cautionary words, it might almost seem like a happily ever after.

The two young women walking arm in arm, fire and ice. Bright and hopeful on a level road that, squinted at in that benevolent summer light, might even resemble one of the Nine Roads to Peace that Princess Eira was so fond of invoking.

Returning to the manor, to the bustle and excitement of the crown prince's arrival, Princess Eira found herself at Lord Berengar's side, her reckless Nordish grin melting away his sudden, crowd-induced yearning for hibernation.

A happier ending to such a dark curse than anyone would dare hope for.

Princess Marjani surprised herself by welcoming Princess Raisa with a fierce hug, which Princess Raisa surprised *herself* by returning. Seeing (former) Princess Eira's open adoration of Saebern's not-so-missing (former) earl, Princess Raisa even managed a gracious congratulations to the Nordish princess on not being quite so dead as rumor suggested.

A happy (enough) ending to a dangerous rivalry.

Which allowed Princess Marjani to slip away for a quiet conversation with a certain handsome reeve. A conversation that may have led to a kiss—a breathtaking and auspicious, if not exactly *unexpected*, kiss.

A nearly exemplary happy ending, though truly just a beginning.

It wasn't until the feast that evening that anyone noticed the Ravninan sorcerer was missing. This might have wounded Rurik's self-esteem if he hadn't already been leagues away (he couldn't truly become smoke and travel on the wind, but he *had* mastered the art of a quick and undetected getaway).

Even then, his friends might have assumed he'd fled to avoid meeting the prince whose brother he'd tried so hard to murder. If only he had not been nudged to believe in something larger than himself by his association with our two princesses. If only he had not left that unfortunate note.

To you, my companions,

Do not mourn my departure nor attempt to follow. The path I travel is too dangerous. I hoped the lifting of Berengar's curse would pay my debt for meddling in dark sorcery. Alas, I have discovered my account is still in arrears.

As I confessed to you, I once sold a curse from my master's book to buy my own survival. I couldn't imagine anyone being fool enough to try it, much less succeed in casting it. In that, as in so much else, I have been proven appallingly wrong.

I never learned the name of the young man who paid for the curse—I guessed him to be a more powerful man's lackey—and I never asked its purpose. Until yesterday, I assumed it had failed for the buyer as spectacularly as it failed for me. Just as I had assumed that Crown Prince Guntram was murdered by his father's treacherous nobles.

Which may yet prove correct, just in a more roundabout manner than I imagined.

For the spell I sold that ill-fated day was the Morai ipakro liomandras—*a spell that turns an assassin into a manticore.*

Although I cannot fault the target chosen, I fear the darkness that has been unleashed, if not properly banished, will strike additional victims, more innocent than its original quarry.

I must again visit the old witch of the Serpents Teeth to discover how to bind the result of another Santian death curse. Surviving the journey will be one challenge. Surviving the witch another.

If I fail, you must find another way to shield yourselves from this evil.

Remember me, your friend and humble servant, in your prayers.
Rurik of Ravnina

Lord Berengar may have believed no one mourned his disappearance, but no one besides Silke had rejoiced, either. Sadly, the same could not be said of Crown Prince Guntram.

Still, although Princess Marjani and Princess Eira might agree that the brutal prince had received nothing more than he deserved, they had learned all too well how evil led to evil and one curse led to another.

If Rurik had not left a note, if his friends had not shared its contents, no one would have thought to follow him. News of his flight would not have reached Newport Castle. King Wulfric would never have learned the origin of the curse that killed his son.

And none of Prince Theodor's knights nor any of the twelve princesses vying for his hand would have been put like hounds on the sorcerer's trail, set on a quest from which not all might return.

THE TWELVE DANCING PRINCESSES

The Blessed Kingdoms

Bellis
Princess Beatrix
Rigas
Princess Dora
Ravnina
Princess Raisa
Aldforth
Princess Ellycia
Venia
Princess Jaclyn
Ilhavair
Princess Lidia
The Fair Isles
Princess Ziva
Montaine
Princess Isolde
Princess Pia
Nordmark
Princess Eira

Almasa
Princess Marjani
Kherem
Princess Anara

ACKNOWLEDGMENTS

This is my chance to thank everyone who made Eira and Marjani's story possible with their support and encouragement.

Thank you, as always, to my wonderful critique group—Sharon Brown, Georgia Salmon, and Jennifer Sowle—for seeing where I wanted to go and helping me find the path.

Many thanks to Nancy Short & Beth Hull for generous and cheerful help with the part of writing a book I hate the absolute most—you know what it is. And to Mike and Deidre Hansen for moral support and for catching all those little details I missed.

Thanks to my amazing co-workers, Jen, Gabby, Katy, and Mike for making my first Princess book a bestseller at the best bookstore in town (and for never batting an eye when I pick up a book on psychopaths or curses and say, "Oooo! *That* looks interesting.")

Thanks, as always, to my family. To Ari and Mom for always being there for me, no matter what. And to my sister (and book coach!), Katherine Longshore, for helping me cut through the chaff to find the heart of the tale—you make me make every book better.

And finally, a heartfelt thank you to all the readers who have accosted me to demand, "when is the next book coming out?" This is for you.

ABOUT THE AUTHOR

Rowan Mallory grew up on the northern California coast, in a world of giant, ancient trees and swirling mists, which may have subtly altered her brain to gravitate toward tales of mystery and adventure. She's in her happy place in the forests and the fog, writing stories about strong, smart, flawed heroines who believe the world can be a better place if they just make it so.

She shares her home with her cool kid, as well as a dog and cat with massive amounts of personality—who may or may not have provided inspiration for a certain cheeky little dragon.

Rowan is the author of *The Twelve Dancing Princesses* series, which began with *The Blacksmith Princess*.